Chains of
Vengeance

E.J. Cain

Arborean Tears Creative Studio

Arborean Tears Creative Studio
Minneapolis, Minnesota, USA

First ATCS digital edition December 2019

ISBN (ebook) 978-1-7343993-0-1
ISBN (paperback) 978-1-7343993-1-8

Cover illustration by Tania Sanchez-Fortun

*To Stephanie, for giving me the courage
to bring my stories to life.*

Contents

(1) Fire and Tears

It was a windy evening in the Aegis Forest where an elf slowed his horse, listening intently to his surroundings. The elf looked much like a human save for his copper-toned skin and slightly pointed ears. His features were smooth and angled, with a hairless chin beneath his large, brown eyes. His frame was tall and lithe.

The eastern reaches of this expansive forest had been this elf's home for many years. However, something was awry in this part of the forest. The animals were acting strange. The quiet scurrying of their tracks seemed odd as they attempted to leave the scene; to silently slip on the eve of the stormy excitement to come. The heavy winds rustled the higher branches of the trees, allowing many leaves to sail on the winds toward the forest's floor. The short elf smiled as a leaf fell helplessly into his dark hair. For a moment, all was serene, all was as it should be. The rushing wind, the wetness of the air, it was just a hint of the natural beauty of the rainfall to come, the continuation of the endless cycles. The millennia his people have spent among the trees seemed both eternal and instantaneous as his mind slipped away from the moment, into the eternal stream and back again.

The elf shook himself from the momentary daydream and climbed off his horse and walked towards the nearest tree. He peered deeply into the woods, sensing something unseen. He knew he should not linger, for he was on an important mission. However, the driving desire to find the source of the unnatural feeling beckoned him. He then lost his smile as his eyes found the disturbance. His jaw dropped in disbelief as he peered at two glowing red points less than a few strides from his position, hidden among the cloaking branches. The red orbs in the distance narrowed.

The elf gasped in surprise and rushed back to his horse. With a quick leap he was once again on the back of the quick steed. He patted the beast's flank and they took off in a great sprint down the broad dirt road. The horse's hooves created a rhythmic patter upon the packed earth.

The elf looked behind him as fear and trepidation overtook his mind. The road was clear behind him, yet it did not ease his worries. He begged the chestnut-colored horse onward into greater speed, hoping to escape the danger he had witnessed. The road ahead was also clear, and the elf prayed they would escape. He could not fail in his mission.

Then it came. Out of the underbrush along the side of the road leapt a giant cat-like beast. It slammed into the rider's horse knocking both to the ground with a painful numbing force as they made contact with the hard earth. The elf felt bones in his body shatter from the impact and he cried out in pain, desperately trying to crawl away from his injured, erratic horse. The mount was now thrashing in pain as the strange creature slashed and bit into the horse's supple flesh. Then the horse's body stopped moving and was silent.

The elf cried vainly as he crawled down the road, his body aching with each effort. He was then violently pulled back, forced to face upward as two red eyes peered at him hungrily from above. Then he felt horrible pain as the beast tore into his intestines with razor-sharp fangs. With no more than a gargled gasp, the elf's eyes stared forever at the cloudy, windswept sky.

*   *   *   *   *   *   *

Many of the wooden hovels built into the branches of the massive trees swayed in the wind this night. The occupants closed their windows and barred doors in hopes of keeping the heavy winds from reaching their warm homes. The elves of the village scurried about, running across the many stretched bridges and branches that connected the tree-top village. Not a light-hearted face could be spotted among the usually cheerful elves, as only a sense of dread filled the air. Nearly fifty archers had found positions among the trees, bows stretched in hand patiently, determinedly. All eyes faced to the northeast, towards the source of that dread. It had only been an hour since a few scouts had returned, fast on their feet, calling the warning that dark elf raiders were on the march.

The dark elves, or shadmar, were once kin to the surface elves of the world of Enelis. Once they joined in the elven revelry among the trees; singing praises to the stars and the moon in a celebration of life; but that was many ages ago. Now they were changed. Many millennia have passed since the shadmar tribes were banished to the deep underground, far below the world of the surface. Only the occasional raid to the lands above would bring their breed of darkness to the surface dwellers. It seemed that the village of Escailar was their target tonight.

Little more than a semi-permanent way-station for the mostly nomadic wood elves of the eastern reaches of the Aegis Forest, Escailar had been the home of elves for quite some time. Permanent residents were mostly hunters and forest-gatherers who gathered the riches of the forest. Others were herbalists and alchemists that traded their potions and elixirs to passing travelers in need. There were a few questionable sorts living in the village as well, especially those that traded with the men to the east of the forest in the land of Eshlien. There were also a few bounty hunters, always willing to kill a few of the unwanted in the lands of men; the poor who sought refuge and perhaps redemption among the forest boughs. They rarely received such luxury.

Another more reputable character was the mystic who lived on the edge of the small village. Magic was a common thing for the elves of the forest. It was a subtle, quiet thing that breathed life and spirit into the trees and mystic places of the world. Practiced druids could beckon a tree to grow into the shape of a living home over the course of many years. This was in fact common practice for the fey folk to dwell in such homes.

Alchemists were common enough as well; finding the secret combinations of mystic herbs to aid in sleep or in the healing of a wound. They knew just the right combination of herbs and roots to elicit near-magical effects.

Wizards, however, practiced something else; something significantly less subtle. The tales tell of wizards who could command the minds of those around them or blast a tree to the ground with a flaming inferno. It probably is this latter practice that had given them such a bad reputation among the elves of Escailar. Only one such wizard lived in this village, though few could claim to have seen him perform any real magic. He was quiet and mostly kept to himself; only occasionally meeting at the community hall for wine and spirits among the evening stars. He was the village's foremost scholar and expert in all things pertaining to the outside world. A seasoned traveler, the wizard had come to rest in Escailar many years ago. Now the village relied much on his skills and expertise in times of crisis.

While most of the elves in Escailar were thunmar, or wood elves, having copper-toned skin and dark hair the color of tree bark, Thesomber Ambreaia was a silver elf; having pale skin with a tinge of a silvery moon and hair that resembled sparkling platinum. His deep blue eyes sparkled with hints of gold, always seeming to be staring off in contemplation.

He was now in the midst of that deep contemplation, peering over the words of an ancient tome, unconsciously stroking his smooth chin.

A loud knock banged outside the wall near his door. "Thes, you are needed at the front lines!" a firm voice

4

shouted behind the tangle of leaves that served as a door to the modest treetop hovel.

A patient, humorous voice answered, "Then, if my services are required to save my kinsfolk, I shall be there before the village is asunder. But for now I must study. I am formulating a plan to allocate my resources."

"Be quick, Master Ambreaia, we fear the shadmar have more numbers than our scouts have guessed," the firm voice said in resolution as the nimble figure leaped his way through the trees.

"And be quick I shall. . .the village must be protected," muttered the stoic elf to himself as he slowly closed his tome in consideration of the actions he must soon take. He eyed the droplets of rain that began to drip down outside his window, knowing the moments to come would not be easy.

*   *   *   *   *   *   *

The battle raged on as copper-skinned elves danced in swordplay with their dark brethren. Numerous crossbow bolts flew into the melee from the dark reaches of the forest, and in turn many arrows sailed across the air from the treetops that formed the village of Escailar. The hopes and dreams of the copper-skinned elves sang out as they fought for their homeland from the shadmar that sought to devour it. The shadmar seemed to have numbers well beyond those of the village. The few aged elves who had lived through a shadmar raid before knew this was the biggest band seen in centuries.

The ferocious dark-skinned warriors were relentless fighters. They reveled in the chaos of battle and the splattering of blood at their feet. The copper-skinned elves were also quite determined. Though the spilling of blood was not in their nature, they showed no mercy to their dark brethren.

Thes found himself standing behind the melee watching the carnage below him as the newest ranks of wood elves charged in, swords swinging mechanically, meeting the charge of the chaotic shadmar. Seeing the approach of another band that sought to flank the wood elves, Thes closed his eyes and began murmuring the incantations of the powerful spell he had been studying.

His lips pursed slowly, in much the same way a person blows upon a sizzling cup of tea. A rhythmic high-pitched hum escaped the wizard's lips slowly gaining momentum, exponentially increasing its volume. Then the song abruptly stopped and the wizard's eyes shot open. A freezing wind engulfed the shadmar warriors and quickly shaped the now pouring rain into a hail of jagged ice crystals. The shards of sharp ice fell down upon the shadmar band like a hail of deadly arrows. Many shadmar warriors screamed in pain as the shards tore through their ranks. Many warriors were impaled by the freezing spears, piercing their skulls, shoulders, and sword arms, soon rendering over half the group useless in mere moments.

The slender wizard stood tall with a determined gaze as the shadmar began to break ranks and the few remaining warriors fled towards the east. At that moment Thes seemed imposing to the fleeing shadmar, standing on the village balcony, high in the trees; his leather cloak waved behind him in the heavy winds. His dark green robes with bright yellow trim were kept untied, which served more as an inner coat than true academic garb. A lightweight green-tinted shirt and deerskin trousers finished the ensemble with a pair of heavy leather boots. A bright leather satchel hung around his shoulder, bearing a few tomes. A dark scabbard was tied to his belt. The wizard appeared more like a disheveled traveler than a mage of any reputation. The shadmar, however, were unaware that Thes struggled to maintain his imposing posture. His mind burned in pain from the recent spell. A spell he knew might be more than he could handle. After a few moments, Thes was able to regain himself and he looked down closely at the ground below him.

The elf's eyes narrowed as another shadmar band rushed in with more ferocity than the previous group, felling many copper-skinned warriors. The shadmar warriors flanked the wood elves, who were caught in the melee between the two shadmar squads. Rage built into the young elven wizard as he saw his friends slaughtered in the carnage.

Thes was unaccustomed to such a strong emotion. He was an academic and scholar, who preferred rational logic over emotional decision making. However, the sight of his friends falling to the shadmar blades brought a visceral anger within him that overtook his better judgement.

Thes's hands fell into the intricate pattern of another spell. The wizard pulled a small shard of iron from his satchel and he gently rubbed it across his chest before returning it to his bag. Thes uttered an archaic phrase, and wisps of blue sparks fell about his body into the shape of a metallic breastplate, but soon dissipated. Thes then leaped down the tree, rushing down the massive branches that curved towards the ground below. He quickly, yet carefully, leaped from branch to branch, always keeping his stern visage on the scattered shadmar below. He drew his long slightly-curved blade and rushed in at the shadmar warriors, shouting an elven war-cry that sounded more like a fierce song.

Thes jumped from the lowest branch into the treacherous battle. His blade met the face of an unwary warrior. Blood sprayed from the dark elf's face as the wizard's steel sliced down his opponent's neck. With two quick crisscrossing slashes, two more shadmar joined the first upon the ground. After downing the few unprepared warriors, Thes noticed three more enemy warriors charging towards him from the north with sinister glares of anger painted on their faces.

Thes rapidly struck a nearby rock with his sword producing many sparks against the stone. Calling upon his mystical powers, Thes began manipulating that static energy, amplifying and focusing those sparks. Two fist-sized missiles of electric energy soon raced towards his target with unerring accuracy. The bursts exploded on the shadmar's skin, but the warrior only clenched his teeth and charged onward.

The shadmar warriors met the wizard in combat, brandishing their dark cruelly-edged swords and using their bucklers defensively. Thes parried an attack from the first and narrowly dodged a blow from the second, but the third warrior struck home. The sword scratched harmlessly off Thes's invisible magic armor bringing surprise to the shadmar's face. Three more attacks came in at the wizard, again two were barely avoided, but the third had a clear shot at Thes's unguarded throat. But luck was with the wizard at that moment, when an ally's arrow was suddenly protruding from the third shadmar's neck and the warrior's sword fell harmlessly across Thes's shoulder. Thes silently nodded his thanks to the hidden form on the village balcony, as he threw an attack from outside in a wide arc against one of the remaining warriors. The shadmar easily blocked the blow with his buckler. Another arrow struck the second shadmar dropping him to the ground. Thes suddenly felt more at ease with only a single opponent to face him, as he set his feet and prepared a defensive posture.

The shadmar warrior rushed in, sword and shield before him. Thes evaded the bull rush with a quick strafe to the right. An arcing sword went in at Thes as the shadmar turned on her prey, but Thes anticipated the strike and parried it with the middle of his blade. With a sneer, the shadmar kicked the wizard with full force in the lower chest, only to squirm a second as her foot made contact with something unseen. Thes gasped for a second as the blow knocked him back vulnerably. Then a few arrows slammed into the shadmar felling her before any action could be taken. Thes waved another thanks to his companions in the trees above. The anger within the wizard pushed him onward as he ran off to find more enemies in the arduous battle.

*   *   *   *   *   *   *

The battle raged for hours, neither group seemed to be doing better than the other. Then a group of archers arrived from Diiera, another wood elf village north of Escailar. Within moments of the archers' arrival, morale had soared for the copper-skinned tree-dwellers and the wood elves soon had the upper hand. After another rush of chaotic battle, the shadmar raiders were sorely outnumbered. It seemed that the wood elves would defend their homeland successfully.

It was then that Thes, exhausted and weary, his cloak and robes covered in dirt and dried blood, decided to begin the hunt for fleeing shadmar warriors. He wanted to prevent them from returning to the mountains and bring the knowledge about the location of his home village back with them. The action would bring the wizard mixed feelings, for he did not like to slay those that did not offer any immediate danger, but shadmar that were allowed to flee would surely invite more to return, and like all elves, their life-spans were centuries long.

After a few hours of chase, Thes had taken out quite a few of the fleeing shadmar. Now it was harder to find the dark-skinned warriors and Thes was quite far to the east of the village. Thes had only one more in his sight as the sun was beginning to peak over the horizon. The fatigued shadmar warrior sat upon a log among the trees catching his breath. He had fled quicker than the others as Thes dispatched his comrades right before his eyes. Little did that shadmar realize was that same elf had a bow cocked with an arrow aimed for his unwary head. Vengeance was but a gesture away.

Thes hesitated to fire, finding it hard to kill any foe unaware. But then again, these were the shadmar. All the tales of his youth preached of their evil and treachery. He released his hold and the wizard's head quickly veered to the side in disgust as the arrow shaft struck home in the shadmar's skull. Dark blood poured from the wound as the body hunched over never to look up again. Thes never saw him hit the ground. It was a long walk back towards the village and he knew he would be needed in the repairs that would be required in the aftermath of the battle. A shadmar raid had not occurred in this area in over a century, so it seemed odd that after all these years the vile shadmar would attack, especially such a small village with so few resources to gain.

Was it truly their wicked ideology that brought them so far from their home? Thes thought. The situation was perplexing to him. He could not fathom the motivations of a shadmar warrior to climb through the deep tunnels of the earth to the surface world, only to slay and pillage a few poor villages. He realized he did not know much about the shadmar's culture. Their relative absence from the surface world made them quite a mystery and perceived nightmare to those living on the surface. Although Thes had heard tales of the shadmar and knew the history that drove them underground, he did not truly understand their motives or their current culture, and as a scholar, that ignorance bothered the wizard.

10

He sighed as he watched the slow wind rustle the dark canopies that glistened from the nightly rain in the pale dawn light.

Things seem to change too fast, he thought. It was only two days before that all was serene and quiet. The occasional traveler would bring news from the great elven cities or from the human villages to the east, but these things seemed so distant to the wizard. He was comfortably ignorant of the wide world around him for perhaps the first time in his life. Blissfully reading ancient texts by day and singing softly to the stars at night. But now, things have changed. The life he knew before had faded instantaneously. Though he knew the village would survive, he also knew things would never be the same again.

Thes sighed again, trying to regain the focus of his weary mind. He knew the walk would be long, so the wizard began to shuffle his weary feet in the proper direction still contemplating the changes to his life. After many minutes of walking, Thes decided to conjure an alternative now that his mind had recovered from his previous spellcraft. The elf whistled quietly into the wind which then began to blow stronger, but ever so gently. Thes's feet soon floated upward into the air, high above the trees. He gestured west and soared with a gentle speed towards his home village.

*   *   *   *   *   *   *

Thes finally reached the outskirts of the village, expecting to see others preparing the dead and giving life back to the trees. Instead, he saw only smoldering trees roaring in tall flames like massive torches. The wizard's eyes grew wide and his breath did not come. An inferno roared as the tree-top village crumbled and burned to ashes. Not a single living creature was in sight of the wreckage and the flames were spreading from tree to tree. The wizard staggered back trying to understand how the shadmar could have won the battle. How those dark, vile monsters could have conquered the humble wood elves of Escailar. The battle seemed a sure victory when he had left to chase after the fleeing shadmar.

The guilt of his absence grew into a lump in the wizard's throat. Tears glistened as they slid gently down the silvery cheek. Hatred began to blaze in Thes's blood. It was a pure burning desire for retribution unlike that of which he had ever known. Minutes went by as the angered wizard stared at fires that mirrored the feelings in his heart. Then, unexpectedly, even to Thes, the elf screamed to the rising sun. He screamed all the pain and guilt and anguish he felt until his throat was sore and his voice was raw. He dropped to his knees as tears streamed down his face, a fountain of guilt and remembrance for the village that had been his home.

"Over here!" a rough shadmar voice yelled to his companions upon seeing the wizard. The three shadmar warriors rushed in at Thes, brandishing their swords, all eager for one last taste of bloodshed. Thes stared at the warriors for what seemed like an eternity, wishing to join in the death they offered; wishing to end his treacherous guilt. But the fires in his heart would not let him, they would not let him die meaninglessly when he had the strength for revenge.

The rage focused within the wizard, gathering energy into his mind. Thes channeled that energy, barely containing the power of his newfound anger. Lightning exploded from the wizard's fingertips uncontrollably, engulfing the shadmar warriors in a torrent of electrical energies. The warriors screamed in pain as their muscles burned and scorched from the inside. Thes stepped over the three corpses after the energies dissipated, stepping determinedly

12

towards the fires of the village. That addictive taste of revenge pushed the wizard to seek more confrontation.

A large band of shadmar warriors came up the nearby hill charging towards the wizard. Thes already felt his mind weakening from the exertion of his magic. He drew his sword, eyeing the coming warriors with only hatred in his eyes.

But then the quiet, rational portion of Thes's mind returned. The wizard began to realize the futility of his violent actions. Self-sacrifice would not bring his friends back to life. He decided it better to return another day, prepared and rested.

With a single gesture, Thes continued his flight and soared straight upwards through the branches, using his sword to guide the way above. Glistening red eyes, with a hint of an amber glow, followed the wizard's path, a mark of trepidation beginning to take form in those menacing orbs.

(2) Unlikely Friends

The lonely elf trudged out of the woods. It had been a few days since the fires of Escailar. Thes had flown far to the southeast, away from that tragedy and the Aegis Forest. Eventually his mind had burned with exhaustion and he was forced to take to the ground. He felt tortured, reliving those feelings of guilt and dread endlessly as he stumbled through natural woodlands and windswept meadows. He knew not how long he traveled nor where he was headed. He knew only that his life was shattered. Everyone he had come to know as friends and companions were gone. He was alone again.

The need for food, drink, and rest grew heavy in the elf. His eyes were red with tears and weariness. His body felt heavy and half-asleep. He had the intuition that he was heading east, recalling the warmth of the sun rising on his face that morning. He knew there was a village in the valley near where he found himself and decided to continue his weary course towards the warm beds they offered.

The winds blew from the northwest into the wide gap between the two mountain ranges, heading towards the wide valleys. For a moment, the cool winds brought his mind into the present as his lungs took in the crisp air. Far in the distance small wisps of smoke blew almost horizontally across the hills from the many small smokestacks that rose from the small village ahead.

Beyond the village would be the green rolling hills and forests of Eshlien. There dwelt the eshmar, or half-elves, with their numerous trade towns along the Moon Lake. Beyond Eshlien lay many feudal kingdoms of men. They were the last remnants of the fallen Nomen Empire. The once powerful empire, with its democratic ideals and virtuous draconic deities, had claimed all the lands along the

15

eastern coast, from the Noradrie lands in the cold north, to the hilly Toldrie lands of the south. It had now become nothing more than scattered kingdoms, all fighting to reclaim the old empire's glory. There was one exception to the madness. The city of Goldwall, the former seat of the old empire. Goldwall maintained a democratic leadership and a fair government, however, the old city could do little more than protect its own borders as it served as a neutral trading hub for the many warring kingdoms.

Thes's eyes looked to the northeast where he saw the shadow of the Eriasha Peaks in the distance. Beyond the mountains was the land of the dwarves, an alpine land of tall peaks and beautiful valleys. The Kingdom of Kalavar could be found there in the mineral-rich mountains. The dwarven kingdom was nearly as old as the elven culture of the Aegis Forest and the dwarves that dwelt there were a proud and talented people. Dwarves were a stout folk, no taller than four or five feet high with long braided hair. Their males usually had equally elaborate braids in their long beards. Thes had little personal experience with the dwarves, for long ago many wars were fought between the elven and dwarven people. The two races were conflicted, lacking an understanding of one another's culture and values. Initially the war came about by the dwarves' deforestation of the forest as they expanded their domain. The philosophical differences between the races only made it worse. For two-hundred years the empires fought. Eventually a treaty was signed, putting an end to the war, but both races still carried a great deal of bitterness for the other.

Thes had lived most of his life in the trees of the forest. Elves were a magical race, believed to be one of the first sentient beings to appear after the dragons. Over the millennia, the ancestry of the elves split into at least five distinct tribes. It is said in the ancient folklore that the bodies of the heavens blessed each of the ancient tribes.

16

The sun blessed the sulmar, the People of the Sun, or gold elves to the menfolk. They had tanned skin tinged with gold, with hair that ranged from shimmering black to radiant platinum. They had built many fabled cities of crystal and stone along a great lake found deep in the Aegis Forest. Though few of these cities remained, the great city of Elienspar, the City of Brilliant Light, still stood as a bastion for elfkind. Thes had visited the place many times, but found the people there to be generally haughty and pretentious. He preferred the quiet humility of the forest.

The thunmar, People of the Twilight, or wood elves, were elves who dwelt in the deep forest. They had copper skin with hair that ranged from the color of bark to greenish tints. They were masters of the forest, expert hunters and woodsmen. Their druids, who still clung to the old spiritual beliefs, created villages among the trees; willing the massive trunks to grow into the shapes of homes for the elves. It was among these wood elves Thes felt most at home. He enjoyed the simplicity and community in their lives.

He was of the ethmar, the People of the Moon, known as the silver elves to the men of the east. His people were master tradesmen, diplomats, and travelers of the many rivers that wound through the forests. They tended to be the most common type of elf seen outside of the Aegis Forest. They had pale skin with a slight tinge of blue or silver. Hair colors ranged through all human varieties, though some had gold or platinum. Thes was not a typical ethmar, for he practiced the academic scholarship of the sulmar, but preferred to dwell deep in the forest with the thunmar.

There once were the stelmar, or People of the Stars. No one seems to recall what they looked like or the manner of these people. They had a great kingdom that reached throughout the eastern coasts long before the coming of the humans who dwell there now. However, the stelmar empire was destroyed by raging dragons, leaving no trace of the star elves except for broken ruins scattered throughout the eastern regions.

Last was the shadmar, or People of the Starless Night, the dark elves. Aptly named, for they were fond of caves and dark hidden corners of the forests. They had deep, ebony skin with hair that ranged from blonde to platinum white. Long ago, the ancient kingdom of the shadmar was the strongest of the old kingdoms, for they were masters of metalcraft. They provided the old kingdoms with tools and weaponry, especially during the wars with the dwarf clans. They once ruled over the valleys in the shadow of the mountains, over the very region where Escailar once stood.

The dark elves desired more, however, and sought to rule over all four of the elven crowns. Long before the Nomen Empire of men arose, the Treaty of Arrow and Axe was signed, ending the war between the elven and dwarven cultures. The elven Emperor and the dwarven High Magistrate met to sign the final agreement and celebrate the coming peace at the shadmar fortress of Valraen. It was there that they were both assassinated by a conspiracy between the shadmar rulers and one of the dwarven clans. Both groups greatly opposed the treaty as they were tempted by wealth and power, of which the continuous war had given both. The truth of the conspiracy was soon uncovered, however, resulting in an internal war between the shadmar and the other three elven kingdoms. In the end, after the civil war ended and the shadmar were defeated, the shadmar were banished using powerful ancient magic. They were forced under the mountains below the earth in the endless caverns of the deep-underground. The might of the remaining elven kingdoms never recovered and the elven people continued to dwindle over the millennia since.

Thes continued his steps, eager to rest in the village. His eyes may have had the village in view, but his mind was still wandering elsewhere. The burning fires of his home continued to ignite before him as guilt and dread overtook his being. Evil shadmar faces snickered and snarled at him from every angle, challenging the wizard to face them. The clash of the battle still rang in Thes's ears. He fought firmly against the tide of these feelings and shook his head hard to regain his focus on the current moment and his current surroundings. The wizard suddenly felt lonely and isolated, a lost soul drifting helplessly in a sea of emptiness. He vowed that he would seek revenge when the time came, for now however, he must find rest.

Thes walked in open fields and rolling hills with scattered woodlands; occasionally sighting a tower or crumbling ruin from some lost kingdom. This area was a lawless land with many bandits and brigands, orcs and goblins, and even the occasional giant or dragon to threaten the common folk who dared to make their life here without the safety of a kingdom's soldiery. These were strong and brave folk, used to relying on grit and determination to protect their homes. As a consequence, the townspeople rarely trusted strangers and often would chase out any perceived threat with pitchforks and torches.

Thes drew his cloak tighter around his shoulders. With a lonely sigh, he pulled in some courage and eyed the human village from the distance. It had been awhile since he had spoken the language of men, and he mumbled a few phrases to remind himself. The rolling words of the old Nomen tongue came easily to the elf. He tightened his cloak again and trudged forward; it had been too long, he decided, since he had spoken with another soul.

Nearing the village, the elf noticed the scattered farms surrounding the small gathering of fifty or so squat buildings that defined the village of Allsvale. The buildings were mostly built of wood with sod to fill in the gaps; thatch and twine covered most of the roofs. Only two of the buildings were made of stone, a small chapel on the edge of town and a large two-story building in the center, presumably the inn.

Thes walked into the village, the hood of his cloak taken down as a sign of openness. A few townsfolk glared as the elf carefully walked past their gardens and into the village proper. The bustle of the common folk surrounded the elf: men and women rushing and shouting at each other, pushing wheelbarrows and pulling carts. Children squealed as they chased each other in the crisp air of the late morning. The wizard tried to remain innocuous as he shuffled his way through the crowd, gaining only the occasional stare from the humans around him. The children were the most excited, for most had associated elves with the sounds of music and song.

Though Thes was glad to have happy, smiling faces around him again, he tried his best to avoid the curious children. His heart was too heavy to fully commune with anyone just yet. The wizard scrambled past a group of youngsters begging for an elvish song, but Thes only smiled meekly and shook his head as he stepped into the inn.

The Allsvale Inn was a simple establishment barely making enough coin from the few travelers that came through from the Aegis Forest into Eshlien proper. They served a simple cuisine featuring mostly roasted birds or venison with plenty of potatoes and yams. Their ale was thin and watery, and the wine tasted more like beets and yeast than most would find palatable. For the farmers and game hunters of Allsvale, the inn offered an easy meal and a chance to vent about everyday chores to family and friends. The occasional outsider provided a bit of news from beyond the fields; and exciting news like that would not be missed.

The inn was homely with a bellowing aura of smoke in the air as a few locals sat with long, curved pipes near the entrance, drowning their worries away in a mug of cheap beer. A few travelers sat at the bar, but otherwise the place was quiet and near empty. The tired elf hardly noticed anything as he found a table in the corner. His body relaxed as he sat upon the chair; a needed comfort for his weary bones. After a moment a young human woman with large blue eyes came toward the elf. Within a few minutes, the elf sat comfortably hunched over a wooden cup filled with some pungent beet wine and a small bowl of porridge.

The memories of the battle still afire in his heart, he sunk his head low with a frown of discord. He felt it would be a long while before a smile would once again stretch across his slender face. Taking a cue from the near silence, the barmaid left him in peace. The elf ate and drank what he could. Lost in the memories of the onslaught, Thes didn't notice the brawny, bear-of-a-man sit down across from him.

"I recognize that turmoil," the big fellow said in his deep bellowing voice. "Seen the tragedies of war, ye have. Why don't ya tell ole' Morstar yer tale."

Thes, now suddenly aware of the stranger's arrival, pulled back from the man, annoyed that his thoughts had been disturbed.

Please leave me alone, he pleaded silently with his eyes as he grabbed his bags and stood, eyeing a new seat at the bar. He managed a grim look of annoyance in the direction of the man as he grabbed his wine and sat upon the wooden stool at the stained counter.

The man thought little of the elf's attempt to avoid him. He soon was sitting next to the elf at the bar, with a smile spread across his thick-bearded face. Thes, now feeling defeated for his chance at solitude, turned to face the man. As his gaze met dark brown eyes hiding behind bushy, black eyebrows, he was actually relieved that he had someone with whom he could confide.

"Please accept my apologies," the elf said, "the battle was a brutal one and my heart still bears the pain. I'd prefer to be alone."

"Aye, ye could do that, or ye could tell the tale and feel better for sharing it," the man said cheerily. "By Rolk's beard! Ye can't let it tear down yer spirits. It'll slowly eat ye away. Believe me, I know. I've been there meself."

At the mention of the dwarven deity, Thes's gaze slowly went to the bearded man's legs and realized they were short and dangling from the stool.

This is no man before me. I am conversing with a dwarf! Thes realized, and he became confused. He peered more closely at the stranger sitting beside him. He was dressed in thick leathers and padded cloths, the kind typically worn under heavy armor. A long, bushy dark beard hung down to the dwarf's thick leather belt. The charcoal-black beard was braided with two long braids to the sides of the central beard. The dwarf's hair was also braided in five long braids down his back. On his face he wore a curious smile beneath a large, rosy nose.

"Why does a dwarf make conversation with an elf so eagerly?" Thes asked curiously.

The calm dwarf reflected in thought for a second, and then replied, "Maybe ye haven't noticed, but we are the only two in this bar not of the menfolk. Strangely enough, I felt more comfortable talking to ye than those others." He chuckled to himself and then added solemnly, "And I sense yer tortured spirit, lad, something of which I know all too well."

Thes was completely surprised at the reaction of the dwarf. *Surely, I have met the most contemplative dwarf known to walk the face of Enelis*, he thought.

"How odd!" the elf replied. "I always pictured dwarves more at home discussing metals and stones with men, rather than listening to what any of the fey-folk would have to say."

"Aye, tis true our peoples have had their problems, but no two stones are ever alike, I always say. Who am I to judge one stone over another, they all have their uses. But before we reach a long conversation regarding metals and stones," the dwarf said with a grin, "tell me the tale of yer battle. You look like you've seen something horrible," his face now showing genuine concern.

The elf sat a moment in thought regarding the request. Then, mustering courage, he muttered the two words that brought clarity to the dwarf, "Dark elves."

A second or two passed before the elf continued, he slowly explained the details of the battle and the role he played in the course of the chaos. Of course, he omitted details regarding his use of magic, fearing any eavesdroppers that might cause a scene. Magic was not a common thing outside the world of the elves. Thes explained his feelings of guilt for not making his way to the village in time, for not dying alongside his friends when the enemies had closed in. The dwarf remained quiet, occasionally nodding and grunting with each tragedy the elf explained, honest concern displayed clearly on his face.

"I have long sought an end to my restlessness and wanderlust," Thes continued, "I had searched deeply for a true home. I felt that I had found it, but 'twas swept away in but a day. So I walk only with my guilt and the fires in my heart, so that one day I can achieve vengeance upon those who have wronged me." The elf's tone became grim and determined. As he relayed those final words, a dark anger bubbled up from the recesses of the elf's heart.

The dwarf snorted at that final declaration. He considered it for a while, and then slowly began to speak, choosing his words carefully, seemingly holding back emotions of his own.

"Vengeance will not repair your heart, elf-friend, nor bring your allies back to life, only spread that pain like a plague." The dwarf's eyes became firm as he stared off to the side, biting back the emotions from his own tumultuous past.

Images of dead elves flashed in Thes's mind. Perhaps it was the great weariness that hung upon him, as he could almost hear the gleeful cries of the shadmar fill his ears in the roar of a battle. His face burned red as anger poured through him. Flames roared behind the wizard's eyes as they bore into the dwarf, though he was not the target of the elf's wrath. The pained wizard only saw the faces of cruel shadmar before him. The dwarf, however, only stared back with true concern.

The elf and dwarf stared off for what seemed like an eternity. Thes then suddenly snapped back into the present, his eyes finally blinking. Tense words dripped from the elven lips as fire still burned in his eyes.

"I will have vengeance, and not a soul in Enelis will stop me." Thes turned from the dwarf, his face hot with ire. He ordered a room from the barkeep, and stormed up the wooden stairs hefting his leather satchel over his shoulder. The dwarf sat quietly at the bar, shaking his head.

*   *   *   *   *   *   *

It was late in the evening. The burly dwarf was chomping down his third helping of venison, eagerly licking the grease off his fingers. He had barely moved from his seat at the bar from earlier in the day. His fourteenth mug of beer was down to its bottom and the dwarf was eagerly awaiting his fifteenth as the bartender filled his wooden mug with the foamy dark-amber liquid. The dwarf nodded his thanks as he grasped the mug and took a hefty gulp of the ale to wash down the bits of meat clogging his throat. Afterward, the

24

mug came down hard on the bar and the dwarf withheld a belch as he took in a lungful of air.

"That hit the spot," the dwarf muttered in his own language, the heavy consonants of the Kalavarian tongue perplexing the bartender as Morstar grasped another piece of the thick, smoked deer meat with his stubby fingers.

A nimble figure sat next to the dwarf and ordered a cup of wine. Thes took a few cautious sips of the sour-tasting drink, trying to gather his thoughts.

It had been a long day for the elf. He'd intended to get enough sleep to let his mind finally acquire the rest it needed, but the dwarf's words had left too strong an impression on the elf. Staring wearily at the ceiling of the dim room, the straw of the mattress poking hard into his back, Thes had contemplated the dwarf's words and his own feelings regarding the tragedy of Escailar. The rational and unemotional, usually-dominate, side of Thes's mind had tried to come to terms with his guilt. Though he still wished to slaughter every dark elf on the face of Enelis, he knew it would be foolish to strike alone against the shadmar in their deep caverns. It was no life to live fighting solely for vengeance.

Thes sighed as he turned to the dwarf and spoke in the tongue of the human traders.

"I'm sorry about earlier, sir dwarf," the elf began apologetically. "Your words had true wisdom. My anger is not for you."

"Morstar," the dwarf mumbled with a mouth full of venison.

"Mor-star?" Thes echoed confusedly.

The dwarf swallowed his mouthful and cleared his throat before he spoke, "Morstar Haglekdon, Slayer-of-Orcs, Hunter-of-Worgs, and Foe-of-All-Goblinkind; at your service." The dwarf bowed his head a moment then offered his greasy hand to the elf.

Thes grasped the oily paw and shook it gingerly with a smile, bowing his head as well. The elf was glad to be smiling again.

"I'm Thesomber Ambreaia, but most folk call me Thes."

The dwarf smiled back at the elf as he released his hand and returned to his meal.

"Anyway, Sir Hag-lek-don, I wish to thank you for your wisdom. I am quite fortunate to have bumped into such a wise dwarf."

"Don't ye mention it, elf. I just happened to experience yer pain some years back. It ain't easy, but ye'll live through it."

Thes solemnly nodded with the dwarf's words, believing them fully, confident that he could find solace in time.

Curious, the elf asked, "What experience similar to my own have you endured?"

The dwarf stopped, swallowed hard, and dropped the meat he held back on to his plate. He sat in thought for a few moments, staring off into space, before he said, "Well, elf, it's a long tale, and it doesn't have a happy ending."

"Nevertheless, I am eager to hear it. A tale for a tale," Thes replied.

"Well, then, I suppose it started many years ago..." the dwarf began. He described his position as a patrol sergeant for the dwarven city of Gorgaddur. It was their task to roam the wide mountainous region above the Hanu-gar Forests on the northern edge of the Kingdom of Kalavar. They would search for goblins, orcs, and dangerous beasts that wished harm on the dwarven commonfolk. More importantly, they protected the vast amount of wealth the dwarves stored deep in their stone halls, nestled beneath the mountains.

One crisp autumn night, Morstar's band of thirty dwarves were preparing their camp in the lowlands. They had tied up their ponies, and were trying to get some sleep. A band of goblins had ambushed the dwarves in the night. The battle was brutal and vicious, for the dwarves were ill-prepared and many of the soldiers were new recruits, without the reflexes of a seasoned warrior.

Morstar recalled awakening to the sounds of screams as many of the soldiers awoke to find crossbow bolts already protruding from their chests. The look-outs were hanging dead from nearby trees, strangled by nooses silently slipped around their necks. Morstar had leapt from his bedroll, warhammer in hand. He pummeled and hammered each goblin within reach with his deadly weapon. Morstar recalled how he had been fighting desperately for survival. The goblins had surrounded him and only a few of his brave soldiers were left still standing. A hard thud suddenly echoed through the stout warrior's body as a huge branch was cut above him, the massive limb slamming him to the ground, his consciousness gone in an instant. In the end, the goblins had slaughtered every dwarf in Morstar's band and the fortunate sergeant had survived simply because the goblins counted him among the dead.

To Morstar's luck, some dwarven lumberjacks had found him among the broken tree several hours later and brought the wounded warrior back to the comforts of the underground city. It was not long before the dwarf had recovered. He recounted how he had requested another patrol to avenge his comrades. The request was denied, however. Morstar explained how his rage soon had him forsaking his post to pursue vengeance on his own. Though the dwarf had eventually succeeded in slaughtering a goblin band single-handedly, an act that would make any warrior proud, he explained how he had no way of knowing if it was the same band that slaughtered his kin. More importantly,

Morstar explained how the killing blows upon his enemies did not quench the fires in his heart. He came to realize a life of vengeance was incomplete.

"So, you see," the dwarf continued, "that's the sad tale of this dwarf. I know the pain ye carry, it'll pass with time."

The elf sighed, "I hope so... "

"At least until ye run into a dark elf again, for the embers shall burn for a lifetime," the warrior added, bringing a look of understanding to both their faces.

"So how did you end up here?" the elf asked.

Morstar explained how the anger in his heart still burned for the loss of his companions. He knew he would never find solace if he remained in Kalavar. He also knew his disobedience to his superiors would bring great shame upon his family. Morstar knew he had to find a new purpose for his life, and so he sought the open road and a new life for himself. He had little skills outside of his knowledge of warfare so he headed south, hiring himself out as a caravan guard to traveling merchants, occasionally using his hammer to defend the wagons from thieves and monsters. Morstar recounted how he had lived the mercenary life for many years. More recently, the dwarf had been a guard for a wine merchant that had just traveled to Allsvale. Coincidently, Morstar's contract expired, leaving the dwarf seeking new opportunities.

"I thought I had had my fill of adventure," Thes said. "I planned to hang up my traveling boots. I had found a home, a place to spread roots and grow tall. Now I don't know what to do with myself."

"Ye can fight can't ye?" the dwarf asked. "I could use another blade for me next little adventure."

"What exactly would that be?" Thes queried.

"Well, I got this map from a local woodsman. It leads to an old ruin not too far into the forest westward. I'm

28

a wee bit doubtful t'will lead to anything more than a crumble of stones, but the locals say it used to be a crypt of a powerful sorcerer from back in the Nomen days."

Thes's eyes lit up, he was always interested in ancient magic. The tingling excitement of a possible adventure rekindled something in the elf. While the elf had truly believed that he had wished to end his traveling days, he felt a resurgence of that curiosity and a thirst for knowledge that had driven him on all those adventures before he had settled in Escailar.

"So would ye like to join an old warrior and go searching for hidden trinkets? Half of any treasure would be yours, of course," the dwarf promised with a large grin.

The reawakened spark exploded and the elf felt a giddy excitement come over him. Perhaps because it was a ready distraction from his heavy heart, but the elf wanted to jump at the opportunity.

"I'd love to," the elf said with a matching smile.

The dwarf chuckled. "And a new adventure begins," he said excitedly. Two wooden cups came together with a dull *thunk*. They were both eager for the excitement that was to come. That night the two shared many drinks and tales of previous adventures.

Morstar was certainly a seasoned warrior, spending much of his life as a soldier for the dwarves of Kalavar. He relayed stories of battles with orcs to the north of his homeland, wars with giants in the mountains, and even a few skirmishes with the Noradrie horselords of the hills and tundras in the cold northlands. He described the Noradrie as the bravest and fiercest warriors of all the tribes of men.

Thes recounted his travels across the eastern regions of Enelis. He described the human cities along the eastern coasts, and the great city-state of Goldwall in all its marvel and beauty. He told of the haunted forests of the Toldrie lands and the dangers of the dragons to the south. He told of the great war between the desert Empire of Arathkelsara and the noble knights who sought to claim the holy land for their own. Thes spoke of his failed excursion through the Freewind Savannah to the unknown western lands beyond. He had met many strange creatures in his expeditions, but never made it to the far side of those wild, unsettled lands.

Despite their clear differences, Thes and Morstar had natural rapport. Their growing bond was undeniable. Eventually, the elf and the dwarf had their fill of ale and wine and thought it best to turn in for the night, though the excitement of the journey ahead made sleep difficult for both of them. The next morning, the two adventurers bought a few supplies for their journey. Morstar donned his thick scaled armor and tied a mighty warhammer to his belt. Thes had no need for armor, relying on magic and speed to save his flesh from harm.

As they made their way out of the village, the townsfolk eyed them curiously, for it was an odd thing to see an elf and dwarf walking together in friendship. Quite a few times, Thes had to stop and share a song with the local children. But now, he was more than happy to do so. At these times Morstar would hum deep low notes with the elf's high-pitched song.

It was not long until they were far from the village, the line of trees stretched before them far on the horizon. The elf was a little nervous about returning to the forest. He was not eager to return near the ruins of Escailar, but he reasoned that the shadmar raid was long finished and the dark elves had probably returned to their caverns deep in the earth, where surface-dwellers readily agreed they belonged.

(3) The Lord of Darkness

It had been a day of celebration for the shadmar of House Niedrie. Their patriarch had arrived from the depths of the deep underground. It was time for him to lead their society into greater glory. They would continue to put their plan into motion.

It had been many decades in preparation, a plan for a massive war between the underground-dwelling shadmar and their hated surface kin. The shadmar of House Niedrie had been preparing for so long that it had become the single purpose that united these otherwise chaotic beings. Rarely did the shadmar noble houses keep alliances, much less actually work together. There were constant power struggles, backstabbing, and new leaders rising to take control, often in new directions.

But Lord Delrith Niedrie had a vision; a golden, uniting vision for all the shadmar. He offered them the surface. With a century of manipulation and struggle, Lord Niedrie conquered all the shadmar houses in the subterranean depths below. Now a throng of shadmar would fight and die at his command. All this because they believed that they could take back the surface world from the elves above; take back the lands their ancestors once called home. This they called the Promise.

At first it had seemed a foolish attempt at control; a pathetic minor house attempting to take command through manipulation. But somehow no other house could stop the prevailing sorcerer of House Niedrie. Every attempt at betrayal or warfare became drastic for the aggressor and Lord Niedrie would always remain on top. Many whispered he had a dark power at his command, others whispered that only a true visionary could remain victorious. It was the greater belief in the latter that slowly brought the legions of shadmar to lay their swords and lives down for the sorcerer.

As his armies grew, the larger houses attempted to unite and squash the minor lord. A civil war tore apart the shadmar houses, bringing great devastation to their home caverns. Ultimately, in the magical aftermath of the war, the ceilings of the great caverns shattered and fell, destroying much of the shadmar city of Dith Derithin. It was then that Delrith Niedrie's dream seemed essential for the future of the survivors. His dream united the remaining shadmar, even those that previously opposed him, and brought them to the surface and the beginning of their new future, their only future.

Captain Velstir paced nervously about the large antechamber. The rough stone had an ebon sheen. Though the ancient shadmar fortress had crumbled over the millennia since it was abandoned, these days its inner chambers were well restored. The captain admired his almost square visage and glistening red eyes that showed a hint of amber in the silver-framed mirror. The shadmar captain smiled at himself, proud of the progress his people were making. Never had the warrior seen his kin progress so far in his two centuries of life. Never had he seen such hope for a brighter future. No more war between the great houses of the shadmar; only peace and unity. The promise of the war to come had been a powerful motivating force.

It had been only a few decades since the shadmar climbed towards the surface. The captain easily remembered the hopeless tunnels and sleepless hours trying to guard the refugees from unseen monstrosities. The lightless caverns housed many vile beasts and expert predators. Now the shadmar dwelt comfortably in the numerous chambers deep under their ancient stronghold. Valraen was the ancient seat of the king of the shadmar during the rule of the Four

Kingdoms. Before the treachery of the light-skinned elves. Before the shadmar were banished to the deep underground over three millennia ago.

The captain dropped his smile and continued to pace, knowing that his impending meeting with the house patriarch would not turn out well. They had razed three elven villages over the past week. He was given strict orders to not allow a single survivor in these villages so that other settlements would not become aware of their presence. But that single elf, that wizard, had defied him. The captain knew he would take the blame. He wondered what his punishment would be for failing his patriarch. His mistake could single-handedly ruin their efforts if that wizard knew the attacks came from not mere raiders, but from a conquering army. The shadmar had planned to slowly establish themselves in this fortress and prepare their defenses. Then they would march to Elienspar, the capitol of the surface elves and the seat of the crown. Lord Niedrie planned to march in no more than a few months. Though the captain wished it were sooner.

Meanwhile, Lord Delrith Niedrie, the high lord of the fortress, sat upon an ancient, obsidian throne. His thin features accented his pale eyes and abnormal height. A thick mane of jet-black hair rolled over his shoulders. He sat alone, slowly stroking a large rat on his lap within the windowless chamber. He arranged for light absorbing blackness on the walls, using his magical prowess, so that he could ease the tension on his eyes. They were sensitive to the light, and he found this his only relief from the bright world above. The darkness was home, so alike to the stone caverns of the deep underground of which he was so accustomed. Although he knew that in time to come, his people would no longer be slaves to the darkness. They would one day welcome the sun and slaughter their enemies amidst the dawn. Once the war began and the traitorous surface elves fell before his armies.

This world will soon beckon to me, thought the shadmar patriarch as he continued to absent-mindedly pet the large, deformed rat on his lap.

A small knock on his chamber door interrupted him.

"Enter!" he shouted to the stone door.

A small-framed servant entered meekly. "Lord Niedrie, Captain Velstir wishes to discuss the results of the raid with you," the scrawny dark elf said.

A menacing grin spread across the dark lord's face as he jumped off his throne, sending the rat sprawling to the floor. He ran to the door and pulled it open in one wide gesture.

"Captain Velstir," he said smiling, "tell me what has befallen our enemies over the past few days." He then stepped into the doorway of the antechamber past the quivering servant.

The captain turned away from his pacing nervously, his voice evading him. The patriarch's eyes narrowed as he stood stern, facing the captain, who stood up straight and looked at his master, into those menacing pale eyes.

"Lord Niedrie," the captain said with a quick bow, "the raid has been largely successful. Our enemies have all been decimated in the three thulmar villages we've discovered. However..." The captain gulped.

"However?" the patriarch echoed impatiently, a tinge of anger growing on his face. The captain searched the hallway, trying to keep his view away from the growing flames in the eyes before him.

"However... an ethmar wizard escaped from the village we raided this week."

Fury flashed across the lord's face, "What!?" he exclaimed.

34

"S-S-Sorry, my Lord," the captain stammered. "We were awaiting your arrival to the surface before we acted. The commander feared that we would be going beyond the boundaries of your orders by sending any armed patrols," the captain recounted.

Pure rage roared to life within the Lord of House Niedrie, *"Why didn't you dispose of him!?"* he asked between gritted teeth.

The captain dropped to his knees, and stuttered, "H-H-He fled from us before we could reach him. I-I-I claim full responsibility in this matter," courage then returned to the old captain's voice, "He did not head toward the sulmar city, he flew eastward. With your permission, Lord, I shall hunt him down, personally."

The patriarch eyed the captain for a long moment, those burning eyes slowly losing their flames. "Have you memory of his face?" the lord then purred.

"Yes, my Lord," the captain said, his voice strong and resolute, "without a doubt in my mind."

Lord Delrith Niedrie grabbed the captain's neck and pulled the burly dark elf to his feet with surprising strength. "Then I will charge you to find him," he said intensely while staring into the captain's face. With a wave of the patriarch's dark hand, the captain fell asleep hard to the floor. The dark lord then turned to the servant cringing near the door, "Take our captain to the spell chamber, he is going to require a new *vestment* for this task."

The servant, knowing the price for sluggishness, quickly obeyed.

*   *   *   *   *   *   *

In the upper chambers of the foreboding fortress of Valraen, blood-curdling screams echoed down the halls. In Lord Delrith's spell chamber, the muscular body of Captain

Velstir lay nude and strapped to a circular table. The circumference of the large chamber featured many large candles and braziers burning with an eerie glow. A red pentagram was drawn upon the center of the three-tiered room on its lowest level. A few small candles burned at each of the five points of the star. In the center of that pentagram, the pained captain shuffled and screamed. Tears of pain dripped down Captain Velstir's cheeks as his cringing body was cut, stabbed, and prodded by a handful of servants. They quietly struck at him with large iron spikes, piercing the shadmar's limbs. A black-cloaked figure entered the room, the hint of a smile hidden beneath the cloak's hood.

"Are we comfortable, Captain?" the excited patriarch said sardonically as he slowly walked toward the small podium just outside the pentagram. He opened the large tome upon the podium and searched unhurried for the proper page. Ignoring the screams from Captain Velstir, the patriarch motioned for his assistants to leave the room.

"Now we begin, Captain. Now you wrestle with real demons," the patriarch whispered quietly, more to himself than to the injured warrior.

The dark lord raised his right hand and closed his fist tightly. The lights in the room all went out, except for the candles upon the pentagram's points, which turned an unearthly red as they brightened. The patriarch raised his other hand and began chanting in a dark, guttural tongue. The flames on those candles slowly rose, separating the fires from the wax bases. The hovering flames grew wildly.

The five flames, now each over a foot wide and three feet tall suddenly shot out at each other above the circular table, creating a flaming rift in space above the now quiet and frightened captain. The rift was a flaming circle with over a six foot diameter. Through the rift, glowing brimstone and hotter flames loomed in the distance. Soon a deep,

36

unearthly voice spoke from the rift in the same dark guttural tongue as the shadmar sorcerer behind the podium.

"Delrith of the mortal house of Niedrie, what services does thee request from the Indomitable Burning Lords of Xelenvar?"

The sorcerer grinned at his success in making contact with the demon-lord. Although it was certainly not the first time the sorcerer had made this connection, there was always the tentative fear of being greeted by silence. Delrith calmly walked towards the rift, but carefully remained outside the pentagram.

"A boon, my Lord Zalkael," the patriarch answered. "A simple request. I need only a lowly seeking-demon to take possession of this ineffective captain, so that our plans may go unhindered."

A low growl erupted from the flaming portal. Then silence. The flames burned around the rift, crackling and popping, slowly feeding off an infinite source. The patriarch felt a slight tingle at the back of his head, knowing that the demon would soon learn all he knew. Delrith waited nervously for the demon's reaction, but the long wait continued. He began counting the rough tiles on the floor, afraid to shuffle his feet even though the strain in his legs were begging for a readjustment of posture.

Suddenly, the demon's deep voice erupted, "I read your mind, mortal. These troubles do not bode well for our plans. Your boon is granted."

Then without pause, the rift closed and all the flames in the room went out as if a gust of wind had roared through the chamber. Delrith slowly began to breathe again, curiously eyeing the captain, who was staring back at the sorcerer with only hate in his eyes. The candles at each of the pentagram's points slowly returned to life. Red-glowing spirits, tiny motes of light, began to rise from the small flames, slowly drifting into the warrior's wounds. The captain returned to his screaming as the spirits began a horrific transformation on the shadmar warrior.

The dark elf's slender ebony hands and feet enlarged into huge raking claws. The square jaw of the captain stretched into a feline jaw with razor sharp teeth. The captain's muscular body gained strength and size. His intelligent eyes brightened into a flare of sinister instincts. Soon the shadmar warrior was replaced by a snarling, demonic, panther-like beast.

Delrith stepped towards the demon in awe as the spirits took control of the warrior's body. A smile spread across the patriarch's thin face as the transformation finished.

"Now, you are ready for the hunt, Captain," he said. The jet-black, panther-like demon snarled in reply as it was released from its bonds. The brawny beast crawled off the spell table and sniffed the air as if trying to find some unknown scent. Then it growled as if its quarry were nearby. The beast raced off down the corridors seeking the forest for a particular pale-skinned wizard.

(4) The Wizard and the Warrior

The boughs of the trees swayed in the increasing winds. Summer had long relinquished itself to the autumn and the weather was slowly preparing for the change to a colder winter. Birds and beasts alike scurried about finding shelter in the brewing storm. Among a small gathering of pines sat two figures huddled against the trunks seeking protection from the rain.

"Blasted, bothersome weather!" a frustrated Morstar muttered to himself. The pale-skinned elf beside him gave a slight nod and returned his gaze to the distant hill where the dark, black clouds of the storm were crawling their way across the horizon. Lightning flashed across the sky simultaneously with a bang of thunder as the rolling mass strode forward. The wind clawed and tore at the adventurer's faces bringing tears to their eyes. The trees grasped at the ground as their trunks swayed heavily.

The adventurers gave each other a worried look and grabbed their wet packs. They ran down the hillside into the welcoming forest below dragging their bags behind them. The wind chased them playfully as they stumbled down the rocky hill. The tired and weary travelers dropped to the ground amid the towering trees. Soaked and weak, hearts throbbing, lungs aching, they crawled under an arched tree root beneath the massive trunk and let weariness overtake them. The storm roared on through the countryside and the hours stretched on as the travelers slept peacefully underneath the thundering storm above.

Later, the aching dwarf climbed from his slumber and rose quickly to his feet. He gave a light kick to his comrade.

"Wake up, foolish elf," Morstar grunted to Thes. The tired wizard slowly rose to his feet as he stretched his arms with a yawn.

The wizard looked at his friend for a second in reflection, and then muttered, "That was a most disturbing slumber."

The dwarf answered with a puzzled look.

"It's nothing..." the elf replied quickly as he gathered his damp bags together. His dreams were haunted by the shadmar, relentlessly tormenting him in the fiery ruins of Escailar. But Thes shrugged off the nightmares as he stood and gazed at the forest around him, glad to be back in his homeland, his place of peace.

"I'll need a moment," Thes said quietly to Morstar, his eyes staring at nothing. He slowly walked away from the dwarf, feeling the rough bark of the nearby trees. The elf's visage showed nothing but serenity.

"Proceed," the dwarf said with a smile, glad to see Thes at peace, though he did not understand why, for dwarves were not known as lovers of the forest. He only shrugged and pulled out his whetstone and began to sharpen his hunting knife.

The next week was of little excitement for the two explorers. The rain had left the forest quite muddy and dreary, at least that was what Morstar thought of the situation. The mist of the gathered moisture seemed to be of comfort to Thes, who occasionally whistled a melodic song. At nights, they continued to share stories and tales from their homelands over a campfire. The unlikely pair were becoming fast friends, their tragedies and histories uniting them against the pain. Each one provided the other with a unique glimpse of each event and insightful wisdom.

The map the dwarf had purchased was quite crude, but the combination of Thes's knowledge of the forest and Morstar's sense of direction soon led the adventurers to

40

where the map indicated, the rumored location of an ancient Nomen crypt. They were climbing up a sloping hill ringed with large pines. On the top of the hill was a crumbled ruin. In its time it couldn't have been larger than a typical barn, but now it was little more than a low wall that ran along the perimeter of the flat plateau at the top of the hill. Grasses and vines had conquered the ruin long ago as the rocks were quite smooth and unremarkable.

"Well, this certainly doesn't seem to be a ruin of any significance," Thes said somewhat disappointed.

Morstar only snorted in reply as he examined the crumbling debris that was once the floor of the structure. He began to circle the ruin, seemingly scrutinizing every rock and stone left by the once prominent building. Thes soon grew impatient, however, and began wandering around the hill, whistling elven tunes to himself and thinking about what might lie inside the would-be crypt.

Over an hour passed and evening was darkening the hillside, the last rays of pink and violet light were cresting the horizon above the trees. The silence was broken with an excited "By Rolk's beard!" as Morstar came to the final corner of the crumbling wall.

Thes rushed over from near the bottom of the hillside, hoping the dwarf had found the entrance to the crypt. "Did you find it?" he asked.

"No," the dwarf replied bluntly, "But I know the crypt is beneath this hill."

Thes groaned as he turned away, returning to his contemplation.

"Maybe there is a cave or something nearby," Morstar muttered, a little frustrated.

Thes turned quickly, "A cave? There is one down there." He pointed to the north end of the hill.

The dwarf's face became agitated, "Why didn't ye say so?!"

Thes shrugged as he led the way down the slope. Morstar mumbled to himself as he followed. Soon the two were staring into the deepening darkness of a cave that led straight back beneath the hillside. Morstar grinned as he lit a torch and boldly entered. Thes followed, his heartbeat rising.

*   *   *   *   *   *   *

Darkness lingered on the edges of the torchlight, grasping for the figures in its protected aura. The stone walls of the tomb were well worn and cracked. The old masonry blocks had shifted, leaving a few gaping holes every few paces along the tunnel, hinting at something unforeseen in their depths. Dust drifted in small motes in the thick air, sailing slowly to the ground with each step of a heavy boot. Every step echoed through the tunnel; and it was the only sound the two heard for what seemed like an eternity.

Morstar decided to break the silence, "So, elf, what do ye think we'll find in here?"

Thes shrugged, "I'm hoping for some bits of ancient texts. But chances are the dead could be lurking in this old crypt, walking once more."

Morstar shook his head and tightened the grip on his hammer. His eyes wearily swinging to the left and right in case something emerged from the broken masonry. Every few paces he swung his head back so they wouldn't be ambushed from behind.

As his eyes centered on the long tunnel behind them, two red points grew in the distance as a brawny panther-like creature raced towards them. Morstar yelled a war cry as he lunged towards the incoming beast. His warhammer made contact with only air as the beast leapt above him and the dwarf fell forward finding the rough ground below.

The monsterous panther landed near Thes with a snarl. A row of razor-sharp teeth glistened in the torchlight

42

and a long, pointed tongue was poised behind in a pool of caustic ichor. With a quick pounce, the monster had its deadly paws on the elf's shoulders and its pointed teeth reaching for the wizard's neck.

Thes, completely surprised by the creature's appearance, made a frantic cry for help as he dropped and rolled downward and to the left, releasing himself from the beast's grasp. The monster's long, razor-like claws tore at the elf's shoulders, tearing a long gash down Thes's backside.

Morstar, after reaching his feet, approached the beast bearing his warhammer, his face angry and determined. The demonic panther growled and lunged. Morstar feigned a bull-rush to meet the attack, but then slid to his knees as he swung his hammer upwards with full force. It crashed into the beast's ribs with a loud cracking sound. Steam poured out of the wound and blood scattered across the floor. The dwarf dropped his hammer and rolled to the side scrambling. He narrowingly avoided being caught under the falling broken body of the beast. Morstar quickly wrenched his weapon from beneath the creature's squirming body and raised it up. He then dropped the hammer hard to the monster's skull, unknowingly releasing Captain Velstir's pain.

"Thanks," Thes said, "Are you alright?" He bent over offering a hand to the panting dwarf. Morstar only nodded and let himself be pulled to his feet.

The dwarf took in a deep breath and said, "We were lucky. I wonder where that damned creature. . ."

He stopped mid-sentence staring at the fallen corpse. In place of the black-skinned, panther-like creature he had slain moments before, laid the form of an ebony-skinned elf, bones shattered across the ribs. Neither adventurer noticed the blood-red spirits streaming out of the corpse into the cracks of the floor.

"Dark elf?!" muttered the dwarf in complete confusion.

Thes's jaw dropped and he slowly stepped away from the corpse. He felt like he had lost his mind. The vivid images of light-skinned elves being slain by the cruel swords of the shadmar warriors re-entered his vision. Burning buildings surrounded him as he stumbled about in the small tunnel of the crypt, trying to find the wall behind him for support. His breathing came in quick rasps of breath as he fell to the floor clawing at the masonry blocks, consciousness leaving him.

*　　　*　　　*　　　*　　　*　　　*　　　*

It was cold. Thes shivered as his eyes opened to see Morstar crouching over a small pile of timbers with some flint. The darkness of the crypt was gone, replaced by the darkness of the night and the glow of the stars; Thes turned to gaze at those shining stars above. He was laying comfortably on the dwarf's bedroll, his own cloak wrapped around him. The chirping of the nocturnal insects could be heard in the forest. The elf sighed, and his weak body shivered again. The wounds on his shoulders felt quite painful, but they at least were bandaged and cleaned.

Morstar was trying to ignite a bit of kindling with a piece of flint and the edge of a small blade. He nicked his thumb with the dagger he was using and muttered a curse under his breath. He tried a few more times until he got a bit of kindling to finally ignite. Confident in his preparations, the dwarf got up and sat on a log near the tired elf. Thes sat up and grinned at him, then reached towards the fire, muttered a few arcane syllables, and suddenly the small sparks began to grow rapidly into a roaring campfire.

The surprised dwarf fell off the log backwards and rolled quickly to his feet, staring wide-eyed at the wizard.

44

"Ye warn me before ye go throwing around that stuff. Could have burned me beard off," the dwarf scolded. He then just shook his head as he began throwing some bigger pieces of wood on the fire, muttering something about *damned elvish magic*. Thes's mind returned to the dark corridor and the dark elf form he saw within.

"So, what ye want to eat?" the dwarf said, breaking Thes's concentration. He grabbed a huge log and dropped it on top of the blaze. It was soon wreathed in flames.

"I dunno," shrugged the elf. "What are my choices?" He smiled to the burly dwarf.

"That depends what ye go foraging for," Morstar teased. He then reached over into his backpack and pulled out a large object wrapped in red cloths. The dwarf's eyes lit up as he unwrapped a huge chunk of cured venison. He smiled at Thes as he began searching in the timber-pile for a few good support sticks.

Thes only replied with a look of disgust. After the dwarf had his meat sitting over the fire with a row of sticks, he reached into his backpack again. He tossed the next cloth bundle he found to Thes. The wizard slowly unwrapped the cloth, expecting to find another dark chunk of flesh. To his delight, Thes found many various dried fruits and nuts cluttered together in the yellow cloth. He found the berries to be especially delicious.

The two ate in silence, watching the fire in peace. Thes was lost in his own mind thinking about Escailar again. Morstar wanted to ask the elf about the monster they had encountered and inquire about the elf's magic, but he respected Thes's space on the matter; so the two ate in silence, gazing at the crackling flames in the early autumn night.

Thes sat wondering about the dead shadmar, and why it was after him. Thes knew of powerful druids who could take the shape of an animal, this did not concern him as much as the shadmar seemingly hunting for him. *Why would a shadmar shape-changer leave the deep caverns below the world just to pursue a wandering wizard?* It didn't make any sense. *What could they have wanted?* Thes's mind circled around these questions endlessly. Morstar stared at the elf, wishing to ask his questions.

Eventually, Morstar couldn't wait any longer, "That's quite the flint ye have there," the dwarf said with a raised, curious eyebrow.

Thes turned to the dwarf, slowly pulling out of contemplation.

"Ye never said ye were adept at magic," Morstar inquired.

"You never asked," the elf replied with a grin.

"Tis a rare gift."

"Maybe. Though it's not much better than a good hammer and a stout heart."

The dwarf's eyes grew wide, "Not better than a hammer?!" he echoed incredulously. "Throwing fireballs and blasting rocks to dust?"

Thes laughed. "Don't believe all the tales," he said. "Though there may be a few powerful wizards that could wipe out entire armies, throwing balls of flame at their whim, magic isn't usually that simple."

"Then how does it work?"

The elf then thought for a moment, hand on his usual chin. "Well," he began, "the energy has to come from somewhere. I must expend the energy of my own mind. Eventually I get too exhausted to do much of anything." Thes gathered himself a moment before he continued, "Much of my power comes from communion with the spirit-world. The spirits of fire, air, earth, and water are a wizard's most valuable friends."

"Spirits? What do ye mean, like ghosts?"

"Something like that," the elf answered mysteriously.

"Ye sound more like a priest than a wizard," the dwarf said with a snort.

"Yes, perhaps I do," the elf explained. "When I was first taught the ways of magic, it was by a druid of my home village. The druids see magic more as a communion with the hidden spirits of the natural world. Whereas human wizards and the elves of the cities see magic as more of a systematic arrangement of thoughts and gestures that produce a desired effect; a science."

"Well, ye have a fine talent lad," the dwarf said smiling.

Thes only shrugged as he stood up, moving closer to the warm fire. "Don't the dwarves have magic? I've heard many tales of enchanted weapons and armors from the halls of the dwarven lords."

Morstar smiled, "Aye, tis true. We are masters of runelore, much like the giants of the mountains. Our runicks can imbue steel or stone with great strength, or hide a stone door on the face of a cliff. But I can't say I've ever seen them blast enemies or throw balls of flame."

"Well, you won't see me do it either. For me, the flame must already exist," Thes said with a smile, gesturing towards the campfire. He closed his eyes a second murmuring to himself as he put his palms together outstretched before him. The burning flames rose from their wood-source swimming and rolling in a large sphere as it rose above the pile of wood.

Morstar's eyes were wide with amazement as he stared back and forth from the flames to Thes. Thes returned the sphere down to its wood, which became its crackling, pointed shape once more. The elf put down his hands and winked at the dwarf. Morstar only chuckled, shaking his head.

Thes stood up and walked to the bed of moss against one of the towering oaks nearby. He laid down his weak body on the soft green bed while pulling his cloak about him.

Morstar soon put their fire out and lay upon his own bedroll near the elf. They stared optimistically at the wondrous sky that enfolded between the wind-swept boughs of the trees. It was only moments later that Thes lay quietly not far from a snoring dwarf dreaming about the next day's adventure.

(5) The Crypt Beckons

Early the next morning, the two brave adventurers were once again slowly creeping their way along that dark and silent tunnel of the ancient crypt. Morstar had dragged the shadmar's corpse out early in the morning, before Thes had finished breakfast, knowing his friend would have trouble seeing the shadmar again. The dwarf had piled rocks over the body of the dark elf, speaking a few words to Lagmud, the dwarven deity who watched over the dead, to guide the elf's soul to the halls of his ancestors. He believed such a prayer would prevent the shadmar's body from rising again from some dark magic. The crypt itself had enough dread without a lingering corpse of a shape-shifting enemy.

After nearly half an hour of walking down the sloping tunnel, they had reached the first room. They had very carefully checked the floors as they walked, fearing traps that may be left for tomb-robbers. Motes of dust floated in the air of the small room. An overwhelming sense of dread seemed to radiate from an unknown source. The square room was small with heavy masonry in tight blocks on all walls, the floor, and the ceiling. Four stone sarcophagi sat on the far wall of the dirty crypt.

The dwarf shuddered as he strode towards one of the stone coffins. Strange runes were etched along its side. One huge rune covered the stone lid. Thes swallowed as he read it.

'*Danger*' it read, in an ancient Nomen script.

Morstar turned to the elf with a look of fear and said, "Think there are traps?"

The elf shrugged, "Maybe not traps, but there could be something inside that may not want to be disturbed."

The dwarf shuddered and took a step back from the sarcophagus. The runes gleamed in the torchlight, beckoning for the two adventurers to explore its contents. After a few moments of gazing and swallowing, the dwarf leaned forward and pushed the heavy stone lid off the dusty coffin. It slammed onto the flagstones below, smashing it into smaller chunks of rock. The dwarf quickly leaped back and grasped his warhammer all in a quick motion, anxious but ready.

Thes raised his sword towards the dust cloud that rose from the ancient coffin. They both waited a few moments nervously; waiting for something dreadful to rise from the sarcophagus.

Nothing. Two sighs of relief echoed in that dark crypt. The two foolhardy adventurers proceeded the same way for the other three coffins. Each was empty. There were no treasures, no useless relics, or even the skeletal remains of the dead. This had the two explorers confused.

"Hmmm. . .I wonder where the bodies went," the dwarf said.

Formulating an answer himself, the dwarf began to look frantically about searching for walking corpses in the corners of the room. Thes glanced about as well, but neither of them saw any dangers.

"Look around, elf. There has to be some sort of secret door or compartment somewhere," Morstar said determinedly.

Thes complied, though he had already assumed that the crypt had been emptied centuries before they arrived.

The dwarf scrutinized every crack and crevasse along the walls and floor of the crypt. When he had finished, all he found was an old finger-bone tucked between two uneven flagstones.

"This is emptier than a stone giant's heart!" Morstar yelled in frustration, his deep voice echoed down the long tunnel. "There has to be at least a scrap of gold or commoner's gem for our troubles." The angry dwarf muttered to himself.

Suddenly, Morstar's eyes grew and his jaw dropped. Thes gave him an unusual look as the dwarf crawled to one of the sarcophaguses and pushed on its long side with all his strength. The giant, stone casket slowly gave way and made a shrieking grating wail as Morstar slid it a few feet to the side. Underneath the coffin was a mostly decayed wooden trapdoor.

Thes laughed with full spirits. The elf came beside the grinning dwarf and asked, "How did you know?"

The dwarf turned to his friend, his grin stretched into a toothy smile. "I noticed the uneven stonework near the sarcophagus. At first I thought it was the flagstones, but then I saw that the flagstones by this sarcophagus were tightly packed. I knew I had to look."

Thes chuckled, "Now that is dwarven magic."

Morstar continued to smile wide as he opened the ancient trapdoor.

*   *   *   *   *   *   *

A sound echoed in the darkness. It was a sound that had not been heard in many, many years. A crumbled skeletal form slowly slid off its broken throne. Its bony arms straightened the thin, golden circlet upon its cracked skull. No creature would dare disturb this ancient wizard's undeath. Unsure of how long he sat hunched in his chair, the ancient lich staggered to a nearby desk.

For years, the lich had simply sat in its crumbling throne, simply pondering about minor details of existence itself. *Why did fools have to disturb his thought process, just when he was coming to a solution to his problems,* the dark wizard thought. Searching wildly, the skeletal form opened each cabinet and desk for the scroll he sought. He was not about to be surprised either.

*   *   *   *   *   *   *

The air was stale in the huge, long hall. Rows of pillars lined to each side of the adventurers. The elf set a spell upon the dwarf's helmet; it glowed with the radiance of a torch creating a light to lead them by. The light added an effect to the darkness that only enhanced their fears, however. The taint of death simply hung in the air. The two explorers felt the intense dread in the mists that surrounded the walls. Fear would have been an understatement. The dwarf had well passed his second thoughts on turning around and was working on his fourth. Both companions were wondering if any treasure or knowledge was worth each dreadful second that passed. Each second that one of their booted feet pressed against a possible trap. Each second that their breaths echoed across the large hall possibly alerting any dangers. Dread was everywhere.

They continued down the stone hall. Two rows of pillars lined each side, the thick stone carved with many worn and dust-covered designs. Darkness hid the far end of the hall and shadows danced along the edges of the walls behind the pillars.

The dwarf took in a deep breath and sighed, trying to release the terror that hung at the back of his skull. The elf simply closed his eyes for a second reminding himself of the knowledge that may remain here. Each of the travelers was completely unaware of what was to come.

Across the long stone hall, a bright flash erupted from one of the many pillars lining the hall to their left. The pillar at the far end suddenly fell over. It began to roll down the row of pillars knocking them down one by one. The rolling barrage of stone tumbled towards the unwary adventurers. The dumbfounded explorers' eyes grew wide as the massive stone pillars fell their way.

With a quick grab for his less agile companion, Thes jumped to the right and rolled. The dwarf stumbled in his lead. They ran past the other row of columns and turned down the hall again, scrambling to their feet. They stumbled down the hall between the right row of pillars and the wall. The ceiling began to rumble, however, knocking them off their feet. Then, the left side of the hall crumbled and caved in. Crawling behind the safety of a pillar, the travelers waited for the shifting stones to stop and the large cloud of dust to settle.

"That was too close for my liking," Morstar grumbled after the thundering crunches of falling stones ceased, returning the dreadful silence to the room.

"Indeed," replied the elf, "I wonder what sort of trap triggered that event. It seemed to be magical in nature." The elf thought a moment, and then said, "I did not feel my feet trigger any trap."

"Neither did I," the dwarf stated, gazing at the wreckage the cave-in had caused. "I only pray by Rolk's beard we aren't trapped in this unearthly crypt. I may be likin' the underground as much as the next dwarf, but I'd be an ogre's breakfast before I die in this gloomy pit."

"Relax, my stout friend. I may have a way to get us out if need be. Just pray to your god's beard that this crypt isn't protected against my magic."

The dwarf gulped and looked about again. He nodded to his slender partner, got to his feet, and began walking down the remnants of the hall. The elf followed.

$$* \quad * \quad * \quad * \quad * \quad * \quad *$$

Since the hallway had been reduced to the small walkway between the right row of pillars and the wall, many of the doors they had seen previously were no longer accessible, however, at the far end of the hall was a single wooden door. Time and decay had its toll on the door, a large hole gaped in its side; large enough for Morstar to easily walk through, and Thes with a slight duck of his head to follow. Beyond the broken door, an elaborate laboratory stretched before the wary heroes.

The large room had bookshelves and cabinets on every wall, covered with cobwebs and tattered pieces of old parchment from books that couldn't stand the test of time. Four tables dominated the center of the room from which mystical lights gleamed within many glass decanters and vials. Thes's eyes lit with wonder when he looked at all the magnificent potions and elixirs glistening in their glass containers. The dwarf ignored the collection of bottles and was more concerned with the door on the far side of the room. Morstar walked to the heavy wood door and stuck his ear to it and listened carefully. A low hiss was all he could hear beyond the oaken slab.

"Thes, do ye hear that," he whispered to his distracted companion, "behind the door."

Regretfully, Thes ignored the magical wonders before him and stepped beside his shorter friend.

His keen, pointy ears allowed the elf to hear the horrible hissing sound before he even reached the door. A look of puzzlement crossed his face as he listened. Thes began to murmur to himself in an archaic tongue as he closed his eyes, concentrating on the door. Wisps of a nearly imperceptible energy seemed to flow through the door to the elf's ears. The sounds in the other room became clear within Thes's mind.

"Yesss. . . .killsss them I mussst. Disturb my'sss rest they doesss," a broken croaking voice said with great disgust and annoyance.

"It is as we feared," Thes muttered.

54

Morstar looked at him, puzzled.

Thes just began to slowly back away from the door and make his way for the hole that led back into the crumbled hallway. Morstar began to feel his hairs on the back of his neck stand on end, as he, too, made way for the other door, eyes still fixed on the closed oaken door, now hissing louder.

Wooden pieces suddenly burst through the air, as the door the heroes had previous stood by exploded into scattering splinters. A dark shape emerged from the shadows of the doorway. It was a human-sized skeleton dressed in the scraps of a once purple robe with a melted golden crown resting on its skull. It stood glaring at its intruders with burning eye sockets. Rage flowed from those burning eyes; rage and death gleamed from those hollows. The ravaged skeleton stepped towards its trespassers with infinite patience. The two frightened adventurers were already at a full sprint down the destroyed hallway.

Booted feet echoed down the long hall after the explorers scrambled up the trapdoor. Like a pounding hammer the sounds increased in frequency as two frightened adventurers ran frantically for the comforts of the trees outside. Behind them a red, haunting light followed. It slowly gathered intensity in light and terror as it began to catch up to the four pumping legs in the dark halls of the tomb.

The bright illumination of the outdoors greeted the dwarf and elf as they ran. A giant ball of wreathing flames shot towards the desperate heroes. Morstar felt his back scorching from the heat and the scales on his armor reached painful temperatures. Thes's cloak had caught aflame and he released its brooch as he dived to the side just as he reached the outside. Many prickling bushes met his face and arms. A deafening explosion echoed through the trees as the fireball reached the ground just outside the tomb.

With weary legs, and an even more weary heart, Thes climbed to his feet. The ground near the tomb entrance had been scorched beyond repair. The cavern entrance had caved in, forever ceasing explorers from entering the dark crypt and disturbing its ancient, undead master. The beautiful bushes that adorned the opening now were slowly-burning, wiry twigs.

Morstar climbed quickly to his feet and stepped out of the small clearing he had leaped into. The dwarf's eyes met the elf's and grins reached both their cheeks. Thes grabbed his burned cloak from the wreckage. Without a word spoken, both explorers sprinted through the trees. Neither of them saw the dark, red eyes that followed them.

After nearly ten minutes of sprinting through the trees, the adventurers stumbled to a halt beneath the welcoming shadow of a huge pine.

Morstar looked to the elf with a wide smile across his face, "Enough adventure for ya, elf ?"

The exhausted elf sighed, "Indeed. Perhaps I shall become a baker."

The dwarf burst into fits of laughter at the thought of the thin elf sticking bread into an oven. The elf soon joined him. After a few minutes of amusement, the two sat up and began to decide what to do next.

"Well, we could check out other sites that are marked on that map," Thes began.

The dwarf grumbled, "I think we've had enough fun disturbin' the dead."

"Well, this little excursion didn't seem to be all that was promised, was it?" Thes said with a smile.

A perplexed expression grew on Morstar's face, "Wait, you hear something?"

Silence greeted the adventurers. Nothing seemed to be stirring in the forest. Not even the chirping of songbirds or the scurrying of little rodents. Silence. Panic seized the travelers as they sat up quickly. Out of the forest's depths many dark shapes came into focus from behind the trees. Many dark-skinned elves surrounded the disheartened adventurers with many crossbows and swords in their hands. Shadmar.

Anger instantly filled the wizard's heart. His rational mind lost in the torrent of rage. Thes tried to contain himself, but his eyes began to glow with an inner energy. The shadmar moved in closer until their shoulders almost touched. They were nearly ten feet from the dwarf.

"RUN!" Morstar screamed as his hammer flashed out and slammed into two unprepared shadmar. Thes then released the energy of his anger into an explosion of electrical energies at the confused shadmar. Lightning ripped through two more unwary shadmar warriors. Their crippled bodies flew into unyielding tree trunks. The two explorers leaped over the fallen warriors and rushed into the cover of the trees. The shadmar simply stood their position.

An ebony hand reached towards the running explorers as dark, slithering words echoed from the owner's mouth. Red flames crackled around the dark hand and blood-red spirits spiraled from the fires towards the adventurers. The dark spirits sped quickly to the dwarf and elf, wrapping around their limbs with magical tentacles of energy. Their grip tightened.

Morstar's limbs suddenly stopped moving. "I can't move!" he cried as he fell to the ground, warhammer falling beside him.

Thes fell as well; his muscles unable to pull free from the curling dark spirits grasping his arms and legs. The wizard's rage burned yet in his body, but he was too weak to release the fury into the air. "No!" he cried in defiance as his face tore through the leaves, desperately trying to rise again. "I will not yield!"

"But you will," a cruel voice said from behind the wizard. A swirl of pain and darkness came over Thes, who felt a heavy club strike his head.

(6) The Tales of Forest-Dwellers

Two curious eyes watched from above. A small maple leaf was slowly curling to the ground. The wind toyed with it like a child does to scurrying ants in the grass. The leaf would slowly drift to the ground only to be lifted by the wind again. The owner of the curious eyes smiled in amusement as he placed another small piece of rough, dry meat into his mouth. The food wasn't great by any standards, but it certainly kept well for a long time.

With a sigh, the man sat up on his branch and leapt to the ground, many feet below. His body landed in a perfect crouch with barely a sound.

The human stood six feet tall and was clothed in quality leathers of deep brown with many iron studs dotting its exterior. A dark green cloak adorned his shoulder and back along with a closed quiver of arrows and a curved, long bow. Two leather scabbards adorned his belt with a few small pouches. Light brown hair lay loosely upon the man's head with a few strands hiding his deep brown eyes. His curious smile was surrounded by the shadow of a full, but moderately trimmed, dark brown beard. The ranger slowly walked through the trees listening to the sounds of the smaller creatures. A small falcon suddenly landed upon the man's shoulder, squawking in earnest.

"What is it, my friend," a warm, concerned voice said to the bird. The ranger concentrated and sensed the fear within the avian creature. "Where to my friend? Show me what disturbs you." The bird leaped from his shoulders and took flight through the trees; the hooded ranger following behind.

It was only a matter of a few minutes until the silent ranger found himself on a branch, ten feet above the ground.

He was quietly watching as seven dark-skinned shadmar warriors led two prisoners through the forest.

Suddenly one of them shouted, *"Tuiave nesuirtir!"* The ranger listened to the elven words.

"Quiet, you fool," a robed shadmar said to the warrior who yelled his victory cry. The words were like a knife and the warrior's mouth came to a close. Malvu'ir hated dealing with such dimwitted fools. Since the patriarch's recent arrival to the surface, it had been his duty to take these idiotic louts with him on these pointless patrols.

At least this time the patrols have proved profitable Malvu'ir thought, glaring at the two adventurers being dragged before him. His patriarch would surely appreciate the elven sacrifice he had brought, and the dwarf would make a good slave. He would be rewarded well. Malvu'ir smiled at that thought as an arrow whistled through the air and pierced his throat.

The ranger dropped many other shadmar warriors before any of them knew what was going on. Morstar and Thes soon felt the soft bed of leaves comfort their sharp fall to the ground as the shadmar that held them clutched at arrows in their abdomens. Fearing that an elven warband was upon them, panic seized the shadmar warriors and the remaining three members fled through the trees without even a fight.

Quiet footsteps, trained from many years in the wild lands, graced Thes's ears. The wizard struggled to turn over and look upon his rescuer. A dark, hooded figure stood over him. Nothing but a row of teeth arranged in a smile could be seen within the dark hood.

"Are you two alright?" a calm voice from within the hood said in the elven tongue. Morstar only groaned as he struggled to his feet with the bonds on his hands and legs still attached.

"We could be better. Could you cut our bonds hooded stranger?" Thes asked politely. The cloaked man bent over and cut each of the heavy ropes that bounded the elf with a curved dagger. He then cut the bonds of the dwarf before returning the dagger to his belt.

"We can't thank you enough. What name do you go by, stranger?" Thes asked, still in the beautiful eloquence of the elven language.

"What are ye sayin'? Can't ye two just speak in the Nomen tongue?" Morstar grumbled, as he grabbed his hammer from one of the dead shadmar warriors.

"My apologies, dwarf," the man said as he bowed slightly, "We must go, I shall explain everything at a later time. I know a sacred spot not far from here where it will be safe to speak." The hooded figure than began to run through the trees with barely a sound. The two adventurers shrugged at each other, grabbed what gear they could, and followed.

*   *   *   *   *   *   *

"So, what is your name, stranger?" Thes asked the unshaven man after giving his own name. They were now many miles from where they were saved; the hooded ranger took them through the forest to a small hut. It was in a glade hidden from view by rising rock cliffs. It was graced with a stream that trickled its way down the cliff side to a small pond. Only a small stair built into the stone cliff led down into the glade. *Enchantingly beautiful* Thes would have put it. This was clearly some sort of sanctuary of the ancient druids.

The hut itself was small, maybe ten feet round; it seemed to be built of deadwood sodden with mud and sticks, with hand-cut boards as a frame. Only a wide table adorned it with four poorly-made chairs. A few barrels and boxes lined one wall, two leather quivers hung from a nail on another wall with many arrows filling their bulk. The man seemed to hang most of his possessions by these outstretched pegs, for his leather jacket and scabbard now both hung from pegs on the other wall, his bow leaning against the corner. One corner held a pile of linens and furs, presumably a bed for the ranger.

"Artemis Mengsk," the man answered the question. "Bane of gnolls and evil kings, and an elf-friend to the woodland dwellers."

"A man of the forest," Thes stated. "I knew some men had been said to dwell within the reaches of the woods, but I thought they were few and far between."

"Yes, few men would seek the solitude of the forest boughs, but I feel it is my place. And it is my duty to protect those that travel within."

"We thank you; your rescue could not have been more perfectly timed," said the elf.

"Aye, thank you woodsman," Morstar grumbled looking about impatiently. "Ye got anything strong to drink here. My mind needs some ease after that little scare we had."

"Scare?" the ranger asked with puzzled uncertainty. "Were the shadmar that horrible to bear?" he added with slight sarcasm.

"Hardly! We faced an angry lich early this morn," the dwarf stated proudly.

The ranger only raised a disbelieving eyebrow.

Morstar began the tale about the lich and the tomb they explored. Thes kept quiet during the tale. The ranger seemed amused by their story but fearful of the lich that dwelt beneath the tomb.

"Liches are nothing to laugh at, dwarf. I have heard many tales of their power and wish not to be visited in the night by an angry skeletal wizard wishing to seek vengeance upon you."

62

Morstar only chuckled and tightened his belt with a bit of bravado.

Changing the subject, Thes suddenly spoke, "Where do you hail from, Artemis?"

The ranger looked solemnly at the elf for a second. "Far from here, in the southern reaches of the Wildren Forest. In a small town known as Layu on the Lilayan River within the borders of Gerdall Kingdom; I once was a protector of that land and the forest within it."

"What brings you so far from your home?"

The man preserved his solemn expression. "It is a sad tale, not to be shared with strangers. I have been within this great Aegis Forest for over five years, and it will be my home for many more."

Thes and Morstar only looked to each other, not wanting to break the solemn silence.

"But it matters not why I am here, only that I am. For if I were not, I could not have stumbled upon the oddest pair of travelers I have ever seen. Nor could I have saved them from certain slavery in the dark caverns of the deep underground." Artemis smiled, "What brings an elf and a dwarf together disturbing crypts and battling dark elves?"

Morstar only chuckled as Thes shrugged absentmindedly. The elf's thoughts were lost as the last two words of the ranger's question echoed in his mind: *dark elves, dark elves.* Again he wondered, *why were dark elves still within the forest? Why hadn't they returned below to the darkness of their caverns after the raid upon the village?*

"Thes?" the dwarf asked, waving his hand in front of the elf's staring eyes.

The elf popped out of his reverie and eyed the dwarf curiously.

"What's on yer mind?" Morstar asked.

Thes sighed and looked at the dwarf and the ranger. "The dark elves," he said slowly, "Why are they still in the

63

forest? I am concerned with the presence of the shadmar on the surface. I fear for the lives of the men that dwell nearby and for the other elven villages."

"Yes, it is strange that the dark elves would remain on the surface after a raid," the ranger said.

Thes looked surprised as he stared at Artemis.

"Yes, I was aware of the raids last week," the ranger began, answering the wizard's unspoken question, "I saw three sets of flames in the distance over the course of the last week. The smoke did not clear until that storm came over the trees a few days past."

"Three fires?" Thes asked bewildered.

"Yes, I saw three fires. I believe it was the villages of Teillina, Escailar, and another I did not know. At least those are the only villages that I am aware of in the region."

"Escailar was one of them," Thes said sadly. "I was there."

The elf began the tale of the battle. He left the magical parts in the story, trusting his new friend. It seemed a bit easier to relate the story a second time, but not by much. Now he understood more too, it seems the archers from Diiera, the third village, had left their village unprotected when they came to the aid of Escailar. *Only to die in the fires*, the wizard thought. Thes then told the tale of the panther-like monster and the shadmar patrol, trying to make sense of the events himself.

"It seems the shadmar have no intentions of returning to their dark caverns." Thes concluded.

"Yes," Artemis said, "They must have fortifications somewhere, perhaps even open war is their intention."

"Aye, it may be so," Morstar mumbled to the room.

Thes's mind wondered. As he thought of a possible war between the shadmar and the surface-dwelling elves, flames of rage and vengeance began to burn in his heart. It was a visceral hatred aimed at the cruel shadmar. This emotional part of him was secretly joyful that the dark elves remained. Vengeance could be his.

The elf suddenly slammed his fist on the table as the joyful rage enslaved him. "It is my duty to save my homeland," he stated determinedly. "I know neither their numbers nor their strengths, but I will not rest until I can put an end to these shadmar invaders."

Thes rose from his chair and looked hard at the two warriors that sat beside him. He turned an eye to both of them, silently beckoning them to join in his quest. His heart was surging with adrenaline and anger.

With a crooked smile, the dwarf laughed "By Rolk's beard! Someone must make sure ye live through this, elf. Ye can count me in to help."

Thes smiled at the dwarf, then turned to the silent ranger, "What about you, will you help me, Artemis 'Aegistrider'?"

The ranger's head lifted and smiled at the elf upon hearing the title bestowed upon his name. "I suppose my arrows can join the fray. This is my home as well. I will protect these forests with my blood if need be."

The three clasped arms to celebrate their newfound fellowship. They then each sat back down at the table, the full reality of the situation dispelling the moment of comradery.

"First we need to find out where they may be hiding," Thes began.

"Yes," said the ranger, "Tomorrow we can search for the tracks of that patrol and follow those fleeing shadmar to their home fortress."

Thes's face lit up, "Excellent! As soon as we have confirmation of a shadmar army, we could head to Elienspar and inform the city's soldiers. I would imagine that the messengers of the destroyed villages will soon reach the city to inform them of the raids anyway. However, if we can also provide strategic details about their encampment, it may help the retaliation. It is likely the crown will only send a small patrol if it suspects raiders."

"Then it is imperative that we verify our suspicions that a dark elf army lies within our midst," the ranger stated.

The elf nodded. "But what do you think three foolhardy adventurers can do against a possible army of shadmar warriors."

The ranger's hand found his chin, "Hmmm, you speak truth. It would indeed be a challenge beyond our strengths if we were to be discovered. They already know that we exist and that we have seen them." The man turned to the dwarf, "Perhaps, Morstar can go to the nearby human towns and find a few like-minded warriors. Maybe even mercenaries if need be."

"Aye, I can do that. I suppose I wouldn't do much good at tracking silently through the forest anyways." He chuckled slightly to himself as he banged on his chestplate. The dwarf then stood up, reached for his hammer, and headed towards the door. Artemis and Thes turned and looked at each other and laughed at the dwarf.

"What now?" Morstar grumbled, turning around to face the two chuckling figures.

"You're leaving now? Do you plan on walking on through the night, dwarf?" the ranger laughed.

"Mayhaps. Unless ye have a keg of ale, I'll be better for it when I reach that inn," with those last words the dwarf was halfway out the door of the small hovel, leaving the other two in fits of laughter before the dwarf heard the popping of a keg's cork and happily returned to the finest berrywine he had ever tasted.

That night the three shared tales of their exploits. The ranger may be a very knowledgeable woodsman, but he had not traveled for much of his life. He had grown up in Layu, a small town within the Kingdom of Gerdall. His father was a hunter and his mother was a skilled tanner, he was an only son and together they made a modest living selling leathers. The ranger relayed tales as a boy playing in the woods and learning to hunt and be silent amongst the trees. He used to practice his archery deep in the forests near the river, and it was during one visit that he met Draken Pendragon, a prince of Gerdall, who happened to be near his age. They became fast friends despite Draken's noble heritage.

King Artean was glad his own son had a trusted friend and treated Artemis like family. The king would often tell the young boys tales of knights and dragons, and other heroics. The rest of the family, however, was quite cruel. Draken's older brother Gaul in particular was a mean, spoiled child. He would spit on the young Artemis, calling him names like 'serf-spawn' and 'mudborn'. Over the years, the friends saw less of each other as Draken trained in knighthood in the Order of the Golden Sword, like his father before him, while Artemis became ever more adept as a ranger in the Wildren Forest.

Their friendship was separated as Draken and the Knights of the Golden Sword left Gerdall to join the crusades in the western lands, fighting for the holy city of Korratus. That was ten long years ago; Artemis was only nineteen at the time. That same year Artemis had joined with the Rangers of Lilayan with the other hunters of the forest. They were a small band of adept archers and woodsmen that could protect the kingdom on its forest-rich western side. During these years, Artemis was very busy maintaining that western border, for raids from gnolls and orcs had become ever so common with the majority of the knights in the distant lands of the west.

Just over five years ago, three large bands of gnoll raiders charged through the forest. The rangers intercepted the middle group and valiantly held them off, though with heavy losses. The other two groups had slipped through the forest's defenses. One band surprised the King's patrol on the southern road heading to the castle, slaying the guards and King Pendragon himself. The other band went to the north and raided the village of Layu, burning it to the ground.

The castle's soldiers forced the gnolls to flee, but the kingdom was never the same. Prince Gaul assumed the throne, demanding larger taxes and tithes to increase protection for the kingdom. Artemis and his band of rangers fled the kingdom, proclaimed exiles by the prince for failing in their duties. It was then that the ranger trudged on alone into the far north, finding the Aegis Forest as refuge. The loss of Layu was still burning in his heart.

At the end of that sad story, Morstar poured himself a fourth cup of berrywine as Thes decided to tell the tale of his own upbringings.

Thes, who was over a century old, had spent most of his life within the trees of the Aegis Forest, letting years trickle by as most men would let a few hours slip by in reverie. For the long-lived elves, some have been known to live over five-hundred years, time was a less precious commodity and things were done with care and patience.

The elf's father was a humble merchant and ferrier, bringing berries and herbs, gathered by the elves and packed in sealed barrels, down the rivers from the ancient forest to the towns and cities of the eshmar of the Eshlien Valley to the east. His mother, an accomplished weaver would work from the home and stay with the children, for he had two siblings: his older brother Judikar, and his younger sister Nisember, or Nissy as she would often be called. The children would run through the village's high walkways chasing each other with wooden swords and long sticks as staves. There were only a couple ethmar families in the village of Muinhen, for it was a village of mostly wood elves high in the boughs of the trees, much like Escailar.

It was during these childhood years that Thes noticed he could hear the voices of the brooks and streams, the crackling fires, the breeze above, and even the rocks below his feet. The local druid, an aged elf named Sulaeren, became aware of his talents and sought to train him. Thes had turned thirty years old, reaching the Age of Skill as it was known amongst the wood elves, for this is when they seek their first trade-skill and pursue their talents. Sulaeren approached the young elf and began the long years that would teach him to be a druid, despite his ethmar heritage.

Thes learned quickly and was fascinated by magic and the spirits of the world. The lessons would take the two through many strange journeys in the woodlands and beyond. Thes did not share completely with his new companions. But he recounted the long years of training, and when he reached his ninetieth birthday he had finished his long study under the druid. His friends and siblings were long gone, having already established themselves in various places long before. For most elves finished their training by seventy-five and pursued a trade on their own. His sister had become a jeweler in Elienspar, while his brother became a silversmith in another town.

Still enthralled by magic, the newly-trained druid left the forest into the lands of men. Thes studied magic in many forms, spending many years under the tutelage of Gharagon the Grey, a wizened, old human wizard that helped to sharpen the elf's skills and teach him new ways to approach magic. After the tragic death of Gharagon, a topic the elf did not elaborate on, Thes went seeking magical lore alone in various parts of the world.

Every druid had an element that they connected to most deeply, and for the wandering, whimsical elf it was the element of *air*. This is why he was so adept at channeling lightning and requesting the spirits of the air to carry him aloft. It was for this purpose he sought the fabled city of

Orno across the Freewind Savannah. The mythical city of many towers was said to have many adept sorcerers who mastered the winds and clouds. But Thes failed to cross the endless plains that separated him from the fabled city and decided that the life of an adventurer was waning in him.

It was then the elf returned to the forests of his homeland where he learned of his brother's accidental death in the silver forges and his sister's mysterious disappearance. Thes knew his sister was talented in the mystic arts, like himself, and figured she had given up on jewelry to learn magic in a far off land, at least this is what he had hoped. There was little information about her whereabouts. But the wizard decided to stay with his mother, who was distraught both over Judikar's death and Nissy's disappearance. It was only a year later that Thes's father was killed by bandits along the river. The heartache seemed too much for his mother, for not long after, she had died a natural death, though it could only be the sorrow that took her.

After many years of grieving and with no family left to tend to, Thes took about wondering the forest and mastering his magic. He eventually settled in the small town of Escailar, finding the small village much like the village where he grew up. The people there came to rely on the wizard for the defense of the village. Despite having some desire to return to his travels, the elf couldn't leave the villagers. He settled into his new role as the village wizard and alchemist. Only occasionally did he venture to the human lands or to Elienspar for books or scattered lore to continue his studies of the mystical and arcane.

Thes seemed to stop the story short, not wanting to talk much of Escailar or the time he spent there before its tragic destruction. Morstar took the hint and began his own tale, in the great mountain-homes of Kalavar.

Morstar was raised in the Hall of Forges in the city of Gorgaddur to be a metalsmith like his father. The

70

underground cities of the dwarves had many sections and divisions, and the smiths held some of the most honored positions in dwarven society. The greatest of the smiths labored in the deepest tunnels where great magma forges burned. These forges produced great steel weapons and armaments, for dwarven steel could be found in no other place. The steel made by men could not match the strength and durability of the dwarven metal. The dwarves also produced weapons made of Kalavarian steel, an iron alloy composed of an uncanny metal found deep in the earth. Only magma could soften that metal, and only the dwarves could master the molten rock to do so.

During Morstar's youth, the Fourth Great Orcish War was underway. The orcs prized the many riches of the dwarves. The forges worked hard for the armies of the dwarves that fought off the orcs. The tusked, green-skinned humanoids seemed to pour through the mountains from the northern lands, bringing giants and goblins and other nasty creatures with them. Though he was still only an apprentice blacksmith, Morstar sought glory and fame in the battles. He left his trade behind and joined the soldiers of the mountain.

The war had little glory for the warrior, for it was mostly a dirty, cold affair. He spent many nights curled in fractured battlements trying to steal a few hours of sleep before his fort was bombarded again by boulders thrown from giant hands. Morstar fought bravely and earned rank quickly, soon he was a sergeant of his own patrol. He had been in many battles, his hammer fractured more orc skulls than he could count, he even boasted of felling a few giants. After spending thirteen years in the war, it finally ended and the orcs ceased their onslaught.

Morstar returned home, finding the quiet life missing the excitements he had become accustomed. He found it hard to relate to his parents, for they had never seen the terrors of battle and the heartache of loss when a friend dies by your side. Feeling estranged from his family, the dwarf returned to the soldiery, spending much time as a guard in the mountain-homes, until he had finally secured a position as a patrol sergeant. It was then he was free to travel the lands around the mountains he loved. But years later, the lesser goblins became more frequent as the wealth of the dwarves began to flow east and southward to the human lands. Morstar related to Artemis the tales of his last patrol and the pain that brought him to the south.

With this last story told, it was now deep into the night and the adventurers climbed into comfortable places on the floor of the hut to sleep the night away, the many tales drifting into their dreams.

(7) Taste of Revenge

It was a strangely warm night in the deep trees of the Aegis Forest. Many storms have left their mark upon the land in the fierce autumn weather. Mud clung to the forest floor and the roots of the trees stretched a little to enjoy warmth before the coming winter. The owls didn't seem to mind as they hooted to each other in the darkening gloom as bits of rain still dripped from the trees. The light of the stars and moon provided some dim illumination.

Thes and Artemis had been waiting in the trees for the past few days, hoping to spot the shadmar patrolling near the area where the ranger had rescued Thes and Morstar. Now the two adventurers were hiding high in a tree peering down on an unaware group of shadmar below them.

"They seem to be waiting for something," the elf whispered to the cloaked man beside him. They crouched patiently upon the high branch of an oak. Thes brought his free hand to his chin in a favored position of thought. Down below, the shadmar warriors were arguing about their orders.

"I tell you, we are to find them and kill them," one of the taller warriors, named Gundal, said to his two companions, rage glowing brightly in his red eyes. *How much longer will I be stuck out here with these fools?* he thought. *Whoever killed the last patrol is long gone and there is no chance of finding them. Why do all of his leaders send him out with impossible orders and fools to follow them?*

"But if we capture them alive we can learn who else knows of our presence," the shortest of the three argued his point again. Gundal shoved him back with a sharp fist and watched the young warrior fall to the forest floor in a none-to-pleasing puddle of mud. But before the younger elf could retaliate, Gundal sword whipped out of its sheath and stuck pointed to the shadmar's breast.

"I'm in charge here. We do this my way," the taller warrior replied enunciating each word as sharp and cold as the sword that held the shadmar to the ground. "We kill whoever sees us. Now move out."

Ruencen pulled himself from the mud with one of the lower branches of a nearby shrub. His eyes suddenly grew huge in surprise as he saw the shadow of two crouching figures in the trees. However, he could only gurgle a startled gasp as an arrow pierced his throat.

"Ruencen?!" Gundal roared, "We're moving out you stupid fool..." He stopped in midsentence as he watched his subordinate's corpse lurch to the side, back into the puddle of mud.

Gundal raised his shield just in time as another arrow pierced its top just above his arm. Another shadmar warrior raised his shield as well and used his sword-arm to pull out a small charm from around his neck. He pressed the small gem upon it. Blood-red spirits soared into the air at lightning-fast speed. A few more arrows pierced their shields. The shadmar warriors remained solely on the defensive as more arrows, now glowing with magical explosive energy, shattered shields and left small dents in the ground at their feet.

Moments later a six-foot wide ring of bright red flames appeared just above the ground not far from the shadmar, who were now taking cover behind the trees. The warriors were trying to return the arrow fire with carefully thrown daggers. Ten more shadmar warriors then stepped out of the ring of fire, firing crossbows and throwing daggers at the two figures huddled in the thick canopy.

"Our luck has run out, my friend," the wizard told the ranger beside him. Thes murmured a few quick incantations and grabbed the upper arm of his friend, just as Artemis

74

released another arrow into a shadmar archer's neck. The two of them disappeared up into the sky as a strong wind soared through them, leaving only the rustling of the branches and leaves.

"By the darkness of Morriga!" Gundal cursed in dismay. "We will find those fools before the day begins."

"Pointless searching won't be necessary," a nearby, newly-arrived robed shadmar replied. He walked calmly and patiently from the ring of flames, which dissipated behind him. He looked to Gundal, sneering, "My spell has traced them. Have your warriors ready to march, we will find these cowards."

Gundal grumbled a reply and barked orders to his soldiers. He did not like the idea of this sorcerer usurping control of his band. *Yes,* he thought, *and when we are finished with them a certain someone is going to have an 'accident'.*

Vralthen spun around quickly and brought his fierce red eyes upon the warrior and whispered, "I don't think so," and smoothly walked towards the northwest, purposely turning his back to the patrol leader. Gundal swallowed nervously and followed behind.

*　　*　　*　　*　　*　　*　　*

The two adventurers soared quickly to their hidden glade, Thes's brow furrowed in concentration. Artemis stared with wonder at the trees below them and the night sky above. He was fearful to let go of the elf, so he returned the Thes's grasp with a firm hand of his own. They then dived down to the hidden glade, easy to spot from above by the rocky outcroppings that rose just before the cliff of the flowing stream.

They landed softly beneath the towering oaks of the glade. Artemis gladly released the wizard and began to wash his face in the pond near the waterfall and cliff-side. Their work had been frustrating. For the past two weeks they had tried to find the shadmar's base of operations, but failed to find anything. Thes had soared over the trees but found no structures that stood out above the boughs of the forest. Artemis had tracked the footprints of the shadmar patrol, but they eventually headed to a point where the tracks simply disappeared in the woods.

The previous day, they had decided to return to the exact place Artemis rescued Thes and Morstar from the shadmar patrol. They had waited all day, perched in the trees above, listening and watching in silence. It was well past midnight when the patrol finally appeared, and now they knew why the other tracks disappeared. They had the aid of sorcerers to hide and transport them.

Thes was lost in thought, trying to piece this new information together. The two entered the cabin seeking a bite to eat. As they entered the hovel, their eyes fell upon a darkened figure in the corner of the room.

A familiar dwarven voice answered, "Just me, foolish elf." The dwarf was keeping his eyes on the sparks circling around the elf's fingertips.

"And it is just us, foolish dwarf," Thes replied sardonically eyeing the dwarf's hefted hammer. Morstar grinned and lowered it to the floor.

"What a horrible turn of events," Artemis muttered with a sigh. "Well, dwarf, I hope your efforts had better results than ours."

"Ha!" Morstar laughed. "Ain't a man, nor a dwarf for that matter, willing to join us against the dark elves. They'd rather wait in their town's defenses than bring the assault to them. Doesn't matter, most of the townsfolk considered me a roaming madman, saying it'll be a bright day in Nembral's halls before dark elves gather on the surface."

76

"Fools," Thes interrupted, "The shadmar could have a great army by then and will sweep the men clean from Enelis." The elf began to pace about the small cabin with his hand stroking his familiar chin.

"Did you find no like-minded folk to aid us in our cause?" Artemis added, returning his attention to Morstar.

"Not a one. Though some of the town-folk spoke of a wandering warrior that came through town just before I arrived, but I didn't find anybody. No one seemed to know where he was headed."

Artemis let out another sigh and walked out the door in frustration. Morstar looked to Thes, but the elf only shrugged and returned to his thoughts. The dwarf reached under the chair nearby and pulled forth a large flask and grinned at it. The dwarf began to sip on the fiery liquor as he began his own pose of thought.

*   *   *   *   *   *   *

Fireflies sparkled in the glade like tiny stars in a spontaneous dance of a mysterious design. The trickling of the small waterfall on the north side of the dell was the only sound accompanying Artemis, except for the occasional owl hoot. The hooded ranger sat on his usual rotted log and puffed on his pipe in deep thought. The tufts of smoke drifted upwards towards the stars.

The ranger thought of his homeland, and the village of Layu which he missed more than anything. He thought deeply about the villagers that used to praise him for his work in the forest. He would give much to return to his homeland and see the village restored. The ranger sighed as his chin hit his chest solemnly, just before a dagger sliced through the empty top of his hood.

Artemis instinctively kicked off the rotted log, rolling backwards to his feet behind an intimidating oak. Several daggers pierced the ancient tree.

"Thes!" the ranger yelled as he grabbed his bow, which was leaning against the tree. He clutched and readied three arrows between his fingers. Many dark shapes were hiding behind the forest edge just outside the glade. Artemis glanced at the shimmering pool to his left. He saw many red points of light in the reflection. He then glanced quickly to his right to another large oak and made his move.

The two shadmar slowly closing in on the pool were spitefully surprised by the three arrows that rushed towards them. Artemis released the bow's taunt string, bow held sideways, just before he rolled behind the other towering tree. Each shadmar warrior took an arrow in the chest and fell to the ground. The third arrow planted firmly in another oak a foot above Gundal's crouching head.

Gundal's eyes narrowed to slits as he gave the hand signal to attack. Three more shadmar came from behind the trees nearest to the ranger. They readied their swords and rushed in at him. By that time, Thes and Morstar were scrambling out of the old cabin with sword and warhammer in the ready. The shadmar warriors scowled at the light-skinned elf and came on with a fierce fire in their red-glowing eyes.

Artemis threw his bow to the side and drew his sword, reaching one of the three shadmar warriors simultaneously with his companions. Each adventurer faced off with one of the experienced dark-skinned veterans, cutting and weaving, and desperately avoiding well-placed blows by their enemies. While the ranger was desperately trying to ward off an outside slash by one of the shadmar's two swords, Gundal rushed in with his deadly flail spinning purposefully above his head, aiming for the ranger's open midsection. Artemis surprised both dark elves when he used the natural slipperiness of the leaves beneath him to slide forward beneath the first shadmar, using his sword to slash the warrior's ankles and push him aside. He then rolled to the left away from Gundal's flail, who was already swinging again for a blow against the prone human. Artemis narrowingly avoided the blow and scrambled to his feet.

Meanwhile, Morstar was grinning at the shadmar before him as his hammer's head blocked every blow the scimitar-wielding shadmar tried to place. Morstar had always been a steadfast fighter, using his endurance and patience to tire his enemy before he made the necessary killing blows. Though once the dwarf eyed the ranger's predicament out of the corner of his eye, he decided a more aggressive stance was required if he was to aid his new companion. The dwarf slammed the shadmar's scimitar to the ground as the dark-skinned elf attempted a low stab towards the dwarf's seemingly open gut. Before the shadmar could pull his weapon back, Morstar ducked and slammed his helmed head into the shadmar's chin knocking the warrior to the ground just as his warhammer swung back behind the dwarf in an arc to slam down into the shadmar's midsection.

Near the cabin, Thes was having a hard time keeping up with his opponent. Thes's thinner sword was not much wider than the shadmar's rapier, but the dark-skinned elf certainly had more training with his weapon than the wizard did. Regardless, Thes managed to keep his defense up, blocking and parrying each swift and subtle stab and slice of the needle-point blade. He was especially careful to avoid striking at the openings he saw, knowing them to be false and misleading; traps set for killing blows by an experienced warrior.

Growing tired of the wizard's defensive maneuvers, the shadmar warrior began a strongly aggressive stance coming in at increasingly fast angles. Thes found he could only rush back on his heels to avoid many of the stabs. It wasn't long before he found his back against the side of the cabin. He then made a desperate roll to the side, just as the shadmar's rapier sliced past his cheek. The blade landed firmly in the crack between two logs, causing the shadmar to push the sword in the hole up to the hilt, greatly overbalancing him. Thes took that moment to slash viciously at the shadmar's exposed side. But before the wizard's sword could slice through that dark leather, the shadmar's other hand brought a dagger from his hilt up and intercepted the wizard's attack. That is when a dwarven hammer slammed into the shadmar's backside, crunching the dark warrior into the cabin wall. The corpse fell to the ground broken and bloodied. Morstar only smiled as he turned to aid the ranger, now nearer the pool on the far side of the glade.

Artemis was desperate, looking for any hope of reprisal. Gundal was a fierce warrior and a master of the flail, swinging the spiked ball again and again, right in the ranger's proposed routes of attack or escape. In the rare moments Artemis found a chance to counterattack, the shadmar's buckler knocked back the ranger's sword. Artemis breathed a sigh of relief as his friends came towards him across the glade. But that moment was short-lived as three more shadmar warriors came from the west end of the glade. It was the unit Gundal had ordered to surround and attack.

Morstar intercepted the first of the three shadmar warriors. These three bore only short swords and bucklers and dark leathers, geared more for scouting than combat, but their morale was no less than expected for a battle-hardened warrior. The dwarf's hammer and shield worked in deft unison as they intercepted all three attacks by the dark-skinned warriors. They only grinned at each other as they circled Morstar, trying to flank the dwarf.

80

Thes eyed both situations, trying to decide how he could help. The wizard called to the magical spirits around him. Scattered stones in the dell began to glow and levitate as they gathered around the wizard, spinning in faster and faster circles over Thes's head. Thes then launched the stones into the shadmar warriors, sending many to each of them. Though the rocks didn't injure them too greatly, they proved to be powerful distracters. One of the warriors facing Morstar decided to strike at the wizard instead, freeing Morstar from their flanking maneuver.

Gundal grimaced as the heavy rocks struck his backside, which caused many bruises. The flail-wielding warrior scowled and took a step back to regain his momentum against the defensive ranger. Artemis, however, used that moment for a desperate attack. As Gundal swung his flail, spinning before him as a make-shift shield, Artemis pivoted and side stepped as he flipped his sword in his hand so that the tip faced the ground. He took a wide step, with his back to the shadmar and slammed his sword behind him, behind the swirling flail. The blade landed firmly in the shadmar's side, striking the shadmar's chainmail shirt with a rib-cracking blow. However, the blade could not pierce into the shadmar's abdomen through the dark iron chainmail.

Gundal scoffed and stepped back from the blow away from the human ranger. In a rage of raw fury, the shadmar rushed at Artemis, who was still overbalanced from his maneuver. Artemis tried to get away but only stumbled frantically as the dark elf's flail slammed the ground near the ranger's foot. The human then rolled as fast as he could, right before the flail swung upwards. The heavy, iron-spiked ball at the end glanced the ranger's side, tearing a hole in his leather jerkin.

Suddenly, a tremendous roar echoed across the glade as a giant-of-a-man came rushing at Gundal with a large circular wooden shield leading the charge. The shield bore the symbol of a golden helm with a faded blue back-drop. A blood-stained battleaxe was raised above the newcomer's bearded head as he rushed inward, roaring a defiant warcry. A twisted, almost savage, visage was depicted on the warrior's face, hidden in his flowing reddish-blonde hair and thick beard.

Gundal had plenty of time to react, however, giving up on the scrambling ranger. The shadmar warrior brought his own shield up for a defensive posture. Then a moment later a loud clang of axe on shield was heard across the glade. Gundal had easily blocked the blow, but soon realized that this warrior had every intention of hitting a shield, but it was the human warrior's pure strength that the dark elf had not considered. The power of that blow nearly broke the shadmar's arm and certainly stunned him far longer than prudence would allow.

This was all the time the new warrior needed, taking a step back from his hard blow and using the back-ward momentum of his axe in a backward swing, cutting upwards into Gundal's right side. The axe slammed into the iron chainmail, tearing through many of the chain links, but not otherwise finding much flesh. The strength of the blow, however, was more than sufficient to break a few ribs and knock Gundal backwards, prone on his back.

By this time, Morstar and Thes had taken care of the other two shadmar scouts. But before anyone could acknowledge the new warrior, a jet of flame slammed into the newcomer, hurling him into the nearby pond. The source of the flames was a robed dark elf standing on the far end where Gundal had entered the glade. He smiled wickedly as he began to prepare another volley of flames.

Morstar, Thes, and Artemis, and even Gundal, managed to scramble for cover behind some trees before a ball of flames exploded in the center of the glade. Gundal then took that distraction to flee towards the robed sorcerer, his broken shield-arm hanging uselessly at his side. Artemis, now in a much better position, twirled the dagger from his belt at the running shadmar, the thin blade sliced the dark elf across the face. Blood sprayed into the air as the dagger landed firmly in the dark elf's nose, just below his eye. Gundal screamed in pain as he staggered towards the sorcerer.

Vralthen, the sorcerer, scowled as the injured warrior's bloody face splattered stains on the shadmar's robes. Thes then stepped up, preparing to hurl a bolt of lightning at the two shadmar. Vralthen scowled again, this time at the light skinned wizard, and murmured something under his breath. A ring of red flames suddenly appeared, roaring behind him. The two shadmar stepped into it quickly before it dissipated, taking the shadmar with it. Thes's bolt of electrical energy struck the ground where they stood, having little effect on the dirt.

Thes had not fought so hard since the battle of Escailar, which seemed so long ago. He felt a new surge of strength in him as his anger towards the shadmar dominated his mind. He felt invincible. For the first time since the battle of Escailar, Thes felt like he was alive again; the taste of vengeance sweetening the moment. Eventually the rage subsided, and the wizard caught his breath. "Is everyone alright?" Thes asked.

Morstar only shrugged at the elf as he clamored towards the pond to see if the mysterious warrior was still alive. A wet and curious face popped out of the water then, smiling oddly at the three adventurers coming towards him. The warrior then reached around himself in the waters, soon pulling out a battered iron helm. He poured the water out of it then replaced it upon his dirty head of long, disorderly reddish-blonde hair that now stuck to his face.

"A fine day for a battle, eh?" the warrior said with a thick, northern accent, as he began to pull himself from the pond. "I needed a bath anyway." The warrior then laughed to himself. He stood before the three on the now muddy bank and began to shake erratically, much like a dog trying to remove each drop of water from its fur. Water droplets splattered in every direction, a few landing on the three stunned brows staring at the armored man.

Artemis stepped forward, "I must thank you, warrior. You came just in time."

The warrior shrugged, "It is the glory of battle I seek, and the chance to prove my valor. No better place than where it is needed most."

"What is your name, noble warrior? And where do you hail from?" Thes asked, curiously.

The warrior stood firm and puffed his chest out as he replied, "I am Bryman Hethroth, Prince of the Hethroth Clan of the Noradrie, and War-Priest to my ancestors, the Kings of Old. I seek battle to test my mettle for the glory of my clan."

Morstar liked the warrior's sense of honor. "Morstar Haglekdon, once a Hammerdwarf of the Kingdom of Kalavar," the dwarf said with a low bow. "I have seen few with such ferocity in battle."

Thes smiled and stepped forward, "I'm Thesomber Ambreaia, known as Thes the Mystic in these parts."

"I am Artemis Mengsk, ranger of the woodlands," the man said with a polite nod. "Come to my cabin and let us speak."

"Aye, we may have more battle for ye," the dwarf said with a grin.

A large smile grew on the war-priest's face as he said, "Then ye have my ears."

(8) A Father's Request

After many cups of the ranger's berrywine, and even more helpings of the roast venison, the large warrior was willing to talk to the very eager adventurers.

"You are a fierce warrior, fiercer than most dwarves I've seen in battle," said Morstar to the war-priest.

"Yes, if you had not come at that time I may very well be dead," Artemis said earnestly.

"How do you come to be so deep in the forest anyway?" Thes asked.

The large man grinned wide before taking another long pull from his wooden cup. "An odd tale," Bryman began, "for I was just passing through Allsvale. The people in town said a raving-mad dwarf was telling the townsfolk that dark elves were gathering in the forest. It seemed like that'd be a good place to find some honor for my clan, so I headed to the forest. Thankfully, your heavy boots left an easy path."

Morstar raised a quizzical look to the warrior and said, "We must have just missed each other in town."

"Aye, but I didn't stay long, I was eager for a chance to wet my axe," the warrior said with a hint of bloodlust in his eyes. "So I wondered through the woods for a couple days in the direction the townsfolk pointed, following your path as best I could, until I saw, between the branches of the trees, two figures flying overhead, barely silhouetted by the stars above. So, I knew I was in the right direction, now I see it is you three that speak of dark elves in the forest. And I was mighty glad the tale was true." The war-priest finished with a hearty laugh. He sat their grinning a moment as he looked beseechingly at his empty cup, until he asked the question that had been on his mind, "What do you know of these dark elves? Are there more of them?"

The other three in the room exchanged glances, but it was Thes that seemed to be the one silently chosen to speak on the matter.

"Well," he began, "It is our belief that the dark elves, or shadmar, are gathering on the surface in a stronghold hidden somewhere in the forest. They have already raided a handful of elven villages but seem to want their presence to remain hidden for the moment."

"Which is why we think they are still gathering their forces from the deep underground," added Artemis.

"We don't have the numbers to deal with an army of shadmar, but every blade helps," the elf said. "We would certainly welcome your skills against these mighty foes."

Bryman hesitated for a moment, taking in the information. "Alright, you can have my axe in your war," he answered. "This glory is as good as any and I never shy from a battle."

"Good. Then that is one more stone in our pile," Artemis said with finality. He then seemed to have remembered something and said, "We might have to relocate, however, for the dark elves are now aware of our location."

"Of course!" Thes said, a thought bubbling up to the surface of his mind, "I shall take care of that, have no worry." With that he stepped out of the small cabin, the others just stared at him, a bit perplexed.

"What ye going to do?" the dwarf asked.

"Wards and protective charms, worry not!" the wizard said with a secretive smile.

With that Thes turned away from the others and wandered out into the center of the glade, closing his eyes. He reached out with his mind, beseeching the magical spirits around him for aid. The elemental spirits of air seemed always most eager to aid the wizard, but for his charms he needed all the natural spirits to aid him. With his mind and mystical energies, he beseeched all the spirits around the area to assist him, and only him.

Soon all the mystical energies in the area would only answer to the wizard's call, so that no others may magically learn of the location of the glade, nor magically transport to its vicinity. Also, Thes would be notified with any information about those that came nearby.

Feeling drained for his effort, Thes returned to the cabin smiling wide despite his somewhat pallid complexion. The group was trying to coax Bryman to tell them how he came to be so far south from his homeland.

"Aye, I have come a long way, you might say. The journey has been long and not an easy one," the large man bellowed.

Seeing the wizard enter, Morstar asked, "Are ye alright?" with a concerned eyebrow.

Thes only nodded and took a seat at the table; sitting back, closing his eyes, and listening to the war-priest's words.

"Well, you might say that it started with my father, Broglin Hethroth. Prior to my birth, he was the last living of the Hethroth clan, the blood of kings flows in our veins..."

Before Bryman could begin his tale though, he was stopped by questions from Artemis about the Noradrie, for he hadn't heard much of the war-priest's people; and so, the warrior began again, starting with the history and struggles of his people.

The Noradrie were a proud, strong people. They, like Bryman, tended to be quite tall and well-built, with hair colors of light varieties, particularly blonde and red. They took pride in physical fitness and physical strength, forcing some in the southlands to call them barbarians, though they were as civilized as any group of men in the south. They were masters of the saddle and could often be seen riding horses in small groups, hunting wild game with short bows and spears across the rocky and rolling hills of the land known as the Barbarian's March. Though, this sacred land was known to the Noradrie as Aelgard.

There was no greater glory to the Noradrie than victory in battle. The Noradric war-priests, comparable to the knights of the southlands, took the honor of battle quite seriously. They usually wielded large two-handed swords, an axe, and a large wooden shield bearing their clan's symbol. The Hethroth clan bore a golden helm upon their blue shields. These war-priests had a code of conduct much like any knight, but it was for the measure of courage and strength of wills, not chivalry. Fleeing from a battle was considered breaking the code of conduct for these warriors, for they believed a true warrior should never fear an honorable death.

Long ago, a great king, Rohard Hethroth, Bryman's ancestor, ruled all the clans of the Noradrie. However, many wars with the nearby orcs and goblins from the north and west tore the kingdom apart. These days the Noradrie lived in nine fortress towns scattered across the cold hills, each one ruled by a powerful Clan-Prince. Each Clan-Prince had a hundred or more riders at their command. There once were ten princes to rule the cold lands, but orcs had raided and burned the town of Helmsmead, leaving the Hethroth clan without lands to rule.

The Noradric war-priests were also the religious leaders of the people, for each town sought understanding and wisdom from the ruling clan's ancestors, though every clan shared worship of the Great Axelord, Rohard Hethroth. Bryman was often called Kingsblood by his people for his close resemblance to the great Rohard. It is because of the people's love of the Hethroth's that all the other Clan-Princes were weary of a Hethroth leader taking over the towns once more. They feared a Hethroth might reunite the old kingdom, usurping their power. That was at least before the people heard of the death of Broglin.

Bryman's father was said to have died fleeing from the battle at Helmsmead, for no one could claim to have seen him defend the town. The orcs were eventually driven off, leaving a broken, flaming ruin behind. There was no sign of Broglin's body after the bloody affair. The Hethroth clan's honor had been shattered that day, also leaving Bryman without any lands to call his own. His people scattered to one of the other nine Noradrie domains. Bryman was then ridiculed and scoffed at by his people; as the son of a coward. So, Bryman left the comforts of his homeland seeking glory and honor in battle to redeem his father's perceived act of cowardice.

"So you see, my way is forged by my father," the warrior concluded.

"Yes, so it seems," said Artemis. "It is good for us that you have come this way, we could use a strong warrior."

"What brought ye to the southlands at all? Why not stay and try and redeem yer father's actions?" the dwarf asked.

Bryman's face turned a bit red with anger, "My father was NOT a coward!" he roared. The warrior calmed down quickly before continuing with frustrated words, "I knew my father did not flee the battle, because he wasn't even in town when it happened, for I was with him. That is why I too survived the onslaught."

The others exchanged glances again before the war-priest continued, "The night before the orcs raided our home my father told me he had a quest to fulfill. He sought to reunite the old kingdom and seemed to know how it must be done. I know he would not have left if he knew of the coming raid. But the snows were harsh, and no news of raiders had reached the town. He told no one else of his departure before he disappeared into the cold winter winds on foot."

Artemis passed the warrior another cup full of the sweet wine, switching out the empty cup the anxious war-priest clutched tightly.

Bryman nodded his thanks, took a deep gulp of the bright liquid before continuing solemnly. "I tried to follow him," he muttered. "I was too young, only sixteen years of age. The frozen winds were deadly in the night, and I was ill-prepared. Finally, weariness overcame me, soon after I had lost the dark shape of my father on the horizon. He was lost to me. His last words before he had left our home still echoed in my mind, '*If I fail in my quest, this task will fall to you.*'"

The warrior sighed, while the others were silently looking at him, listening intently. "I still don't know what task he has set for me, but with time, and with the guidance of my ancestors, I will follow the path my father has set before me." He was silent for a moment. His next words came subdued, "At the least, I shall die honorably in battle as a warrior worthy of my clan's glory." With these last words, he finished his cup of wine, offering the cup again to the ranger for filling.

While Artemis handed him another full cup of the sweet wine, Morstar pressed on, "So what have ye been doing since those dark days?"

"Well," Bryman began, the sorrow leaving his voice, "I've been traveling and fighting. Offering my axe to any just cause I could find; mostly mercenary work for trade caravans. It's been many long years since I left Aelgard. Since the tragic day I was left without a home."

"That is a long time to leave one's country behind," Artemis said, feeling a shared connection of exile with the warrior.

"Aye, but I have no land or family to go home to. I just pray to the spirits of my ancestors to grant me the strength to return, and the courage to face and break the lies that have been told over my father's grave."

Silence took the room for a moment. Thes was thinking of his recent loss of home as well. Morstar thought reminiscently about the mountainhomes of Kalavar. Poor Artemis thought only of the burning town of Layu. The ranger clasped the shoulder of the war-priest earnestly, believing that he too would find the courage to return home and face the accusations against him.

That night the group shared many tales with the Noradric prince. They shared their own tales of sorrow and travels, as well as the interesting adventures that had made their lives exciting. It was soon late into the night, and sleep seemed to be on the minds of many. Thes and Bryman had arranged beds outside, Thes's up in one of the large oaks of the glade, Bryman's at its base, while Morstar and Artemis slept within the cabin, though Artemis decided it would the last time he shared a room alone with a snoring dwarf.

The next morning, after a meal of dried meat, wild berries, and roasted nuts, the group decided to begin planning their next move against the shadmar. They were again huddled around the table, this time with a makeshift map of the southern forest spread about. The map was sketched by Thes and Artemis on the pale skin of a doe. A light breeze blew in through the open door. The air was a bit crisp and cool, but it brought an aura of purpose to the small planning room.

"So here is where we have searched already," Artemis said pointing to forested areas on the map that Thes and himself had painstakingly looked for a possible hidden fortress of the shadmar.

"There is no sign of a large structure that stands above the trees," Thes added.

"Yes, and the patrols use their sorcerers to transport to and from the place," said Artemis.

"Couldn't the fortress be anywhere then? They might be coming from the caves deep beneath the earth!" Morstar said frustratingly.

Thes thought a moment. It could be possible that the shadmar were slowly increasing their presence on the surface, but why the patrols?

"No," Thes then said. "They would not be trying to be so discreet or bother to patrol if there wasn't some significant group of them already here near the surface."

"Yes," agreed Artemis. "It also seems that they must be waiting for something too. Why else would they not march to war immediately?"

"It is peculiar," agreed the elf.

Bryman only sighed. He was not one for making plans and sitting cloistered in a room. He wished to walk headstrong into the shadmar camps and demand a fight from their finest warriors. He was listening only mildly as he daydreamed of a glorious battle where he and the others at the table vanquished an army of shadmar upon the rolling hills of Aelgard.

"We still have the problem of people," the dwarf added grumpily. "We don't know the shadmars' numbers, but tis certainly more than four."

The others nodded in agreement, curious about how to acquire more for their small band. Bryman only interjected, "Four!? I'll take on any number of the vile creatures, point the way and my axe shall lead."

Artemis chuckled, shaking his head.

Thes smiled at the warrior, "I appreciate your enthusiasm, but we still don't know where they are, or even if they are centralized to one location."

"And the loop continues," said Artemis absentmindedly. They had been going in circles for nearly an hour. It seemed they would not get anywhere until they knew two pieces of information: where the shadmar were hidden, and how many there were. They also, except for Bryman, seemed to agree that they would need more warriors to help them in their task. A few warriors would be nothing against an army of fierce shadmar.

"We must search again... it is the only way we'll get any information," Artemis said finally.

Thes sighed, ran his hand over his face with the strain of the situation, before he answered, "Yes, I suppose we have no other options."

"Who'd think that finding an army of dark elves'd be so difficult," grumbled the dwarf.

"Aye, perhaps we should roar out a challenge to those creatures to crawl from their dark holes and face us with courage," Bryman said in his gruff, throaty voice.

There were three pairs of rolled eyes at this comment, for neither of the others were fond of the warrior's bold determination for combat. However, they also knew when battle did come he would be a powerful ally. So, they just shook their heads at the brawny man.

"There is one other thing bothering me," the ranger began, "Where is the patrol from Elienspar? Surely they would have arrived by now had they received word from the raided villages."

"Yes. That troubles me too," agreed the wizard. "But I would not wish to make that long trek ourselves until we have more information about our foes."

"Agreed," the man nodded.

"I think the best course of action, would be to relax and prepare ourselves for the day ahead and begin the search tomorrow morning," Thes said, wishing for some time to dwell on the questions that they had posed on his own.

The dwarf nodded eagerly at this thought, for the food was running low and he knew some hunting and gathering would be required to restock the supplies. Luckily, the ranger kept many barrels of berrywine fermenting in a small cavern on one side of the glade, otherwise the dwarf would have left that moment to bring an ale-laden pony back to the cabin, and the war-priest would have certainly joined him in the effort.

Bryman and Morstar were both quite adept at melee combat and shared an equal love of ales and spirits. Morstar was by far much more organized, but the war-priest had a certain chaotic spirit that was not easily quelled.

That day the two warriors decided to spar in the glade. They grew to appreciate each other's fighting skills and shared many laughs as neither seemed to dominate the other in the competition. Thes watched them sometimes, though his mind was preoccupied and he decided to be the one to gather the autumn fruits and nuts they would need before it got too cold to find such ample food. Artemis took care of the hunting, bringing a few deer carcasses to another cave off the glade that served as a smokehouse, using Bryman's strength to help haul them around. The ranger was the happiest he had been in years, despite the circumstances. He had spent so much time alone in the past few years that he had forgotten the company of good friends. He wished days like this could go on forever.

The day seemed to go by much too quickly, however, and soon evening approached as the four of them each sat on logs around a burning campfire. They shared baskets of fresh berries and nuts as well as long slices of roasted venison. Thes preferred the taste of the frog-legs from the few frogs he pulled out of the pond. The group was heartily laughing and singing songs from their homelands. The next day's frustration seemed an eternity away as they sat there in the cool breeze of autumn near the warming fire.

Artemis had become quite quiet as Morstar and Bryman seemed to share in a dwarven drinking song, the deep chorus accented by the clanking of their wooden cups, spilling droplets of the sweet berrywine to the forest floor.

"I'm going to gather some air," the ranger said to Thes as he made his way to the sloping side of the glade. The air was much cooler as he left the soft glow of the fire, but the woodsman only tightened his cloak around his shoulders as he silently strode around the winding path to the top of the rocks just above the glade's waterfall.

The ranger soon stood at the peak looking down into the glade. He saw the fire down below and the shadows of three figures swaying in song. Directly below was the pool of water below the waterfall dropping nearly thirty feet. Artemis then turned around. From this rocky outcropping, he had a good view of the valley of trees to the north. The stars were beginning to shine brightly, though there were some clouds slightly to the east. To the west, the hidden sun was giving off its final glow before departing for the night. He looked out smiling over the forest that had been his home for half a decade, secretly wishing it was the more familiar forests of his own homeland.

He stood there for many minutes, watching the light slip away below the horizon into the darkness of night. The moon was hidden, but many stars were shining and they twinkled above the ranger. Artemis caught a glimpse of twinkling below as well, deep in the forest to the north. He looked keenly at the light in the distance.

The ranger's eyes grew wide. He knew that sight, he had seen it three times a few weeks past. It was the beginnings of a forest fire.

(9) A Fire in the Forest

Artemis turned back to the campfire below, looking down on his companions from the high peak of the rocky outcroppings above the waterfall. The three shadowy figures were now trying to imitate one of Thes's elven dances. If the ranger's mind wasn't racing with the stress of what he had seen, he might have laughed heartily at the dwarf continuously stumbling over his own two broad feet.

"Thes! Come hither! Fire in the forest!" the ranger yelled down, snuffing out the merriment in an instant.

Thes leaped towards the ranger and seamlessly floated on the air to the top of the rocks next to Artemis, whispering to the air spirits as he soared upwards. The other two simply readied their weapons watching the slender forms of the ranger and wizard stand silhouetted by the stars behind them.

Thes's eyes stared intently at the twinkling lights in the distance. His elven eyes were much sharper and able to see more clearly than even the keen-eyed ranger. He could barely make out the shape of the burning flames as the tree-top's glowed like candles in the distance. There was much smoke and haze, but there could be little doubt a large fire was consuming the forest. With such a clear night, this fire must have been set intentionally.

"We must go," the wizard said determinedly to Artemis, anger beginning to rise through his body.

"What is it? Another attack?" the ranger asked.

"Yes, come on!" the elf urged as he raced off down the trail towards the others, beckoning for the ranger to follow.

Morstar and Bryman stood there, armored and armed as the other two rushed down the slope towards the cabin.

"We must go! A village is under attack by the shadmar and there is no time to waste," Thes said to the two warriors as he slung on his own sword-belt.

The ranger handed an extra bow and quiver to the elf as he asked, "Can you take all of us aloft?"

"Not easily," the wizard replied, "I will be quite drained for the effort, but no time to worry about that. Everyone be ready."

Thes closed his eyes and concentrated hard. The air spirits were beckoned from all around and were soon lifting the four of them up into the air and slowly towards the north. They moved effortlessly over the tops of the trees, picking up more and more velocity as Thes continued to call the aid of the spirits in each area they passed through. Soon they were soaring like birds through the night sky, just above the tops of the highest trees.

Thes's mind was focused hard on the task at hand, maintaining his concentration on the magic surrounding him and his friends. In the back of his mind, however, was a mixture of guilt and anger. During all his time searching for the shadmar, he never thought to look for other elven villages that might be in danger. The somewhat xenophobic wood elves had many villages hidden in the forest's boughs. Being self-sufficient, they rarely had need for trade or travel. Thus, many villages were hidden and forgotten except by those who lived within them.

Thes was quite angry at himself for not considering the possibility that other hidden villages could fall prey to the shadmar war parties.

Morstar watched in awe as the branches of the trees whipped past below him. Bryman, however, was not fond of heights and it was only the excitement of the battle ahead that kept him from closing his eyes and praying to his ancestors for a safe journey.

After many long minutes of flight, the twinkling lights of the fires became clear to Artemis. He could see the flames above the trees and a few forms leaping from balcony to balcony in a treetop village, firing arrows down on darker forms. They were still far off, however, and time was winding down as the cold air clawed at their faces above the trees.

*   *   *   *   *   *   *

Meanwhile the wood elves of the village were nearly defeated; only a handful of their deadly archers remained in the village of Cwendilin's high treetop balconies. For every arrow that felled a shadmar warrior below, the desperate archers saw at least three more blade-swinging warriors fill in the gap. It was a tragic and terrible defeat that was slowly enveloping the single remaining group of light-skinned soldiers. They stood defiantly in the last towering tree even as more flames engulfed the village around them.

"Let's fall back!" shouted Svendian at the top of his lungs. The last captain's throat was raw and his breath now came less easily as the smoke of the burning woods became ever thicker. The heat of the nearby fires had left him soaking in his own sweat, coloring his fair skin as the drifting ash clung to the sticky layer. He wiped his brow to save his already pained eyes from the dripping ichor, the smoke leaving them red and stung.

He looked down at the coming entourage of blood-thirsty shadmar warriors, their deadly blades pointed upwards as they climbed up the spiraling balconies towards the last group of light-skinned soldiers. With a nod of Svendian's head, two soldiers cut the supporting ropes nearby. Svendian then led them towards the southern edge of the village. He only heard the satisfying clash of bodies, weapons, and clattering armor as the dark warriors fell far to the ground below.

The remaining band of Cwendilin's archers was no more than twenty now, and, with their village and friends under flames, only survival was on their minds. It was for this reason they followed Svendian's lead towards the south, for the aged captain had experienced a shadmar raid before. They leaped, dived, and dodged after the ancient elf, carefully avoiding crossbow bolts, flaming arrows, and falling tree limbs. Many were surprised at the captain's agility given his many years upon the world, but they had little time to consider it, so they kept their eyes and feet moving, careful of the dangers around them.

The soldiers raced down a spiraling balcony, wrapped like a ribbon around a towering tree. They watched their footing carefully for many of the branches that made the descending stair had been smashed and broken in the initial assault. As the shadmar had swept under the village from the south, Svendian's group held the north end. As the village fell to flames, the village soldiers had to scramble their way across the burning village over the heads of the shadmar, causing chaos beneath them. Now they were descending on the south side, far from the majority of the dark warriors.

Svendian gathered the group together after they had reached the forest floor. "We make for Ensia Pond for a quick rest before we flee to one of the southern villages," he ordered the soldiers. The archers nodded in agreement following the captain's lead through the woods.

Soon they rushed into the clearing surrounding the still pond. It was usually a site of great rejoicing during the midsummer feast, however now it was ringed with flames, blocking all exit out of the clearing save where the light-skinned archers had entered. Svendian cursed and turned around. He commanded his archers to form in a line behind

100

him, facing their only escape from a fiery death. Shadmar warriors were rushing in at them, their blades reflecting the red glimmers of the flames.

"Fire!" the captain shouted. His soldiers released a volley of arrows into the dark warriors. The shadmar platoon fell to the ground as arrows pierced their vital organs through tiny holes in their sleek chain-linked armor. Still Svendian saw many more shadmar rushing towards the small gap into the flaming circle surrounding the pond. Many of the archers were out of arrows now, drawing their long knives and short swords for what they believed would be their final stand. The shadmar rushed in quickly, a few falling to the last remaining arrows. Svendian braced his feet in the ground for a firm stance, took a deep breath, and held his shield high as he readied his sword behind him for a heavy blow.

Suddenly, from the sky above, soared down three bulky, weapon-wielding figures upon the shadmar band. There was an unheard splash as a fourth figure dropped into the pond behind them. The fair elves of Cwendilin gasped in amazement as blade, hammer, and axe tore through the center of the host of warriors. The confusion stunted the shadmar's furious charge. Svendian charged in with an elven warcry, his soldiers behind him. Soon the shadmar were seeking every possible escape as Svendian's soldiers came in upon them.

Blades clanged upon shields and chain for a long while as the battle raged. Morstar and Bryman held the north end, slowing the tide of shadmar into the clearing. Svendian's band of warriors cut through the few disoriented shadmar that made it past the deadly hammer and axe of the seasoned dwarf and Noradric prince. Artemis had put away his sword and was now pelting fleeing warriors with arrows.

Soon the battle was finished and only a couple of Svendian's soldiers had fallen. Svendian wasted no time however and approached the three adventurers as his soldiers exited the pond's clearing.

"We don't know how two men and a dwarf made it this far into the elven realms, but we are thankful for our fortune that you had come to our aid," Svendian said sincerely, using the Nomen tongue. "I did not know a dwarf could take to wing, but it will ever be a favorite story of our people if we live to tell the tale."

"We have come to aid the village," Artemis said in the tongue of elves. "But we soon learned that we were too late. It is good to have at least saved some of its fair people. As for the flight, it was the work of our wise wizard..."

It was at this point that Artemis and the others became aware of Thes's disappearance.

"Thes!" the ranger shouted in panic, searching frantically around. Hoping the wizard was near at hand performing some magical trick and not dead amongst the many shadmar corpses.

"I heard a splash in the pond... before the battle began," added a young archer. Svendian eyed the pond, finding the ripples no longer disturbing the still waters.

"Yes, the pond, let us fetch him," he said as the captain would give any order.

Bryman paid no notice, for he was already ankle deep in the cool waters, stomping forward into the deep center. His head dropped below the water's surface as he dived below, his large arms propelling his bulky mass surprisingly fast through the clear liquid. Soon he felt something strange. The Noradric prince squinted his eyes seeing what seemed to be a swirling mass of bubbles and currents spiraling around a frail figure.

Though it was beyond the warrior's sight into the realms of magic, he was actually seeing a horde of irritated magical energies spiraling around the wizard who beckoned them. Thes was now barely conscious and too weak to order

102

them away. He had bent his mind solely on propelling him and his friends across the miles that separated them from the burning village, but towards the end he had lost control of the magic. All he could do was release his friends from their influence before they slammed him into the pond. Now he could only hope the energies would dissipate and leave him in peace before he drowned.

A large burly arm wrapped around the elf, and pried him free from the swirling cyclone. The swirl of air then fired upwards like a vortex through the water into the sky above the pond, out of sight.

Bryman crawled from the water, Thes on his back, both dripping, but drying fast from the ring of flames circling the pond. Morstar and Artemis sighed in relief seeing the elf's ragged breaths and initial shivers of cold. However, soon the war-priest and the wizard were warm and near dry.

Svendian looked upon the wizard for a moment before turning to Artemis with a sense of urgency in his voice, "We haven't time to wait here; the village is lost. We must flee to one of the southern villages. You and your companions are welcome to follow."

Artemis looked to Thes, who was lying weakly upon the warming ground, finally succumbing to unconsciousness. The ranger nodded to Bryman, who gently threw the wizard back over his bulky shoulders.

"We are ready to follow. However, perhaps you should instead follow us," he suggested to Svendian cautiously. The ranger did not wish to undermine the captain's authority.

Svendian, however, only raised an eyebrow awaiting explanation.

Artemis continued, "There is a secret glade a few days' march to the south-east, from whence we came. There is ample food and security there. From there the southern villages shall not be far off." Artemis involuntarily averted the elf captain's powerful stare. The ranger knew that these villages had already succumbed to the shadmar raids weeks before, but he did not have the heart to tell the captain in front of his soldiers. Not after they had already lost so much.

Svendian caught this gesture, but seemed to understand its meaning. "That will be our heading then. Lead on stranger, we shall follow you."

"Wait!" Bryman said angrily, "Shouldn't we be following the dark elves to their lair. We have them!"

"It is not the time, we are still outnumbered," the ranger reasoned with the war-priest. "These elves need escape and solace, there is little battle in them and not enough of us to fight."

Bryman only grunted his reply, seemingly giving up on the argument as he straightened Thes on his shoulders.

"Then we are away," the elven captain said to his patrol. With a wave of his hand, they began to march.

*   *   *   *   *   *   *

The band of elves marched in a chaotic pattern behind their captain, weaving past each other, crisscrossing, using the trees as natural cover as their soft feet made neither a crack nor rustle sweeping through the underbrush. Morstar marveled at their effort, knowing that if he had not been walking among them, he would soon lose the elven band. They blended perfectly with their surroundings. The dwarf began to feel guilty for his own heavy steps as he trudged on with them.

Bryman, however, made even more of a clamor as he pushed aside low-hanging branches and the stretching reaches of nearby shrubs with his free hand. His other hand held the still unconscious form of the wizard to his shoulder. Artemis was leading the way with Svendian at his side. The

104

two had begun to speak quietly as they continuously marched towards the ranger's hidden glade.

"I must thank you again for your timely rescue, my patrol would have surely found death at that pond," the captain said in earnest to the ranger.

Artemis turned and smiled at the elf captain, "It is only what we could do to help. But the thanks must go to our dear wizard, who made the effort possible."

Svendian nodded to the ranger, turning his head over his shoulder a moment to regard the frail form draped over the war-priest's arm. "I have not seen such a feat of magic in my long years. I hope he has not sacrificed himself for the effort."

Artemis only nodded to the captain, trying to avoid that line of thinking. He had been vigilantly concentrating on the path ahead, trying not to let his mind wander to places of gloom and despair.

Artemis introduced himself and his companions to the elven captain. Svendian was quite surprised at such an odd collection of people.

"I am Svendian Lua'ela. Captain of the Third Archers Unit of Cwendilin," the captain paused for a moment, and then continued sadly, "Or we were of Cwendilin. It seems that village is no more."

"I'm sorry for the loss of your people and homes," said the ranger solemnly. "If only we would have arrived earlier."

The elven captain shook his head, "Had you arrived earlier, friend, you would have burned in the flames of the village. I have never seen such numbers in a shadmar raid."

"Have you seen such raids before?"

"Yes and no. Usually raids are performed by smaller bands of young shadmar recruits, eager to make a name for themselves among their dark kin. The raid we witnessed this night was performed by veteran warriors, and at least three times as many were present. No." The captain swallowed hard as a realization came upon him. "This was no mere raid to inflame a young warrior's spirit; this was an act of true war."

"War? You think the dark elves are seeking to gain territory on the surface?" the ranger asked the captain, though he and his friends had already come to this belief.

"It would appear so. I never thought that after all these millennia the shadmar would wish to fight for the surface. Not since the crown of the Fourth King was shattered."

The ranger gave a puzzled look to the aged captain, but Svendian seemed lost in thought. Artemis decided not to press the issue. The ranger concentrated on the path ahead once again, avoiding his own thoughts of darkness.

The long hazardous night ended peacefully with a rising sun. The marching patrol, now heading mostly southwards, had to blink their eyes as the shimmering red and orange lights filtered through the trees as if the forest was a great cathedral greeting the morning through stained glass. The tired warriors had been marching all through the night.

The warriors stopped and rested through the morning after they made some distance from the village. However, Svendian was not willing to rest too long for fear of any shadmar following their retreat. So they marched all the next day and night, with only short rests.

The following morning the sight of the glade before them was quite comforting. The band circled around and entered the glade from the east side. Svendian ordered his archers to rest through the morning as he made plans with their rescuers. The band of fifteen elven soldiers climbed up nearby trees to find comfortable places to rest as Svendian,

Artemis, Morstar, and Bryman (still carrying the wizard) entered the ranger's cabin to discuss what could be done.

The war-priest laid the wizard upon the ranger's bed of blankets in the corner of the wooden structure. The elf had not awoken at all in the past day. However, his complexion began to look better the previous evening and he seemed to be recovering from his exertion. Bryman joined the others surrounding the table as Artemis passed around cups of berrywine. Svendian smiled warmly. The cool drink danced on his tongue and, for a moment, it took the captain's mind away from his current situation.

Morstar sat with a deep grunt, "So now what?"

The others just looked at each other slowly, each wondering what course of action would be best. Svendian was considering fleeing towards Elienspar and the safety of the elven city. The captain broke the silence as he questioned his new friends.

"How long have you dwelt here, friend?" he asked the ranger.

"Many long summers, though by your reckoning I would think it would not seem long at all," he answered, half-smiling.

"Perhaps," the captain replied echoing the smile. "Are you aware of the other villages in the area: Teillina, Escailar, and Diiera?"

"I was aware of the first two you name. Thes, our wizard, hails from Escailar," the ranger answered cautiously.

"We should proceed to the next village, they may be next for the shadmar's conquest," the captain told his new companions.

The others, knowing of the other villages' destruction, avoided the captain's eyes. Artemis swallowed as he turned to face that stern visage.

"I'm sorry to tell you this," he said solemnly, "but those villages are no more."

The aged captain dropped his head at this news. Despite suspecting as much, it was hard to bear the gravity of the situation when he was told directly. Silence ensued for a while. The others stepped out of the cabin to leave the old captain in peace for a moment, stepping quietly into the morning light. Svendian was left to the gloomy thoughts that hung on his mind.

The villages near Cwendilin were somewhat isolated in the eastern reaches of the Aegis Forest. For a long time, they had been the only villages to reside in the former shadmar territory after the shadmar were driven from the surface. In addition, the area was also closest to the ever-expanding land of men. The kinship of this isolation, however, had waned over the past couple centuries, and communication between the villages had almost halted entirely. Svendian was one of the few who remembered the days when the villages would meet each year to celebrate the midsummer's day. He felt a deep sadness for what that loss of contact had done to his people. In the old days, the villages would have united against the threat, just as they had done when human loggers of an ancient human kingdom threatened the safety of these lands.

"I'm sorry for your loss," said Thes in the elven tongue, now solemnly leaning against the cabin wall upon the bed of blankets and furs. He had been laying there listening to the conversation for awhile. "I too have lost my home and friends to this new threat. In the days of the ancient kingdom, this would be trivial, but I fear the days of the elves have long diminished. Dark days are ahead of us."

The surprised captain eyed the younger elf for a moment, but then nodded at this wisdom. "Yes, I feel if our people do not unite as we did in the old days, our forests will fall prey to this threat as well. But, alas, we are such small birds in the sky to make such changes."

108

Thes shook his head, thinking deeply. Reverberant courage birthed from the desire for vengeance flowed through the wizard suddenly, "You are wrong; for even a pebble can ripple through the lake with time. This threat that has fallen upon us is for us alone to overcome. There are no more alliances and kingdoms to come to the People's aid; it is up to us to reunite our kin against this threat."

Svendian sighed and looked at the hopeful, younger elf, "Who, young elf? Who would help us overcome the shadmar? Men? Dwarves? The villages are alone and all but conquered. The People are scattered, there is no place left. We must go west and at least let Elienspar know of the tragedies that have befallen the eastern forests. Perhaps the elven crown still cares for these lands."

Thes stood up, using the wall to maintain his upright position in his frail state, "No, if a single village remains we have a duty to warn them. Perhaps with every able-bodied warrior in that village prepared to withstand the shadmar, there is hope of victory. They will not have the advantage of surprise. We do not need to flee to the city just yet."

"Perhaps, but to what end? The shadmar will simply strike another blow, their numbers are paramount," argued the captain. "I know of one more village in the area, if there are still elves that dwell there. But the shadmar could already have struck. That village could be burning at this moment!" Svendian raised his voice, his words gaining force with rising anger. "Cwendilin, Teillina, Escailar, Diiera, they all have been burned!" The captain's fist slammed down onto the table. He then sat back ruminating on his frustration and anger.

"What village do you speak of?" Thes asked tentatively.

The aged captain eyed the wizard keenly for a moment, his irritation threatening to dominate his words. However, Svendian quickly released his anger and calmly answered, "Harpien, the hidden village. It should be farther south and west of here".

Thes nodded. "Then there is still hope for a resistance. I believe in our people." He smiled at the captain.

Hope coursed through the captain as well. "I haven't seen its deep valley since I was a youngling, but they say the village is practically invisible by the high walls of the valley surrounding it. If there are elves that still dwell there, we may be able to unite a defensive against the shadmar. In the meantime, perhaps they could send more messengers to Elienspar and plead for aid from the crown."

Svendian smiled warmly as he helped Thes to a seat at the table. The other companions returned to the room, hearing the yells of the captain. Now they saw Svendian smiling with Thes, as they began to discuss their immediate plans.

(10) The Aegistriders

A number of days had passed with many discussions among the fellowship over the plan. A scout had been sent to the ruins of Cwendilin to find the hunters and gatherers who had been safely away from the village during its demise. Later that night ten more elves had joined the ranger's encampment. They had brought more food and supplies from the village's hidden caches.

"We shall leave for Harpien at midnight," the elven captain commanded his archers late in the day. The hunters from Cwendilin were eager to join the captain's squadron, each excited for a chance to strike back against the dark scourge that had taken their home village. Now Svendian commanded twenty-three archers, each with fresh arrows and fresher spirits as they prepared to leave the encampment. The other five elves, food gatherers from the village, offered to serve by carrying the squadron's extra arrows and food supplies.

Artemis was busy preparing his own blades and bows as Bryman sharpened his bloodied axe. The ranger looked at the faded metal blade as the brawny man rubbed it with a large whetstone. The grating sound carried a high-pitched tone that only hinted at the deadly sharpness of the axe.

"Do you ever clean the blood from your weapon?" Artemis asked Bryman.

The burly warrior bellowed a laugh. "It is not our way, friend. The Noradrie cherish each spot of blood of their enemies that falls prey to their weapon; the darker the blade, the greater the warrior."

"Won't the blade rust?" the ranger asked.

Bryman shook his head, "Not a chance, this is dwarven steel. My father was fortunate enough to trade with the dwarves of Kalavar for this precious weapon. This axe was handed to me when I came of age." The warrior paused a moment smiling reminiscently at the blood-soaked blade. "Aye, it has been many long years together," he said quietly to the axe, still appreciating its perfect form.

Artemis nodded, smiling at the warrior's sentiment. He examined his own sword, a weapon he had used little. He could not immediately recall where he had acquired it. His bow, on the other hand, he had made himself just last winter, and it was one of his proudest creations.

Artemis looked back to Bryman and his axe, curiously examining the blood stains. A thought then came to his mind. "Wouldn't unseasoned warriors be tempted to spill the blood of a goat upon their blade to appear more experienced?"

"Aye," the warrior answered, still sharpening the axe, "but tis a grave offense against one's ancestors. A noble warrior would never do such a thing. Although, bandits have been known to do so, to encourage the exchange of coin without bloodshed."

Artemis shrugged. He eyed the axe once more, finding only a few spots where the shimmering steel still glimmered. Noticing his gaze, Bryman winked at him.

"I hope we never fall on opposite sides of conflict," the ranger said smiling to the warrior respectfully.

"Aye, but I believe you'd have an arrow in my skull before my axe ever left my belt," the warrior said, returning the respectful smile.

Artemis chuckled heartily. "Then let us avoid such conflicts." He returned to adding more grease to his bow string.

Meanwhile, Morstar was trying to negotiate with the supply elves to carry more of the wine. They did not seem to think that kegs of wine were necessary for their march. To calm the dwarf, they insisted that there would be plenty of wine and spirits upon reaching the village. The dwarf eventually agreed with the elves and began his own preparations. He had cleaned his warhammer and shield earlier that morning, but his scale armor was in great need of care. He found a good sized log lying about the glade and placed his armor over it.

"Getting too slow…" Morstar murmured to himself as he noted each of the bent and missing scales. The dwarf pulled out a small smithing hammer and began to correct some of the bent scales. It was a precise and tedious work, but dwarves were renowned for their patience and skill when working with metals. Morstar thought back to when he left the mountainhomes of Kalavar. He had left home with the weapons and armor that had been commissioned to him as a patrol-sergeant. Taking them was a serious crime against the city. At the time he hadn't the coin to purchase such fine equipment. It was something the otherwise law-abiding dwarf had always regretted. He admired the scale armor shimmering in the evening light which reflected off a thousand small teardrop shaped scales; each one overlapping others in a subtle pattern that seemed to maximize both the comfort and perceived strength of the bearer.

"How's the armor, friend?" Thes asked curiously.

Morstar broke from his musing and turned to see the wizard standing behind him, sword and whetstone in hand. "It goes well, however, I wish I had a forge and some spare steel to set to it proper. Then I could have a shimmering piece to be proud of, eh?"

Thes only smiled in reply, appreciative of the steel armor hanging on the log.

Morstar still stared blankly at the wizard, "So… how are yer own preparations coming?"

The elf glanced away from the dwarf for a moment, belying his words, "They are going well."

Morstar only chuckled at the elf. "Ye should hurry yourself, won't be too much longer before we be marching."

Thes nodded, his hesitancy for the coming war clear on his features.

"Don't ye worry about it, lad. Ye can't reason with dark elves," the dwarf said, knowing the elf cared little for bloodshed. The dwarf, himself, had feared his long years of battle had made him dispassionate and uncaring of life. However, his days with Thes, and more recent time with the elves of Cwendilin, assured him his morals had not been tarnished by war and conflict.

Thes sat near the dwarf as he began to sharpen his sword. It was not a particularly special weapon. He had purchased it in a small village in the human kingdom of Astonia from a traveling merchant. The blade was clearly human made, with no particular design or style, simply utilitarian. An unknown crafter's sigil of two diamonds was found at the bottom of the simple leather hilt. The wizard was more concerned about his book of spells and scrolls he carried in his satchel. He had spent much time examining them lately, keeping the complex rituals and gestures fresh in his mind.

The thought of the coming clash currently dominated the elf's mind. It was not the fear of bloodshed that worried the elf, as Morstar suggested. Thes was fearful of himself. He feared that the coming fight would only strengthen the hate and anger deep within him, until he was consumed by the rising fires of ire. For so many years, the wizard had been logical and rational, almost completely dispassionate. This anger he carried towards the shadmar felt out of his control. He was illequipped for such emotion.

It was getting late in the day as the large group of elves and the others had finished their preparations. They all came together over a large bonfire and had a mighty feast with the food and drink they could not take with them. They shared berrywine, roasted venison with berries and nuts, and stews with various combinations of fish, venison, and herbs. After the feast, they shared song and dance, most of which told tales of great wars and wonderful triumphs. There was much merry-making throughout the late evening as the moon rose over the treetops.

Afterwards, Svendian went over the plans the group had drawn together early that morning. The squadron would march for three long nights to the village of Harpien. They would march through each night until late afternoon and rest until darkness fell. They would continue until they reached the village's high outer cliffs. Svendian went over some details with his own soldiers as the squad of archers grabbed their belongings.

Thes was still mentally preparing himself. He had never marched to war before, and he was still quite nervous about the upcoming diplomacy that would be required to form a formidable defense with the villagers of Harpien. However, he noticed a growing positive demeanor in the dwarf's mood, and he found comfort in it. Morstar had seen much battle and the eve of its approach put the dwarf in good spirits. Bryman, too, was extra cheerful as he finished collecting his gear and stood with the elves. Artemis, however, seemed to share the wizard's reluctance and held a serious expression as he joined up. Thes knew it was the fires of vengeance that pushed him to seek this path, but he had not the strength to deny the option of fulfilling it. It had felt far too good to kill shadmar lately.

$$* \quad * \quad * \quad * \quad * \quad * \quad *$$

It was a long march through the forest and Thes was worried that the large group would be spotted by the shadmar patrols. The marching elves had little choice, however, since only Svendian knew the way to the hidden village. Svendian, Thes, and Artemis led the way, followed by ten archers, the five of the supply crew, and then five more archers. Bryman and Morstar held the rear of the squadron, quietly laughing and sharing tales of battles they had fought in. The last eight of the elves tried their best to hide signs of the groups passage, always just out of sight behind the squadron.

It was now deep in autumn. Cool winds chilled the backside of the patrol as they headed southwest towards the hidden village of Harpien. Leaves sailed in the winds and a few trees could be seen in the night that began to change their colors from dark and cool greens to bright yellows and reds. To Thes, the changing of seasons and weather seemed to mirror the changing of power, from the vibrant, cheerful elves of the surface to that of the dark, cruel leaders of the shadmar. The wizard's thoughts were now dominated by the coming battle, even though no one was sure when the shadmar would find and attack Harpien. If they found it at all.

According to Svendian, Harpien had been the smallest of the eastern villages in the Aegis Forest. The town of wood elves was completely self-sufficient within a deep valley. Its citizens rarely, if ever, left to the wide forests outside the bounds of the high cliffs that surrounded the hidden retreat. A high waterfall brought fresh water to a large pond within, where fish and turtles could sometimes be caught. There were also many varieties of flora and fauna gracing the valley in great abundance. It was quite the paradise for the inhabitants, especially considering the high cliffs surrounding the valley kept most predators and enemies away.

It had been a long time since Thes had made any excursion westward. In fact, it had been a long time since Thes had made any trip outside of his home village. That point became clear to him as he marched along through the forest.

116

Had I been so entrapped in a domestic life? the wizard thought, the idea troubling him. He had always considered himself a traveler and seeker of knowledge and hidden cultures, but he could not ignore the fact that it had been many years since he last left the comforts of his village home. In fact, he now considered it odd he even considered himself permanently settled in the village of Escailar. Thes tried to dwell on this realization and the emotions buried within it, but the events ahead of him soon dominated his thoughts again.

Svendian and Artemis were forming a kinship as they shared tales of hunting, scouting, and the ways of forest creatures. The ranger was surprised by the captain's vast knowledge of the forest and felt there was much he could learn from him. Svendian was growing fond of the human as well, having never met a man so concerned for the forest. The captain never had children of his own, and had always considered the many squadrons of elves he taught to be his progeny. However, Svendian knew there was much he could teach this man and hoped he would have the time to do so after the coming danger.

Bryman and Morstar were both excited for the battle ahead, but for entirely different reasons. Bryman was quite eager to shed blood with his axe and reign in the glory of the victory he knew would come. Morstar, on the other hand, was more eager for the chance to prove his capability as a leader and warrior, eager to prove to himself that he was still the capable soldier he once was. Somewhere deep inside, the dwarf felt this was the chance to make it up to those poor recruits who died under his command. It had been quite a long time since he fought in a sizable conflict and he knew his experience would be needed to prepare for the effort.

It was late in the afternoon of the third day, when Svendian suddenly stopped. He then raised his hand for others to do the same. As if by magic, there was suddenly a drop in front of them, a great cliff where the tops of trees were visible. The trees bestowed the impression that a leafy ground cover filled a shallow valley. However, when they looked through some of the breaks in the trees, they could see that the valley was quite deep. The tree tops below them were exceptionally tall.

"Now how do we find our way down?" Artemis asked, peering around the cliffside for a safe path to the bottom.

"I'm afraid that is one fact I do not recall about my childhood journeys here," Svendian said hazily, as if sequentially searching through those memories for a clue.

"Perhaps I could patrol around the valley's exterior?" Thes offered, as he motioned upwards towards the sky.

Svendian nodded. "Good idea. I'll also send two small groups to circle the valley on foot."

Thes summoned the energies that would bear him aloft, flying upwards. Svendian ordered six archers, three to each side, to circle the valley.

"I shall join the northern patrol," Artemis stated.

"No," interjected Svendian, "The elves of Harpien are more cautious of strangers, and the sight of a man might lead to unnecessary hostility."

Artemis nodded, pursing his lips. The fact that he was probably the youngest of the group suddenly dawned on him. Maybe it was the threat of impending war, but he was feeling restless and the idea of waiting here wasn't helping.

Although, if Artemis was restless, Bryman was outright agitated. The idea of waiting and hiding in the woods did not appeal to the warrior. He found a nearby log and sat upon it while grumbling to himself, pulling a whetstone from his bag. He began vigorously sharpening his axe, much to the dismay of the nearby elves, who eyed the warrior a bit wearily.

118

Morstar grinned at the burly man as he pulled out a small pouch and offered some smokeweed to Artemis. The frustrated ranger pulled out his pipe and took a pinch of the fragrant dried herb, joining the dwarf sitting on the ground. The other remaining elves were quite patient, some resting upon the ground while others guarding their perimeter with their eyes.

While the two scouting groups rushed off through the trees, Thes was rising into the sky. The late afternoon sun was bright and the wind was cool. The wizard rose quickly into the clear air. Many crows were scattering about from tree to tree below him, calling occasionally to each other. There was a hawk high in the air that took an alternative route upon seeing the elf reaching its altitude.

Thes took in the fresh air as he surveyed the valley below him. The valley was a long depression stretched out southward with a wild stream running through its length. He could see glimpses of a vigorous waterfall on the northern end that gushed down into the valley below. A long pond could be seen not far south of the waterfall. Most of the valley, however, was covered in the thick tangle of tall trees. There was no sign of a village or any dwellings within the opened arms of the rocky bluffs surrounding the valley. Thes peered closely at the edges of the valley, but could not see any navigable paths along the high cliffs. Although, the high trees blocked much of the cliffs from view as well. The elf sighed as his eyes followed the edges of the cliff towards the southern end. Thes took one last view of the vast forest around him before descending back towards the others.

Thes landed gracefully in the middle of the other elves, despite feeling a bit exhausted from the effort of his magic. Svendian came to the wizard with a hopeful look in his eyes.

"Well...?" the captain asked pointedly.

Thes shook his head and said, "I'm afraid I cannot see any route into the valley from this side. Our only hope is to enter from the far southern end along the river, just before the land rises."

"And what of the village? Did you see anything?" Svendian asked keenly.

"No," said the wizard. "I dared not go below the tree line, however. If these elves are as intolerant as you indicate, I would not wish to intrude so boldly."

"A wise decision, wizard. Let us then make camp here for the night. Perhaps one of the patrols will have better luck."

Svendian then began giving orders to the nearby elves. Soon they were all bustling about the perimeter of the area while Thes sat upon the ground with Morstar and Artemis. He was keeping a wary eye on Bryman, who was still sharpening his axe. The action was creating a frequent shower of sparks.

Thes whispered to Morstar, "Is he okay?" His eyes still upon the Noradrie warrior.

Morstar nodded as he handed his smokeweed pouch to Thes, who was pulling out his own pipe. "Aye," the dwarf whispered back, "a man like that isn't made for waitin'."

Artemis, who overheard, snorted, as if this was a mighty understatement. However, Bryman seemed to take notice that the three of them were talking about him. His fierce blue eyes glared back at them for a moment. Then his hand shot out.

With a blur of steel, the razor-sharp axe flipped end-over-end into a nearby tree with a loud *thunk*. The warrior grinned mightily at the three surprised faces as he stood up and strutted towards the tree. The elves around them shook their heads, visibly disappointed that a tree was harmed. Bryman ripped the blade from the trunk with a quick flex of

120

his burly arm. He then sat down next to Artemis. The ranger seemed more than a bit apprehensive.

"Might I have a try?" Bryman asked the ranger, in his thick voice. He pointed to the short pipe now hanging from Artemis's mouth.

"Uh... sure," the ranger responded, still taken aback. He handed Bryman the still smoking pipe. The others seemed a bit uneasy, hesitant of the warrior's intentions.

Bryman put the soft wood to his face, curiously eyeing the device, obviously confused on how to go about smoking from it. Artemis carefully grabbed the pipe, gave the warrior a quick demonstration of a careful intake, then he bellowed forth a near-perfect smoke-ring to the upper boughs of the trees. He then handed the pipe back to Bryman.

Bryman took it carefully and tried to replicate the ranger's actions. He was soon robustly coughing as he attempted to take in much more smoke than was sensible. The previous tension dissipated instantly as the other three laughed heartily while Artemis patted the warrior on the back. After the coughing fits subsided, Bryman joined in with roars of laughter.

*   *   *   *   *   *   *

It was past nightfall when the two patrols returned to the camp. Neither group was able to find a safe way down to the bottom of the valley. It seemed the only hope was to walk in from the southern end, where the land around the valley became equal in its depth. The patrol elves enjoyed some fresh provisions while Svendian talked with the others. They soon decided to stay put for the night and make the trek in the morning, when there would be less risk of inadvertently falling to certain death.

The next morning the band of elves, men, and dwarf set out for the southern end of the valley. The journey took most of the morning and as the sun began to peak, the travelers reached the valley's entrance. They continued within, sending scouts ahead of the main group to keep an eye out for traps and other obstacles.

The valley expanded around them as they left the narrow southern entrance behind. The rushing stream flowing beside them as they marched their way through the tall trees. The many layers of foliage shimmered in the dappled light as some of the green leaves had given way to tinges of gold and bronze. The company was quiet, as if all its members were entranced by the ancient trees towering above them.

After an hour of slow progress, Svendian's hand went up and the company halted. He had a strange foreboding feeling at the base of his skull in conjunction with the fact that the scouts should have checked in by now. The aged captain peered through the trees ahead, trying to catch a glimpse of the source of his anxiety. However, the way ahead was clear and quiet. Only the muffled sounds of the birds above and the rushing water to their left could be heard through the trees.

"Something wrong?" Artemis whispered near Svendian.

The captain only responded with a slight nod as he continued to peer about, his soldier's instincts expecting something to happen at any moment.

Something then did happen. The nearby river pulled itself out of its bed like a snake arching its coiling body into the sky. It quickly wrapped and swirled around the company forming a barrier of rushing water, magically contained in a great wall that flowed around them. The wall rose at least twenty feet into the air as it swirled on itself, eventually closing the top, forming a watery dome. They were surrounded and the roar of the rushing waters around them masked their shouting voices.

122

Thes closed his eyes and reached deeply into his mind, reaching out to the elemental spirits. He could easily sense the water spirits swirling about in the dome and focused his mind on the faint chanting which bound the water spirits to their task. The voice was firm, yet soft, perhaps sweet. The female voice was not the commanding arcane words of a sorcerer, but the gentle persuasion of a practiced spirit-speaker. Whomever conjured the dome of flowing water, was a druid, not a wizard.

Thes focused again, ignoring the cries of his friends as the dome continued to roar and whip around them. His own magical words penetrated the noise and persuaded the water spirits to let him pass. The elf boldly walked towards the roaring water just as a doorway appeared, soon filling in again as he stepped through.

Behind the wall of water, Thes saw two almond-shaped eyes the color of shimmering chestnuts. The eyes displayed surprise, then curiosity. They belonged to a beautiful thunmar woman with tanned skin clad in thick leathers with a long, hooded cloak of gray wolf furs. She raised her hands towards Thes as her temporary smile dropped into a stern and vigilant visage.

"Halt. State yourself and your business in this valley," she said in a thickly accented Elven dialect. Her words firm as she eyed Thes searchingly.

Thes calmly looked into those auburn eyes and softly said, "No need for hostility. I am Thes Ambreaia of the village of Escailar. We seek those of the village of Harpien. We bring word of an eminent threat to the region."

"Eminent threat, indeed. You have marched into our valley with a raiding party from the looks of it. Bringing men and dwarves in to plunder our possessions and defile our sacred places," the elven druidess replied, her tone still stern and unwavering.

"Please," Thes pleaded. "We mean you no harm, I assure you." Thes opened his arms, his palms open to the sky in a gesture of peace. "We are not raiders, but survivors. Escailar, Diiera, Teillina, and Cwendilin are no more. Shadmar have returned to the surface and now raid upon the land. We seek sanctuary from war. We offer to help defend your village from those that wish it destroyed."

The druidess began to stalk in a circle around the wizard as if she was trying to find a lie hidden on his form. Thes stood firm, palms open, facing forward, as she stepped behind him. When she reappeared on the other side, Thes couldn't help but notice a bit of concern in her face. She stepped in front of the wizard, her arms crossed as she continued to stare at him, peering deep into his eyes.

As that piercing stare bore into him, Thes felt a flutter in the upper reaches of his stomach and he swallowed uncomfortably. The world was momentarily forgotten as those shimmering auburn eyes laid bare all he was and would ever be. The wizard lost himself looking into infinity. Thes's mind then sharply returned to the present. He blinked heavily, trying to dispel the lost moment. However, he had a strange feeling that a lingering enchantment was upon him. He knew he would have to be wary around this mystical thunmar.

The druidess raised her arm in a gesture and numerous elven archers stepped out from behind hidden places in the trees. In that same moment the great watery dome dissipated, splashing upon those inside. Soaking wet elves, men, and a dwarf stood dumbfounded and unprepared as the archers of Harpien surrounded them with arrows at the ready. Bryman reached for his axe, ready to slip into a warrior's rage. However, Morstar wrenched the man's arm away and gave him a stern look. All was then quiet.

"Take the men and the dwarf, have them bound," she ordered the elves around her, still speaking in the Elven tongue, such that Bryman did not reach for his axe a second time. "Escort the People to the valley's entrance." She then turned towards Thes and said solemnly, "I'm afraid we cannot help you and you cannot help us."

"Please, stop!" cried Svendian as the elves reached towards Bryman, Artemis, and Morstar with bindings. Bryman looked to Morstar seemingly for permission to defend himself. The dwarf could only shrug in equal confusion, but he was not eager to begin hostilities.

Svendian then addressed the druidess directly, "Please, I beg you. My village was burned to the ground before my very eyes. We have come seeking refuge and offer assistance so that you do not suffer as me and my friends have. Find Meaia or Roswin! Surely they still live! They can vouch for me. I am Svendian Lua'ela of Cwendilin."

The druidess gestured for her guards to step back from the captives and she stepped towards Svendian, peering at his face closely. She spoke quietly to him, "Roswin has passed on decades ago, but Meaia Oganta still serves this village as an elder. How do you know of her?"

"She once caught me stealing fruits from her garden," the old soldier said smiling. "I use to visit this village every five years for the midsummer solstice. It was before your time, when I was a young and curious child."

The armed elves turned to the druidess, seeking orders as their arms tired from drawn bowstrings. The druidess nodded to them and their bows descended. She looked around at the soldiers from Cwendilin, the men, and then at the dwarf. She then stared into Thes's eyes again, but only for a moment. She then turned back to Svendian.

"I will bring you to her if you take responsibility for these outsiders," she said, clearly referring to the non-elves.

"I do. I owe them my life and would entrust it again in their hands," the captain stated, smiling at Artemis, Bryman, and Morstar.

"Then follow us to Harpien where we shall confirm your identity and the truthfulness of your story." She then began to lead the elves into the woods northward. The soldiers of Cwendilin began to follow with Artemis and Thes right behind them. Thes's eyes watching the druidess closely, still feeling somewhat enchanted.

The men, elves, and dwarf willingly let the thunmar archers take their weapons and were led to follow the druid down the forest path.

Bryman leaned down towards Morstar as they followed the others. He whispered, "Are we prisoners or guests?"

"Not a clue," the dwarf replied as he grinned wide at the warrior. The two chuckled as they followed the elves down the forest path.

(11) A Warning of Peril

As the group followed the winding forest path along the river towards the hidden village, Thes stepped forward to talk to the mysterious druidess.

"You are quite adept in the ways of magic," he commented as he stepped in stride alongside her.

The druidess made a sidelong glance at the wizard as she continued to lead the group through the trees. She nodded and said, "Yes. I have studied much of the ways of nature and the spirits that govern Enis's domain." She turned to Thes and smiled, "I see you too commune with the spirits."

"Yes. I do." He answered, returning the smile. "I am learned in many ways of magic." The druidess seemed slightly suspicious of his last comment. Thes noticed her smile subside, so he introduced himself to break the tension. "I'm Thesomber Ambreaia."

"My name is Sia Harlow," she replied tersely.

Thes could sense the hostility. "I know you do not trust us, but I assure you we mean you and your people no harm. I think you will appreciate our help in protecting your village."

The druidess stopped and turned fiercely towards the wizard. "Yes, I do *not* trust you. We have many threats in this part of the forest and we have grown weary in our struggles. Whether it be orc or dwarf that walks in this valley, it makes my stomach cringe to see my land tainted by outsiders." Her eyes were wide with anger as she took in deep quick breaths, holding back her inner frustration.

Thes simply looked back with concern in his eyes.

She continued, her anger growing with each statement, "When contact with the other villages dissipated, we have survived here on our own. When the crown stopped sending regular patrols to this region, we learned to defend ourselves. When orcs invaded our valley from the mountains, we protected our homes without help from outsiders. Now you say another threat is at our borders and you offer your help. We do not need it, ethmar." Her last statement delivered as a spear thrust at the wizard.

Thes stood firm, searching into Sia's reddened face. He noticed her eyes glistened with withheld tears. Perhaps it was the enchantment, but he did not wish to see such pain in the emotional thunmar's features.

The druidess turned angrily away and marched on down the old forest path to the north. Thes followed quietly behind her, keeping his distance. He couldn't help but notice that she was wiping her eyes as she marched.

After a while, the forest path gave way from the thick foliage and thorn-bearing thickets to an open woodland with a few sun-lit patches dotted by tall, majestic trees. In the distance, there was a large pond at the end of the forest stream. Many small hovels could be seen tucked into the woodlands by the pond. The newcomers were brought to a larger clearing, which was surrounded by numerous totems. As they entered the clearing, many thunmar began to gather around them. The villagers' stern faces were not comforting to Thes and his companions.

The thunmar of the village dressed in a wilder fashion, with feathers and artistic beads adorning their clothing. They seemed to have a few dozen warriors among them as well, drawing bows and arrows, or long curved knives, as they came out to view the outsiders. Soon an aged ethmar woman with an elaborate headdress made of raven and blue feathers entered the clearing. The many villagers grew quiet.

Sia walked towards the old elf and whispered quietly into her ear. The druidess then stood to the side with her arms crossed, facing the outsiders. Svendian walked hesitantly towards the old woman, dropping to his knees in front of her as a sign of respect. The others remained quiet and watched.

"Meaia?" the old soldier asked as he gazed into the old elf's face. It was hard for Svendian to be sure, but his memory stirred as he looked into the elder's dark eyes.

The old elf nodded slowly. She smiled at the old soldier and offered her hand to help him to his feet. Svendian stood up and smiled at her.

"Are you here to rummage in my garden, Sven?" Meaia asked sweetly.

Svendian laughed. "Certainly not. I learned my lesson." The crowd of people joined in the laughter and the general tension of the moment released. The warriors near the men and dwarf, however, kept their weapons drawn and ready.

Sia seemed to visibly relax as well, although she still bore a troubled expression on her face. She then found that Thes was staring at her across the clearing. She turned away towards Svendian and Meaia, hiding an embarrassed smile.

"It is good to see you again and other People from the northern villages," the elder elf began. Her voice became more serious, "But why do you come here after all this time, with men and dwarves in your company?"

Svendian replied, his face dark and grave, "Times are dire for the eastern villages. The People I have brought here are all that remain. The others are travelers and friends that continue to aid us in our plight." Svendian then turned away from the elder elf and addressed the growing crowd of villagers.

"We are all at war. Our dark brethren have returned from the deep underground. They return with fire and hatred aimed to destroy our homeland. They wish to see us punished for the transgressions of our ancestors."

"Pah!" came a gruff challenge from one of the older warriors near Meaia. "We have fought shadmar raids before, we are not afraid."

Svendian stared down the interrupter for a moment before he began, his eyes fierce, "It is not of a mere raid of unseasoned shadmar warriors that I wish to warn you. We believe there is an army of shadmar hidden among the roots of the mountains, ready to reclaim their ancient lands."

The crowd was silent, seemingly absorbing the warning of the old soldier. The interruptor still wore a skeptical look upon his face, but he had seemingly decided not to challenge Svendian again.

Meaia looked grave as she peered deeply into Svendian's eyes, looking for truth in his words. Eventually she solemnly nodded to the soldier. "If what you say is true, then the elders and I wish to learn what you know."

Svendian nodded and walked with the old elf towards the largest of the hovels near the clearing. Sia followed them, while Thes and the others stayed back with the archers of Cwendilin, still surrounded by armed warriors. However, the local guards seemed less inclined to be forceful towards the outsiders.

A few hours went by and the sun was beyond its zenith. Thes was learning much from the villagers that were willing to talk to the outsiders. He learned that Harpien had undergone many hardships over the years. Many of the original thunmar and ethmar villagers from Svendian's visitation days were killed in goblin attacks, shadmar raids, or simply old age. The village's population dwindled with the loss of visitations and trade from the outside. However, the village received some new life when a tribe of wild thunmar elves from the south settled in the village many decades ago. These wild elves were used to living without the luxuries brought in from the elven cities. Their culture

130

and survival skills helped the village thrive and take advantage of its prosperous valley.

Morstar and Bryman were sitting near the pond. Bryman was taking another attempt at Artemis's pipe, puffing out wide clouds of smoke. The other elves, like Thes, were chatting with the villagers of Harpien, learning and laughing with their distant kin.

Thes's eyes then followed Sia as she quietly left the elder's meeting hovel and strode into the woods behind.

Thes interrupted the old elf he was listening to and asked, "Who is she?" He pointed to the druidess as she marched deeper into the woods.

"That is Sia, our spiritual advisor and healer. She was taught by the great Shihara, a legendary druid among our people. It was Shihara who led the wild thunmar to our village and revived our populace."

"She seems to carry a great burden," Thes replied as his eyes watched the last of the druidess disappear behind the trees.

The old woman smiled, "Yes, she is the only one who knows the ancient druidic arts after Shihara was killed during an orc raid. The village relies heavily upon the poor girl. She is wise beyond her years, but she has too many responsibilities."

Thes nodded absently as he still stared off to where Sia was last seen. "It is not simply her duties that trouble her. Her heart is heavy with loss."

The old elf eyed the wizard curiously, "Yes, I fear she never mourned the loss of her parents, who were also felled during the orc raid. She took up Shihara's mantle without hesitation to serve the village. I remember her as a young and eager elfling when she and her parents arrived with the other wild thunmar. Now, she is always serious, her heart is wrapped in ironwood. "

Thes turned to the elf, concerned. Before he could say anything more, however, Svendian exited the hovel and walked pointedly toward the wizard.

"The elders wish you to give your account of Escailar," the old soldier said, beckoning Thes to join him. Thes thanked the old woman for her time and joined Svendian into the expansive long hovel.

Inside, he found three aged elves, including Meaia, sitting cross-legged upon the floor in the center of a round chamber. A small, smoking fire burned nearby with many fragrant smells emanating and filling the chamber with sweet tones. Thes sat down next to Svendian across from the aged elves. The elders sat stoically looking upon the wizard purposefully. Thes felt somewhat uncomfortable at the idea of recalling the painful events of the shadmar attack. He did not want to be consumed by the rage he felt deep within him. However, he knew he must share his knowledge.

Thes recounted what he knew about Escailar before the raid. The infrequent trade down the forest road and the many villagers who dwelt there. The elders, however, seemed impatient behind their stoic expressions, so Thes continued his story into the day of the raid. He recounted how the scouts were fortunate to have some knowledge of what was to come and the foresight to send a scout to Elienspar to warn the city that a shadmar force was striking Escailar. He then explained the battle and his role, even his use of magic and eventual escape at the end of the raid.

After he finished his story, Thes found tears upon his face and his fist trembling. He wiped his face and took a few deep breaths before facing the elders again. Meanwhile, the aged elves were whispering among themselves, sorting out the details of everything he shared with them.

Finally, Meaia broke the silence. "Thes, do not feel discouraged for your departure," she said reassuringly. "You could have done nothing for those villagers. But for what

Svendian says you have done since then, you should be proud of your actions."

The wizard simply nodded, still trying to regain his composure and push the swelling anger back into the deep recesses of his heart. He continued, telling the aged elves of what he and his friends had discovered since the destruction of Escailar.

The old elves stood up and quietly conferred with each other following the wizard's exposition. After many minutes of hopeful silence, the elves sat back down to speak with Thes and Svendian.

"The shadmar attack on the surface does make us wary for the safety of the village," Meaia began.

"Then let us prepare the defenses," Thes interjected, standing to his feet.

"However," she continued deliberately, "we are not convinced that a conquering army of shadmar exist upon the surface as you have said."

Thes and Svendian looked at each, both disappointed and in disbelief.

"What proof have you that a conquering army threatens us and not simply a prolonged raid?" she questioned the two outsiders.

Svendian began, a bit angry and terse, "I told you what we know. Do you not think it odd that all the eastern villages were raided and destroyed in a short period of time? Do you not think it strange that veteran warriors attacked our homes, not mere adolescent warbands? Do you not think it odd they had powerful sorcerers among them? These do not seem like raiders to me. This is an army with an intent beyond mere looting and terrorism."

"Perhaps," Meaia replied slowly, "but perhaps not. We are not convinced."

"Not convinced!?" Thes echoed impatiently. His anger simmering.

Meaia simply nodded as Thes and Svendian both looked at the elders like they were on fire. "I'm sorry," she said solemnly, "our years of experience do not lead us to believe that this threat is as serious as you deem it to be. We have seen many such raids in our time, even those as large and dangerous as you have described. It would not be the first time that sorcerers have accompanied the warbands either. Since you have found no fortress for such an army to be housed, it is likely these raiders are simply a greater force threatening the area from the deep caverns in the mountains. These are quite unfortunate circumstances and we are willing to offer refuge for your people."

"And what of the men and dwarf," Thes asked pointedly.

The elders looked at each other uneasily. "They..." an elder thunmar answered, "must stay indefinitely. Now that they know the location of our home, we cannot have them telling others of their kind."

Both Thes and Svendian were shocked by this final statement.

"Please tell me you will at least send word to Elienspar," Svendian pleaded.

The elders looked at each other again, nodding to each other. "No," Meaia answered, "We cannot spare anyone to make the long journey; and few here remember the way. Besides, the elven crown has shown little attention to this region in the past century, we doubt they would show any concern to its plight."

Thes stood up and exited the hovel, his heart was racing. Deep anger threatened to swell up and consume him. He marched headlong into the woods behind the hovel, unseen by his companions near the pond.

*   *   *   *   *   *   *

134

The singing of birds overhead, the babbling of the stream in the distance, the dancing of the branches in the light winds; they all served to calm the wizard as he slowed his pace and began to lose himself in the surrounding ambiance.

"They are a tough committee," spoke a quiet feminine voice above the wizard.

Thes looked above to see Sia sitting comfortably in a high bough, her curved body reclined in a perfect niche. The wizard looked upon her and could not help but smile.

"Indeed they are," he answered. "They choose ignorance and prejudice over the reasonable warnings of outsiders." His statement bitter and sardonic.

"Not that my words can sway the elders, but I believe you," the druidess said as she swiftly descended the tall tree to stand beside him. She then looked into the wizard's eyes. "I am sorry for what happened to you and your village."

Thes was mesmerized by her eyes, feeling that lingering enchantment again. However, his mind managed to wretch free. "How did you hear of my story?" he asked her curiously.

"The spirits echoed your words to me," she responded, with the somewhat apologetic expression of one caught eavesdropping.

Thes only smiled, knowing that this druidess must be quite adept in her magic to hear quiet words spoken from so far away. He was careful looking back at her, trying not to look too deeply into her eyes. He was trying to avoid feeling enchanted by her magic.

"I take no offense," he said. "I am glad you were willing to learn of me. I hope I am no longer the dangerous outsider you at first perceived."

"No," she stated. "However, if you are not a liar, then I must worry about your tale and the true threat facing my people. We are fierce and strong, but a shadmar army would be more than a match for us."

"Then perhaps together we can convince them," the wizard offered. His gaze reflexively went deep into her eyes, for a moment trapping his attention inside.

Sia smiled back at the wizard, "Perhaps, but I doubt it. They are as stubborn as they are aged. In my many years serving as druid to the village, I cannot recall a single time when I was able to convince them of my convictions."

Thes sighed as he leaned back against the trunk of a tree, his gaze breaking free. "Then our coming here has brought only ill to my friends. I am not eager to tell them of the elders' decree. They will not stand for staying here."

Sia eyed the dismayed, platinum-haired elf for a few moments. Her gaze then looked to the sky and the coming setting of the sun. She then reached out and grabbed his hands.

"Come with me," she beckoned as she pulled the wizard to his feet. The playful smile on the druidess's face immediately released the tension in the wizard, her eyes captured his gaze again. He could not refuse her beckon. Soon he was chasing after her as she raced through the trees towards the river's edge.

After many minutes of chasing Sia through the woods, Thes finally caught up to her as she leapt out over the stream. Immediately a tendril of water, like an outstretched hand, rushed to greet the druidess's feet. She landed gracefully upon the impossibly solid water's surface and rose into the air as the column of water swiftly rose high into the branches.

Thes watched in awe as the wild elf disappeared into the canopy above. He summoned his own magical energies and was soon flying upwards after her. The two mystical elves continued to rise until they breached the upper canopy.

136

The wide valley was in full view, with the upper reaches of all the trees shimmering in the evening light.

Sia was gracefully holding to a high branch, her arms crossed to hold herself to the tall tree. Her watery tendril was swiftly descending back to the stream below. Thes perched beside the druidess and looked at her. The sunlight danced in her wide almond eyes as she looked out to the golden landscape. Thes turned to see what brought such awe to her face.

Above the canopy, a majestic dance was underway. Numerous butterflies, moths, birds, and insects swirled and swished in the yellow light of the evening sun. The trees had small red and white berries as an offering for the many birds who dashed and darted to grab the precious packets of sweetness, ever careful to avoid attracting the attention of the birds of prey watching the tentative feast from the trees along the high cliff. The large orange butterflies danced with each other in a dazzling array, a mating dance fit for such a delicate creature. The entire event was like an animated symphony where nature's music accompanied the finest dancers.

Thes swallowed and caught his breath as he gazed at the wondrous splendor. He turned to Sia to thank her for sharing this sight with him. He found that she was watching him curiously trying to see how he would react, as one does when they share something intimate and personal.

"Thank you for sharing this with me," the wizard said, turning back to face the majestic view. "This is so beautiful."

"I'm glad you like it," the druidess replied, also turning to take in the scenery. "This is my favorite place in the early autumn."

The two elves found more comfortable perches on their respective branches and continued to watch the marvelous natural beauty play out. Not a word was spoken and the two sat comfortably listening to nature's orchestra. After a while, the sun was shrinking behind the cliff wall behind them and darkness was beginning to stretch out across the valley's canopy, putting an end to the evening's show.

*   *   *   *   *   *   *

Meanwhile, back at the village near the pond, Bryman was starting to get eager for action. He was pacing back and forth near his companions, wishing he had his axe in hand. There were no longer many villagers in the clearing. Most had headed to their respective homes for dinner with the setting sun. Only a few village warriors, reluctant to stay and watch the outsiders, occupied the area.

"Careful there, ye might dig yourself a pit," Morstar said to the pacing Bryman. The dwarf sat comfortably against a log with Artemis. Both of them were smoking pipes. Artemis was shaking a small wooden cup with his palm pressed over the top. Wooden dice rattled inside and he threw them upon the dirt. Morstar cursed under his breath as the little wooden cubes stopped rolling on the hard ground.

Bryman turned to the dwarf, clearly frustrated. "I cannot wait for these elves to decide their actions. *We* know what we face. Why not set the battle plan and prepare for the coming assault?"

"Aye, that we do," the dwarf agreed. "But I'm sure Thes and Svendian will convince them soon enough. You should have joined us in this game of chance." He turned back to the dice game, cursing under his breath again as Artemis smiled widely. The ranger had added a mark to a growing column of marks in the dirt. A deep line separated these marks from an adjacent column, which had only a few such marks.

138

Bryman then turned eagerly toward the elder's hovel as Svendian walked out solemnly. The aged soldier seemed to be carrying the weight of his years upon him as he stepped out into the clearing towards the others. Svendian walked past the relaxed guards and came to the men and dwarf.

Morstar could see that something was wrong the moment he saw the elf's face. "Seems grim. What's the news?" the gruff dwarf asked when Svendian reached them.

The old elf released a sigh of defeat as he looked upon Morstar, Bryman, and Artemis. "They don't believe us," he said matter-of-factly.

Bryman's face turned red and his body visibly tensed. But before he could shout in rage, Morstar leapt up and aimed his palm at the burly warrior. The dwarf was not in the mood for the war-priest's proclamations of battle.

"Quiet," Morstar said tersely. Amazingly, the large man seemed to obey the dwarf and shut his mouth. Morstar turned and questioned Svendian, "What did they say? What's going on?"

The old elf told them what had happened in the elder's hovel as the others intently listened. He then ended on the elders' final decree concerning the outsiders, "And thus, you must remain here until the end of your days."

Bryman was again filled with growing rage. His face was flushed red again and his hands was out in front of him as if he was preparing to strangle someone. Artemis tentatively patted the tall warrior on his back to calm him and looked helplessly to Morstar and Svendian.

"Well... we can agree that won't be happening," the dwarf stated.

"These elves threaten our honor to imprison us without battle!" Bryman growled, trying to contain his anger. Upon hearing angry words, the guards at the edge of the clearing came to attention and grabbed their bows. They were eyeing the situation from afar with a tense interest.

"Relax, friend," Svendian quietly said to the enraged warrior. "We have neither blade nor bow to fight. Let us try to resolve this diplomatically before we come to blows with potential allies."

"Aye," agreed the dwarf. "And if that doesn't work, we can always unleash an enraged Noradrie into their midst." Morstar smiled wryly at Bryman. Bryman returned a grin, bottling his rage for later.

"Where is Thes?" Mortstar then asked Svendian, noticing the wizard's absence.

Svendian looked around confused. "I am not sure. He left in a foul mood upon hearing the elders' decision, but that was quite a while ago."

"I am sure he will join us when his mood has improved. We should let him have his space," Artemis offered.

A few minutes later, the elders exited the hovel, sending over a few of their guards to escort the visitors to a vacant hovel for the night. Svendian and the others quietly complied, having just decided they would wait until morning to argue for their freedom. The accommodations were simple, but comfortable. The beds were piles of soft spruce boughs covered with a thick, weaved reed mat. The guards had brought the visitors dried gourds filled with fresh water and bowls of dried fruits, venison, and nuts. The tired travelers thanked the elves for the food and prepared themselves for rest.

Along the forest path, not far from the village, Thes and Sia casually walked towards the village together. They had been sharing tales of wondrous places they had seen. Thes told tales of the many sights in his travels of the world, while Sia talked about the many creatures and sights she had seen in her time in the river valley.

140

"You have such wonders in this valley," Thes said to Sia, still somewhat in awe of what he had witnessed in the canopy above.

"Yes, there are wondrous things here on occasion," she replied. "However, with each year I look upon them, they lose some luster to my eyes. I yearn to see wonders that lie outside this sheltered valley." Her words were solemn with a hint of defeat. Sia knew she could not abandon the village for her own pursuits, as too many here counted on her skills and magic to heal and protect them. She stopped in her tracks as the realization of this fact subsumed her emotions. She then looked at Thes, realizing the greatest danger of outsiders was hearing about all the splendid things she was missing in the world.

Thes turned back to look at Sia, seeing her sunken posture and that unseen burden upon her shoulders. Since he now knew what burdened her, he looked into her eyes willingly, expressing his distaste for the responsibilities that kept such a strong, intelligent women bound to serve those who seemed unappreciative.

"Pity me not, ethmar," she said quietly to the wizard, turning away from him to wipe growing tears in her eyes.

Thes strode to her and gently held her shoulders as he turned to look into her eyes.

"I do not pity you," he said quietly and earnestly. "You have willingly served your village with such honor and selflessness all these years. You could have abandoned them at any time to pursue your own wanderlust. Yet you did not. Even if they take you for granted, your intelligence and strength goes not wasted. This village thrives because of you." Thes was convinced of this after speaking to the other villagers earlier in the day. He was also sure such assurances were words that the overworked druidess did not hear often enough.

Sia surprised Thes by wrapping her arms around him in a hard embrace. Her heart was fluttered by the words she needed to hear, even if an outsider had spoken them. Tears continued to bead down her cheek as she was overwhelmed by both self-pity and self-admiration for her many hard choices over the years. Thes held the druidess softly, gently rubbing her back. He thought of his own choices over the years, and his own choice to stay in Escailar even when his wanderlust threatened to pull him away. He suddenly recalled why he had chosen to stay, why he ceased to be a traveler those many years before. He too had felt needed and obligated by the villagers.

Sia whispered softly into Thes's ear, "Thank you, for your kindness. I do not deserve it for the way I treated you earlier."

Thes pulled back from the embrace, grasped Sia's shoulders and looked into her eyes again. "Everyone deserves kindness, especially those who are afraid to give it."

The druidess smiled at Thes. She looked up at the darkening sky. "I must rest and prepare for the morning rituals," she said solemnly, wishing this night would not end. She kissed the wizard softly on his cheek before stepping back. She breathed deep, feeling her emotional spirit satisfied and renewed.

"Until the morn," the wizard replied. Sia pointed out the visitor's hovel to Thes as she left towards her own home.

Thes stood for a moment and pondered the druidess predicament in relation to his own choices. He too might have felt similarly had more years gone by in service to Escailar. Although now he might be considered free from that burden, Thes felt ever more bound to serve the memories of the village and gain vengeance for the villagers. He wondered if it was guilt that had him seeking vengeance. Guilt for his own prior feelings of wanting to leave the village, yet not wanting to disappoint those he helped and cared for. The destruction of the village may have freed him from one burden to be replaced with another. He was surprised at how out of touch he was with his own emotions on the matter. Feelings he was sure were buried deep within him, in order to carry out his daily tasks. All of the changes in the past couple weeks only served to release a cacophony of complex emotions, many of which the wizard did not feel ready to face. It was then that Thes knew Sia was much stronger than he to face such realities and still choose the selfless path. Thes was unsure if he had the virtue to make such a choice had it not been made for him.

The wizard cleared his mind and walked to the visitor's hovel, smiling and nodding to the nearby guards around the small home. The wizard was soon quietly sneaking into the short building, finding an empty bed near a snoring dwarf.

(12) Sweat and Blood

His dream had been filled with strange images of shifting smoke and burning embers. The oppressive feeling of drowning was the dominate emotion as a deep, guttural voice uttered incomprehensible words. Then all was quiet. He awoke to the stern prodding of his half-brother.

The dark cavern walls had their characteristic dull color to the eyes of the awakening shadmar. Over the millennia of living in the deep underground, the shadmar had adjusted to seeing the faint infrared spectrum of reflective heat. The cold cavern walls reflected this heat in such a specific way it was easy for the dark elves to use their own warm emanations to see details in the walls around them.

Kinrithir was shorter than most elves, with dark, ebony skin as characteristic of the shadmar. He had tufts of short white-blond hair that stood defiantly upon his head. He had near-black eyes that glowed with a hint of red as he peered at the reflective heat of the chamber. His face was handsome, yet gentle, bearing the semblance of one who smiled often.

His half-brother, Kryther, had a similar shape and build as Kinrithir. The shadmar's blonde-white hair hung down to his shoulders and was kept neat and brushed. Kryther's face also belied the fact that he often wore a scowl, with hints of unfavorable lines around his eyes and mouth.

The dazed Kinrithir sat upright and peered around him. His half-brother, a bright glow of heat to the shadmar's eyes, was mixing some mushrooms with water to make a thick paste to serve as breakfast. They often ate this mushroom gruel with red-fan leaves, rolling the paste in the wide leaves as a convenient wrap to eat on their way to the mines.

The muscled Kinrithir stood up and drank deeply from a nearby clay bowl. The fresh water perked his senses and immediately removed the foreboding feeling that his dream left upon him. Kinrithir folded back both his and his half-brother's woven sleeping mats, making room for them to sit and eat together. The tiny alcove that they shared was of average size compared to the many others that were given to the shadmar miners. It had a small entry to store what few items they owned, then a small sleeping area with two raised platforms cut into the stone to serve as both bench and bed. Kryther offered a mushroom-wrap to Kinrithir and they sat down, slowly eating and enjoying the morsel in silence.

Kryther and Kinrithir had a trying relationship. Kryther was a few years older and more stern and pessimistic than Kinrithir. Their shared father, Thirinar, was a tyrant and womanizer, always serving his own ends. He showed little attention to either of his sons throughout their lives. He had a knack for using their desire for his affection to get them to serve his needs. In equal measure, the two sons cared little for their father, or the fact that he was now counted among the many dead in the old caverns of Dith Derithin.

Despite their shared heritage, there was little else that bound the two shadmar half-brothers to each other. There varying temperaments made arguments common and their domestic life difficult. Kryther was quick to anger and was often complaining about some injustice or another. Kinrithir preferred to see the brighter sides of things, always eager to find common ground and hope for a better future. The two shadmar had been working together for many years, doing their best to survive in the dark caverns since the destruction of Dith Derithin.

"What do you think the news will be?" Kinrithir asked Kryther. It had been announced that the shadmar miners would be summoned to a great assembly today. Kinrithir was eager to hear the news, hoping it meant that

146

their work was coming to an end. He was equally eager to walk freely among the surface as had been promised to them for so many years.

"Nothing good, I'm sure," replied Kryther disdainfully. "New veins of ore to mine," he offered.

"Surely not," Kinrithir disagreed. "They would not have called off work for the cycle if it was just another promising vein discovered."

Kryther only shrugged, not wishing to argue as he finished his breakfast. Kinrithir finished as well, and the two of them cleaned their culinary utensils in silence. The two shadmar half-brothers then strode out of their personal alcove, through the thick woven cloth that hung from the stone above and separated their home from the wider tunnel outside. There were many other miners slowly shuffling their way down the long tunnel to the far end where a faint phosphorescent glow shimmered in the distance.

"Off to the assembly?" said a fellow shadmar miner to the two half-brothers as they stepped in line in the tunnel.

Kryther simply grunted a reply to the inane question.

"Yes, Vlidvir," said Kinrithir with his usual friendly tone. "I am eager to hear the words of the counselor."

"As am I," said Vlidvir excitedly. The younger shadmar was smaller and thinner than most, but seemed to blossom with more enthusiasm than his small frame could contain. "Do you think it is time? Are we going to the surface?"

Before Kinrithir could respond, Kryther interrupted, "No. Don't be a fool," he said harshly. "They'll keep dangling that promise in front of our noses until we work ourselves to death."

Vlidvir's eyes went wide with astonishment. Kinrithir stepped over to the small, gullible shadmar, placing his arm around his friend. He whispered, "Do not listen to my half-brother, he is more bitter than a bitterroot." The two snickered to themselves at this comment. The optimistic shadmar continued, "I still believe in the Promise. If not today, then tomorrow, or the next day. When it comes, I'll be ready to see the bright lights upon the surface world."

Kinrithir's true feelings, however, belied his words to Vlidvir. He knew all too well there was truth to Kryther's statement. He and his half-brother remembered how the Promise came to his people. They both were directly involved in the civil strife between the noble houses that led to the destruction of Dith Derithin. They were the last living members of House Velmir, a noble house believed to be vanquished by the indomitable force of House Niedrie.

Kryther was still bitter and angry for the loss of his status, he despised being reduced to hiding among the common miners. On the other hand, Kinrithir was simply glad to have survived the ordeal and to have a chance to make a new life for himself. Although, Kinrithir still held hope for an opportunity to present itself that would allow he and his people true freedom from the rule of petty aristocrats and self-declared rulers.

"Do you think today is the day?" Vlidvir asked Kinrithir hopefully.

"Perhaps. We'll soon find out," Kinrithir said smiling. Kryther only cursed under his breath, already finding his half-brother's optimism reaching its peak annoyance for the day.

The three of them followed the crowd into the larger connecting cavern. Many miners were filling the large chamber looking upon the far wall where a high catwalk marked the entrance to the upper caverns and the chambers of Valraen above. The caverns beneath the ancient seat of the shadmar were dug out from the earth many millennia ago. The caverns were numerous, featuring many large spaces such as the meeting chamber the miners now gathered in. The original purpose of these chambers may have also

148

been for mining, as in the ancient days the shadmar were the primary source of metals for the other elven kingdoms. However, these days these caverns were used for both mining metals for the coming war and for feeding the populace with mushrooms, cavern flora, and the few livestock that dwelt in the deep underground.

Kinrithir looked upon the catwalk, expecting only to see the work counselor, Gharin, in his grey robes and stoic expression. However, there was a new figure next to the old shadmar. The new shadmar was abnormally tall with thin pale eyes and a flowing mane of jet-black hair rather than the characteristic white or blonde of most shadmar. The figure wore red robes, shimmering like flames caressing its fuel source. It was Delrith Niedrie, patriarch and leader of the displaced shadmar.

Kryther and Kinrithir looked at each other somewhat apprehensively. Vlidvir's eyes were wide with awe upon seeing the patriarch. He was trying to get closer to get a better glimpse of the leader, but then looked back at the half-brothers, beckoning them to follow.

Kinrithir simply smiled uneasily to the young shadmar and waved him to go ahead without them. Soon the young shadmar vanished in the crowd as many others pushed to the front to see Delrith. The half-brothers simply stayed near the back of the crowd, trying to keep some distance from the high catwalk.

"Do you think he can see us?" Kinrithir whispered to his half-brother, nervousness in his voice.

"No," replied Kryther, his own apprehension betraying the conviction of his response. "We probably look like the other common rabble."

The two half-brothers had not seen the shadmar patriarch since the fall of the city. They knew that Delrith believed them dead when the great city's ceiling came crashing down. House Velmir was one of the primary antagonists to Delrith's rise to power. They directly opposed the Promise and the growing power of House Niedrie. In order to combat Delrith's growing power and religious zeal, House Velmir and a few other minor houses managed to gather an opposing force by promising political reforms and democracy to the shadmar commonfolk. While the half-brothers' father, Thirinar, had no intention of actually giving power to the people, Kinrithir did believe the people deserved to govern themselves. Kryther, on the other hand, did not believe the commonfolk had the aptitude to do so. However, it was because of this direct opposition to House Niedrie, the two half-brothers pretended to be of the commonfolk themselves when the people marched towards the surface years ago. The ruse had so far worked perfectly since they had not the fame of their dispassionate father.

"I hope you are right, brother," Kinrithir whispered as the hall began to quiet.

Delrith raised his arms to silence the crowds, however, that only encouraged them to shout praises at the shadmar leader.

"Silence, my friends," the patriarch said warmly, his voice magically enhanced to fill the chamber and reach every ear. Silence then did come and everyone listened intently to the coming words. Hopes were high and many expected to soon charge out of the caverns to the surface world in a matter of minutes.

"You have all worked hard and bravely over these trying years," he began, his words seemingly warm and empathetic. "The surface is almost ours!" he shouted with enthusiasm that matched the crowd as he clenched his fist in front of him. Roars of cheers echoed in the mass of miners. After a few moments the shouts died down. Delrith was smiling wide and confidently.

"However, I bring some ill news to my brethren," he continued, feigning sadness. The crowd gasped and went

150

silent. "Those vile surface elves are trying to thwart our return!" he shouted again, with rehearsed anger. The crowd, however, seemed oblivious to the dramatizations of the patriarch. In a furious populist chorus, the miners shouted for the death of the light-skinned elves.

Kinrithir hated to see his kin so enraged against an ancient enemy. He believed that the elves above had far more reason for hatred than those below the ground. The practice of sending young warriors to strike at surface villagers over the past millennia only fueled that ancient anger. The wild fanaticism of the shadmar's hatred of the surface elves were born of misinformation and ignorance rather than true animosity. Even the pragmatic Kryther knew it did little good to strike at the surface elves, particularly when aid and alliance may benefit the shadmar more than war and strife in their people's vulnerable predicament.

"The time is near at hand, my friends," the patriarch continued. "The time for war is coming and we shall claim the ancient seat of the People for the future. For *our* future." He made a dramatic pause, seemingly taking in the shouts and outrage of the miners to heart. "Work hard, my friends. Gather the metal for our army. In the coming weeks, we will find those of you who are willing to fight and join in the war effort. Until then, focus your anger on the task at hand. Remember how those vile surface traitors left us to die in the underground caverns. Remember how we prospered despite their attempt to subdue us. Remember how we rose from death to glory and will reclaim the surface world!" The patriarch's words grew to a great crescendo surrounded by a wild chorus of shouts, mostly vulgar and discriminatory chants, as the miners were inspired through the united hatred.

Kinrithir and Kryther only looked apprehensively to each other as the many shouts echoed in the wide cavern. Delrith had his arms outstretched above him again, encouraging the intolerant taunts and spiteful enthusiasm. He then waved his farewell as he exited the chamber through the wide door off the catwalk.

Gharin, an old, plain-faced, shadmar took to the center of the catwalk and raised his hands to calm the miners. It took many moments for the enraged crowd to quiet, and Gharin had not the magical aid on his voice. However, his voice still boomed in the caverns when he spoke.

"My friends," he began, "you have heard the words of our leader. We must work hard in the coming weeks if our efforts are to succeed. Recruiters and administrators will be sent down to meet with each of you over the next week to find those who are capable of joining the infantry and to take a census of our populace. However, today belongs to you, my friends. The patriarch has declared today free from work. A feast will be prepared in the chamber later today. Give congratulations to yourselves and your kin, for you have earned this break. Dismissed."

More cheering erupted from the crowd as Gharin waved his good-bye as well. He entered the adjacent door on the catwalk, leading to his personal chambers. Kinrithir and Kryther feigned excitement when others congratulated them and shook their hands, as such actions reverberated throughout the cavern. However, the half-brothers were both worried. They believed that the administrators might expose their true heritage. They had managed to remain hidden by pretending to be Kinrir and Kryn, simple miners with a common, but unknown father. However, they knew well the precision of the administrators, those who delighted in documenting and cataloguing details about a person's background and lineage.

In the city of Dith Derithin, such information was paramount in determining who was of the worthy nobility, pampered with the best living spaces, food, and say in the governance of the city. The chaos following the destruction

152

of the city had diminished the meticulous recording of births, deaths, and lineages of each citizen. Now, one was either of House Niedrie and its allies or they were nobody important. There was anonymity in belonging to the latter. The half-brothers feared a return to an organized census would expose them.

They walked quietly back to their home alcove as the crowds began to disperse. When they reached their home, they each sat down on their respective bench, each worrying about the speech and the coming events.

"What should we do?" Kinrithir asked his half-brother.

Kryther shook his head, "I don't know."

"Perhaps we can still fool them," the optimistic shadmar offered. "We just need to rehearse a story together. Craft something believable, yet of no significance."

Kryther looked up at Kinrithir, still shaking his head with a doomed expression on his face. They both knew there was little hope in that. The administrators of the city often used magical means to help determine who was related to whom, with the detection of falsehoods and blood traces.

"No, we will be found. Dead as a slave," the pessimistic shadmar replied.

Kinrithir's face then lit up. "That's it!" he replied enthusiastically. "We just need to convince them that our parents were slaves."

Kryther gave a disgusted expression. It was demeaning enough for the proud shadmar to pretend to be a commoner. However, he knew there was some sense to his half-brother's logic. When the city fell, all the slaves were freed and given common status with the other workers in order to help unite the masses. Slaves were never tracked in the census in the old city. Kryther expected there would be many new lineages due to the former slaves.

"But how do we pass the falsehoods and blood tests?" Kryther asked, beginning to find this plan more palatable.

"We shall have to hope they do not perform one. And why would they? We are but mere slaves reaching for common status. We only experienced such tests as nobles, I bet they will reserve such magic for those claiming to be of House Niedrie," Kinrithir said confidently.

Kryther nodded in agreement. "Then Kinrir and Kryn will need to choose a surname for their new lineage," he said with as much humor as the moody shadmar could attain.

That evening the two half-brothers joined the entourage of miners in the main cavern. There were many tables set up filled with the many favored dishes that the shadmar have come to know in the deep underground caverns. There was also plenty of dancing and music, as a few musicians had kept their prized instruments from the lost city. The festivities went late into the night, until Gharin shouted down from the catwalk, dispersing the crowds with empty threats of extra work the next day. Kinrithir was sore from dancing and fell quickly to sleep upon his mat. Kryther, however, who spent most of the night brooding at a table, was still anxious about the coming census. He had trouble finding sleep for much of the night as thoughts of torture dominated his mind.

The next day, the half-brothers performed their usual morning rituals, this time eating their wrapped mushrooms on the way to the mines. Below the catwalk in the main cavern was a series of tunnels where the shadmar had been mining for the past few years. Each miner was given a pickaxe at the entrance and assigned to work in one of the offshoot tunnels. Kinrithir and Kryther were rarely assigned to the same tunnel, but today was one of those rare occasions. They set to work, throwing their body and muscles into decisive strikes at the stone walls. The labor was certainly

154

hard work, however, after the many years, the miners' bodies were honed to their task. The two tended to work well together, despite the constant bickering that usually accompanied their joined efforts.

Thankfully for the shadmar, there were still many thick veins of iron and coal in the caverns. The many shipments of ore were sent to another, well-ventilated cavern up one of the long tunnels where it was smelted and fashioned into tools, weapons, and armor. Giant cave-lizards were used to haul the ore and goods throughout the underground complex beneath Valraen. Such creatures also made an important food source due to their quick growth and large clutches of eggs.

After a hard day's work, the half-brothers were released from their duties. They ate what they could of the evening's mushroom stew, served in the large cavern, before retiring to their home alcove. However, upon reaching the thick cloth separating their rooms from the adjoining tunnel, they heard unfamiliar voices within. The two half-brothers stopped, both anxious and uncomfortable as they tried to listen.

"I think I hear someone approaching," a shrewd, unfamiliar voice said.

The half-brothers looked at each other, trying to gather their resolve, before stepping through the cloth.

"Greetings," said Kryther in an uncharacteristic sing-song voice. Kinrithir almost laughed, but managed a friendly smile to the two robed shadmar standing in their home.

"There you are," the shrewd shadmar said to Kryther, "we have been waiting." The other administrator was short and quiet, holding a stack of parchment in his hands. He simply nodded as the two miners entered their home, offering a seat to the visitors on a bench as they sat upon the other, facing them.

The shrewd one spoke again, "As you know, we are conducting the census and conscription. I hear your names are Kinrir and Kryn. Is that correct?"

The two half-brothers nodded.

"Excellent," he continued, without pause, "Could you please tell me about your family and how you came to work in the mines here?"

Kryther began a fictitious tale about an unknown slave father who worked the mushroom fields of Dalrin's Rise, a modest-sized field on an upper portion of the caverns of Dith Derithin that supplied food to the many taverns and public houses of the city. The half-brothers pretended to not know his name, but their mothers had known him before his demise when he was cut down for insulting a passing soldier. Kryther then explained how they in turn came to work the fields as slaves until the city's caverns collapsed and they followed the survivors to the Valraen caverns.

The two half-brothers made sure to use eye-contact sparingly, believing that former slaves would be reluctant to look their "betters" in the eyes. However, the two inspecting shadmar seemed rather uninterested in the story. The quiet one jotted a few notes down at the end of the tale.

Then the shrewd one asked, "And have you chosen a new surname for you and your brother?"

"Half-brother", Kinrithir corrected apologetically.

Kryther gave him a side-long glance. He then nodded, "Yes we have. Veridia. To honor the green places we expect to see on the surface." The two had decided they should appear as fervent believers of the Promise. Although their chosen name was the term often given to the caverns of mosses and red-leafed flora found in the lightless caverns, the ancient word had once been applied to the forest above.

The quiet shadmar administrator recorded the name on some parchment.

156

"And is there any military duty you do not feel you are fit to perform?" the administrator asked pointedly at the two healthy shadmar.

"We are both fit to serve in any capacity," Kryther said, as if rehearsed. Kinrithir nodded in agreement.

"Excellent," said the shrewd administrator as they both stood up to leave. "Thank you for your time, Kinrir and Kryn Veridia." The clerical shadmar exited their chamber and could be heard entering a neighboring alcove with greetings to its occupants. The two half-brothers dared not celebrate the moment and both laid silently on their benches, the anxiety of the encounter slowly diminishing. Kinrithir could not hide his smile.

The next few days were uneventful. The half-brothers worked the mines by day, rested and bickered by night. Everything seemed to be back to the way it was before the census. There was some excitement by the other miners, as former slaves were given surnames of their own. Vlidvir, particularly, was celebrating over his new surname. However, since he was unable to come up with a name on his own, the administrators assigned one to him: *Brantrusin*, meaning stone-breaker. Kryther nearly laughed upon hearing it, expecting there would be many who shared such a name. Nothing, however, could diminish Vlidvir's excitement.

After one long day of mining, the two half-brothers were bickering about the day's work as they approached their home alcove. There was a soldier standing at the entrance to an alcove just past their own. He was talking to the occupants about their military assignments.

Kryther's heart dropped has he caught sight of the soldier's face. It was Kalvin, a noble of House Ridwalin. It was one of the first minor houses to fall in line with House Niedrie's plans, likely seeking protection from the larger house. The brutish nobleman was a constant rival for Kryther when they studied at the academy together. They had an immediate dislike for each other that often resulted in bitter fights in the hallways of the academy.

The half-brothers quickly slipped into their home before the soldier saw them. They were both quite anxious, on the verge of panic, knowing that Kalvin would recognize them instantly.

"What is he doing here?" Kryther asked Kinrithir angrily, as if his half-brother was to blame.

"I don't know," Kinrithir replied weakly, deflecting the unnecessary aggression.

"They probably couldn't find any other use for that damned fool," growled Kryther as he began pacing in the entry chamber. Kinrithir sat on his bench, fervently trying to think of a plan to repel the brutish soldier.

However, they were out of time, as Kalvin was soon standing behind their cloth calling their false names, "Kinrir and Kryn Veridia?" His constrained voice belied his smug belittlement for the names of mere slaves. The half-brothers looked at each other in panic, their minds whirling, but their bodies still.

Without an invitation, the stout head of the soldier popped through the cloth, "Hello there, future soldiers…" he started, but his voice trailed off and his jaw dropped in disbelief. His eyes transfixed on Kryther for a long moment as they both stared at each other.

Kryther then sprang into action and grabbed the soldier's neck, wrapping his burly arm around and squeezing tight. Kalvin, too surprised to react, struggled vainly as Kryther wretched him into the alcove, slamming his head into the cavern wall. Kinrithir was too astonished at his half-brother's actions to do much more than scramble out of the way, backed into the recess of his bench. Kryther pulled the soldier's disoriented body into the wall at the back of the

158

alcove, nearly falling over their feet in the cramped space. He slammed the soldiers head into the wall, again and again. Blood and brains splattered on the wall and on the face of the enraged shadmar. Kryther's eyes were wild with fury, venting his emotional tensions of the past few years all into this one sadistic act.

After a few moments, Kinrithir calmly placed his hand on his half-brother's arm. The wild shadmar looked fiercely upon Kinrithir for a moment, but then slowly gave way to reason, releasing the bloodied corpse upon the ground. The angry shadmar could not hear his feral grunts that roared in the small chamber, but they had attracted the attention of neighbors who now peered into the alcove seeing the bloody mess and the traitorous act. Vlidvir's eyes were wider than either half-brother had ever seen them. The scrawny shadmar soon fled down the cavern screaming for help.

Soon more soldiers arrived to arrest the half-brothers. They had simply cleaned themselves of the blood and sat calmly on their benches, awaiting their demise in silence. Their neighbors were arguing and shouting at the entrance as the soldiers arrived. The two traitors were beaten to the ground and their hands bound behind their backs. Blindfolded and gagged, they were then taken to an unknown cavern, not too far from the mining caves. One of the soldiers vainly tried to get information about the murder from the two captives, however, they remained silent and resolute, even when separated. They were then tortured for a few hours, but this too proved only to release screams of pain rather than explanations or confessions. The two half-brothers were then branded as slaves, a fiery mark upon their back, then sent to the slave pens in the bottom-most cavern.

The lowest caverns were the compost caves. The many buckets of urine and feces, both of the shadmar and their lizard livestock was dumped there. It was added to the bits of stale food and agricultural waste in large pits. The slaves of the pits worked to stir the vast piles with long sticks, helping it compost into a rich manure to grow more mushrooms and cavern flora. It was these foul dark caverns the half-brothers would now spend the rest of their years along with the other prisoners and slaves of the shadmar rulers.

(13) Error of the Experienced

The beautiful, though slightly chilly, morning came upon the valley of Harpien. Thes and his friends slept quite well listening to the quiet stirrings of night creatures and the babbling of the nearby waterfall and stream. Had they not been ordered to stay in the valley, Artemis and Morstar agreed it would be a peaceful place to spend one's final days. However, given the current situation, the proclamation of their forced stay combined with the impending war in the region, these outsiders had far more pressing matters to address.

After each of them had awoken, they huddled in the hovel to discuss their plans to both convince the elders of the impending danger and to prepare proper defenses should that danger arrive. The discussion began with ways of providing evidence of their claims to the elders, and whether an attack on Harpien was truly imminent.

"Can we be sure they will even find the valley?" Svendian asked, curious if the shadmar would likely find the hidden place.

"I believe so," Thes replied, "They seem to have cunning sorcerers among them. I have little doubt their magic will expose the village's location eventually."

"Can't you use your own magic to hide it?" Bryman asked, already eager to get out of the small chamber and stretch his tall frame.

The wizard shook his head, "I cannot hope to throw a cloak over such a large location. It is simply a matter of time before they discover it. If we assume they had been searching for all nearby settlements, Harpien is likely the last one they would have discovered. However, given the timing of the other attacks, it is quite likely they have already dispatched raiders to this location."

"Then we must assume an attack is forthcoming," Svendian replied.

"Perhaps we can begin some defensive fortifications on the south end of the village?" Morstar asked. "Certainly, the elves can't complain about that?"

"I would not think it wise to blatantly disregard the elders' decision on this matter," Svendian answered the dwarf. "Your presence alone makes them nervous, best not perform actions they may deem against their decree. They would not want you wandering off."

"Bah!" exclaimed the dwarf. "We only wish to help."

"Perhaps the art of subterfuge can aid us," Artemis interjected.

"How so?" Thes asked, "We do not wish to strain our relationship with these people."

"Indeed," the ranger replied, "therefore you and Svendian, and the other elves, who are free to move about, can help prepare defenses at the valley's entrance. Bryman, Morstar, and I can remain in clear view here in the village. Perhaps there are preparations we can perform here."

Svendian added, "The elders do worry about a raid, even if they do not think it is an army behind the aggression. I think offering free labor, be it elf, man, or dwarf, will appeal to them regardless."

Thes nodded. "Sia, the druidess, may be willing to help as well."

"If you think we can trust her to help," Bryman interrupted. The war-priest was quite wary of the magic she possessed after the watery sphere he experienced.

The elf turned to the man, "I do. She is as worried about this threat as we are." The large man stared at the elf for a moment, trying to glean why Thes responded in defense of the druidess. Blue eyes faced blue eyes in firm observation. Then Bryman smiled at the elf, his round cheeks showing a slight blush. The war-priest had watched

162

the elf sneak into the hovel last night wearing a wide smile. Now he knew why.

Before Thes could respond to the war-priest's allusions, Svendian interrupted the silent exchange, "I will go speak to the elders immediately to see if they will allow us to improve their defenses. Failing that, I can always speak with the tribe's warriors. Perhaps some will come to reason and assist us."

"Aye, sounds like a plan," Morstar agreed. "We'll be here, waiting like a boulder," the dwarf mumbled sardonically.

The group then exited the hovel. Svendian rushed off to speak with the elders, while the others stayed near the small building. Bryman stretched his tall body, reaching for the tops of the trees. The morning sun was still hidden just below the edge of the valley's walls. There were a couple guards posted not far from their hovel, but they seemed rather relaxed in their duties. A few wood elf villagers soon came to offer the outsiders more fresh water and baskets of dried meat, fruits, and nuts. The group graciously accepted, sitting around the entrance of the hovel as they ate.

Thes only grabbed a handful of the fruits and nuts as he also headed into the village. He wanted to search for Sia and get her assistance in convincing the elders. He walked through the trees past many scattered hovels tucked into the woods, as he munched on his breakfast. Many of the thunmar eyed him curiously, as he quietly wandered through the village.

The village was larger than the wizard imagined and he took a long winding walk through the trees. Most of the hovels were well hidden among the trees and underbrush, the occasional garden betraying the existence of subsistence living. However, he also noticed many of these small buildings were disheveled and likely abandoned. He searched each face he came across, trying to find the

163

sparkling brown eyes and the gentle expression of the druidess.

Thes suddenly became aware of how eager he was to see Sia again and continue their talk from the previous night. He had such a strong desire to be in her presence again. Thes was growing worried that whatever magic she cast upon him when they first met had grown stronger.

She has charmed me, he reasoned. *She did not trust me at first, so she charmed me.*

He decided he would ask her to remove the magical charm when it was appropriate. While he did not care to use such enchantment magic himself, he could not deny that whatever magic was upon him was potent and effective.

She will have me as a willing slave within a week, he thought. He laughed to himself. Mostly because he felt, in his enchanted state, such a prospect would not be so undesirable; he felt willing to do almost anything for Sia.

Thes looked throughout the village before returning to the pond and the elders' meeting hovel. It was there that he finally found her. Sia was exiting the hut with a wide, confident smile on her face. She saw the wizard coming toward her and she rushed to him with an enthusiastic spring in her step. Svendian was following behind her.

"I have wonderful news, friend," the druidess said to him.

"Pray tell," Thes requested, his eyes entranced by her presence. Her good spirits filled the wizard with a giddy sensation as his heart reveled in her joy. He tried to shake off the feeling, trying to stay resolute against the lingering charm.

"The elders have agreed to accept your help. We shall help you and your friends prepare defenses for the village," she said beaming.

Svendian nodded. "Indeed. Sia was able to convince them before I even arrived. It seems they at least understand

164

there is no harm fortifying ourselves should the worst arrive. As I expected, they wish to take advantage of the available labor. The others are free to move about as well. Escorted, of course."

"This is excellent news," the wizard replied, both excited and uneasy about the preparations for battle.

Svendian continued, "I will be sending out my archers to patrol the region. I hope that will give us some advanced warning of an attack. I plan to organize two defense plans, a first line at the valley's entrance, and a fallback here in the village. I presume the two of you will plan the best use of your magic."

"Yes, indeed," the wizard replied, smiling at Sia.

Svendian went off to organize the defensive efforts with the others while Thes and Sia stayed to begin discussions about how their magic could best be applied defensively. The two sat down near the edge of the pond. The morning light now shimmering in the water as the sun crested over the valley's edge.

They quietly sat down, neither speaking a word, as if the comfortable silence from the night before still lingered between them. They smiled at each other for a long moment until entrancement gave way to awkwardness.

They both then began to speak at the same time, empty false starts that faded into over-enthusiastic apologies. Then back to smiles and awkwardness.

Sia finally managed to break the deluge of inelegance, "Thanks again for your words last night. You are a kind soul."

Thes's heart leaped at the compliment. He now forgot all about protecting himself from the lingering charm. "I meant every word," he replied sincerely. "You are an amazing asset to this village. Even now your effort with the elders' amazes me."

Sia blushed slightly as she turned to look out over the pond. The yellow light was sparkling in the smooth water and bubbles infrequently bobbed to the surface. Thes still looked at her, appreciating her fine features as she was bathed in the morning shine. She then turned back to face him, catching his admiring expression.

Thes then swallowed uncomfortably, his eyes wandering for a moment. He then cleared his throat. "I guess we should talk about tactics before the day gets away from us," he offered.

Sia smiled and nodded, eager to clear the awkwardness between them.

"I wish to stay in the village during an assault," she began, firmly. "I will hold the second line. If their forces are as great as you say, then I expect they will overwhelm the entrance."

Thes agreed, "That is likely. I intend to provide what assistance I can at the entrance and help them retreat when the time comes to fall back to the village."

The two continued their discussion of battle tactics, talking long about what magic might be useful in a conflict. Villagers who required a ritual or minor healing from the druidess often interrupted the two as they sat near the village pond. However, Sia took the interruptions in stride. Thes noticed how kind and generous she was to those that came to her. She listened intently and kindly to each request, no matter how foolish. She offered many hugs and encouraging words to lift their spirits. Her kindness and optimism was boundless and Thes could not help but feel inspired by her selfless role, even though it stirred up unresolved emotions in the wizard.

That initial awkwardness had long passed and their discussion continued for many hours. Although they did manage to come up with a basic defense plan for their magic, they were often sidetracked with stories of unrelated

166

experiences, learning much more about each other in the process. The wizard felt a great kinship to the druidess and a growing desire to spend more time with her. Although, internally, he was worried that the entrenched enchantment was responsible for his growing devotion to a woman he had just met. However, since there had not yet been a moment when this magical compulsion was dangerous to himself or his friends, he decided to ignore the feeling and bury his worry with other emotions he dared not explore.

Over the next few days, the outsiders did their best to fortify the defenses of the village and its sheltered valley. Morstar and Svendian, both experienced in warfare, took leadership roles in the effort, organizing the patrols and the labor of the other elves and men. They first constructed archer posts and a long catwalk in the high trees along the southern entrance, with Thes and Sia using their magic to help in the construction. The local elves were reluctant to modify the beauty of the area, but they did their best to blend the high catwalks with the trees. They then gathered many stones near the stream's edge to build low walls to impede the forest path, the only safe passage through the thorny brambles at the southern entrance. Next, they built more catwalks near the village as a second line of defense for Sia and the remaining archers of the village.

Bryman and his great strength was greatly appreciated by the elves. They marveled at his ability to carry small boulders and pull supporting ropes impossibly tight. He and Morstar had a lot of fun working together, both appreciating the honest work under the forest canopy. Artemis was his usual quiet self, but joined in the laughter when he could. He did not have the strength of the other two, but his knowledge of knots proved useful for the catwalk's supporting structures. He also provided strategic advice for how the archers should be positioned above the wall.

Svendian spent much of his time working out the patrol rotation for his archers and organizing the defense plan with the warriors of the village. He even took the time to help instruct the other villagers in the ways of battle should they be forced to defend themselves. Many of the villagers had some experience, but were eager to learn additional techniques and the discipline of a soldier from the experienced captain.

The elders were especially gracious and appreciative of the effort the outsiders provided to help the village prepare itself. While they still did not believe a conquering army posed a threat to them, the elders were ever more confident that the village would be quite effective at defending itself from raiders. Each morning and night, they had food and drink brought to the outsiders in thanks.

Thes and Sia were quite busy during those days, providing magical aid for the constructions, and fulfilling the villagers' needs. They had not had a chance to speak privately again since that first day. However, some of the tribe's warriors and the druidess joined the outsiders each night for their evening meal, laughing and sharing stories with the group over a roaring fire. Svendian seemed particularly joyful that everyone was getting along well. Additionally, Thes's friends came to appreciate the druidess for her kindness and outspoken candor as much as the wizard did. Thes, however, had not told anyone about the enchantment she placed on him and had yet to find a private moment to discuss the matter with Sia.

It was late on the third day when Thes and Sia finally found some additional time for a private discussion. The sun had just sunk below the wall of the valley as the two sat relaxed against adjacent tree trunks near the village pond. They were trying to find ways to confuse the shadmar raiders. They had previously discussed ways of using their environment to their advantage, but were curious how they could use magical trickery to perhaps have the raiders attack each other. Thes suddenly had an idea.

"Your enchantments!" he exclaimed, "You could use your enchantments to trick them to fight their own. Would they obey such orders if enchanted so?"

"I do not follow. Of what enchantments do you speak?" the druidess asked perplexed.

"Your magical charms," he continued, excited by the idea, but hesitant to broach the subject. "Like the one you put on me when we first met. I know you have not acknowledged it, but I am more than aware of its growing strength," the wizard said insistently.

"I'm afraid I do not understand you," Sia replied, somewhat insulted.

"I am not angry at you. I understand your suspicion of outsiders. However, certainly now you have no use for such a charm upon me. We are friends and allies."

Sia had no response as she stared at him in confusion. Thes looked at her, growing increasingly agitated, waiting for her to confess as an uncomfortable silence grew between them. He did not like the idea of his mind being bound by her magic anymore.

"Do not feign ignorance," he continued, anger slipping into his voice by her refusal to admit her actions. "I am aware of the magic upon me. Since the moment I met you, there has been a lingering charm upon me. With each day, my mind increasingly wavers, thinking of you. I yearn for the time when I am in your presence. Certainly, that is the work of magic upon my will."

Sia simply looked at Thes with an expressionless face, her eyes somewhat wide. She was joyful of Thes's admission of his affection for her, but saddened by how this seem to bother him. There was a hint of tears at the edges of her eyes.

"I would ask that you remove this vex from my mind," Thes continued pleadingly, the anger absent from his voice, "Free me so that my mind is clear for our strategies." He sighed. "I do not blame you for trying to allure my servitude."

Sia continued to stare expressionless at Thes, her own mind was racing with confusion and mixed feelings. Her eyes watered, but her expression remained stoic.

Thes stood up, still staring at the druidess, waiting for a response. His anger was returning. He then spoke abruptly and clearly, "When your eyes looked into mine upon our first meeting, did you not put an enchantment upon me?" His tone was thick with accusation. However, as he looked at her confused and hurt expression, doubt grew heavy in his mind.

Abruptly the sound of pounding feet came rushing towards the two elves. It was one of the village warriors. He looked strained and out of breath.

"They're coming!" he shouted to them. "The shadmar are coming!" He then rushed into the elders' meeting hall to relay the news.

Sia stood up and looked into Thes, a mixture of hurt and remorse in her expression. The fear of the coming battle vanquishing any sadness.

Thes looked at her dumbfounded, finally coming to a realization. "I'm sorry," he muttered to her. "I do not know my own heart." He felt a strange mixture of confusion, embarrassment, anger, and trepidation at that moment. The many emotions he had buried since the burning of Escailar, and possibly from earlier in his life, threatened to bubble over. Again, he felt so confused and lost amid his own feelings. In the ways of the world, he was knowledgeable and confident, but in the ways of his own heart and feelings, he was lost and muddled. Now he stood blind to his own affections.

170

Sia reached out to the wizard, placing her soft hands upon his cheek and looked deeply into his eyes. "I may feel as you feel, Thes." Her eyes beaming with her characteristic empathy. "But I assure you no magic sways my heart or yours."

Thes tried to form words, but he could not speak over his strained heart and the choking feeling in his throat. He just looked at her, helpless.

"I hope we live this day, lest these words be our last," she said solemnly. Sia then rushed into the village to organize the defenses, leaving the wizard frozen.

Thes felt a welling of tears within him, a primed wellspring of aching sentiment, buried deep in his soul. For a few moments, his mind battled with his heart. His mind fought to free itself from the clutching agony pausing him in purposeless self-pity. He tried to urge himself to rush off to help his friends and defend the southern perimeter. He took a few deep breaths and his mind finally broke free. The cyclone of emotional turmoil cascading down into its deep pit, for the moment. The wizard then reached out to the air spirits with his mind, floating aloft through the trees towards the valley's entrance in a hurried flurry.

*   *   *   *   *   *   *

Meanwhile, Morstar, Bryman, and Svendian held the newly built southern wall, as Artemis and a few of the archers held the catwalks above. One of the patrols had returned with news of a marching force coming from the northeast. There were still two patrols out in the wild woods beyond the valley, but most of Svendian's archers were on the high catwalks, bows at the ready. Morstar was growing nervous, as it was only the three of them standing at ground level. Many of the village warriors were to come and join them as the news of the attack reached the village.

Thes soon landed on the catwalk next to Artemis, many of the warriors from the village not far behind him.

"I am here, friend," the wizard whispered to the human's ear, trying not to startle the man. The ranger was peering deeply into the forest beyond the wall, but the growing darkness made the difficult task ever more challenging.

"It is good to have you," Artemis replied, smiling. "Praise Zallus our arrows strike true," the ranger whispered. Whether the Nomen dragon-deity heard the man's plea remained to be seen.

The situation was tense as the village warriors took their positions along the wall and brambles on the ground. Village archers took their cover on the camouflaged catwalk. Bryman was quite eager to scream a battlecry and rush out at the first sign of activity, but he tried to calm himself, as he promised Morstar he would stick to the dwarf's plan. He smiled down at his trusty axe, knowing that his talon of steel would soon cut down his foes, each felling blow adding a morsel of honor to the tarnished Hethroth clan.

Soon there was a flurry of activity as many elven archers came into the clearing, their hands above their heads to indicate their allegiance. It was Svendian's patrols. They had returned and soon clamored over the low wall. They all took positions on the catwalks with their bows readied, but not drawn taunt. Everyone was in position and the forest was tense and quiet.

It was over twenty minutes before any sign of trouble could be heard. A loud explosion then echoed back towards the village. Bright lights of flames roared to life on the northern end of the valley. The archers and warriors began to panic, fearing for their friends and family. Svendian and Morstar shouted for them to be steady, both knowing the wave of raiders would soon follow.

172

Thes, however, could not wait. He never considered that the shadmar sorcerers would strike from above, and immediately felt guilty for not preparing for an aerial assault in their plans. He was angry with himself for letting his feelings get in the way over the past few days. He then thought of Sia. His heart sank in momentary terror. He leapt off the archer's catwalk, taking to the air towards the village. Artemis softly called out to him, but the wizard was too focused to hear the ranger.

As Artemis watched Thes disappear into the tree's canopy, he heard a rustling in the underbrush down towards the forest path. The ranger turned back to see scores of shadmar warriors cutting their way through the underbrush onto the cleared trail. Svendian pulled his hand down in command and a volley of arrows from the catwalk pierced many of the leading shadmar warriors. The initial strike only enraged the dark warriors behind them as they broke their slow march and rushed out in a wild charge. The archers above could only strike so many of them as the furious wave got ever closer to the low wall.

It was then that a crimson shield of translucent energy appeared in front of the charging warriors. The archers' arrows ricocheted and deflected uselessly off the magical barrier. Artemis called out for the archers to halt and save their arrows. For a moment, the village warriors, hiding below the wall, watched the wave of angry warriors charging towards them. They braced themselves and steadied their minds for the coming assault. The band of shadmar warriors then neared the low wall. Morstar nodded to Bryman and the large man leapt out from his tree cover screaming a Noradrie battlecry.

The sight of the large burly man, with his wild eyes and furious temperament, slowed the shadmars' pace. When Bryman landed at the small entrance through the low-wall with his round shield in front and his axe brandished, a few of the shadmar even tried to turn around and flee. His axe flashed out in a furious strike at their brave leader. It shattered the magical barrier before the elf, not even slowing the momentum of the blow. The shattered energy rippled through the translucent barrier, shattering it throughout as if it was red glass. The blood-stained axe then cleaved the leading shadmar's head clear off of his torso in a wild sweep.

It was then that the Morstar gave the command. The dwarf, Svendian, and the other elven warriors then leapt up, shields at the ready. The sight of the defensive force broke the momentous charge of the shadmar, and many tried to scramble back over their companions and avoid the promised death before them. The waiting line of warriors quickly felled those that did charge through; Bryman at the head with his blood-stained axe at the ready.

*   *   *   *   *   *   *

Meanwhile, back at the village, Sia was climbing to her feet. She had fallen out of the catwalk with many of the other archers. One of the supporting trees had fallen over and was wreathed in flames. Thankfully, she was mostly unharmed by the fall. She assumed that the sorcerers must have conjured the balls of inferno from the eastern cliff-side. There was panic all around her as villagers fled to the western end of the valley, across the pond, away from the burning trees and ruin. Many of the warriors tried their best to help carry the injured and weak.

Sia was desperate to put the fires out before the whole valley was consumed by the flames. The druidess concentrated on the river and pond calling the water spirits forth to aid her. Soon many globes of water bobbed through the air, sealed by a thin layer of ice. The floating orbs then stopped above an open flame. The icy bubbles burst, dropping the water and quenching some of the flames. Sia

174

worked tirelessly, sending many of these icy bubbles to the flames around her. However, she found the flames resisted extinguishment due to their magical nature.

Thes then appeared in the trees, not far from the druidess. He landed gracefully in the clearing near the pond. Upon seeing her ash-caked, sweat-covered face, he ran to her. The momentary terror leaving him, replaced by joy and relief. The fires were growing around them, consuming the village and the trees.

"You should be helping the warriors!" the druidess screamed at him over the rising roar of the growing flames and the screams of the last fleeing villagers.

"The village needs my help, as do you," Thes called to her. "Summon your water and we shall make it rain," he directed.

The druidess did as he asked and summoned a thin curtain of water to rise from the pond nearby. It stood firm and straight like a translucent mirror. Thes concentrated hard, focusing his mind on the air above the valley, directing it into a spinning motion. Soon the curtain of water was pulled ever so slightly. Tiny droplets on the curtains surface gave way to the pull and zipped into the swirling air like many tiny raindrops falling upwards. The vortex of water and air began swirling faster above the treetops. More and more tiny droplets poured into the vortex. A large foggy cloud soon took shape and began darkening as water continued to stream into it from the vertical sheet.

Both Thes and Sia had to concentrate hard in order to keep the cloud growing. Their magical talents working in tandem; air and water mixing in a fierce tempest. Thunder and lightning roared above as the storm kept feeding from the pond. The two mystics were fully subsumed in their magic, carefully monitoring the flow of water and air, using their wills to shape and grow the mounting anvil-shaped cloud.

*　　*　　*　　*　　*　　*　　*

Back at the battlefield, Morstar was barking orders to the elven warriors, fully absorbed in holding the defensive wall. The shadmar force was large and kept pushing into the wall of defending warriors. Bryman was uncharacteristically keeping to his place in the wall, swinging his axe wildly. The fury of the Noradrie warrior was enough to keep the shadmar at bay near the entrance; however, they simply pushed their marching force sideways, forking to the sides of the warrior's rage. The shadmar were slowly cutting their way through the thick tangles of the thorny thicket that flanked the low wall and forest path. Svendian became aware of this and knew they would only have so much time before those that breached the thicket would flank them.

High on the catwalk, Artemis urged his archers to target the side squadrons, hoping to slow the tide. The sun was set and the valley was cloaking in darkness. A storm was gathering on the north end of the valley, blocking the final glow of dusk and the coming stars. The ranger was finding it harder to see the action below him and hoped the keen eyes of his elven allies were unaffected.

The ranger was now making fewer shots as each arrow became more precious and each shot became less assured to find its mark. He looked about at the other archers who were still firing away into those shadmar trying to flank the low wall through the thorny thicket. Unfortunately, the thick brambles slowed the arrows as easily as it slowed the shadmar warriors.

Morstar, who could still see just fine in the darkness, was beginning to grow worried. The shadmar forces were not slowing, despite the many dark-skinned corpses that lay just beyond the wall. Those who still marched at them

176

simply strode up the mound of bodies, slowly eliminating the advantage of the low-wall. Svendian seemed to be thinking along similar lines as he and the dwarf made eye contact, nodding to each other.

However, before Svendian could make the call to fall back, another explosion of fire burst behind them. The power of the blast rumbled the earth and a few members of their defensive line lost their footing. It was then that the shadmar surged forward, breaking the defender's wall. An all-out melee broke out as the thunmar and shadmar intermixed and faced off in a wild battle.

The powerful, sorcerous fireball destroyed the middle-section of the archer's catwalk. Thankfully, Artemis was far enough to the side of the inferno. He was blown back into the tangled branches of one of the supporting trees. Many of the thunmar archers, however, were not so lucky; their scorched and broken bodies falling into a heap below. The ranger held tightly to the branches as he could hear the running feet of fleeing warriors and the shadmar chasing after them. The commotion of the battle beneath him soon drowned out all sounds as Artemis tried to climb down the tree, though his bruised and battered body gave much protest to the effort.

As he reached the ground, the ranger had difficulty telling thunmar from shadmar in the dim light. Thankfully, frequent flashes of lightning from the nearby storm illuminated the battle enough for him to get out of the way and head towards the second line in the village. He stuck near the thick brambles trying to sneak his way out of the melee, occasionally scraping his clothes and his skin on the sharp thorns.

Morstar was amid the raging battle swinging his warhammer in careful blows, breaking many bones in the chaos. Bryman was out of sight and Svendian was just to the warrior's back. The two of them were trying to keep the throng of shadmar warriors at bay as they poured around them. Svendian had been calling for the village warriors to retreat to the second line, but there was no way to know who could hear those orders in such a cacophony of shouting voices.

"We need to pull back!" Morstar shouted from the corner of his mouth to the aged captain.

"Yes, follow my lead," bade Svendian as he began to step around Morstar slowly, keeping his back to the dwarf.

Morstar discerned the elf's intentions and did likewise; the two of them rotating together like cogs on the same revolving gear. They began to pick up speed and rotate faster, swinging warhammer and sword, bashing and slicing, in a deadly two-step dervish dance. They slowly moved northward, cutting through the many shadmar around them, always keeping their vulnerable backs to each other for protection.

After many paces, Morstar spied Artemis hiding by a tree, his sword drawn, but seemingly waiting for the right time to reveal himself. The dwarf called out to him, motioning with a nod of his head.

Thankfully the dwarf's shape was quite obvious to the ranger, as Artemis could barely make out the gesture. He could see the success of their maneuver and knew it was his only hope to get to the second line. The ranger waited for the right opportunity then scrambled his way between the two swirling warriors adding a third sword to the deadly gear. Svendian adjusted his pace as he saw the ranger join them and soon the three of them were cutting their way through the last group of shadmar that still dared to face the three of them.

As they reached the north end, the battle thinned and they could abandon their constant spinning. Both Morstar and Svendian needed a second to clear their head from the pertinent dizziness. The shadmar seemed to be regrouping

178

on the forest path behind them as the rest of the village warriors fled to the second line in the village.

"Where is Bryman?" Artemis asked as they began to rush northward.

"Lost 'em in the chaos," Morstar said solemnly, as he tried to keep pace with his taller companions.

"If the shadmar were able to stem his fury, then he will at least have died a noble death," the ranger said respectfully.

"Aye, Rolk bless his axe," Morstar murmured reverently.

(14) The Dark Sorcerer

In the burning village of Harpien, the mighty anvil-shaped cloud above the scorched hovels was beginning to break shape as Thes and Sia prepared to release the waters on the raging fires. Thes nodded to the druidess and she dropped her sheet of water over the pond and concentrated on the water within the storm cloud. Soon the column-like cloud partially collapsed into a wide swirling vortex. The two magic-users did their best to control the powerful energy of the cloud. Sia then let a shower of rain release from the vortex onto the burning village. The flames sizzled and smoked as their temperatures dropped and the energetic wisps were no more.

Now the area was empty. The villagers had already fled leaving a smoking ruin behind. Many of the trees were scorched to death, leaving their high majestic canopies open and barren. Thes and Sia could now make out a group of shadmar high on the eastern cliffs. The vile sorcerers were easily discernible in the growing dark by the balls of flames in their hands, occasionally releasing jets of fire beneath them on the trees. They were still trying to ignite what trees they could from their high perch.

Rage grew in Thes as he saw the sorcerers responsible for burning the village. He leapt into the air as his eyes flickered with latent electricity. He soared through the seared and smoking canopy, his hands out to the sides, palms upward as he slowed down and gathered the remaining storm cloud around him like a cloak. He heard the faintest call out to him from below as Sia desperately shouted his name. However, the wizard was subsumed in his path for vengeance.

The shadmar high on the cliff suddenly became aware that the storm cloud was swirling into a spherical shape. Its tendrils twisted around something unseen in its depths. It was now sweeping upwards and coming straight towards them on the eastern cliffs. The sorcerers dissipated their tendrils of flame and scrambled away from the approaching maelstrom. Bolts of lightning flashed out of the shadowy, swirling sphere, striking one of the sorcerers in the back. His body shook violently as the electrical energy tore through him, his dead body tossed hard into a nearby tree.

The remaining sorcerers screamed as they got a glimpse of a humanoid shape inside the dark cloud. It seemed to be composed of nothing but crackling electricity. Lightning struck again and again, felling more of the fleeing shadmar, the storm gaining on them. However, with each strike, the cloud became slightly more transparent and the wizard within became ever more corporeal.

Thes's mind surged with rage, subsumed by the hatred and energy he carried. As he felled the final sorcerer in sight, the cloud broke and dissipated into a wisp of fog and the crackling of energy faded into mere static charge. Thes stepped lightly to the earth, looking to catch his breath. However, he soon heard the sound of murmured incantations just off to the side. The weary wizard then dived out of the way just as a roaring ball of fire exploded where he once stood.

A shadmar sorcerer stepped out of the darkness, the faint starlight illuminating his sinister features as he prepared yet another blast of flames. Thes was in a dangerous position. His mind burned from the excessive use of magic and even his body ached from being used as a conduit for that energy. He summoned what strength he had left and ran headlong to another larger tree. Flames licked at his flank as the sorcerer then unleashed a jet of searing blue. Thankfully, Thes narrowingly avoided the fires. He then peeked around the tree trunk to view his aggressor again. Thes then

182

recognized the shadmar as the sorcerer that led the attack on Artemis's grove.

Fury again got the better of the wizard. He unleashed another bolt of lightning at the sorcerer. However, the electricity struck some unseen shield and dissipated into the ground, harmlessly. The shadmar laughed confidently as his hands moved in complex gestures, seemingly preparing more demonic fires to throw at the weakened wizard.

Thes's mind burned with a growing agony as his powerful magic began to catch up to him. The world began to get a bit blurry and his sense of balance faltered. Thes stumbled and held the tree tight as the world begin to spin. He felt as if the blood in his veins was draining, as his head was light and his consciousness was fleeting.

Thes concentrated and bit his lips hard until blood began to accumulate at his teeth. The pain jolted him enough not to faint and he tried to stand tall. He knew he could not relinquish himself to the silent sleep and the shadmar's mercy.

The murmurings of an incantation echoed around the wizard as he stood, trying to regain control of his muscles. He knew he had to leap, to dodge the incoming pain. Yet his body would not obey, it was too weak. The desperate wizard turned around and pressed his back into the tree's trunk for protection, knowing this was the best he could do.

Soon flames roared and whipped around the massive trunk, licking and tickling the wizard's skin with tongues of searing heat as it jetted past the occlusion. Portions of Thes's clothes smoldered and smoked and he covered his face with his hands, trying to keep the stinging pain out of his eyes. The roar of the flames lasted for many moments, tearing at the last threads of stamina possessed by the wizard. When the flames finally died down, Thes was beyond exhausted. He collapsed to the ground behind the tree, vainly trying to move his pained limbs.

He heard slow footsteps coming for him behind the tree. He tried to muster some strength to rise to the coming sorcerer, but again his body refused to obey. From behind the tree came the robed, shadmar sorcerer, his face in a wicked grin as he looked upon the collapsed elf.

"Looks like the storm has cleared," he said sneering in the elven tongue. "Eh, ethmar?" he asked derisively. His booted foot kicked Thes hard in the side, the cracking, numbing crunch of a rib echoed through the fallen wizard's body. The shadmar flipped Thes over and threw him propped against the trunk of the tree, so that the wizard would be forced to look at the shadmar face-to-face. Thes's eyes rolled in his head as the pain in his side and his general exhaustion threatened to overwhelm him. He tried to remain resolute and conscious and not give the shadmar the satisfaction of defeating his spirit.

The sorcerer's black eyes stared down at Thes as he hunched down to peer over the wizard. "Finally, I have caught you. You have no idea how much trouble you have been." Vralthen had been savoring this moment since Thes and his friends thwarted his attack at Artemis's cabin. He patiently drew a jagged knife from a scabbard on his belt, looking at Thes for any sign of fear.

*　　*　　*　　*　　*　　*　　*

Back on the road to the village, Morstar, Svendian, and Artemis were gathering what warriors they could as they headed towards the village. The three were soon informed that most of the villagers have fled to the west where a well-hidden stair led to the top of the valley.

Upon hearing this news, Svendian turned to the outsiders, "You should go with the villagers. Flee this place and its torments. You need not die for the lives of the elves."

184

"Pah!" exclaimed Morstar. "Nice try, elf. But ye won't be dying here alone. Ye send what warriors you can to help the villagers, and I'll help ye hold off those damn dark elves."

"Yes," agreed Artemis. "You can count on me as well. We must give the villagers time to escape."

Svendian expected as much and simply smiled at the two warriors. He then called out for volunteers from some of the village's warriors to help them form a new defensive line at the entrance to the village. The rest of the warriors went to help with the evacuation of the villagers.

The strange storm cloud seemed to have dissipated, but there were occasional flashes of light high on the cliffs to the east. The sight of which made Morstar fearful for Thes, not knowing what became of his friend. He murmured a quick prayer to the dwarven deity, Brog the Hearthmaster, to watch over the elf. The dwarf was beginning to fear that he would lose all the friends he had made these past few weeks.

The warriors that remained didn't have much time to prepare their defenses, nor did they have the benefit of a stone wall. However, they did manage to quickly prop a few pieces of broken hovels between the trees to somewhat restrict the enemy's direction of assault. With the river on the one flank, and the smoking village on the other, it wasn't the worst defensive position. The defenders braced themselves with readied bows and spears peering into the darkness for the hints of the coming shadmar.

Then it was bright. Their eyes stung for a moment as a shimmering light began to grow far ahead of the defensive line. Svendian's heart nearly stopped as he realized what was coming.

"RUN!" he shouted, leading the group to plod into the nearby stream. The others rushed to follow as a wall of flames began to move quickly towards them. The flaming inferno was consuming trees as it came onward.

Svendian cursed himself for not expecting such a tactic when he had seen it used on his own village. They expected them to die in a flaming valley with no escape. He suspected that the shadmar had no knowledge of their escape route, however, or it would not have been worth the effort to burn the entire valley. That thought comforted the elf as he led them through the waters, then rushing through the trees on the other side.

*　　*　　*　　*　　*　　*　　*

Vralthen was about to press the point of his dagger to Thes's neck, but a bright light down in the valley gave him pause. Flocks of birds scattered from the woods soaring into the night sky. A menacing laugh was aimed at the fallen wizard as Vralthen understood that the valley and its villagers would soon be no more. He pointed towards the growing conflagrations.

"See there, ethmar." he snided. "It is over. Your friends and villagers are soon but mere ash and smoke. Like the knights that came knocking at our door, you will all be slaves. The fires of war now claim the elven demesne." His hands reached high above him. "Your selfish kind has claimed the stars for far too long. Now the shadmar reclaim the night... and the glory of day. We dwell beneath your feet no more." He brandished his dagger again as he came closer to Thes.

The wizard was barely able to maintain his consciousness as he felt the cold dagger faintly pierce the pale skin on his neck. The slightest trickle of blood dripped down the jagged tip onto the ethmar's scorched clothes. Vralthen grinned as he pulled the blade back and casually watched the last drops fall from the steel.

186

"Unto death I give your soul to the Lords of Xelenvar," the shadmar whispered in ritual as the dagger then plunged deep into the wizard's abdomen.

Thes gasped in pain, his eyes wide with final sensations, before he slumped into unconsciousness and the slow ride to death's door. His blood slowly oozed from the point where the blade pierced his vital organs, just below his ribcage. Vralthen then pulled forth the dagger and cleaned his blade with Thes's robes as he watched the ethmar closely, eagerly waiting for the wizard's final breath to fuel his latent magic.

As the shadmar stood to his feet, he began to make complicated arcane gestures to aid the dark ritual he had prepared. His eager voice began to release a guttural incantation. Blood red wisps of energy appeared around the sorcerer as his chorus began to gain momentum, his voice slowly driving to a crescendo of dark utterances.

*   *   *   *   *   *   *

Morstar chased after the elves, secretly wishing his legs were longer, as the increasing heat of the inferno began to warm his backside. Everyone was pounding their legs with determined rhythm as they came to the cliff-side on the northwestern end of the valley. There were a few of the village warriors up on the wall, the last of the village's band. From Morstar's angle, it was nearly impossible to see the stair on which the elves were using to climb their way up the cliff.

As their band of warriors reached the wall, Svendian sent up the village warriors first, then Artemis and Morstar. He looked back down at the valley for a moment, seeing the ancient trees fall prey to the flames of destruction and a great sadness came over him. He saw in those flames the end of his civilization.

The aged captain then began to climb the high stair, reaching carefully for each hand-hold. After a minute of careful climbing, he turned back to view the forest. He caught sight of a large figure rushing through the flaming trees. It seemed nothing more than a wet mound of shadmar cloaks bounding aimlessly in the direction of the stair, steam was swirling from the heap. Yet, it was far too tall to be a desperate shadmar warrior. Svendian paused, placing his hand on his dagger for a moment. Then as the mound turned and bounded for the elf on the stair, the elf saw a glimpse of bright blue eyes hidden in the folds. The piles of cloaks came flying off the figure, immediately being consumed by the flames behind him as he reached the bottom of the stair.

"Bryman!" shouted Svendian with awe and amazement, beckoning the warrior to climb with haste. Soon the Noradrie warrior was clamoring behind the aged captain up the stairs. He was covered with a layer of dried blood, his armor was missing many of its protective steel bands and the underlying leather was covered in many breaks and chinks, dyed with the warrior's own dried blood. He seemed to be in poor shape, but otherwise unencumbered by his wounds.

The flames roared beneath them as they climbed the cliff side. They had to carefully watch each step, crawling on hands and feet to brace themselves to the narrow ledge. Svendian wanted to ask the warrior how he survived and came to find them, but he knew there was no time for such discussions.

As for Bryman, his body ached with the many bruises and cuts from the battle, and his large bulk seemed oversized for the cautious task of climbing, but he did not survive through battle and fire to give up now. He trudged on behind the aged captain, mastering his resolve. Svendian had a renewed sense of hope and could not help but smile as he listened to the bulky warrior whispering prayers to his ancestors behind him.

188

The two were far behind the others who had long passed over the ledge into the woods above. As Svendian neared the top, he stopped before coming over the ledge. There was sounds of shadmar warriors shouting to each other. Svendian's sense of hope shattered as he realized the shadmar were waiting for them. The captain gently tapped Bryman on the shoulder with an outstretched foot. As the warrior, ever afraid of such heights, looked up to curse at the elf, he saw the captain's finger on his pursed lips and a worried look in his eyes. The warrior went silent and his battle instinct took over his mind. He waited and listened. Svendian peered over the ledge stealthily to see the situation.

Up on the ledge was a small band of shadmar warriors. They had many of the villagers and village warriors in bindings, strung together in a line with Artemis. It was not a particular large group of shadmar, maybe a dozen or so, but they must have taken the villagers by surprise when they reached the top. Thankfully, with the flames roaring in the valley below, the shadmar did not expect any more elves to come clamoring over the ledge. Their attention was fixated on keeping an unruly dwarf in line. Morstar fought and pulled on his bindings as two shadmar tried to pin the dwarf to the ground. The captain of the shadmar was shouting at them.

Svendian turned back to Bryman, who was looking up at the elf with a thirsty anticipation. The captain nodded to the warrior as he silently drew out his sword and summoned his remaining vigor. His hand then reached out to pull himself up over the final ledge, sword in hand.

*   *   *   *   *   *   *

Vralthen continued his dark ritual as Thes lay upon the ground bleeding. The dark utterances had reached their peak and many blood-red swirling motes of light surrounded the sorcerer. They swirled in a particular archaic pattern, everything precise and perfectly arranged. It was time. The ethmar wizard's body and soul would be possessed by the demonic powers of Xelenvar ready to serve Vralthen's whim. Although his mind was locked in fervent concentration on the ritual, the shadmar was giddy with excitement as he awaited the power he was about to receive.

The sorcerer was so consumed in his sinister task that he failed to notice that he was not alone. In the shadow of the trees, a large silver beast prowled, eyeing the sorcerer with feral intent. A silver-haired wolf then bounded towards the shadmar growling and snarling. It lunged towards the sorcerer. Vralthen screamed as the wolf's teeth tore at his leg, tearing the skin around his ankle and crushing the fragile bones beneath. The swirling motes of blood-red light scattered, swirling chaotically; the ritual had been ruined.

Vralthen vainly tried to fend off the wild beast as it tore into his leg. They rolled and flipped together as Vralthen kicked with his free leg and stabbed at the creature with his ritual-dagger. The agile beast avoided the piercing stabs of the dagger and accepted a few of the kicks with resolve as it continued to crush and tear through the sorcerer's brittle leg. It dragged the sorcerer away from the fallen wizard. Vralthen was trying his best to keep distance from the enraged monster, but he was unprepared and unfocused. His mind was too distracted and he could not bring a spell to fruition. Vralthen then managed to kick the beast away. He scrambled further from the creature, gaining little ground due to his mangled leg.

However, the beast simply leapt upon him again. Vralthen was forced to drop his dagger as his hands grasped desperately around the creature's neck. The beast snapped and snarled near his face, its dark chestnut-colored eyes glaring with anger, its deadly teeth edging closer and closer with each snapping bite. The thin shadmar, who had forgone

190

physical conditioning in favor of magical study, struggled to keep the beast from edging its sharp canines closer to his face. The beast's claws then dug hard into Vralthen's side as the creature used its superior strength to climb upon the shadmar.

With a desperate push, Vralthen threw his body to the left, rolling away from under the beast. He took advantage of the momentary escape and scrambled up on his good leg. He then prepared a spell with a few quick gestures. However, the wolf leaped high upon the sorcerer before he could finish the incantation.

The two then rolled towards the edge of the cliff. Panic hit them both as they realized the dangerous situation they were now in. Desperate swirling limbs of both creatures reached for salvation as their bodies flung out towards the open air above the valley. Vralthen was kicked hard by the wolf's back legs. He was soon weightless as he soared towards the renewed flames deep in the valley below.

The wolf, however, was clawing desperately at the edge of the cliff, but was unable to grasp the loose stone. Ineffective canine paws then slowly gave way to grasping elven hands. The wider hands and sprightly form were at ease to halt the momentum. The elven woman hung over the edge for a moment before carefully pulling herself up and away from the ledge. Sia's body had returned to its normal form.

The druidess rushed desperately to Thes's side, her mind was in sharp focus. She was scared that she was too late, that she would lose this new person in her life. Sia performed a few ritualistic gestures, summoning many elemental spirits to her aid. She then knelt down beside the dying elf, placing her hands firmly to the wizard's bleeding wound. With a low hum of magical energy, her hands released a bright light into the wound. The tissue began to slowly coalesce and rejoin. Sia watched Thes's face desperately as she poured more of her mental energy into the dying elf. Thes, however, showed no signs of recovery; even though his wound was mended, his pale face resembled that of a corpse.

*   *   *   *   *   *   *

Morstar had lost his strength as three shadmar pinned him to the hard ground. A fourth shadmar held a dagger to the dwarf's throat. The dwarf finally gave in to his captors, his sore muscles giving in to their torment. Tears dripped down his rosy cheeks.

Artemis felt defeated as well. The ranger's body was still quite sore from the battle and explosion. After the horror they had just witnessed, he felt there was little hope in their current predicament. He was worried that Svendian had fallen from the cliff behind them and that he and Morstar were all that remained of his friends. Now it seemed they would soon be slaves to the shadmar.

As hope gave in to despair, the ranger caught a glimpse of a shimmer of light. It was starlight reflected on a steel blade. A dark silhouette climbing over the ledge could barely be seen. The burning flames glowed behind the dark lithe form, presenting what seemed to be a shadow wielding steel. Hope had struck again in the ranger's heart.

Svendian stealthily leapt upon the shadmar. His blade sliced off the unfortunate hand holding the dagger to the dwarf's throat. Chaos erupted on the cliff side as the few remaining soldiers of the village tugged and pulled at their bindings in unison. The captives rushed at their keepers using the ropes between their bindings to knock over the shadmar guards. Then a roar echoed off the trees as Bryman's intimidating bulk lunged towards the confused guards.

The sound of that bellow brought a surge of strength in Morstar. He pushed off the distracted shadmar upon him and kicked one of the others hard in the face. The dwarf then rolled to his side cutting his bindings on the fallen dagger. He then clamored to his feet, brandishing the dagger as he rose. The guards kept their distance, but began circling around the dwarf with their drawn swords.

Svendian was fighting off three shadmar guards while Bryman was holding back four. Artemis was leading the kicking assault on the two guards knocked to the ground. One shadmar was simply kneeling on the ground, screaming and clutching at a blood-gushing hole where a hand once stood.

Artemis and the villagers managed to knock out the two guards with furious kicks. They quickly cut their bindings with the fallen shadmar's daggers. The ranger then grabbed his sword and the dwarf's heavy warhammer, rushing to join the dwarf. Morstar seemed to need assistance more than the others did. With great effort, Artemis managed to toss the hammer through the circling shadmar. It landed at Morstar's feet, distracting his adversaries. The dwarf then flung his dagger into the nearest guard's chest and reached for the warhammer. The maneuver made the dwarf vulnerable to one of the guard's slashing blades, but Artemis arrived just in time to deflect the blow and push back the guard with a fury of aimless cuts.

With the dwarf armed and the ranger at his side, the two quickly cut down their foes with teamwork fueled by renewed hope. They then aided Svendian and Bryman in finishing the rest of the shadmar guards. The shadmar were dead and the remaining villagers were safe, for the moment. The flames in the valley lessened somewhat and the cold night air chilled the bare skin of the survivors.

Svendian talked with the villagers and soon learned that the elders were killed in the initial fire attack upon the village. The fleeing villagers were then cut down here on the ledge. The shadmar surprised and ambushed the survivors as they reached the top. After a quick scuffle, the shadmar had most of the villagers bound. When the village warriors arrived, with Artemis and Morstar behind them, the shadmar had their bows aimed and pointed. They were forced to surrender. The shadmar then proceeded to kill all those they deemed to be unfit slaves, mostly those too young or too old for manual labor. That horrid act is what ignited Morstar into a fighting rage against his captors. The piles of lifeless elven corpses were scattered, the bodies unceremoniously left where they fell. Only five warriors were left; two remained from Svendian's own band from Cwendilin. In total, there were only twenty-six elves standing on the ledge.

Svendian's heart was broken. He had now witnessed two elven villages suffer the flames and slaughter of the shadmar army. He gazed at the pile of corpses for a moment, consumed in grief. Morstar and Artemis stood beside their friend, bowing their heads in reverence to the lost elven lives. Neither of the two had words to offer. They both felt the loss as keenly as the captain. Bryman, however, was sitting upon the ground, catching his breath. His gaze was aimed above, to the clear, cool sky. Stars twinkled behind the swirling clouds of smoke and glistening motes of ash.

Svendian then broke the silence, as he turned to the villagers. "Listen up," the captain called to the elves around him. Tears glistened in his eyes, and for a moment it seemed as if his words would escape him. He tried to regain his confidence as he looked upon the war-weary elves. "War has come to our forest home," the aged captain stated, driving the emotion out of his voice. "You must find safety in the elven capitol. Elienspar is your only hope. Tell them what has befallen here. Quiff and Kalen can lead you there," the captain then nodded to his remaining soldiers.

"What about you, captain? Are you not coming with us?" Quiff asked.

The aged captain looked to Morstar, Artemis, and Bryman. "No," he answered. "We must find what became of our friend and do our best to ensure you are not followed." Bryman turned and aimed a toothy grin at the captain, glad he had not given up the fight.

The villagers then gathered what supplies they could find among the fallen, before heading to the southwest. They would find the old forest road to take them on the long journey to Elienspar.

Morstar then turned to his three companions and said, "Let us find what became of our wizard."

(15) Ancient Enemies, Common Fate

His body ached with so much pain and toil. The horrid smell of the thick manure still managed to enter his nostrils, despite the wad of clay shoved into those discontented slits. Even with those conditions, Kinrithir continued to flip the mounting feces with his long wooden fork as he stood in the knee-high waste.

He was in a long, deep cavern. From one end to the next, it was filled with the foul-smelling manure. Numerous other slaves worked throughout the chamber, each working the refuse as a handful of shadmar guards observed from high walkways on the rim of the cavern.

The shadmar had reserved these lowest caverns for this foul purpose, serving as both a slave-pen and a vital component of their agricultural production. It took extensive training and skill to ensure high quality production from the mushrooms, flora, and beasts the shadmar relied on for nourishment. Therefore, slaves assigned to such duties were always selected based on their prospective longevity and ability to be trained. They would only take the healthy and most fit among those they subjugated, killing the rest without remorse. However, sometimes they ended up with unruly or untrainable subjects. These slaves were assigned here in the manure pits. A place where minimal skill was required and the unrelenting stench and constant toil would eventually tame the most disobedient.

It was here that the shadmar sent their murderers as well. For this reason, Kinrithir and Kryther now joined the many slaves working the manure pits. The two half-brothers had little time to talk since they were sent down here, after Kinrir and Kryn, their alter-egos, were sentenced to slavery for the murder of a respected nobleman. The past few days were filled with nothing but toil, surrounded by the merciless stench. At the end of the day, they were given a bowl of cold mushroom stew, likely the leftovers from the miners and farmers above them. They would then collapse in a small cavern where all the slaves were chained and linked for the night.

There were all types of humanoids here. Kinrithir saw goblins, orcs, humans, and many wood elves, or thunmar. There were only three other shadmar slaves, also punished for crimes committed in the caverns above. There was one unfortunate female sulmar in the caverns as well. A member of the elven elite and most hated of the surface-dwelling elves. The sulmar had tanned skin and long blonde hair. Kinrithir found her features quite beautiful, and even the manure caked to her skin failed to diminish her allure. However, she carried herself more like a soldier than a courtesan, cloaking herself in an aura of hostility. The shadmar guards were particularly sadistic towards her, but she managed to hold her ground and even roughed up a few of the guards in small bursts of defiance. In the end, she would still take their beatings in silence, never giving them the satisfaction of hearing her pain. When Kinrithir looked at her and her rebelliousness, he was filled with hope.

One night, after the tired and worn slaves ate their meager portions, they were each chained to a random post in the side sleeping cavern. Kinrithir found himself chained next to the defiant sulmar. The guards had left for the night, leaving the slaves in the absolute darkness. While the other shadmar, orcs, and goblins could see well in the lightless cavern, the surface elves and humans were as good as blind. Kinrithir would occasionally hear the quiet whisperings in the corners of the cavern with his keen ears. Most slaves were usually too exhausted to talk during this time. Additionally, they knew if they were overheard by the guard at the cavern's entrance, they would suffer greatly. For these reasons, it was usually near silent during the resting period.

198

Thus, Kinrithir was quite surprised when the shadmar heard hushed words directed to him.

"One of the new shadmar, is it?" the sulmar asked Kinrithir. Her eyes were closed as she sat with her back to the smooth wall, her arms wrapped around her knees.

"Yes," Kinrithir answered. "How did you know?"

"I may not be able to see, but you still smell like a shadmar," her response derisive.

Kinrithir was surprised at the hatred in her voice. "Have I done something to disturb you?"

"Haven't you? You attacked my people and dragged me down here," her whispers scathing with hatred, eager for an argument.

Kinrithir felt his heartbeat rise, ready to meet the opposition. However, he calmed himself. He did not want to fall into the quarrel aimed at him. He was used to Kryther trying the same tactic.

"I believe you are mistaken," he answered peacefully. "I, personally, have done none of those things. Nor do I condone the choices of those who have."

"As if the shadmar would possess conscientious objectors among their villainous rabble. You now add lies to your list of crimes." Her harsh words were still fishing for an argument.

"I am called Kinrithir. What is your name?"

Silence was her response. She did not even move to acknowledge the query.

Kinrithir waited a moment, then gave up trying to reach out to the sulmar. He turned away from her to sleep, trying to find the least objectionable body position on the uneven stone.

The next couple of days were as uneventful as the previous. Only the occasional skirmish with an irritated guard to break the monotony of the work. However, luck was with Kinrithir as he soon found himself shackled next to

Kryther one night. He had been quite concerned for his half-brother. They had had little contact since arriving in the caverns. When Kinrithir did manage a brief glimpse of Kryther's face across the cavern, he seemed overly solemn and filled with despair.

"Brother, how are you doing?" he asked in the quietest of whispers.

Kryther did not immediately answer. After a long pause, he turned slowly towards Kinrithir, but did not make eye contact with his half-brother. Kryther's eyes were cast down to the ground between them. He mumbled something incoherently.

"What is it, brother?" Kinrithir asked, straining to hear those quiet words.

"I'm sorry, brother. I'm sorry I brought this upon you." His words were still quiet and strained, but now audible. Before Kinrithir could respond, Kryther continued, emotion breaking through the strained words, "I'm sorry for my attitude all these years, for pushing you out of father's inheritance, for being ungrateful, even as you ensured our survival and accepted my company. I never deserved you as a brother or a friend." Tears were now dripping down to the cavern floor as Kryther contained quiet sobs. "I'm... so sorry, brother. This is all... my fault." His sobs were now slightly uncontrolled, quietly echoing off the cavern walls.

Kinrithir had never seen his half-brother in such a state. Tears now dripped from his own eyes as he looked upon Kryther's bout of unashamed emotional release. He tried to console him, not wanting his half-brother to give up hope. "It'll be okay, brother. We will... we will... get out of here." Kinrithir's words were uncertain and he did not sound overly reassuring.

Kryther huffed between sobs as a remnant of his cynicism emerged. His wet, red eyes looked up to Kinrithir. The shadmar then released broken, quiet giggles between

200

sobs as he looked at his ever-optimistic half-brother. It was as if years of bottled emotions all burst forth at once. "I love you, brother."

"I love you, brother." Kinrithir said as he stretched and reached to grasp his half-brother's hand. Kryther did likewise and they clasped the ends of their fingertips together. Kryther then pulled back quickly as a shadmar guard peered down the chamber. Kinrithir did likewise, feigning a repositioning on the hard surface. The guard said nothing, but peered for a few moments before leaving.

Hope had resurged in Kinrithir. He was determined to escape from these caverns and escape with his half-brother. The two shadmar quietly whispered for over an hour, trying to come up with a viable escape plan. Kinrithir believed that hope was their greatest asset and suggested recruiting other slaves for a revolt against the guards.

"They would kill us," said Kryther, in typical tone.

"Then we would die with hope in our hearts," Kinrithir replied. "Let us embrace our noble heritage and die with courage." He knew these words would appeal to his half-brother.

Kryther reluctantly agreed, and the two shadmar decided they would start recruiting slaves for a revolt. If they could take out the guards they might be able to gather the slaves together. Only with significant numbers could they fight their way to the surface and possible escape. They decided that each night they would attempt to recruit their neighbors in the sleeping caverns, until all were ready to strike at once.

The next day, Kinrithir noticed Kryther's face was no longer filled with despair. While they did not get a chance to speak again that day, they were content smiling to each other across the cavern, both knowing they would bide their time until an opportunity presented itself. They would choose the path of hope.

The following night, Kinrithir found himself chained next to a goblin on one side and the antagonistic sulmar on the other. He debated on whether he should try to speak with her again and share his plan with her. Eventually he decided if there was any chance of escape, they would need the feisty sulmar on their side.

"My name is Kinrithir," he whispered to her, trying to be friendly despite their previous interaction.

"I heard you the first time," she replied quietly, her response like the poisonous sting of a scorpion.

Kinrithir sighed, trying to think of a way to gain the sulmar's trust. "Do you want to escape or not?"

"No," she said sarcastically, "I'm beginning to find this inn's accommodations just delightful." Although her surface-accent reduced some of the sarcasms sting, Kinrithir understood her meaning.

The shadmar was trying not to let his growing anger get the best of him. "Well," he began carefully, "if you *do* want to escape, my half-brother and I have a plan."

A quiet, sarcastic laugh escaped from the sulmar's lips. "How do I know you aren't some shadmar spy trying to root out escapees?"

"You don't," he responded, matter-of-factly. "However, unless your master plan is to break each guard's nose, one by one, I don't think you have any other options."

She smiled, but just for a moment. She was proud of her small acts of defiance.

Kinrithir continued, "We can help you and you can help us. Perhaps together we can get more of the slaves to strike a revolt. You can help convince the other surface-elf slaves to join us. My half-brother and I know many of the caverns above this level. We can help you escape to the surface."

She huffed. "What then, shadmar? If we reach the surface, then what? Will you just go about your merry way?

202

Or will I hear of elves slaughtered by rogue bands of surface-dwelling shadmar?" Her words were filled with anger. She seemed to have great hatred for the shadmar.

"I think you misjudge my kin," he replied solemnly.

"I've seen what your kind has done," anger rising in her harsh whispers. "You are nothing more than raiders and murderers, beasts of caves and shadow."

"I suppose to you that would seem so." The shadmar thought for a moment, trying to find the best words. "You might have only seen the fervent bands of the affluent young warriors sent out to terrorize the surface in nighttime raids. They attack out of ancient tradition and a misguided hatred for all that dwell above us. You cannot define my people by the actions of those who live without consequence. I can tell you, their religion is not shared by all, especially among the lower classes. Many of the shadmar I know care little for the ancient feud. They want security and safety above all else. They only wish to raise their children and work diligently for the common good of their community."

Kinrithir paused, noticing the scowl was fading from the sulmar's face. She was listening.

"We lost that," he explained. "We lost everything. Through erroneous decisions and poor leadership, we lost our home caverns and the great city within. All the shadmar here, above you, have nowhere else to go. You are not interned in a military fortress, but the last bastion of hope for the refugees of a lost civilization."

"Then why do I hear whispers of war?" she asked. "Shouts for the blood of surface-dwellers? Why do you raid our villages with your armies?" She no longer seemed combative, but actually interested to discuss the situation.

"My people are under the sway of a powerful sorcerer. He is a skilled demagogue, using hatred and fear to bind people to his will. I do not know his reasons for a full-scale assault on the surface. To me it seems folly given our desperate predicament. We live on limited rations, dwelling in cold, unfurnished caverns, with no assurance that the next day will be any better than the last. We should be asking for aid and compassion from the surface elves. Perhaps we could put an end to the ancient feud. However, that is not the case. Our leader intends to march my people into war and annihilation."

The sulmar was silent. The news seemed to have struck her uncomfortably.

Kinrithir continued, "This sorcerer has made himself as a savior to our people, even though I suspect the destruction of our city was part of his own doing. It disgusts me to see my people blind to his manipulations."

"So why are you here? Did you resist?" she asked him.

"In a way," the shadmar responded vaguely. "It's a long story."

They both sat in silence for a few moments, each pondering the situation. The gravity of his people's plight now weighed heavy in Kinrithir's heart. Describing the dreadful situation out loud to an outsider made the reality more prominent to him.

The sulmar finally broke the silence, "My name is Edras."

Kinrithir turned to her, seeing the faint glow of her eyes upon him "I'm…"

"Kinrithir. Yes, I remember," she said, smiling for the first time.

He returned the smile. "Tell me, Edras. How did someone with such strength and spirit come to be caught in here?"

Edras was quiet for a moment before answering, "I was captured by your sorcerer's armies… a few weeks ago. I am the leader of the Knights of Song. We were a small contingent of warriors who protected the eastern extent of

204

the Kingdom of Three Crowns. We had gotten word of a raid on one of the eastern villages and rode in to help. However, instead of the small band of shadmar warriors we expected, we ran into an army with hundreds strong. We were greatly outnumbered and unprepared." She paused, trying to push back the emotion tied to the memory. "My band was slaughtered before we could even attempt a retreat. I was knocked out and captured. Then I found myself down here."

"I'm sorry for the loss of your friends," the shadmar replied sincerely.

"They died valiantly, protecting their kingdom and kinsfolk. I wish I could join them rather than rotting down here." She signed heavily. "This is perhaps the perfect torture devised by your kin. Forcing me to live and breathe, sitting idle, while the shadmar armies attack the rest of my kin above." Her face looked solemn and broken for only an instant before her hard exterior returned.

Kinrithir empathized with her helplessness. He had watched his kin follow Delrith on this mad crusade to the surface, forced to remain quiet and uninfluential, only to protect himself and his half-brother's identity. Kinrithir suddenly had a thought. "You are a knight? Does the leader of your people have your ear?"

Edras seemed puzzled by the question, "Why do you ask?"

"It is one thing for us slaves to escape and leave this war behind," he began as his mind was racing, "The shadmar here would simply be fleeing into a wilderness where they are unwanted and unlikely to find solace or tolerance. However, it would be far better to lead a rebellion from within, to offer my people another option to oppose this mad sorcerer's schemes."

Edras turned fully to face Kinrithir. Though she could not see him, she felt the sincerity in his voice.

The shadmar repeated his question, "Does your liege have your ear? Can you vouch for my people if we can end this war from within?"

"You wish to strike a rebellion?" she asked, still unsure if the dark elf was serious about such a bold and spirited plan.

"Yes," he said with an enthusiastic nod, forgetting she could not see him. "I believe there are enough of my people here that would denounce the sorcerer's conquest if there was hope of a peaceful option."

"But you are a slave! How will you strike a rebellion from here?"

"We start with the slaves, then we bring in the miners and farmers, then the craftsmen, then the soldiers. From the bottom to the top the numbers grow smaller in the shadmar hierarchy. We will always have the advantage. This is a war of principles, not of arms." The shadmar was filled with hope, dreams of victory, but reality began to sink back into him, and he saw how far they needed to climb to reach freedom. He calmed himself. "Now I ask again," he continued quietly, "will you vouch for the safety of my people?"

Edras sat quietly for a moment, somewhat enamored by the shadmar's boundless optimism. "Yes," she said, "In the unlikely event that you get us out of here and can break this sorcerer's hold on your people, I will speak to my queen on your behalf."

Hope surged in Kinrithir. For the first time since the fall of Dith Derithin, he had a plan to help his people fight back against Delrith's war. The shadmar turned over to look at the sulmar knight. She was sitting back into her customary pose, with her hands wrapped around her knees. He looked at her for a long moment. There was something about her that made him feel strong.

She likewise turned to face in his direction, catching the faintest glimpse of two red lights looking back at her, "I will join in your plan, shadmar."

Kinrithir was excited and he began to whisper to her what he and his half-brother had discussed. An hour of quiet whispering passed before the two elves ended their plotting. With a plan of action in place, the two conspirators finally laid down upon the stone and tried to get some sleep.

The next day, Kinrithir and Kryther were working the manure pits in somewhat proximity to each other. The shadmar guards, paced back and forth on their high catwalks, keeping a lazy eye on the events in the pits below. The two half-brothers were able to whisper to each other, although they were careful not to make their conversation obvious, leaving their lips still and faces in parallel orientations. They continued to use their forks to lift and turn the rotting piles.

"I have recruited another to our cause, brother," said Kinrithir, pretending to work especially hard at a rough patch of tangled garbage.

"You are ever the silver-tongued," Kryther replied sarcastically.

"Well, my mother did have a better way with words than yours," Kinrithir teased.

Kryther ignored the comment, eager to share his own news. "If you must know, I too was successful. One of the other shadmar will join us. He will spread the word as well."

Kinrithir smiled. With each night, they would recruit more to their cause, spreading like a flame through the ranks of the slaves. It would only be a short time before they would be ready to strike.

(16) Recovery and Fission

Morstar trudged through the tangled undergrowth. A loose branch of a rogue spruce whipped him hard in the face. The dwarf ignored the momentary pain, as his focus was on each hurried step of his large booted feet. Behind the marching dwarf, Svendian and Artemis lightly followed, Bryman taking the rear with his long strides and heavy footfalls.

Morstar was worried about his friend. The sight of those fires up on the eastern cliffs drove the dwarf onward. He was clinging to hope with nervous desperation. Hope that Thes and Sia survived the flames in the valley and whatever challenge awaited the two elves on the high cliffs. He also was hoping that the remaining elves of the village would find a safe route to the elven city. Perhaps they would even bring reinforcements to aid them against the shadmar. Such hope guided each hurried step and the occasional burst of energy the anxious dwarf used to force himself forward.

It had been a few hours of hasty travel through the dark forest, with Artemis and Bryman frequently tripping in the darkness that now covered the area like a thick blanket. The smoke from the now dwindling fires had blocked out most celestial light, such that even Svendian's keen eyes had trouble seeing their surroundings. They were all exhausted and the others did not possess the dwarf's uncanny endurance.

Morstar then halted suddenly, urgently stopping. He stretched out his arms to hold back his companions. Thankfully the others were so helplessly tired, that they were in no danger of passing his outstretched arms. A surging torrent of swirling smoke rose from the deep valley ahead of them. They had reached the eastern cliffs. Morstar hiked a few paces away from the cliff's edge, following it southward with his eager steps. The others breathlessly followed, summoning the final remnants of their diminished strength.

Soon the dwarf came across a clearing in the woods. There were many obvious signs of fire and explosive blasts. One tree seemed to have been heavily damaged by a powerful jet of flames, its side blackened and tinged with ash. The dwarf knew this was the spot.

"Thes!" he shouted, in spite of the danger should his words be heard by the shadmar. The shout startled Artemis out of his hazy existence and he grew worried.

"Quiet," the ranger begged the dwarf. "We are in no condition to fight."

The frustrated dwarf turned back to face Artemis, ready to argue with the weary man. However, he heard a voice behind him.

"We are over here," said a sad, female voice. Her words just barely loud enough to be heard by the group. They quietly walked over to her, peering around a large blackened tree. There they found Sia propped against the tree with Thes laying serenely in her arms. His face was quite pale and motionless. Blood-stains covered the wizard's robes, dried blood was caked on the druidess's hands.

Morstar dropped to his knees in front of them, tears trickling down his face. Hope was lost in the dwarf. "No, Lagmud. Let it not be his time," he sobbed. "Not yet..."

Sia shook her head calmly to the dwarf. "He has not yet passed from this world."

The dwarf's face brightened into sobs of joy, "Blessed elf," he said quietly. He looked the injured wizard over, almost expecting him to awaken any moment. The dwarf smiled at the elf's visage of serenity as he sat upon the ground next to Sia.

"Is he okay?" Artemis asked as he sat down beside them. His weary body was eager for rest. Bryman too dropped to the ground to stretch his tired legs.

210

"I think he will live," Sia said unemotionally. "I was able to pull him from Arawna's grasp, but he will need to rest."

"I'm sorry about your village," Svendian said remorsefully as he sat beside the others. "Know that some of your people yet live. They are on their way to Elienspar with the last of my soldiers."

Tears of sadness and joy intermixed upon the druidess's tanned cheeks. "Thank you. Such news brightens my heart." She took a moment to relish in the knowledge that some of her kin still lived. She then added, "The shadmar have left."

"Have they marched from the valley? Did you see them?" Bryman asked, his eyes glinting with eagerness that his body did not share.

"No," the druidess replied, "I only heard them leave. As Thes and I lay here helpless, I could hear the marching army coming toward us from the south. They made little effort to hide their presence. I expected death to come swiftly. But suddenly there was a red light in the distance. When the light finally faded, the sound of the army was no more."

"Magic?" the dwarf asked.

"Yes, it would seem so," answered Sia. She then looked down upon the sleeping elf in her arms, unable to stop herself from caressing his pale face. She was thinking of the last words the two of them shared.

"Damn cowards," Bryman muttered, spitting to the ground behind him in disgust.

"Aye, well," began the dwarf, "I be glad they left us be." He then looked at the large warrior in earnest. "Look at ye!" he exclaimed. "Yer in no shape to be fightin' anyway."

Before Bryman could retort, Sia said, "Let me tend to your wounds." She then scrutinized the others, seeing their many cuts and bruises, and added, "All of you."

211

Sia carefully laid Thes down upon the ground, wrapping him in his scorched cloak to stay warm. She then went to each of the injured warriors, skillfully tending to their wounds with a combination of herbs from her pouch and a touch of magical healing when necessary. The water spirits were ever willing to mend tissue at the druidess's call. The scent of the fragrant aromatics also calmed them all immensely. After Sia finished tending to each warrior, they were all too tranquil and relaxed by the heavenly scents of her herbs and oils to do more than wrap their own cloaks about them and sleep away the rest of the night. Sia pulled her own heavy fur cloak over herself and Thes's motionless form. She pressed her body tight against his, hoping her heat would warm his cool skin and help revive him. As her mind faded into sleep, she dreamed his arm stretched across her waist, pulling her closer.

The next morning was cold and windy. An endless expanse of gray clouds stretched from horizon to horizon as if the world itself was in mourning. Svendian was the first to awaken. He crafted a fire nearby to help the others warm themselves when they arose. His own body was quite stiff from the chilled sleep and eventful days.

The tragedy of the previous night seemed like a nightmare drifting on the edge of his consciousness. The emotional strain and adrenaline-rich memories blended together in a blurred mosaic with the tragedy of Cwendelin. The aged soldier was beginning to wonder if his heart could take more of these catastrophic experiences. How could he go on living when so many other young elves have died? *Surely continuous accumulation of these tragedies would lead to insanity*, he thought.

The soldier sighed, trying to dispel his hopeless thoughts. He wondered what he should do next. It seemed pointless to stay in the eastern forests with the threat of the

212

shadmar army hanging over him, especially if they have the means to appear and disappear at whim. *I should have marched to Elienspar when I had the chance*, he thought. He had good intentions, of warning Harpien and helping them defend themselves, but he could not ignore that his involvement seemed to make little difference in the end. Many have fallen and war was inevitable. He grossly underestimated the might and size of the shadmar forces. It seemed as if all the shadmar in existence had assaulted them. At Cwendilin, he believed their loss was due to lack of preparation. He had no such excuse this time.

As the aged captain sat warming himself by the fire, a burly dwarf sat next to him. Morstar tried to bring warmth into his stubby fingers as he stretched his arms over the meager flames.

"How are you feeling?" Svendian asked him, looking to the dwarf's many bandages.

"My body be fine, elf. Tis my spirit that is broken."

The elf simply nodded in agreement.

Artemis sat down beside them. "Yes, I cannot help but feel defeated. My wounds, however, are no more. Sia is quite the skilled healer."

"Yes," agreed Svendian, eager to change the topic. "I have seen few with such skill in healing and magic."

"Thank you," said Sia behind them, "I am glad you are all feeling better." The druidess was stretching her stiff legs. She joined the others at the growing fire, warming herself.

Thes was still laying on the ground with Sia's thick fur cloak wrapped around him. His face was quite pale, but his breath was barely visible in the chill morning air. Not far from him the large Noradrie warrior was stretched out on his back on the forest floor, his own burned cloak extended over him. A peaceful expression was on the slumbering warpriest's face, his mouth was wide agape.

They all sat silently for a while, enjoying the warmth of the fire. Although they knew that they needed to discuss their next course of action, no one was willing to begin what might be an uncomfortable conversation.

The ever-forthright Morstar broke the silence with a blunt question, "What ye all wish to do now?"

Svendian had already made up his mind, so he answered, "I wish to head to Elienspar. I will try to catch up to the village refugees and ensure the queen knows what has befallen in these lands."

Artemis added his opinion, "That course seems best given the strength of the army we face. However, I doubt us men and dwarves would find much welcome in the elven city."

"Aye," agreed Morstar. "Not a place I'd be eager to visit."

Svendian nodded. "I understand. You all have done so much for my people already. I could not ask you to stay involved anymore. Return to your own lands and be free of the troubles here."

Artemis and Morstar looked uneasily at each other. They both felt deeply involved already, and the idea of leaving the elven forests did not sit comfortably for either of them. For Artemis, these forests had been his home for quite some time. He did not think he would find the serenity and solace he enjoyed here outside of these lands. For Morstar, the idea of quitting on something unfinished was against his nature. He wished to see this war to the end.

"They won't be leaving," stated Bryman's boisterous voice. The warrior was still laying on the ground, but his eyes were open and he had clearly been listening to the conversation. "We have fought hard battles together, and that makes us all kin as far as I'm concerned." The burly man rose to his feet. "As much as you'd like to be rid of the stench of these men and dwarves, I think we are all in this to the end." The warrior then squeezed in next to the fire, eyeing each of them with a defiant smirk.

"No," a strained voice responded. Thes had sat up slowly, holding Sia's cloak tightly to his ravaged body. "You cannot risk your lives for us anymore. I dragged you all into this and the burden of loss is my liability."

Sia rushed to Thes, throwing her arms around him in a tight embrace, and kissing him on the neck. She then helped the weary elf to a place by the fire to warm himself.

As Bryman was about to protest the elf's words, Thes simply raised a hand to quiet him. Surprisingly, the man closed his mouth.

"I apologize to you all. We now know the true severity of what we face. We cannot stop them without an army of our own. I will not let my personal anger and desire for vengeance be used to convince you anymore. We all faced death in this battle and I will not sacrifice your lives for my own agenda."

There were beginnings of protest on each of their mouths, but Thes simply raised his hand again for silence. He was still quite weak and wanted to speak his words before he lost his chance.

"That being said, I feel I have come to know you all quite well over these past weeks. Your friendship is something that I have never known and will always cherish. I know, too, that each of you are as bonded to me as I am to you. However, I want you to make up your own minds. Do not follow me, follow your own hearts."

Sia seemed slightly taken back by the wizard's words. "What if we want to follow you? And where do you think you are going?"

Thes looked to her, mesmerizing himself in those shining, chestnut-colored eyes. "I am going to head east and continue my search for the shadmar stronghold."

"What?!" Morstar exclaimed with an exasperated expression. The others all began to speak in protest to the elf's decision

"Please," Thes pleaded meekly. "I know it seems foolish, which is why I cannot ask any of you to come with me."

Svendian implored the elf. "Why not come with me to Elienspar? Surely your skills would be useful in preparing a counter-attack."

Thes shook his head. "I cannot. There is something much bigger than the elven war going on here. I must look into it."

"Ha! The wizard's got more courage than all of you." Bryman boasted. "He wants to take the battle right to the source, and I'll be there with him."

Thes just shook his head again. "It is not a battle I seek, but information. There is some dark magic at work and I intend to investigate. I have a foreboding feeling in my heart."

"If yer goin' into the belly of the beast, you can count on my axe to join you," Bryman reassured him.

"Thanks," said Thes, smiling to the war-priest. "However, like I said before. I want each of you to make your own choice, and think well on it. This is what I must do, you are free to follow your own path."

Morstar eyed Thes pointedly. "Face it, elf. Ye ain't goin' in there alone."

"Well, please each of you think it over. I must rest before I am able to leave. If you wish to join me on what will most likely be a perilous venture, that is your decision." The wizard then pulled off the heavy fur cloak, placing it around Sia. He then wrapped his own scorched cloak tighter around himself and laid down near the fire and closed his eyes.

"You better believe I'm coming with you, elf," Mostar grumbled.

216

Everyone got quiet suddenly, seriously pondering where they wanted to go. Artemis, Morstar, and Bryman were all eager to follow Thes. There was an adventurous kinship between them that neither wished to see separated. Svendian's mind was still firm. He had little doubt that whatever worried the wizard was important, however, he felt he had a duty to his people to fulfill. He was heading to Elienspar, and soon.

Sia was the truly conflicted one. Should she go off with this wizard, whom she just met into what he describes as certain peril, or should she head to the Elienspar, a place she had only heard about in campfire tales.

Elienspar was practically a myth to her people. She grew up in the very tribal culture of the Aulathunmar (wild elves) from deep in the southern end of the Aegis Forest. There was little contact with those outside the tribe. The stories of a great city of shimmering crystals seemed too fantastic to be true. She certainly did not think a forest dweller like her would feel welcome or comfortable in such a place. Staying was not an option either, especially with the constant danger of shadmar attacks.

On the other hand, Sia had just met Thes less than a week prior. She certainly had feelings for the wizard. He had a thoughtful demeanor and an adventurous spirit that excited her. Yet rushing off to certain doom was not one of the romantic trips she fantasized about. She wished they could just leave these troubles completely and explore the wider world together, unshackled from the responsibilities presented to them.

And yet, she understood why Thes had to investigate better than anyone. His curious mind would not ignore the strange enigmatic energy they witnessed. She had felt it too. The sorcerer that tried to kill the wizard had command over a malign presence. It was a dark emanation in the magical spirit world, an evil that did not belong in this land of living, growing things. When the druidess thinks back to that moment, a cold fear resonates with the memory. It was like glimpsing the spirit of malevolence itself.

It was now late in the morning. For the past few hours, they all sat quietly trying to rest their tired bodies. They had little to say to each other, as there was a growing dread that the group was splitting up, no one completely sure what course of action anyone was considering. Sia had left the others to gather more firewood. In truth, she needed to be alone, to make her decision in the quiet of the forest. Meanwhile, the tired warriors sat clustered near the fire.

Morstar broke the silence again with a blunt assertion, "Peril be damned, I'm going with him." The others turned to regard the dwarf, who was reclined against a nearby tree trunk. "I can't let him face those shadmar on his own. Truth be told, he's the best friend I've had in many years." The dwarf cast his eyes downward. "I've been a rotten drunk these past years. I was a reckless mercenary and just a plain pain in the arse. Who'd think that gettin' bobbed with cheap ale in a rustic village would be the best damn thing that ever happened to me." He paused, lamenting his traumatic past. "When I saw that elf, battle-worn and weary in that inn, I saw a reflection of my own turmoil. Spending these past few weeks with him has really bolstered my spirits." He chuckled suddenly. "By Rolk's beard, I'd follow that elf into the den of Nuegar himself."

The dwarf stood up and looked at his friends, "This fight made me feel on the true side of justice for the first time in many years. I feel like a soldier again. I'm honored to have fought along all of ye. Ye all are starting to feel like me clan."

"Aye, and to you, clan-brother!" said Bryman as he rose to his feet. He rushed over to the dwarf, bending down and grasping Morstar in a giant bear-hug. The dwarf's legs

218

tried to protest, but he soon gave up, patting the tall warrior on the back as he hung limp. However, he was soon positioned back on the ground, as the dwarf was like a small boulder and even Bryman's strength had trouble elevating him for long. Morstar's face was flushed with embarrassment.

Artemis laughed at the display. "Yes, I too feel as kin," said the ranger, who preferred to remain sitting by the fire, enjoying his pipe. He also reckoned that an embrace from Bryman might crush his spine. "I also intend to join Thes on his search. I would not see our fellowship part ways so soon."

"Then it is I that will bear the divisive news," Svendian added stoically. "I still intend to head to Elienspar."

"Yes," said Artemis, turning to the elf. "I understand your duty to your people." He clasped the elf's shoulder, who was sitting near him. "It is not a parting of the ways. Tis but a hunt from which we will return with tales to share."

Svendian smiled at the ranger. He wished that he had more time to share with Artemis, time to share their knowledge of the forest, ways of hunting and tracking in the wild woods. "Then I will look forward to your return and the stories you shall tell."

Sia returned at that moment, throwing her collected wood onto the fire. The air was still quite chilly as the gray-covered sky let in little warmth and encouraged the breeze to blow. Thes was still sleeping, an absent expression on his face.

The others were eyeing the druidess, seemingly eager to hear what she had decided. Sia quickly caught on, but only smiled at them. She slowly sat down, checking on Thes and tightening his cloak around him. Their eagerness was diminishing their patience.

"Well?" Morstar interjected. "What have ye decided, lass?"

"I have decided to join him," she stated. "He will need my help to confront this evil."

Artemis was puzzled, "Do you know what he searches for?"

"I believe I do," she answered. "There is a sinister presence working with the shadmar. I believe he wishes to find out what that presence is and why it feels so troublesome."

"How do you know this?" Svendian asked her.

"I felt it too. The shadmar sorcerers command a dark power. It is like no magic I have known. It scares me. Yet… I will not yield to fear."

"Ha! Such courage in these elves," Bryman exclaimed. Sia simply smiled to the warrior, appreciating the compliment. Truth was, in the company of Thes and his friends Sia did not feel she had much to fear. She already was more than confident in her ability to defend herself. More so, these new friends were some of the most capable warriors she had ever met. Thes's cosmopolitan approach to magic was remarkable and she was certain that they'd soon understand whatever dark force was at work. Perhaps then, she could fulfill her dreams and travel the world with Thes, free from these burdens.

"Then we have all decided," Svendian said sadly. "It is time for me to go. My legs must take me far yet this day."

The aged soldier stood up and stretched. He then embraced each of his companions, except for Thes, who was still fast asleep. He wished them good fortune on their quest saying his final farewells. The elf then hefted his small bag, grabbed his sheathed sword and unstrung bow, and disappeared like a shadow into the forest.

"Well, I suppose we wait," said Morstar, looking down at the sleeping wizard. Bryman grumbled something

220

unintelligible. The dwarf turned to him, "If ye want something to do, ye can gather more firewood. Put that axe of yours to good use."

Bryman nodded. "Aye, fine. But my axe takes offense spilling sap rather than blood." As the warrior set out to gather more wood, Artemis was ensuring the fire stayed warm and strong. Sia was taking the moment to look over Thes's abdomen, ensuring that his wound was healing properly.

"How're our food rations lookin'?" the dwarf asked Artemis. He pulled out his small leather flask, looking at its emptiness in dismay.

"Not so great," the man answered. "We lost most of what we had at the village. I would guess we shall need to forage for supplies if we expect to live more than a day." He stood up and reached for his bow. "I'll see what I can find, but I doubt there will be much game out there in this weather."

"Head to the southeast," said Sia to the ranger. "There is a small marsh where deer like to gather. If you are lucky, there will be a final crop of berries there as well."

The ranger nodded as he headed into the woods. Sia got up and headed into the woods herself, looking for acorns and other tree-nuts. Morstar took over tending the fire.

An hour had passed and the others were still away from the camp. Bryman had returned a few times to drop piles of wood. He seemed to be enjoying himself, venting his frustration on chopping logs. Thes stirred and awoke, finding Morstar tending the fire in deep thought.

"Hail, friend," said the elf as he sat up slowly.

"Greetings, elf. How are ye feeling?"

"I feel rested, yet my body is still sore. Where are the others?"

The dwarf told the elf about Svendian's departure and the whereabouts of the other companions. He also told the elf that the rest of them intended to follow him on his mission.

"So, what're our next steps, elf?" the dwarf asked.

"I think we should return to Artemis's glade. I believe the shadmar are operating closer to that area."

"Aye, makes sense," agreed Morstar. "We ran into walking patrols in that region. They would want to avoid any surprise attacks. If they had the power to transport themselves with magic, they would have little need for patrols anywhere else."

"It is also the area they struck first. I imagine they have been sweeping their attacks slowly westward."

"Do ye have an idea where they are striking from?"

"I believe they are further north and east than I anticipated, near the mountains."

"Not in the mountains!" the dwarf stated incredulously. "If they were any deeper in the mountains, they'd be in Kalavar."

"Not quite that far, dwarf-friend. Yet, perhaps not too far off. Do you know your history? Particularly concerning the end of the war between both our people, the Elven-Dwarven Wars?"

The dwarf thought for a moment. "Only the tales told in taverns, t'was many ages ago."

"The old shadmar kingdom once dominated these eastern forests. It is said they had a fortress at the root of the mountains to the east; it was the seat of their kingdom. In lore, it is written that this fortress was destroyed at the end of the civil war, before their banishment from the surface. But perhaps…"

"…it's been restored?" the dwarf muttered, finishing the elf's statement.

222

"Yes. That is what I believe. It is written that the fortress Valraen held a great underground city during its peak. Perhaps the shadmar dwell within its walls again. I feel a fool for only now thinking of this possibility."

"Wouldn't ye and Artemis have spotted such a fortification when you flew over the trees?"

"We did not search so close to the mountains. In addition, it may be that the surface portions of the fortification are truly destroyed and remain unseen from above the forest's canopy. Perhaps, they merely operate out of the lower portions, using their magic to travel to and fro."

Morstar was concerned by these possibilities. "What do ye intend to do then?"

"I'm not sure. We can at least return to the comforts of Artemis's glade and take advantage of his remaining stores while we consider our options."

The others returned shortly thereafter. Bryman had chopped enough wood to last for a few days. Sia had filled her cloak with numerous nuts, herbs, and edible greens. She heaved the large bounty into the camp. Thes and Mortstar helped her sort the contents into various small sacks and bags. Artemis then returned, bringing a half-dozen large forest-rabbits and a small bag of over-ripe berries.

The adventurers helped prepare what food they could for their journey. They roasted the nuts and smoked the thin slices of meat over the fire. Thes told the others what he had told to Morstar earlier, explaining his desire to return to Artemis's hidden glade.

"Do you believe that place is safe?" Artemis asked.

"I am not sure," replied Thes. "I do not believe there is any place that is safe anymore in this part of the forest."

"True enough," agreed Morstar.

"But we will at least have food and shelter there."

"When do we leave?" asked Bryman, eager to be moving. He was pacing around the campfire, axe in hand.

"As soon as our provisions are ready," said the wizard.

It wasn't long before the nuts were sufficiently softened and the tender rabbit cuts sufficiently dehydrated for the journey. They packed their provisions and gathered their few possessions.

During the bustle of the preparation, Thes approached Sia away from the others.

"I'm glad you are coming with me," he said as he took her hand. Sia turned to him, her slight blush accentuated by her smile. "I only pray that I am not leading you to your death."

"I do not fear death," she stated, looking into his blue eyes. "Were it not for your coming here, I would have burned in my village with no knowledge of the dangers."

Thes tried to say something, but then closed his mouth, finding the words hard to vocalize. He looked to the ground to hide his eyes from her gaze.

"What is it?" she asked.

"I'm... I'm... sorry," he said. "I'm sorry for accusing you of bewitching me. You have brought a stirring in my heart that I have not known in so many years. My heart has awakened from years of slumber and I do not know how to listen to its desires."

Sia reached out, touching his cheek, pulling his gaze back to her eyes. She smiled at him as their brows come together. She whispered, "Listen to it, Thes. This feeling is real."

Thes looked deeply into her eyes as his heart thumped in his chest.

"Kiss 'er already, elf!" Morstar said, grinning at them from the side. The two elves turned their head to find the dwarf watching them. Embarrassment washed over them as they realized their intimate moment was rather a public affair. Despite the intrusion, Thes caressed the back of Sia's neck and drew her in, kissing her passionately. Sia was surprised, but soon kissed him back, losing herself in his embrace.

As they drew back, the two of them were lifted up into the air as a set of large burly arms grasped each of them. They found Bryman hefting them aloft in one of his bear-hugs.

"Welcome to the clan, lass!" the man bellowed as he put them back to the ground.

"Aye, tis a fine fellowship we have here," Morstar said.

"Then let us be away to certain doom," Artemis added light-heartedly.

The adventurers then set off on their journey to the glade.

(17) Rebels and Slaves

The dark caverns of the compost caves could hardly be called homely or comfortable. Yet, the numerous days of hard labor and whispered conspiracy brought a curious enjoyment to Kinrithir. The shadmar had to do his best to hide his inner hope and excitement as he continued to work diligently, his face a mask of despair and depression. The number of conspirators were growing with each day as the message was passed on through the ranks of slaves.

Kinrithir had not spoken to Kryther at all since they laid out their plan together. He could only hope that everything was going well. He took the infrequent winks and nods he received from various slaves as they passed each other in the dark caverns as a sign that things were going well. He had been able to enlist the help of every slave who happened to be resting next to him in the sleeping caverns. He could only hope that Kryther and Edras were as fortunate as he had been. If the other two had been as convincing as he had, he reckoned that they now had a majority of the slaves in the conspiracy. They would be ready to strike soon.

That night, Kinrithir had just finished a difficult pair of negotiations, recruiting a sadistic goblin on one side, and a reluctant wood elf on the other. The tired shadmar was finally laying down to the hard stone for some much needed sleep. He then heard a yell down the cavern.

"Traitors! Traitors!" screamed the male voice. Kinrithir sat up quickly, looking desperately down the tunnel for the source of the shouting. In the shadows of a small alcove, he saw a scrawny shadmar vainly pulling on his chains as he roared again in fear and anger. Apprehensive and shocked with eyes wide, Kryther sat next to the bellowing slave. Kryther was panicking, not sure what to do about the shouting shadmar.

The slave continued to bellow, "Traitors! Friends of surface elves! Vile traitors!"

Kryther's eyes caught Kinrithir and the two half-brothers looked at each other for a moment. Kryther then nodded. He slowly sat up, edging closer to the screaming shadmar, whose attention was focused on the two guards that were unenthusiastically peering down the tunnel with sleepy eyes. Kryther then pulled hard on the shadmar's leg, knocking the shadmar to the ground. This action also slackened the length of chain between them considerably. Kryther grabbed the chain and looped it around the panicked shadmar's neck. The screaming ceased instantly and was replaced by gargled gasps for air.

The guards, seeing the fighting between the two slaves, rushed into the tunnel while brandishing their clubs. By the time they reached Kryther, the other shadmar was a breathless corpse. The guards then began beating Kryther with their clubs. Kryther vainly tried to protect his head from the blows, but the guards were unrelenting.

Kinrithir could not watch the display. He was glad that Kryther was able to save the conspiracy from the bigoted loyalist. However, he could not watch his half-brother be sacrificed for the action. Kinrithir crouched up as best he could, given the length of his chains, and tried shouting down the corridor to those nearest Kryther.

"It is time! Let us free ourselves!" he shouted.

The ruthless beating that Kryther was enduring did not invite other conspirators to leap to action. However, a green-skinned goblin near the violence stood up to his full three-foot height and growled at the shadmar guards. Then a half-elf nearby crouched up and began chanting for action. A few thumar soon did the same. The cries of outrage and violence began to echo down the tunnel as the slaves began to rise and shout. They were defiant and angry. The revolt was primed.

228

The two guards looked up from the bloody and bruised Kryther. The sight of the angry slaves surrounding them brought an uneasiness. The long tunnel was filled with crouched elves and orcs, standing goblins, all shouting and threatening them. Before the guards could take solace in knowing the slaves were all still chained to each other and the ground, their heads were slammed together from behind. The guards had been too close to the orc next to Kryther. The green-skinned orc had leapt up and tore into the guards. He was a bulky, extremely strong figure and used his weight to drag the guards to the ground. He soon had pulled the guards by their feet, flinging one back to the wall where some thunmar soon pounced on him. The other guard he pulled closer squeezing the shadmar's neck with a sadistic pleasure. The two guards were down.

The two copper-skinned thunmar fumbled for the guard's keys. They then unlocked themselves and started down the sleeping cavern, unlocking all the surface elves they came across. The burly orc, after snapping the neck of the shadmar guard, grabbed his key and unlocked himself. He then looked about, unlocking all those around him. The thunmar had unlocked their kin next to Kinrithir but had skipped over the shadmar.

"Wait!" cried Kinrithir. "We are all in this together!" His words paused the thunmar for a moment. They hesitated, looking at the shadmar, seemingly weighing their trust.

Then the burly orc came to the shadmar and unlocked him. He growled at the thunmar, who stepped back, but otherwise held their ground.

"Thank you," Kinrithir said to the orc, using the Nomen tongue.

"Together," the orc grunted in broken Nomen. The orc sneered at the copper-skinned elves before turning around to help release more slaves. The thunmar, either overcoming their distrust and racial predispositions, or not wanting to seem more callous than an orc, turned around and began unlocking all those nearby.

Meanwhile, Kinrithir had rushed directly to Kryther. He found that Edras was there, doing her best to check his wounds. Kryther gazed up at the sulmar and his half-brother with a dizzied expression. One of his eyes was blackened and swollen shut. A few teeth were missing from his bloodied gums and his body was covered with dark bruises.

"Are you okay, brother?" asked Kinrithir.

"I'll live…" the shadmar muttered before spitting blood to the cavern floor.

"Perhaps we can find healing for him later," Edras said hurriedly, "We must gather our forces and strike at the entrance. If we can hold the entrance to the cavern we will have won the day."

"Yes, go forth, brother," Kryther insisted. "I'll follow when I am able."

Kinrithir was hesitant to leave his half-brother in this state, but he knew that he had to help organize the freed slaves if they would have any chance of keeping their momentum.

Many of the slaves were rushing to flee upwards, out of the compost caverns. Kinrithir and Edras ran to the front of the caverns, shouting in both the elven and Nomen tongues, telling those attempting to leave to stop and return. Thankfully, the burly orc was already standing guard at the top of the long ramp to the high catwalks. He held another shadmar guard by the throat and nonchalantly tossed the corpse to the ground below. The fleeing slaves at the front of the bunch, a few goblins, dared not try to pass the orc. Edras and Kinrithir clamored through the crowd and approached the orc.

"You fight bravely, warrior. What is your name?" the shadmar asked.

"Owkba of Okgrukk" he said proudly.

230

"Your tenacity makes dragons quiver beneath your strength," Edras said using the guttural language of the orcs. The compliment was one of the greatest among the orc tribes known to the sulmar. Owkba grinned and bowed slightly to Edras.

Before Kinrithir could ask what she had said to him, Edras pushed Kinrithir past the orc who continued to guard the top of the catwalk. The two elves went around on the catwalk, looking down to the gathering of slaves below them.

"Fellow slaves," Kinrithir shouted in the Nomen tongue. "Freedom is not quite within our reach. We must put aside our differences and work together if we are to see the sky anytime soon. The guards will be found missing before long and they will send soldiers to investigate. We must be ready to hold back the tide of warriors and stand our ground as one. After the first group of soldiers have been dealt with, we'll have time to strike upward and claim the farming and mining caverns." Roars of anticipation were growing below Kinrithir.

"We will find more allies than foes above us! The shadmar farmers and miners are little more than slaves themselves! We must gather their forces to join us and end the war that has brought us all to this torture and misfortune."

"To death with the shadmar!" shouted an enraged thunmar among the crowd.

Kinrithir frowned. "You are right to be angry, thunmar. However, it is not all shadmar that deserve your anger. There is but one shadmar that deserves your wrath! The vile sorcerer that has enslaved and manipulated my people. We will start this day as slaves, but we could end this day as rebels and heroes. We can put an end to the long war between the elven people! We can put an end to this mad sorcerer's conquest!"

There was now much frenzied shouting among the elves. The few shadmar were enthusiastic about putting an end to Delrith and his corrupt leadership. The surface elves were eager to see the coming war end before it expanded further westward.

Owkba turned to the shadmar, "What of me and my kind? What you do with orcs?"

"Fair question, Owkba," Edras answered in Orcish. She turned to the crowd to address the men, goblins, and orcs, "Those among you who are enemies of both surface elves and underground shadmar, if you aid in this effort, not only will you ensure your own freedom, you have my promise as a Royal Knight of Queen Alilledra that you will find safe passage to the edge of elven lands."

More enthusiastic shouts echoed from below from the humans, goblins, and orcs of the slave band. Kinrithir then spotted Kryther leaning near the entrance of the sleeping cavern. His broken-toothed smile was all the encouragement Kinrithir needed.

"Let us fortify this entrance and prepare for our enemies!" Kinrithir shouted. The slaves cheered and climbed up as Owkba opened the way.

An hour later, the freed slaves had built a wall at the entrance of the compost caverns. They had torn down many of the observation catwalks for the required materials. They had also pillaged what few provisions the guards had horded in their quarters, ensuring that everyone had received adequate food and drink. There were about a hundred or so slaves, the majority of which were surface elves (primarily thunmar), with humans being the greatest minority. There were ten goblins, seven orcs, and only five shadmar (including Kryther and Kinrithir) among the band.

Kinrithir learned that many of the surface elves had been captured during recent raids and attacks. The shadmar had no idea that Delrith was already waging war on the surface, gathering slaves from the fallen elven villages. There were surface elves from Escailar, Diiera, Cwendilin, and Harpien. Many of these pour souls had watched their family members and children slaughtered before them. Many of them had little to live for and an equally dismal desire to fight for freedom. However, the thunmar from Harpien seemed to be the least discouraged and most war-ready of the bunch.

The rebels were fortunate that the soldiers had not yet sent a patrol down to the lowest caverns. Their wall was in place and the former slaves were armed with clubs, ready to defend themselves. Kinrithir knew he now had little time to continue their plan. After ensuring that Kryther was cared for, the shadmar was hoisted over the makeshift wall and was sneaking his way towards the mining caverns.

The shadmar clamored his way up the rising cavern tunnels, doing his best to stick near the cool walls to hide his body heat. He came upon a fork in the tunnel. He knew that one way headed to the long mushroom caverns where the compost was hauled. He could hear the sound of large lizards scrambling about, likely bearing shadmar farmers as they tended the numerous rows of well-tended fruiting mushrooms and slow-growing red-fan plants. The bright light of torches shimmered down that corridor. The light of the torches was essential to aid the red-fan's growth.

The sound of two sets of feet could be heard ahead, coming down the other fork from the mining caverns. Kinrithir threw himself into a small alcove in the broken rock, praying that he did not make too much noise in his desperation. Two shadmar, who did not falter in their movements, were heading down the tunnel towards the farming cavern, their conversation unrelenting. Kinrithir breathed a sigh of relief and continued up towards the mining tunnels.

Kinrithir soon found himself sneaking to the side as he entered the large main cavern where he and Kryther once heard Delrith make devious proclamations of war. The cavern was near empty and Kinrithir suspected that the miners were working in the tunnels. There were only two guards near the entrance of the mining tunnels. They seemed to be engaged in conversation and not otherwise paying much attention to their surroundings. However, the large echoic cavern only had the distant sounds of pickaxes on stone to hide Kinrithir's presence. The shadmar sat behind a few clay pots in the corner, waiting for a moment to present itself.

After many minutes went by, the guards seemed to be reacting to something in the mining tunnels. They turned and went down the tunnels. Kinrithir leapt to action and scurried his way across the wide cavern and up the catwalk towards Gharin's quarters. The shadmar slipped through the door, finding an empty dining area. There was a simple stone table and bench built into the sidewall and a dozen or so clay pots in the other corner. There was a hanging cloth dividing the room from the next.

Kinrithir approached the cloth quietly and slowly pulled it back. The shadmar found a sharp steel dagger pointing at him from the other side. The gray-haired Gharin was standing firm with the dagger pointed at Kinrithir's throat.

"Watch yourself, lad. Let's not do anything hasty," the old shadmar said with a sneer.

"Gharin, please," Kinrithir begged. "I do not come to harm you. I simply wish to speak to you."

"Shouldn't you be mining with the others?" the old shadmar remarked, his blade still firm.

"Gharin 'Grimblade', I am not who you may think I am."

234

The old shadmar seemed shocked for a second, but his blade did not falter.

"No one has called me by that name in many years. Who are you?" his voice was now more curious than angry.

"I am Kinrithir Velmir, son of Thirinar. One of the final two of our House."

Gharin dropped his blade, it clattered on the smoothed stone floor. "House Velmir?! It cannot be." The aged shadmar scrambled for his bed behind him, sitting himself down. He looked up at Kinrithir, who was simply standing at the doorway with his hands out in peace.

"It is so. Kryther and I yet live."

"Kryther?!" he repeated, somewhat shocked by the revelation. "I haven't seen that boy in ages. How is this possible?"

Kinrithir sat down next to the old shadmar and took his hand. "I don't have time to explain everything right now, Master Grimblade. I know you once served my father and helped lead the armed resistance in the civil war. I simply want to know if you still hold your allegiance to democracy and the goals of House Velmir, or have you been beaten into submission and serve House Niedrie?"

"Hardly," the old solider huffed. "I've always been with the resistance, young Kinrithir. After the war, and the destruction of the caverns, Delrith offered me a proposal. He wanted me to lead his future armies and bring glory on the surface. I refused. I could not fight for such a dishonorable man. So, they took away my dignity and sent me to lead the miners instead."

"It is good your heart has not swayed to him."

"Never. Thankfully, I was too popular among the common people." Kinrithir knew this to be true. Gharin was a decorated general of the shadmar military. He rose up through the ranks without the benefit of enrolling in the nobleman's war academy. He was the only known commoner given special dispensation to join the ranks of officers, eventually rising to the top of their ranks.

The old shadmar continued, "My popularity kept me from death, but I've been nothing but Delrith's pawn down here. Each week he increases the mining quota, threatening to kill miners that fail to reach their numbers. I have been cooking the books for many cycles now, distributing the amounts between miners to keep the impression that all were working well. Although, this week, I am sure we will not reach the quota. I expect Delrith is expecting it."

Kinrithir clenched his fist, the deviousness of the shadmar patriarch angered him.

"Anyway," Gharin continued, "What in the darkness of Morriga are you doing here? Have you been hiding among the survivors this entire time?"

Kinrithir nodded to the old general, "Yes, you might recall the names Kinrir and Kryn from your logs."

The old shadmar laughed aloud. "You've been under my nose this entire time! Why reveal yourself now?"

"I must apologize for not making ourselves known sooner, Master Grimblade. Kryther and I were too apprehensive about revealing our identities to anyone. And truthfully, I wasn't certain about your allegiance after the war."

"So, what is this all about? What's going on?"

"Rebellion," Kinrithir stated.

"Rebellion? Are you crazy, boy? We can't just start a rebellion." The old solider seemed uncomfortable, his eyes darting towards the entrance of his quarters.

"It has already begun, sir. As you might also recall, Kinrir and Kryn were sent to the compost caves for murdering a nobleman. We have now roused those slaves and have an angry band of surface elves, humans, and others waiting to strike."

236

"My goodness! What have you gotten yourself into? Just like your father, he was always leaping before he looked." The old soldier stood up and began pacing in the small chamber. "You have really gotten yourself into a mighty bad situation. What do you want from me?"

"I need your help rousing the workers to join the rebellion. My band of former slaves will help take out the soldiers in these caverns, but I need you to motivate the miners and farmers and help lead them to victory against our overlords. They will listen to you."

Gharin shook his head. "Nah, Delrith has them in his hand. I'm just the old fool who tells them to keep working, spewing hopeful nonsense."

"Then don't be Gharin the Taskmaster anymore. Be Gharin 'Grimblade', the People's General, the war-hero of the Lake Wars. Be the person every one of those people down there once looked up to. You were a symbol of hope. Living proof that grit and determination can allow someone to ascend social rank. A true hero."

Gharin bit his lip. His eyes were hard on Kinrithir. "I know what you're doing, boy."

Kinrithir smiled. "Sometimes the motivator needs motivation."

The old soldier sighed heavily. "Fine," he muttered. "Gather the slaves. The second civil war shall begin this day."

Kinrithir embraced the general like a father, then raced off out of his quarters. As the shadmar quietly stepped out onto the catwalk, the two guards below looked up at him. They shouted at him as he raced down the stairs. The guards chased after the fleeing shadmar who was now at a full sprint down the corridors towards the compost caverns. The guards continued to give chase, likely assuming it was simply a miner or farmer trying to avoid work duty.

When Kinrithir reached the makeshift gate, he stopped and turned around. A fellow rebel on the other side threw the shadmar a wooden rod and Kinrithir brandished it as the guards came rushing down the corridor. They halted and stared at the strange barricade, trying to figure out what was going on. Then a hole was opened in the side of the wall and a horde of furious slaves came pouring out, brandishing clubs and staves of reclaimed wood. Kinrithir screamed a warcry and joined the chase. The two guards, slowed down by their heavy leather armor, could not escape the quick feet of the thulmar. A score of the thunmar soon reached them and leapt upon them, dragging them to the ground. Kinrithir did not want to watch what would follow.

The shadmar turned back to the compost caves, looking for Kryther. He soon found his half-brother sitting at the guard's table with Edras and Owkba. Kryther still looked poorly, but the fact he was sitting upright was encouraging. Kinrithir motioned to them. They each got up to join him in the march upward. Kinrithir grabbed his half-brother's arm to help him walk beside him.

"Gharin is with us," Kinrithir told them.

"Ole' Grimblade. I'm glad he hasn't lost his bluster," Kryther said with a gapped smile.

"I hope this friend is trustworthy," Edras stated cynically. "The last thing we need is a score of armed guards blocking our exit."

"Gharin is with us to the end," Kinrithir reiterated.

They then marched up towards the farming caverns where they found the rest of the slaves waiting for them. For a random band of strangers, the slaves were surprisingly working well together and staying true to Kinrithir's orders.

They then marched into the farming cavern where they had to kill a few guards and a few farmers who could not be convinced to consort with surface elves. However, Kinrithir was able to at least convince the farmers to stop

238

their work and follow them to the mining caverns where he promised they could choose to participate or not. And so, the slaves and farmers marched into the wide mining cavern where Gharin was already standing high over the gathering of miners. The guards were tied up and gagged in the corner. The door on the upper portions of the chamber, that lead up into the old fortress was barred with barrels, large pots, and pieces of furniture. Kinrithir, Edras, Kryther, and Owkba climbed to the catwalk to stand with Gharin.

The old general stood tall over the crowd, brandishing a guard's spear. He no longer seemed like a stale old man, but a warrior and hero of the people. He nodded to Kinrithir, expecting the charismatic, young shadmar to warm up the crowd.

"My friends," Kinrithir began. "The time has come to shed the veil of lies that has been placed over us. To free ourselves from tyranny and injustice. We have all suffered much since the war that divided our people, since the destruction of our home city. We were then afraid. We made a choice that we now regret. We selected a leader that does not have our best interests in mind."

"Traitor!" shouted a shadmar miner from the crowd.

"Yes!" responded Kirithir with vigor. "I am a traitor! I am a traitor to my own morals, to my own sense of being. I have given my silent consent to bestow power upon an individual who is not worthy of it. I have done nothing while my friends and family suffered under the rule of a selfish tyrant. I am a traitor, because I was once afraid." He paused as silence came over the crowd.

"But I am afraid no more!" he shouted. "Together we are strong! Together we can rebel against this tyranny. Together we can forge a new realm built on the peace and democracy my father once fought for. I am Kinrithir Velmir. Many of you once followed my father's call to justice. I ask that you pick up your arms again." Now the murmuring of voices was growing in the crowd.The shock of the nobleman's heritage spread, but they were obviously hesitate and fearful for action.

"Fear not, my friends. We may have lost the first war, but we cannot lose the second. This time our very livelihoods are in jeopardy. The life we have here is but a ploy in Delrith's plot. As we work to mine the iron and forge the steel for that mad sorcerer's war, he is burning and slaughtering the homes of our surface kin."

"To hell with the surface elves!" screamed another shadmar. There was a chorus of agreement among many of the miners.

"And what have they done to you?!" Kinrithir screamed back rhetorically. "Have they invaded your villages, burned your homes to the ground, slaughtered your friends and family? Because that is exactly what we have been doing to them! We have been forging the weapons and feeding the soldiers that have been out killing numerous, innocent surface elves. We are as guilty as the blades that cut the necks. These slaves here," he pointed to the gathering of slaves in the corner of the chamber. "They are victims of our war. Delrith has convinced us they are our enemies, when they could be our allies and friends. They could help our people return to the surface, give us solace after our years of exile. They could offer forgiveness for the crimes of our ancestors and call an end to the long pointless feud that has been used to manipulate us for centuries!" The crowd was quiet again, seemingly thinking about the possibility.

"Delrith promised us the surface, but we do not have to take it by force. Let us show the people of the surface that the shadmar are more than the noble-born raiders that terrorize their villages. We are a people with useful skills, high morals, and a benign community. We are a people that value hard work, loyalty, and taking care of each other. This

240

is how I would like to be known to this new world above us. Not as the bloodthirsty raiders they would have us be."

"Let me ask you, friends. When is the last time you weren't being riled up with racist chants or told to focus on the future? It has been far too long, friends. They want you to forget your dismal present and the tortured past. They want you to keep working and toiling until every last bit of strength is drained from you."

As Kinrithir continued to speak from the heart, he began to remember things that had been forgotton. It was as if a spell had been broken over the memories, releasing them into his mind. Unbeknownst to Kinrithir, Delrith's magical influence over all the shadmar was weakening.

Tears began to swell around Kinrithir's eyes. A sad and prominent memory came over him. He wiped his eyes and continued his speech. "When is the last time you saw your children? Remember when they were taken from us, years ago. When we came to Valraen we were told there wasn't enough room for the children in the working caverns. We were promised we would see them regularly. Let me ask you, when is the last time you saw them?" Now there were many disgruntled voices among the crowd. The shadmar could now remember this fact.

"They have taken our children. They will train them as soldiers to wage a war that benefits no one here among us. Do we want to be complicit to this madness? Or do we want to fight to free our friends, our families, and our children?" Shouts began to grow among the crowd, they were finally embracing the rebellion. The spell over their minds had been shattered.

"We do not have to join Delrith's war on the surface. There is another way! I stand here with a knight who speaks for the leader of the surface elves. She says that her queen does not wish for war with our people. If we can overthrow this bloodthirsty tyrant, the monster that has subverted our minds and taken our families from us, they will offer us a new home. We will have won the surface just as was promised to us. Except we will have done it ourselves, without owing fealty to anyone." There were many cheers.

"You do not have to join us in this fight, I only ask that you stay out of our way. But if you do choose to join this rebellion, you will have fought for your own freedom and a real chance at a new life for you and your families." There were now a chorus of shadmar eager to join in the rebellion, shouting for Delrith's head. Kinrithir had finally broken through and reached the hearts and minds of the workers.

"We shall not fight alone or leaderless. We have the great People's General, the indomitable Gharin Grimblade to lead our rebellion!"

Gharin raised his spear high to an over-exuberant chorus of shouts and cheers. He stepped forward and was prepared to begin a rousing speech. He looked down on the crowd of miners, farmers, and former slaves. It was a ramshackle bunch of unseasoned and untrained workers. The general knew they would be up against formidable soldiers and completely outmatched in skill. However, he also knew that the folk he saw below him had far greater numbers and a much superior reason to fight.

(18) The Search

The chill overcast gave way to a cold rain over the next few days. Thes and his friends traveled through the woods, cloaks wrapped around them as a light, but steady rain drizzled down. Their fingers were white and trembling and the wetness ensured constant discomfort. In the evenings, they even risked small fires to help warm their chilled bones. By the time they neared the glade, their spirits were a bit strained and their bodies exhausted.

They did not elaborate on their plans in any detail. Thes seemed constantly in deep thought, ignoring the grumblings of his companions. ia was the only one able to rouse him out of his contemplation, although she only succeeded in extracting a few sweetly whispered words each night.

Late on the third day of travel, they finally came to the top of the stone ridge, where the small stream poured down to the pond. Hidden steps led down the side of the cliff to the glade below. The stone steps were slick with the rain and they had to be careful as they climbed down. To their relief, the place seemed undisturbed since they left it weeks before. Thes and Sia worked together to add protective enchantments on the area. Though they had no assurances, they hoped their efforts would be enough to stop the shadmar from suddenly appearing upon them.

Artemis checked on the small cavern's stores, and much to Morstar's pleasure, there were still a couple casks of berry-wine remaining. They built a large fire down near the pond, less worried about attracting attention with the magical wards in place. They were happy to be able to thoroughly warm their bodies and dry their wet clothes. They passed around the ranger's wine as Morstar crushed soaked acorns with light taps of his hammer. Sia used the crushed inner meats to mold small flatbreads that soon baked on the hot coals. Artemis crushed the over-ripe berries they carried into a jam-like spread to smear on the bread. Combined with the spicy herbs and bits of smoke meat, it was a delightful meal.

The group then sat around the fire, sipping on the wine. They were resting against large logs and rocks, lounging in the warming, dry heat of the fire. The rain had ceased and the night sky was relatively clear, the stars shining bright above them. They were looking up, quietly enjoying the serenity above them.

Thes was again thinking deeply about his plans to unveil the shadmar's location. He was eager to learn more about the location of the ancient fortress of Valraen. He unfortunately did not recall any details about the locale and wished he had access to his old books to aid his memory.

"Tomorrow I will fly to the ruins of Escailar," he said to the others suddenly, dispelling the relative silence.

"Why would ye want to go back there?" Morstar asked, somewhat worried.

"I had books of ancient lore that might aid our search. If they survived the fire, they might help me figure out the shadmar's location."

"Then, we'll go with you," the dwarf stated.

"No," replied Thes. "I wish to make the journey quickly and I dare not try to fly all of us again."

Morstar grumbled. Though he could not refute the elf's reasoning, he still did not like the idea of the elf going there alone.

"Then I will go with you," said Sia. She was lying in the wizard's arms, comfortably wrapped in her cloak with the back of her head upon his chest. She looked up at him with a pointed expression that implied there would be no refusal.

244

Thes smiled at her determination. "Alright," he said. "It should not take us long."

Morstar seemed to be eased by this decision.

"I am curious," began Artemis, "what do you think the shadmar are involved with? What is this dark energy you spoke of?" The ranger was eager to finally get some answers from the pensive elf.

"I am unsure," replied Thes. "It is a dark presence, something not of this world." Sia shivered in the wizard's arms and he held her tighter for reassurance. "I honestly don't know what it is we face. It is something that I cannot fathom. Yet, I must seek it out."

"Your words confuse more than instruct," the ranger responded.

"Dark magic," Sia said to the ranger.

"Yes," agreed Thes.

The others were a bit uneasy about the situation. Magic was a strange and foreign concept to them. Even the time they had spent with Thes and Sia, seeing the miracles they performed, did not help them understand the unseen world to which the two elves were ultimately attuned.

"Some believe there are worlds beyond the mortal realm we reside," Thes began. "All cultures have tales of gods and goddesses that reside in mythical realms beyond the stars. Many of these worlds are believed to be benign paradises, while others are wretched hellscapes. I fear the magic that the shadmar work originates from one of those dark worlds. They do not commune with the natural spirits of our realm, as Sia and I do, but of entities of a more sinister world."

"How is such a communion possible?" asked the ranger.

Thes shook his head. "I do not know. Ancient stories say that Enelis was somehow cut off from the influence of the realms beyond, protected from such interference in the earliest days of the world. The mythologies of elves, men, and dwarves all share such a story. Perhaps now you know why I am so troubled by this. It is not just the shadmar and their mortal armies I fear. If they have breached the mystical protection of our world, all of Enelis may be at risk from otherworldly influence."

Artemis was skeptical. "How do you know that these stories are more than that? Can you be sure there is truth to these ancient tales?"

"No," the wizard replied solemnly. "I cannot be sure of anything. All I do know, is that Sia and I have felt a strange alien essence in the shadmar's magic. A malign entity that both of us have never encountered on Enelis."

"Yes," added Sia. "I have attuned myself with Enelis and the natural world. Their magic is not of Enis's creation."

Morstar was troubled. It had little to do with the dire news he just received, rather, the dwarf was more troubled with what Thes intended to do about it. "Then what is your quest, elf?" he asked in a disturbed tone. "To stop the shadmar from using this dark magic?"

"Perhaps," Thes responded sincerely. "I at least wish to understand what is going on here. To see if there is indeed truth to the ancient tales."

"The War of the Ancestors may be upon us," Bryman chimed in.

"What is that?" Artemis asked the warrior.

"The War of the Ancestors. Tis' a tale told among the Noradrie about the end times. When the walls of this world are shattered and the world of our ancestors connects with this one. When the worlds of light and darkness connect with the mortal realm. Mortal men and the spirits of ancient warriors will unite in a grand, final war against all the evils of the dark worlds."

"Sounds rather bleak," the ranger replied.

246

"Nah, we Noradrie rather look forward to the glory of that final battle."

Artemis simply rolled his eyes. The ranger was beginning to find Noradric culture particularly single-minded.

"I hope it does not come to that," said Thes. "We shall have to break this riddle soon or the Noradric prophecy may come to pass."

"Don't be ridiculous!" interjected Artemis. "The end of the world?"

"I don't really know what could happen," the wizard reiterated. "Prophesy or not, if there really is a protection upon this world from the influence of dark forces and the shadmar are in danger of breaching it, it could truly mean the end of our world."

Silence ensued as the gravity of that statement resonated with the group.

The rest of the night, they spoke little before piling into Artemis's small cabin to sleep. Sia and Thes opted to stay and sleep near the warm coals of the fire. The two lovers wrapped tightly in Sia's thick fur cloak.

The next morning, the two elves took to the air, soaring across the autumn-colored leaves towards the ruins of Escailar. It took them some time to reach the devastated area of the forest, however, it was obvious when they were near. Burned piles of ash and charred wood piled around bare and scorched trunks. Many blackened skeletons could be seen sticking out of the ruins here and there. The sight was bone-chilling to the wizard. The elves landed on the edge of the ruins.

As Thes viewed the destroyed village, he could feel a surge of emotion trying to crawl up his throat, but he swallowed hard in an attempt to push the feeling away. Then a soft hand rested on his back between his shoulder blades.

247

The resistance was broken, his sorrow swelled up like a torrential storm. Thes dropped to his knees, sobbing. Sia knelt down beside him, wrapping her arms around the wizard. She withheld her own tears.

"It's okay," she whispered to him. "Let out the weight of your sorrows. Let it be free." Those words unburdened the elf and Thes let out the pain of his loss. His sobs went on for a few moments as the druidess caressed the back of his head. At last, Thes looked up to Sia and embraced her. He stood up and wiped the final tears from his eyes. He did feel unburdened, as if the weight of his guilt had been taken off of his shoulders. He looked back out to the carnage of the burned village. He still felt sorrow, seeing the ruins before him. Yet, the emotional weight no longer overwhelmed him.

"There," he said, pointing to the scorched remnants of a shack still clinging to a great blackened tree trunk. Sia looked out through the ruins and found the shack. It was odd that it seemed to be the only dwelling still aloft and relatively intact. The wooden structure was of a natural timber, grown from the side of the massive trunk, much like a gigantic version of the old knots seen on ancient trees. Most of the tree was scorched and ruined, but the area near the shack had perfectly preserved sections striped with burned and broken sections.

The wizard grabbed the druidess hand and they quickly soared towards the high building. Thes landed gingerly, ensuring the structure would hold his weight. It groaned a moment under the pressure of the two elves, but otherwise stood still.

Thes was still a bit wary, "Better stay close to me."

"Always," Sia replied with a loving smile.

The two elves carefully treaded across the shack. Their eyes were transfixed on the uneven scorch marks, as some places seemed nearly untouched by the flames. Thes walked over to his old desk where a handful of books were piled up. Some of the books were burned beyond legibility. Other books, however, seemed to be in good condition.

"What is going on here?" Sia asked the wizard.

Thes only shook his head. He concentrated for a moment, letting his eyes slip into the magical realm. He saw a strange aura of energy surrounding the shack. The magic seems to have been pierced with a few holes, lining up perfectly with the portions of the room that were burned and blackened. The wizard smiled.

"See it?" he asked Sia.

"Yes, it is quite the ward you have created. Yet, it seems you missed a few spots."

Thes laughed. "Not bad for an accidental ward. I had nearly forgotten about it. I had been experimenting with some new spells the day we heard about the shadmar raid. I had acquired a copy of a spell-tome from Goldwall on my latest travels. Many of the spells were so archaically explained that I think I had foiled a few of them in practice. It is a shame the book did not survive." The elf pointed to the scorched tome resting on the center of the desk.

The elf shrugged and carefully pulled out the few books that were in good condition. He carefully searched through them, dusting the ash off the covers. The two searched the nearby bookcase as well, but most of those books had succumbed to the flames. Thankfully, the tome the wizard was seeking, *The Nomen Expansion*, was intact.

Thes untied his cloak and wrapped the books within, tying the ends together into a large parcel. He grasped the heavy bundle, took Sia's hand, and they floated off back towards the hidden glade.

When the elves returned to Artemis's cabin, they found only Morstar chopping some wood by the pond. Bryman and Artemis were off hunting and gathering for the day. The dwarf was glad to see the elves unscathed. He went back to his labor as the two elves sat down near the pond to go over the tomes.

"What is this one?" Sia asked Thes as she picked up a small leather-bound journal.

"You might find some use from that one," he replied. "That is my poor attempt to outline and codify the druidic teachings from when I first learned the ways of the spirits."

The druidess was flipping through the pages of carefully sketched diagrams of hand-movements, intonations, and phrases. "These are fantastic."

"Thanks, it's just an incomplete journal," he said modestly.

"Do you mind if I read through this?"

"Please, do. In fact, you may get more out of those spells than I did. My teacher, Sulaeren, also had an affinity to water." He laughed. "He always said those who were air-minded, like myself, never had the patience for deep magic."

Sia smiled at the wizard, not believing that Thes could have any ineptitudes with magic. The druidess found a comfortable spot to read the detailed spellbook.

Thes pulled out *The Nomen Expansion* and also found a spot to read. Morstar chuckled as he watched the two elves laying back with books in their hands. He wiped the sweat from his brow and returned to chopping the firewood while muttering about 'lazy elves'.

Many hours went by and the sun was near setting. Bryman and Artemis had just returned to the glade. A moderate-sized stag was resting on Bryman's shoulders while Artemis hefted a few bulging sacks. The two shared the tale of the hunt with their comrades as they prepared to skin the beast. They also displayed the sacks of acorns and nuts they gathered.

250

Meanwhile, Thes had scanned through his tome numerous times, but he could not find any significant references to the location of Valraen. He was annoyed that his memory deceived him. The only sections where the fortress was mentioned was in small segments touting what the elf already remembered about the place. There was no mention of location, neither relative or absolute.

Sia, on the other hand, was having much success in learning the spells from Thes's journal. Although she found Thes's approach to magic to be more regimented and orderly than her own, Sia was able to parse the information into her own style. She was also excited to be learning new ways of employing her magical talents. Her previous teachings had mostly centered on the arts of healing and cultural ritual, and she had had no chance to seek out a new teacher after Shihara passed away. She was the only one who knew the druidic tradition among the people of Harpien. Thes's spellbook presented a wonderful new opportunity for Sia.

The druidess was concentrating on one particular spell that seemed rather complex. Its intricate descriptions and extensive diagrams spanned over many pages, describing a complex setup procedure involving a body of water. After Sia read it over carefully, she stood up holding the book out to Thes in a frenzied excitement.

"I found something!" she cried out.

"What? A spell?" Thes asked as he rushed to her side. Sure enough, there on the pages, scrawled in the wizard's own hurried script, was the complex recipe for a powerful divination spell. It involved numerous ingredients and hours of preparation. Thes recalled watching his former mentor, the druid Sulaeren, prepare this ritual as he watched and took notes. The ritual relied deeply on the reflective quality of water, a feature the air-aligned elf never truly mastered. Sia, however, was quite attuned to the spirits of water. If the spell worked as intended, she would be given a vision that may direct them to Valraen and possibly show glimpses of the future.

"This is a fantastic idea," the wizard said with excitement. "I can help with the preparations, but you'll be on your own for the final trance."

"I can do it," she said confidently.

They shared the news with the others, asking them to help clear the area near the pond. They were skeptical at first, especially Bryman who never had much interest in magic, but he helped with the preparations anyway. Thes and Sia had to gather numerous herbs to use in place of the required incense. They dried the leaves carefully by the fire, then crushed and grinded them. Each pile of ground herbs was then placed on top of flat rocks in a circle near the pond.

Sia then sat with her legs crossed in the center of the circle of rocks, looking out over the pond in front of her. She concentrated on the quiet rustling of the leaves above her, trying to block out the other sounds in the glade. She focused her eyes on the surface of the water, gazing at the faint ripples emanating out from the small waterfall. Her body was relaxed and ready. She nodded slowly to Thes, ready for the incoming vision.

Thes hesitantly ignited the ground herbs nearest him, using a snap of his fingers to produce the necessary spark. The smoking herbs released a heavenly aroma that induced a somewhat cloudy feeling over the wizard's mind. Thes, however, concentrated on his task and proceeded to ignite the rest of the herbs on each rock. Sia was then surrounded by a circle of smoking rocks. The strong incense allowed the druidess to give into the magic of the ritual as she continued to gaze at the nearly smooth surface of the water.

The water then began to ripple from the center. Sia no longer could see the small rocks below the surface. Instead, she perceived a faint scene, somewhat distorted by the water's refraction. The scene slowly gained clarity as if

252

a light provided illumination from the underside of the water's surface.

As Sia gazed at the unfolding scene, Thes watched her with concern from outside the inducing vapors of the incense. The druidess's eyes were cloudy with the magical mist of the ritual. Thes could not see any scene unfolding in the waters, only the changing expressions of the druidess as she sat within the smoking circle.

The scene was now clear to Sia. She saw herself as a bird high in the sky. She was soaring above the forest on the high westward winds towards the mountains to the east. She swirled around the white-capped peaks of the mountains before spiraling toward the western roots. The forest was thick at this part and the tendrils of the mountains were barely visible by the undulations of green trees. Sia now dived deep at the root of the mountains, between two long furrows. As the ground rushed towards her, the druidess gasped as her view collided with the ground and her vision contained only blackness. However, her vision was reawakened as she found herself scurrying along the ground of a dark corridor, as if she was now a rodent in some unknown ruin beneath the mountain.

The walls of the corridor were made of well-fitted stone. There was very little illumination, but many sounds could be heard. There were many elf-like figures rushing back and forth in the corridors, hinting at a distant chaos in the tunnels. Sia saw herself quickly rushing down dark tunnels, swirling and twisting through the corridors, as the sounds of battle echoed around her. There were screams of panic with the ringing of metallic weapons against stone and steel. The cacophony made it difficult for the druidess to keep track of what was going on; the sensory input was becoming overwhelming. She then got a glimpse of what was happening: there were shadmar soldiers trying to hold back a mob of shadmar workers. The soldiers were vastly outnumbered and many fell to improvised weapons as Sia scurried under the mass of feet, making her way into another side passage.

Sia then found herself sneaking through a small rodent-sized hole in a wall, then into a large ritual chamber. There were blasts of flames and electricity illuminating the chamber as two figures circled each other and attempted to fell the other with magical energy. One of the figures came close to Sia's view and the druidess gasped. It was Thes. Her heart beat with increased anxiety as she saw the stressed face of the wizard. This reaction also reduced the druidess's concentration on the vision and the scene began to get blurred and indistinct. Sia furrowed her brow and concentrated, determined to see what would happen to her beloved wizard. When her vision refocused, she saw a tall, dark shadmar pressing a hand coated in red and black energy into Thes's chest. All signs of life were snuffed from the wizard in an instant. Sia screamed.

Thes ignored the circle of burning incense as he leapt into the circle to comfort Sia. The druidess snapped out of the vision immediately leaving her confused and frustrated. She was quickly comforted by Thes's arms around her. She had trouble removing the image of his face, pale and lifeless, from her mind. The vision was untrue. She knew it was not something that had happened nor something that would be guaranteed to happen. Yet, she could not remove the emotional pain of watching Thes die.

"Fear not," the wizard said to her, lightly caressing her back. "It is just a vision. You are unharmed."

"It is not for me that I fear," Sia responded as she pulled back to look Thes in the eyes. Tears gathered around her own eyes as she looked at him. "It was your end that I saw."

Thes only looked back to her, swallowing as he considered facing his own demise. "Worry not," he

254

reassured her. "Such visions do not always predict the future." However, the wizard suspected that it was unlikely that the water spirits would deceive the druidess. Thes embraced her tightly while he continued to consider that his final adventure may be upon him.

The others, having heard the druidess's scream, came towards the circle. Bryman kicked at one of the stones, knocking its smoking contents to the forest floor. Morstar pulled at the hulking warrior, trying to restrain him from performing another brash action that might make things worse.

"Tis alright," Thes told them. "Sometimes these visions show unwanted events. She will be fine."

With that reassurance, the others slowly went back to their activities. Thes and Sia moved away from the intoxicating aromas of the burning incense. After Sia's mind found clarity and reality completely, she recalled her vision to Thes. The wizard was transfixed on the beginning of the sequence and disappointed that the vision did not show the direct route into the shadmar fortress. Sia, on the other hand, wanted Thes to take heed of the warning she foresaw.

She tried to persuade him, "You cannot continue on this quest, you will be unsuccessful."

"You do not know that," he replied tentatively. "Perhaps my demise is even integral to our success."

Sia became anxious, "You should leave here and pursue this doomed journey no more. Perhaps there is nothing that can be done to stop the dark forces from invading this world. Perhaps we have already failed."

"I refuse to believe that. I will not stop pursuing this, Sia." He fixed his eyes upon her sternly. "There is too much at stake to give up, especially if it is only my life that may be in peril. Please," he pleaded, "tell me more of your vision and let us use this information wisely."

Sia decided to give into the wizard's pleading and described her vision with all the detail she could recall. Thes asked many questions, trying to figure out what the vision was showing them. He knew that if the caster was successful the spell would provide the most useful information as possible. Given Sia's aptitude with magic and her affinity for water, he presumed that everything the vision showed her was important.

After an hour of discussion, the two elves gathered the others to discuss what they had learned. Sia explained how she flew to the mountains and found the fortress at the western roots. However, since she appeared to fly through the earth, they believed that there are no clear entrances to the fortress from the outside. As they previously suspected, the shadmar are likely using their magic to transport to and from the underground stronghold. As dismaying as that seemed, Thes did not seem concerned by the news.

"We simply need to draw the enemy to us, and either capture one of their sorcerers, or sneak through one of their portals behind them," the wizard explained.

"Aye, or maybe if we ask'em politely they'll open a door for us," Mortsar grumbled sarcastically.

"Ha! I say it's finally time we start facing the enemy head on," Bryman exclaimed.

The elf continued, "I can use some magic that will likely attract any sorcerers that are monitoring the area. Hopefully, they'll send a patrol to investigate."

"Then we can ambush them," Artemis added, now seeing the elf's plan.

"Precisely," Sia said, nodding with the wizard.

The next piece of information Sia conveyed to the group was the infighting between the shadmar soldiers and the workers. Though they doubted that either group of shadmar would be welcome allies, the distraction from the infighting should serve them well as they sneak into the fortress.

"If the shadmar are fighting among themselves, then perhaps their armies will collapse in on themselves," commented Artemis.

"I doubt it," replied the wizard. "Besides, we will still need to confront the shadmar leader…"

Morstar interrupted the elf, "So… what exactly is our mission here? We sneak into the fortress… then what?"

"Well," Thes responded hesitantly, "That comes to our final piece of news."

The wizard then explained the final part of the vision and his fateful confrontation with the tall shadmar sorcerer.

"I believe that this sorcerer is the source of the dark magic we've witnessed," Thes said. "He must serve as some sort of conduit between one of the dark worlds and our own. If we can defeat him, I believe we will end the threat on this world."

"We must stick together and ensure that Thes does not face him alone," Sia added. "In the vision, this sorcerer killed him with magic." There were many wide eyes after this last comment.

"Ye going to rush into this madness, even knowin' that yer going to be killed?" Morstar asked Thes, his voice demonstrating his irritation.

"Yes," he answered simply.

Bryman stood up and roared, pounding his fist into the air. "You face your death with courage, elf-friend. I'll fight by your side to the end." The warrior seemed even more eager now that their death may be prophesized by the vision.

Before the wizard could reply to the warrior, Morstar interjected again. "This is outrageous! Ye can't be goin' in there to die."

"It is his choice, and it seems he has made it," Artemis said calmly to the dwarf.

"Yes," Thes asserted. "I have made up my mind. We have the knowledge of this vision to guide our actions. I also have limitless faith in the capabilities of my friends."

"I ain't gonna let ye die in there, elf." Morstar said pointedly.

"I know, and I'm counting on it."

(19) Dark Magic

Zeneris stepped lightly onto the forest floor. The scene was quiet and serene, with little more than autumn leaves slowly falling to the forest floor in a shimmering dance of golds, reds, and yellows. The dark sorcerer stepped to the side as a half-dozen shadmar soldiers stepped out of a magical gateway of blood-red energy behind him. The portal closed and they proceeded to march through the woods, with the sorcerer following the band of warriors.

Zeneris was eager to make this mission a quick one. He and his fellow sorcerers had sensed a magical disturbance in the area. While many believed it to be nothing more than a wandering magical creature, such as a unicorn or satyr passing through the primal forests, he was ordered to investigate.

His fellow sorcerers were somewhat fearful of the world outside their fortress since Vralthen failed to return after the most recent raid. Lord Niedrie pronounced the sorcerer dead, as his life essence was no longer detectable through the chain of dark-essence that bound the sorcerers to their patriarch. Zeneris, however, was not afraid. He still had the brash swagger of youth and was generally unconcerned with his mortality. He was also overly confident in his own capabilities.

The group marched for a few minutes before the soldiers stopped and turned toward their sorcerer. Zeneris strode to the front of the band with an aura of arrogance. On the forest floor, many paces ahead of the band, sat a figure. It was a large hulking humanoid shape. Though it was hard to tell for sure what it was. The person or creature was covered with numerous hides, skins, and tattered cloaks. It was hard to tell whether it was a mound of clothing in person-shape, or a very large person wearing far too many cloaks. A large hood obscured the figure's visage and a low, somewhat musical hum could be heard beneath the hood.

The soldiers were a bit apprehensive from the sight. There were already stories being told of a wizard felling shadmar in the woods outside their fortress. Now this figure appeared, unconcernedly sitting on the forest floor, in a place well within the boundaries of their patrols.

Zeneris, however, was not concerned. He stepped forward to address the heap of hides, "Hail, traveler," he said in the Nomen tongue of the surface. "You trespass on our claimed lands. You will surrender yourself to the shadmar."

The figure made no movement and the song-like humming continued unabated. Zeneris turned and nodded to his soldiers to apprehend the figure. When they hesitated, Zeneris snarled the order at them.

The soldiers cautiously approached the large figure, their band of eight circling around the heap with their swords drawn. The leader of the group cautiously used his sword tip to pull back the figures hood. Inside, a handsome and reddish-blond-haired Noradrie smiled wryly at the soldier.

Many things then happened at once. Numerous animated, tangled vines beneath the layer of freshly-fallen leaves came to life and wrapped around the soldiers' ankles and legs, yanking all of them to the ground. Bryman stood up tall, throwing off the pile of hides on the soldier behind him and slashing out with his concealed axe. Morstar suddenly appeared out of some nearby bushes, his warhammer and shield at the ready. The dwarf charged at the distracted soldiers.

Zeneris suddenly felt a tinge of fear as the trap was sprung. He scrambled to prepare a deadly spell for his foes, but hesitated on deciding where to throw his blast of flames. He decided to take down the charging dwarf and aimed a growing ball of fire at the warrior. However, an arrow pierced the sorcerer's hand as he aimed to throw it. Rather

260

than dissipating, the flaming orb lobbed upward and struck an outstretched branch of a nearby dying tree. The orb exploded in a small inferno and began to engulf the dried tree quickly.

Zeneris scrambled away from the carnage, barely forming a protective spell as another arrow sought to pierce his leg. The arrow ricocheted off an unseen shield as the sorcerer broke off the arrow embedded in his hand. He looked for his soldiers, but found that Bryman and Morstar were finishing them off after the vines had pulled them to the ground.

Zeneris then spotted Artemis up in a tree with an arrow cocked and ready. The sorcerer smiled up at the ranger, knowing those arrows could not penetrate his magical shield. He prepared another blast of fire to throw at the ranger. However, before he could throw it, a great wall of water appeared around him. The confused sorcerer let his flames dissipate and instead summoned a blast of intense heat around him. The shockwave of heat slammed the watery wall which immediately evaporated into a blast of hot steam.

Zeneris was now quite frightened. The Noradrie and dwarf were stalking towards him with their weapons readied. Two light-skinned elves came at him from the other side, one with electricity crackling around his fingers, the other with swirls of freezing energy around hers. Zeneris knew he had to escape. He summoned a swirl of dark energy, rotating his arms in wide circles to create a portal back to Valraen. As he did so, an axe came end-over-end hurtling toward him. The sorcerer abandoned his spell and dived beneath the far side of the burning tree as Bryman's axe purposefully missed the sorcerer. The axe blade slammed hard into the base of the tree.

The combination of the fire burning through the last remnants of heartwood and the hefty axe-blow striking its base, caused the barren, heavy trunk to shatter and topple over. The substantial weight of wood slammed down upon the cowering sorcerer's head. A loud crack could be heard as the shadmar's neck snapped.

Morstar and Bryman looked to each other and started chuckling at the unfortunate turn of events.

"So much for capturing him alive," said Artemis with a smirk as he joined the others.

"Yes. I suppose this ruins our plan?" Sia asked, turning to Thes. The wizard, however, was paying little attention to the others. Anger dominated his features and his heart beat with the vibrant triumph of rage. His eyes were locked on the battered corpse of the sorcerer as his fingertips still crackled with energy.

"Thes?" The druidess asked, placing a comforting hand on his arm.

The wizard's mind snapped to the present, his anger immediately dissipating. He nodded at Sia. "Yes. Fortune does not favor us. I doubt they will continue to send sorcerers for our traps." Thes crouched down near the fallen sorcerer looking for anything that might help their quest.

The wizard then noticed a faint glow beneath the leaves. Sia noticed it too. The druidess then carefully pulled up the fallen sorcerer's arm. At the tips of the shadmar's fingertips circled numerous small globes of blood-red energy. Their intensity pulsed randomly with innate power. Thes quickly put his own hands together, cupping one hand over the other. Electricity sparked between his cupped palms as he pulled his hands apart slowly. A glimmering sphere of electrical energy grew as he spread his hands apart. The wizard then concentrated on the blood-red orbs. His brow furrowed and beads of sweat began to drip down the sides of his face. Soon his efforts began to bear fruit, as the blood-red orbs slowly moved away from the dead sorcerer's fingers. The wizard grit his teeth as he continued to strain his mind, trying to gain control over the orbs of energy.

The tense situation had everyone staring at Thes in silence. Only Sia was able to see the blood-red orbs of dark energy. The others only saw the stressed elf and his globe of electricity.

"Is he okay?" Artemis whispered. Sia only nodded to the ranger as she continued to carefully hold the dead sorcerer's arm for the wizard.

Thes then pulled hard with his mind and all the little orbs were vacuumed into the wizard's sphere. Inside the hollow ball of crackling electricity, the orbs continued to bob around randomly, seemingly trying to escape the magical prison.

The wizard visibly relaxed and fell into a seating position upon the ground. "That should do it," he said, catching his breath.

"What exactly did ye do, elf?" asked the dwarf, somewhat concerned. Thes only nodded as he tried to regain his breath and mental strength.

"He captured the dark spirits the sorcerer's use for their magic," Sia replied, carefully taking the globe of energy from the exhausted wizard.

"I'll have to take your word for it," Artemis said. Bryman stepped closer, squinting into the electric sphere trying to see the invisible globes.

"Will they help us get into the fortress?" Morstar asked, still puzzled why Thes was making the effort to capture them.

"Perhaps," Thes replied. "I shall have to study them, but that will take some time. We best be out of here before they learn of our deeds."

Bryman helped the wizard to his feet. The adventurers then began their long hike back to Artemis's hidden glade.

When they returned to the glade that evening, Thes and Sia immediately set about examining the orbs inside the electric prison. They probed and prodded the mystical energies with magical spells and divinations. They were careful to ensure that the orbs were unable to escape, growing or shrinking the prison as each experiment required. Thes made extensive notes as they investigated, scribbling their findings down in an excited flurry.

Sia was unaccustomed to the wizard's scientific approach to phenomena. Her druidic background focused more on training her intuition and spiritual connection. She learned how to feel and empathize with the natural spirits, to persuade them to do her bidding. She cooperated with the natural spirits and guided them to action.

Thes's approach to magic was a strange cosmopolitan collection. At times he seemed quite druidic in his approach, gently persuading the mystical energies toward an objective. Other times he seemed commanding and pragmatic, compelling powerful effects from the forces of nature with the precise control of a disciplined scholar. Yet most of the time, he seemed to operate somewhere between the two approaches. Sia's short time with the wizard had already altered her vision on the ways of spellcasting. She now saw the magic she worked as more than just a spiritual connection to the natural spirits, but also as Thes saw it, a methodical collection of thoughts and gestures that moved the unseen forces of the world.

It was now late in the night. The elves had studied the dark energies for many hours. The others were growing restless while waiting for the elves. They each saw the merit of studying the dark energy, but found there was little they could do to help. As the cold winds of the autumn night began to pick up, Thes called the others together around the campfire.

264

"My friends, I have good news," the wizard said somewhat proudly.

"'Tis about damn time," Morstar said, making no effort to hide his impatience and frustration.

"I apologize for the wait, but you must understand, this is the first time I've encountered magical energies from another world before."

"Tell us what you and Sia have learned," said Artemis, eager to hear what made the elf smile so confidently.

Thes nodded. "I shall begin in the very beginning," he began. "Each race has its own mythology, stories about the creation of Enelis, and how each race came to be. According to the elves, it was Enis the Earthmother who sought to breath life onto a new world; to let green things grow and wild creatures stir in an endless wild beauty.

To create this dream, the four faerie queens, each born of the raw elements, created a world for Enis to thrive. Brana the Stone Queen formed a solid core of rock. Mara the River Queen filled the crevices of the stone with deep waters and running rivers. Atha the Storm Queen breathed upon the land setting air and sky in motion. Then Fara the Flame Queen ignited the furnace in the center of the core to warm the new world and set it to spin within the void. Then the goddess Eostre set her bright light upon the world. With this light, Enis became one with the world, filling it with flora and fauna at her whim."

"That is not how the Noradrie tell the tale," Bryman interrupted, somewhat offended by the elf's story. Artemis rolled his eyes pointedly to Morstar. The dwarf had a wide smirk upon his bearded face.

"Yes, as I said, each race and culture varies the telling of the story," the elf continued. "But the details are not important. Each story also has an antagonist, an entity who wishes to halt this creation."

"Aye, Nomtt the Shadow," the war-priest added.

"Ahh, yes," Thes replied, gesturing toward the warrior and smiling. "The cultures of dwarves and men all point to a shadowy being, the personification of evil and darkness: Nomtt to the Noradrie, Nalit to the Arathians and Seliceans, Nuegar to the dwarves of Kalavar, and Nembralus or Nembral to the eastern men from the Nomen tradition.

However, to the elven culture, this personification was Morriga, the Queen of Darkness. However, she had only a relatively minor role in the creation story of our people. For the elves, it was Xellethon the Destroyer who served as the major antagonist to the creation of Enelis."

"Aye, so what?" Morstar asked, eager for the elf to make his point.

"Xellethon did not like the creation of Enelis, the demon-lord thrived on chaos and destruction. He despised the very existence of the somewhat orderly system of plants and animals, living by day and night. So, he created an army of demons, monsters composed of feral, beastly mockeries of Enis's creations. He released his hordes upon Enelis to destroy it."

"And I suppose he failed to do so," Morstar added irritably.

"Obviously," Sia interjected sarcastically. She decided to take over the story-telling. "Xellethon turned a portion of Enelis into a smoldering wasteland as his monsters poured over the land. To protect the rest of her creation, Enis cast off the ruined portion of Enelis into the void between worlds, separating Xellethon and his demons from Enelis. She then used the perfect reflections of Mara's waters to reflect the light of Eostre to the night sky, creating the moon goddess Arianha to forever protect Enelis from Xellethon's dark influence."

"Dagda the Rider we call it. She is a mighty warrior who rides a silver steed of the purest breed. She protects our people from the evil lurking in the night-time shadows," Bryman interrupted again.

"Yes," Thes agreed. "Each culture views the lunar light as a protector, an entity who circles our world as a guardian. I do not think this is a coincidence."

"Then what is the meaning of all these tales? What does this have to do with the dark elves and that magic you found?" Artemis asked.

"Well, my friend, this magical energy is clear evidence that Xellethon's realm of Xelenvar exists, and worse still, the shadmar have found a way to make use of the malign force that resides there. The energy we found has a foul affinity for fire and destruction."

Everyone was quiet a moment as they took the news in. "The shadmar," Thes continued, "were cast to the deep underground at the end of the civil wars, over three millennia ago. There were stories that dark magic was somehow involved, that the shadmar leaders were communing with demons of another world. Now, it seems that tale was true, and that such practice never ceased among their kind."

Artemis was astounded. "I thought you said you had good news,"

"I do," Thes replied less solemnly. "The good news is that Sia and I have found a way to use the energy we captured to open a portal into Valraen."

"Then why are we telling tales?! We could be defeating our enemies!" Bryman roared as his jumped to his feet. Morstar stood up beside him, placing his hand up to keep the warrior from mounting his rage towards the elf.

"Before we jump into this," the wizard replied as he stepped back away from the angry war-priest, "we must make our choice carefully. There is only enough energy here for us to enter. We will not be able to leave unless we find an alternate exit."

"There's nothing to think about, elf." Morstar stated, as his own irritation was etched into a bushy 'V' above his eyes. "We settled this, we're going with ye. Ye will not face that sorcerer on yer own."

Thes looked to his friends, seeing their ready and determined faces. They were each prepared to follow him into uncertainty and danger. Although he had never felt more loved, he also had never felt so guilty. He believed he had somehow coerced them to follow him. It was hard for him to accept that they did so out of pure love and admiration. He did not feel deserving of that kind of friendship.

The team had separated to gather gear and provisions for the covert assault on the fortress. Thes was busy wrapping his treasured tomes into a cloth and burying the package beneath the ranger's shack. As he layered the floorboards over the hidden books, he silently prayed that he would be able to retrieve them.

Sia entered the shack, closing the door behind her. She took one of his hands between hers. "Before we go, I wanted to talk once more alone."

Thes took her other hand. They looked at each other with a feeling of distance.

"Are you afraid?" she asked him.

"I am strengthened by your presence," he said, smiling at her. "Are you afraid?"

"Not with you beside me," she replied. "Your presence also gives me courage."

They drew close, wrapping their arms around each other. "The divines torment us with destiny," Thes whispered playfully.

"Do you believe in the divine beings?" Sia asked. She pulled back to look into his face.

Thes smiled. "I've never had much faith for invisible forces controlling my destiny. I suppose that's why I study magic, to understand and make sense of something that otherwise seems unexplainable." He paused for a second. "Yet in moments like these, where I must do what I feel is true and just, I cannot help but feel like there is little freedom in my choices."

Sia sighed. "I have known that feeling for most of my life. All seemed set in course, as if by divine foresight. Now I feel both unrestricted and equally restrained by guilt for feeling so." She became solemn. "My friends and kinsfolk were all taken from me. I mourn for them. I do. Yet I cannot help but also feel like a great weight has been lifted from me. The divine river of fate has split into endless branches for me to explore." She drew closer to his face until the tips of their noses just crossed

"When I was young," she whispered softly. "I dreamed I would fall in love with a heroic knight who would rescue me from my village." She laughed. "A silly dream for a young girl."

"Indeed," Thes looked deeply into her eyes. "You have rescued me as much as I have rescued you." Sia blushed at the comment, looking away.

"Yes, well…" her words trailing off. Her eyes slowly turned back to him. "In my dreams, my knight would take me out of the forest. He would bring me to a grand castle where I was protected from harm and danger."

Thes snorted. "That is what people do with their treasures, their tokens, keeping them private and secure, away from the experiences of the world." His bright blue eyes looked deep into her chestnut-colored eyes as their foreheads bent close.

"Yes. Instead, you bring me directly into peril," she teased.

"I love you as you are and what you choose to be; your talents, your strengths, your wisdom. You do not need my security or protection. I would share the world with you, through adventure and fellowship, until old age sends us both on a final voyage."

Sia held back the joyful tears around her eyes as her chest went tight and her breath fell thin. A matching, glistening halo of moisture shimmered around Thes's eyes. For a moment they looked at each other trying to extend a needle-tip of time into eternity.

"And yet," the wizard whispered. "My fate carries a heavy course."

Sia pulled in until their breath was shared. "I choose that course with you. Together."

(20) The Pact

Flames burned in the air. The flaming portal to Xelenvar stood open high in the spell chamber. Delrith Niedrie was pacing in a circular motion, just outside the red pentagram inscribed on the lowest level of the three-tiered room. The patriarch wore a scowl as his anger was surging. For the first time in many years, the sorcerer was somewhat nervous and fearful for the future. His plans had been going perfectly, until now. His allies in the dark world were silent, leaving his summons standing empty and quiet.

The patriarch's reserves of dark magic were growing thin. With each speech he gave to his people, the enchantment of his words would compel them into a magical compliance. He would use their own blind hatred to enthrall them, using a touch of magic to push them into obedience. However, the power for such enchantments was running out. The sorcerer needed more energy from the dark world, and only the demon-lords of Xelenvar could give that power to him.

They had been his secret source of power for over a century. Ever since he found and stole forbidden tomes from the academy in Dith Derithin. After many years of study, he had made his first contact with the burning realms and exchanged dark magic for pacts to create chaos and destruction upon his own world. Besides his trusted inner circle of sorcerers, no other shadmar knew of this foreign influence, nor that his rise to power was entirely due to that dark energy.

However, without a constant supply of the malign force, the sorcerer could not maintain the enchantments over his people. He would slowly lose control over those with greater will, eventually his entire hierarchy of power would crumble into pointless in-fighting. The sorcerer also knew that those with personal feelings and connections to him might overcome the enchantment more easily. Thankfully, Delrith had ensured that all his personal rivals were killed during the city's fall.

The plan to destroy his home city was one of the many pacts the sorcerer made with the demon-lords. Each time the sorcerer asked for greater reserves of the dark magic, the contract for destruction grew in tandem. Delrith only wanted power and dominion over his people and cared little for the individual lives lost along the way. He wanted to be loved and feared, to have the world at his beck and call. The demon-lords simply showed him the path to that power.

The sorcerer was quite adept at magic long before he came across the dark energy of Xelenvar. He had felled rivals in spell-duels and was at the top of his class at the academy. But spell-power only got him so far. He was born to a minor noble house, with little if any influence in the city. He yearned to be celebrated by the greater houses, to be invited to the prestigious social gatherings. Yet despite his incredible talents, he never could gain social capital among the elites. His first pact with the demon-lords was to gain that recognition.

The demon-lords delivered on their promise. When he used his newfound dark magic to destroy a rival house, some greater houses finally paid him heed. Even if it was more fear than admiration, it trickled into the void of the sorcerer's heart, feeding his desire, and growing his thirst for more. He would be loved and respected at all costs.

More rivals were soon destroyed by his hand and he would inadvertently gain appreciation from the lower classes, who desired a champion against those who wielded power over them. Delrith only wanted more authority over those who would admire him. It was then that the demon-lords offered a path to ultimate rule, a conquest of the surface world. In order to gain the power that he would need, the demon-lords wanted a great commitment to destruction, the city of Dith Derithin must be destroyed.

Thus, over decades, Delrith instigated a civil war between his people and fueled the battles that would destroy the city, making the caverns of his people uninhabitable. Delrith was then infused with a surplus of dark energy, which he used to bind his people together with powerful enchantments. He now had a war machine poised to conquer the surface world, and the demon-lords would be his allies in this conquest, relishing in the destruction his war would cause.

Until now, his allies ensured a steady supply of dark energy, which Delrith could also channel to his inner circle of sorcerers. The demon-lords also offered lesser demons to help the sorcerer ensure that no word of his forces would reach Elienspar. These lesser demons hunted along the roads running westward, keeping a steady silence from the crown's forgotten, eastern lands. The plan was working perfectly, until now. Now, Delrith felt his hold over his people was waning and his reservoir of dark energy diminishing. For the past few days, the sorcerer had tried to make contact with the demon-lords. Yet, his allies were silent.

The burning portal flickered and crackled in the room, but no dark, guttural voices could be heard in the hellscape beyond. While such silences had happened before, Delrith never met such repeated failed attempts when in dire need. The demon-lords had been reliable whenever their plans were in jeopardy.

"Delrith of the mortal house of Niedrie, what services does thee request from the Indomitable Burning Lords of Xelenvar?" said a dark voice.

The familiar, deep greeting melted the sorcerer's woes. *Finally*, the sorcerer thought. He turned to the portal eager to commune with the demons.

"Your mortal sense of time betrays you. The Lords will commune as they wish," the dark voice replied to the sorcerer's unspoken thought. The dark energy that bound the sorcerer to the demon-lords also allowed them to sometimes see into his mind.

"Yes, of course, my lord." Delrith swallowed uncomfortably.

"Speak, mortal."

"My lord," Delrith bowed slightly. "My magical reserves grow low and the enchantments upon the shadmar people grow weak. We are nearing the time for marching upon our enemies. I request more power to fulfill our plans."

The portal burned in silence for a moment. The tense air crackled and burned. "Our pact has ended, mortal. You shall receive no more power without prior compensation."

Anger surged in Delrith. "Lords, our pact was to conquer the surface. That deed is not yet done."

"You stand near the surface, mortal. Your people haunt the halls of your ancestors. That is the end of our pact."

"We had an agreement!" the sorcerer screamed at the portal. "My war is mounting. Is the destruction from my conflict not enough to fulfill your contracts?" Delrith tried to hold his rage, knowing that the demons thrived on instilling such emotion.

"Your war is now uncertain; the tides of fate have been shifted by your mistakes."

Delrith was surprised and even more angry that he could have done anything wrong. "What mistakes? I have made no mistakes!"

"The Lords foresee a powerful force rising against you. Your own subjects plot your demise."

"Which is precisely why I need more power! I cannot stop their hearts from straying from our cause without the dark energy." There was a pleading tone to the desperate sorcerer.

274

"That is not all. An external force will soon infiltrate your stronghold. Unexpected enemies will see to your demise."

Delrith was truly shocked. He could not think of who or what from outside his fortress could stop him. Their plan was executed with such precision. No news of their exploits should have reached Elienspar. There was no foreign power aware or ready to deal with their forces.

The sorcerer's mind was racing, "Who? Who strikes at us?"

"The Lords have foreseen. An ethmar wizard will be your end."

"What wizard!?" he screamed in desperation. His mind raced. *How could the wizards of Elienspar know of our presence?* he pondered. Delrith then suddenly recalled the mission he sent a lesser demon to complete, to kill an ethmar wizard that escaped a raided village. He was growing fearful. Vralthren, one of his best sorcerers, had also been killed recently. *Was this wizard responsible for Vralthen's death as well?* he wondered. Rage mounted again in the sorcerer. "Did the demon you provided not deal with the wizard of that village as I asked?"

"The demon was defeated." The voice remained stoic, no hint of emotion.

Anger, however, was surging through Delrith. His blood flowed like a violent river. He kicked over the nearby podium, knocking the stack of books to the floor. "Why did you keep this from me!?" he roared at the burning portal. He suddenly felt like he was being played like a pawn.

The portal was silent.

Delrith continued shouting, "You would jeopardize our plan!? Why!?"

"The Lords desire a sacrifice, one attuned to powerful magic."

Delrith was confused. "So, you let this wizard live? So, that he could be sacrificed to you?"

"The Lords need a sacrifice in a proper ritual, at the proper time. You will prepare this ritual in exchange for more dark energy."

Contempt burned in the sorcerer. He did not like this feeling at the back of his skull. He felt like the demon-lords were manipulating him toward some unseen end. They had always found a way to modify the plans towards some hidden goal. Yet, so far, they have never let the sorcerer suffer, nor did they ever fail to deliver on their promise of more power.

Delrith calmed himself. He would deal with this change as he had the others. He knew he must focus and ensure he got what he wanted out of the new agreement. "I may agree to this new pact; however, I desire protection. I will not have my life taken by this wizard as you foresee."

"Agreed," came an immediate reply. "You will not be killed by the wizard's hand. You will prepare the ritual here, and he will come to you. We shall also grant as many lesser demons as you desire to help you keep your people oppressed."

"Why not give me the dark energy I need to maintain the enchantments over them?"

"No more energy until the sacrifice has been made." The dark voice was firm.

Delrith was still frustrated by the unnecessary restriction. "You have put all we have orchestrated into jeopardy. I expect a vast reservoir of power for this pact."

"After the sacrifice is fulfilled, you shall never want for dark energy again."

Delrith smiled, as his desire for power surged. "I accept this pact, my lord."

(21) Demons and Traitors

The shadmar miners and farmers marched. The dark caverns echoed their footsteps like the beat of drums. There were many shouts and war-cries among the excited shadmar commonfolk. Kinrithir and Gharin's voices still echoed in their minds as they climbed the long corridors that extended upwards.

It was not long before the band of eager rebels burst through a large steel door into a guardhouse that separated the work caverns from the old fortress's living quarters. The most enraged participants of the rebellion were at the front of the group. They raised their makeshift weapons high over their heads as they charged into the chamber.

The guardhouse had a high, vaulted ceiling and was composed of small bricks stacked tightly together. The large room was more than two-dozen paces long where another large steel door stood on the far wall. There was a makeshift low-wall of metal tables placed midway in the room, just before a side corridor exited on the right. Huddled behind the tables were numerous shadmar soldiers clad in form-fitted chainmail featuring rounded steel plates over vital areas. They wore curved, horned helms that seemed to extenuate the dull, red glow of their eyes. The soldiers wielded spears and crossbows, but were hesitant to strike.

The rebels screamed a battlecry as they charged into the room, using their rage as a shield against fear and pain. The captain of the soldiers waited until the rowdy group reached about half-way to the wall before giving his command. A volley of crossbow bolts came screeching across the chamber, felling the first few rebels swiftly.

Those behind the fallen hesitated for only a second. Seeing their friends fall before them heightened their fear, but the ensuing anger also gave them the courage they needed to continue their charge. They closed the gap between the door and the makeshift wall in a matter of moments, too quickly for the armed soldiers to load another volley of bolts. The enraged rebels threw themselves over the wall at the soldiers. Some were pierced by outstretched spears, others swiftly cut down by readied blades. However, in the end, the rebels were too numerous.

The soldiers were quickly subdued and beaten into unconsciousness by improvised clubs. Gharin and Kinrithir sent another wave of rebels into the side corridor where a few more soldiers and officers were encountered and killed. They had won the guardhouse.

The rebels tended to their wounded as best they could and the dead were sent back down into the caverns as feed for the mushrooms, as was their tradition. The victors quickly set to reversing the makeshift wall to face the other door and set guards armed and clad with the armaments of the fallen soldiers. Fortune was with the rebels, for an armory also existed in one of the side rooms. It contained many steel swords, spears, and crossbows.

There was not enough room in the guardhouse chambers to house the entire rebellion. Rather than continuing their march up into the next set of chambers above them, the leaders decided to hold the guardhouse and give time for the rebels to rest. Many had worked long hours in the mines or mushroom caves and had not the chance to recuperate since the rebellion began.

While Gharin and Kryther commanded the garrison at the guardhouse, Kinrithir, the group of former slaves, and many able-bodied miners proceeded back down to the mining and farming caverns. There were at least four other branches where shadmar were working that were similar in size to the complex that Kinrithir and Kryther had worked in. They had all been former mines from the ancient days, but many were now devoid of useful metals and were

278

converted to caves for farming and livestock. The shadmar that worked these caverns were easily persuaded to join their cause and the ranks of the rebellion swelled with new recruits.

Since the rebels controlled the food supply, they expected the response to their rebellion would be strong and swift once word reached the upper chambers of the stronghold. However, they had not heard any sign of enemy activity all night. The few rebels that were willing to scout ahead, however, had not returned. It created a puzzling situation for the rebellion. Gharin, Kryther, Kinrithir, Edras, and Owkba gathered to discuss their tactics.

"Something isn't right here," Kinrithir stated. "Why don't they strike at us?"

"They must have some upper-hand we haven't considered," Gharin suggested.

"You mean other than an army of experienced warriors and powerful sorcerers?" Kryther asked sarcastically.

"If they are ready to march on the surface, perhaps they no longer have need of the stores in these caverns," Edras offered.

"No," Gharin answered. "They haven't gathered what they need for that conquest. There is something we aren't considering." Silence ensued for a moment as they tried to consider their enemy's motivations.

Owkba then offered a reasoning, "When warriors need not enemy lands, warriors burn villages and food, so no more enemy warriors may grow strong,"

"They cannot burn us out of these caverns," Kryther stated.

"No," Kinrithir responded sharply, "but they can flood us out."

"It is a possibility," replied Gharin. "The Ebony Lake is housed in a deep granite basin above these caverns. If they found some way to unleash it upon the caves, or breach the bottom of the basin, we would be sure to drown."

"It would certainly be an easy way to deal with the rebellion," added Edras.

"Yet, why wait?" Kinrithir asked. "I presume they will use some sort of magic to perform this task. Why haven't they done so already if they wished to wipe us all out?"

"Perhaps it is not flooding. Poisonous air? Pack of rabid monsters? Or some other magical attack." Kryther's usual pessimism was apparent.

Before Kinrithir could respond to his half-brother, shouts echoed from the defensive wall down the small hall to the back room they gathered in.

The rebel leaders quickly grabbed their weapons and charged down the hallway. Screams followed the initial shouts, followed shortly thereafter by the feral sounds of large beasts. As the leaders scrambled into the chamber they found the rebel guards being overrun by two large panther-like demons with razor-sharp claws and over-large jaws beset with pointed incisors dripping poisonous ichor.

The initial sight of the melee stalled their charge into the chamber. Kinrithir expected to see shadmar soldiers, not demons. It was a major shock to see these other-worldly creatures. Stories of demons had been a part of the shadmar ancient past, of their dark heritage that drove them underground. Consorting with demons had been outlawed and scorned. Understanding began to dawn on Kinrithir as he saw the bestial forms. He now understood why Delrith had been so successful in his rise to power. He had broken one of their most important laws. He looked to Kryther nervously. His half-brother was smiling arrogantly, despite the danger. Kryther loved being right.

Kinrithir and Gharin shouted for the rebels on reserve to join the fight as they charged in, determined to hold the demons back long enough for reinforcements. Kryther stayed back in the corridor, since his injuries still made it difficult for him to move quickly. He fired his new crossbow at the beasts from the shadows. Edras brandished a sword and charged in with Kinrithir and Gharin, who also drew swords. Owkba raised a large mace over his head as he came in behind the others.

By the time the leaders reached the broken wall of tables, the guards were either dead or dying of cuts and gashes that tore right into their newly-acquired armor. It seemed steel was of little use against the claws of the demonic beasts.

Kinrithir and Gharin circled around one of the demons while it was busy devouring the dead guards. When they were ready, they nodded to each other and made their heavy strikes. Their blades, however, struck hard and throbbed, as if they had struck the firm heartwood of a dense tree. The blades made but minor cuts in the creature's hide. The blows did, however, gain the beast's attention. Its claws lashed out wildly and fiercely. Thankfully, Gharin's years of experience were still with him, he parried the strike with the side of his blade and stepped back. The old general was put on the defensive as the beast tried to bite at him. Kinrithir continued to hack with his full strength at the beast, but produced only negligible scratches in the dense skin.

Meanwhile, Kryther had managed to land a few bolts into the other beast. Likewise, the bolts seemed ineffective. One bolt managed to stick in the beast's hide, but was no more than a finger's breadth deep. The others simply ricocheted off the creature's flank. By the time Edras and Owkba confronted the other creature in melee, they were extra cautious and curious about their weapon's effectiveness. While the beast snapped at Edras, Owkba attempted a heavy-handed, wide-armed blow to the beast's snout. The mace connected, but the creature's head only tilted slightly from the blow. It snarled at the orc and began furiously clawing and biting at him. The orc grasped the large mace in both hands and used it to deflect the blows. Edras took advantage of the distraction and circled behind the creature.

In the corner of her eye, she saw how ineffective Kinrithir and Gharin's attacks were on the other demon. She could not believe such powerful beasts could exist. However, she was determined to make it out of Valraen alive. She decided to test her blade on the beast's twitching tail, to see if a smaller, fleshy portion might be more easily severed. She raised her sword high and cut down hard at the base of the tail.

A sizzle of steam, like hot steel thrown into a basin of cold water, issued from the demon's wound. The tail lobbed off effortlessly, so much so that Edras nearly fell over from her unnecessary exertion. The demon howled in pain and rage as it turned around to face its assailant. Edras had recovered from her strike and brandished her sword in both hands, ready to strike. The demon leapt at her, its ichor-dripping fangs extended for Edras's seemingly vulnerable throat. The knight, however, anticipated this move and dropped to the ground as she maneuvered her blade behind the demon's neck. Her body weight drove the side of the blade into the back of its neck. Before it could lock its jaw onto her own neck, the beast's body fell limp. However, instead of the beast's head, Edras watched the severed head of a shadmar roll off the torso.

The knight gasped in astonishment as she climbed to her feet, staring at a beheaded shadmar instead of the demon she had felled. Owkba called for Edras's help, snapping her out of the daze. The orc was trying to help Gharin and Kinrithir keep the second demon at bay. The beast took turns snapping and clawing at the trio that surrounded it. Kryther just stood off to the side, feeling rather useless due to his injuries.

Edras charged in with her sword leading the way. The blade pierced the demon's flank and immediately sizzled the creature's flesh as it sunk deep. The knight pulled hard on the pommel, tearing the sword out the side of the creature. A rolling mass of steam escaped from the wide gash and the beast fell limply to the ground. In the creature's place lay the sundered body of a shadmar warrior.

Kinrithir and Gharin stared at Edras and the collapsed body on the ground.

"Why do these soldiers take the visage of demonic beasts?" Kinrithir asked the room.

"Indeed. And, why does your blade penetrate their flesh, while ours do not?" Gharin asked, looking to Edras.

The knight shrugged and looked at her sword uncertainly. The blade seemed mostly unremarkable compared to the others. The styling was different than the two held by Gharin and Kinrithir and the metal had a lighter sheen. She brought the sword closer to the torch burning on the wall. Upon closer inspection, she noticed the sword had square-like geometric stylings in the hilt, and the tip of the pommel bore a pair of dwarven runes, likely the smith's initials. The blade shimmered in the torchlight hinting at a silvery glow within the cool metal.

"It is a dwarven blade, Kalavarian steel," she said to the others. As she looked at the shimmering glow of the sword, a thought occurred to Edras. She turned abruptly to the shadmar. "Where did your guards take the belongings of their prisoners?"

A chorus of shrugs was her response.

"I do not know," replied Gharin. "The prisoners were all stripped when brought down past my chambers."

Edras cursed. "I must find my sword. It is an heirloom of the Knights of Song, an ancient blade composed of star-metal. I believe it, too, will be able to harm these demons." The elf had not previously considered recovering her missing equipment. However, now that escape was a possibility, she knew her implements could prove useful.

"If your blade was deemed special or valuable, it has likely been claimed by one of Delrith's greedy captains," Gharin responded. Edras sighed and tried to admire the blade she held.

"Are these demons we face?" Kryther asked. "They seem to be beast-shaping guards to me."

"Yes, they are both," Kinrithir replied. "These are simply soldiers, not sorcerers. Delrith must have done this to them. He forced them to serve as vessels for these demons."

Kryther shuddered at the thought of being forced into a bestial form.

"Delrith has broken the ancient law." Gharin stated. "I had no idea he was capable of such treachery."

The rebel reinforcements then arrived at the guardhouse, helping their leaders drag off the fallen. They then assigned more guards to replace them in securing the door. The leaders gathered again in their small, meeting room.

"I'm going to head into the upper chambers," Edras stated eagerly.

Kinrithir was shocked. "No, it's far too dangerous."

Kryther only shrugged. "Let her go. With that sword, she'll be fine."

"Perhaps demons pose little threat to her, but the soldiers won't be felled so easily by Kalavarian steel." Kinrithir looked at Edras. Her blue eyes shimmered with determination.

"I don't intend to face off with anyone if I can help it," she said. "I hope to use stealth and darkness as my cloak."

284

Kinrithir sighed. "You don't know your way. Let me come with you," he pleaded.

"What about the rebellion?" asked Gharin. "I cannot lead this people without you."

"Nonsense. You are more than capable, General. Plus, you have Kryther here."

"What?!" Kryther was astonished that Kinrithir would leave his side. "Where are you two going anyway?"

"I'm going to find my sword," Edras stated. "We will need all the advantage we can muster against these demons."

Kinrithir offered his own explanation. "I want to find out what happened to our scouts and see if I can bring back any useful information."

Gharin nodded. "That would indeed be helpful. We know little of what may face us in the upper chambers."

Kryther still bore an expression of protest. "Brother…" He then sighed somewhat exasperated. "Be careful."

Kinrithir grasped his half-brother's arm, "And you."

Owkba simply nodded a farewell.

The two elves headed to the large steel doors. They pulled the large door open slowly and quietly before slipping in through the crack. The long corridor upward was composed of the same finely crafted masonry bricks as the guardhouse. Carefully crafted stairs led upward into darkness at a modest angle. Kinrithir found the measure between stairs to a perfect, comfortable step. Edras, however, found her enhanced height and gait made the steps at the worst interval for mindless stepping. She had to carefully work her way upward with Kinrithir to guide her. Additionally, the sulmar was mostly blinded by the impenetrable darkness of the dark hall.

After a long, arduous climb, the elves reached another steel door at the top of the stairs. They both drew their swords, ready for a barrage of crossbow bolts to greet them on the other side. Edras cursed for not bringing a shield with them.

Kinrithir carefully opened the door, pushing it outward. After the door opened a measurable crack, the shadmar stuck the tip of his blade out the opening.

Silence. Nothing happened for many moments. Kinrithir looked to Edras, hoping to gain some insight for his next action from her eyes. However, the sulmar just stood blankly, waiting for him to take an action.

Kinrithir took a breath and edged the side of his head along the closed half of the door. His eye just barely passing over the edge of the steel slab. He saw only a wall and a sliver of a column of well-crafted stone. Emboldened by his success, the elf exposed more of his face to the open line of the room. Silence.

Kinrithir whispered to Edras, "Wait here." He then quickly rushed out of the doorway, rolling on the ground until he was behind the column, then straightened his body to be safely behind the stone structure. The shadmar expected bolts to have pierced him by now, but still there was silence. The shadmar then took somewhat bold looks down the chamber.

It was a huge avenue that stretched on into darkness and out of the range of his heat-sensing sight. The columns carried walkways above them as part of an overhang from a second level of the chamber. Above that the chamber stretched on higher, out of sight. Kinrithir had vague recollections of passing through this chamber when the shadmar arrived from the deep underground. In the ancient days of Valraen, this was the main nexus for the underground city and stronghold, a main avenue that connected to all the other major portions of the multi-leveled complex. Kinrithir knew there were numerous stairways, bridges, and walkways high above him.

286

The shadmar could distantly hear activity going on above them. The sound of armored soldiers hustling around, frantic shouts, and the occasional ricochet of a crossbow bolt. However, these sounds were distant, coming from high above him.

Kinrithir quickly went to the doorway and pulled for Edras to follow him. The two elves carefully stepped along the side of the chamber, following the dark corridor behind the columns that lined the path. The columns were beautifully designed, depicting various shadmar leaders etched eternally in the stone. Some bore proud curved armors and weapons, other held scrolls or staves. The eyes were so delicately etched, they seemed to follow those who looked upon them.

They eventually came across a large plaza where the columns formed a wide circle. Above them were walkways that encircled the top of the plaza. A small globe of light floated in the air in the center of the circle. Beneath it was a large statue of an ancient shadmar noblewoman. She wore a high tiara and a large, swirling cloak carved of shimmering obsidian. The cloak seemed to be composed of shadows with long tendrils that seemed to move and shimmer in the light cast from above. There was some magic upon the statue to make the cloak appear alive.

Edras was lost in awe at the statue. The figure was quite beautiful and the magical effects made the artwork quite surreal.

"Lady Ralmena," Kinrithir whispered to the sulmar. "It is she who brought our doom."

Edras gasped and stared at the statue once more. She had heard the name before. Lady Ulma Ralmena was the leader of the ancient shadmar traitors who conspired to assassinate the elven Emperor and the dwarven High Magistrate. It was the Lady, herself, who personally assassinated them, appearing out of the shadows with her magical cloak. "She is beautiful," Edras whispered.

The two elves then heard a loud commotion. It was the sounds of battle. Thankfully, it seemed to be many levels above them. Kinrithir pulled Edras towards a nearby stairway and they climb to the second level on the other side of the commotion. They then ducked behind the elaborately carved stone railing.

"Do you know where we can find the guard chambers and armories?" Edras whispered.

"I do not," Kinrithir replied. "I am not sure how these chambers have been allocated since my half-brother and I were escorted to the farming caverns."

"Perhaps we should take advantage of this distraction and search the nearby chambers." Edras began to shuffle her way down the hall.

"No, wait," he said. "If there is a battle going on up there, then perhaps we have allies."

Edras wasn't convinced. "I thought you said there were only guards, the infirm, and children in these chambers."

"Do not underestimate a shadmar child," Kinrithir smirked. "Regardless, let's try to get a look."

Edras shrugged. "Fine, but let's at least explore the chambers on the way."

Kinrithir nodded. The two elves then began to shuffle their way unseen between walkways and corridors, slowly heading towards the sounds of battle above them.

(22) Vault of the Shadmar

A burning ring of flames appeared within the darkness, bringing heat and light to the empty chamber. At first it was a small circle, no wider than a hand's breadth. But soon it expanded to the size of a doorway. A shimmering sheen of blood-red energy crackled between the flaming edges belying the magical source of the portal.

A figure then stepped out of the portal. It was a bulky person, tall and broad. Bryman stumbled into the chamber, nearly tripping over his own two feet. The hulking warrior brandished his sharp axe, swinging wildly around himself in the darkness. A moment later, the bright spark of a lit torch illuminated the chamber, and the warrior was satisfied there were no enemies to slay.

Morstar patted the war-priest on the back as he held the torch high. The two warriors looked about the small chamber. It was composed of form-fitted masonry blocks with similar slabs for the chamber's floor. The stonework was nondistinct, but well-constructed. There was a steel door that exited the chamber.

The two warriors stepped towards the door and readied their weapons on either side. By this time, Artemis and Sia had entered the chamber through the portal. Thes then came last. The portal closed behind him, taking the faint heat and light with it.

The group remained quiet, sticking to their plan. Thes summoned magical energy and cast a dweomer upon himself and his friends, leaving Morstar untouched by the magic. The dwarf then put out his torch as Artemis crept to the door. Morstar pulled it open with infinite patience. The ranger then crept his face to the doorway and peered into the hallway as Morstar prepared his hammer behind the steel bulk.

The ranger could not see any dangers within the dark corridor behind the door. It was a short corridor that stretched to either side, with similar-looking doors lining both walls. Artemis was thankful that Thes's magic enabled him to see in the dark as the shadmar and dwarves, making the space easy to discern. A faint light could be seen emanating to the left, where the corridor connected to a much larger chamber.

"We are safe for the moment," Artemis whispered to his friends. There were a few sighs of relief as the others became less tense. They knew their entry could prove quite dangerous. Thes had magically altered their arrival point in the shadmar fortress from the original magic. But without personal knowledge of the fortress, he had to estimate where it would be safe to open the portal.

"We should work our way upwards," Thes suggested. "I believe we will find the shadmar's sorcerous leader in the upper chambers." The others nodded. Sia gave Thes an uneasy expression. She was still uncomfortable with the confrontation she had viewed in her vision.

The adventurers quietly left the small chamber and stepped towards the doorway to the large connecting chamber. After they reached the end of the corridor, they looked into a huge, multi-leveled avenue. Far below them, a faint light glimmered from a floating orb. There were numerous walkways, bridges, and corridors connected to the long chamber. There were many doors and entranceways into chambers along the far wall. They could not see the top, but could identify more than ten levels climbing above them and an equal number below.

Artemis then pulled the others back, noting the faint sound of marching soldiers echoing somewhere in the large chamber. The adventurers shuffled slowly back into the hallway, crouching against the wall. The echo of metallic feet grew louder in the avenue. Soon a few soldiers marched past the opening to the dark hallway. The soldiers wore curved, horned helms giving them an austere, dangerous appearance. The soldiers marched by without turning their gaze towards the hallway.

After the last solder passed by, Artemis crept forward to the doorway's arch and peered down the avenue's wide bridge. He saw six shadmar soldiers continuing their march, although one at the rear was peering over his shoulder. The shadmar's eyes locked with Artemis for a moment.

"Intruders!" the soldier shouted. As the words left his lips, Artemis had landed an arrow into the soldier's eye, a moment too late. The ranger scrambled back into the hallway, taking a rear position with Thes and Sia. Mortstar and Bryman rose and stepped forward to hold the front line with their shields.

Moments later, the remaining five soldiers marched into the corridor with sharp spears leading their charge. The shadmar were quite surprised to see surface-dwellers in their halls. The temporary confusion provided Morstar and Bryman an opportunity to close the distance and fell the leading soldiers. The three remaining soldiers quickly dropped their spears and drew swords. Artemis felled the far soldier with a well-placed arrow, leaving Bryman and Morstar engaged in melee with the last two. For a few moments, the sounds of metal striking metal echoed through the halls. Morstar remained defensive, while Bryman was consistently aggressive with his strikes. Eventually, Bryman felled his foe and helped the dwarf finish the final soldier.

The adventurers then heard more soldiers marching above them in the wide, multi-leveled avenue. From the commotion, it seemed like many enemies were closing in on them. The intruders decided to flee the coming onslaught with Artemis leading the way down the wide balcony. They passed many steel doors and open archways leading to more dark hallways. However, the halls seemed largely unoccupied and quiet save for the sound of the enclosing soldiers.

*   *   *   *   *   *   *

Meanwhile, Kinrithir and Edras continued to explore the lower chambers, careful to avoid the view of the many marching soldiers above them. The soldiers had closed in on the location of the battle they heard above. However, after some tense shouting among the soldiers, they have since spread out, looking for intruders down numerous corridors.

The two elves were crouched behind an archway leading down a dark hallway from the main avenue. Kinrithir was eager to follow the soldiers, believing it was their missing scouts that fought against the soldiers above them. Edras, on the other hand, was not willing to engage in combat. She still had hope in finding her missing armaments, however, she was somewhat discouraged by the large number of chambers that connected to the avenue. So far, the two had only discovered empty rooms or crude storage chambers. It was uncertain which areas were in use by the shadmar and which were simply still abandoned by the former ancient occupants.

Nevertheless, the two elves continued to sneak along, checking chambers that seemed more likely to house something of interest. Kinrithir was growing restless that their scouts may be in danger and pressed Edras to seek higher floors.

"We cannot leave them to be cornered by the soldiers," he pleaded.

"Fine," Edras conceded. "We are finding nothing down here. But we should only engage if there is a guarantee of victory. We cannot give up our stealth."

292

"Agreed." Although in truth, Kinrithir was not sure if he was willing to remain idle should he find the scouts in danger.

The two elves then found a stairway and ascended towards the sounds of marching soldiers. They continued sneaking their way up until they found soldiers marching at the same level. The shadmar seemed to be searching for intruders, shuffling hurriedly past open corridors and occasionally opening doors. Kinrithir and Edras found it more difficult to remain out of sight, especially since Edras could see little of their surroundings this far from the glowing orb below them.

The two carefully ascended another level away from searching soldiers. As they reached the next balcony, they could see across the avenue two groups of soldiers marching from left and right down a far balcony. There was an arched doorway into a hallway opposite of where the two elves stood. Kinrithir could see through the darkness of the hallway; there was a group of armed intruders with weapons and shields drawn, preparing for the upcoming fight against the converging soldiers. The shadmar could not mistake the broad physique of a man and the stout build of a dwarf standing before three, more lithe figures.

Kinrithir's jaw stood open as he tried to understand the situation. Edras could barely make out the shadmar's surprised expression.

"What is it?"

"We have strange allies it seems," he whispered. "I see a tall man and a dwarf bearing shields in the hallway. Behind them are two elves and another man."

Edras was full of hope, yet perplexed. "How would outsiders find their way into the fortress?"

"I do not know. Perhaps if we aid them we can learn how they came to be."

Edras hesitated, still not eager to give up their position to the roaming soldiers. However, her desire to see these surface-dwellers overwhelmed her natural caution. "Yes, perhaps they can aid your rebellion and show the slaves a way to the surface."

The two elves drew their blades and crept along a connecting bridge towards the hallway. The two groups of soldiers reached the hall and converged upon the intruders. Arrows ricocheted off shields and walls and the sound of battle echoed through the wide avenue again.

Bryman and Morstar were on the defensive as numerous spears attempted to pierce them from the first and second rows of soldiers. Artemis continued to volley arrows over the melee, but found it hard to hit a target through the chaos. Thes and Sia were conservative with their magic, but attempted small blasts of lightning and ice shards when openings were presented. However, the narrow, short arch provided few opportunities.

Many fierce moments passed and the two leading warriors were able to fell some of the shadmar soldiers, but there were many more to take their place. Things seemed somewhat grim for the adventurers as they stood defending themselves with nowhere to flee. The soldiers became aware of Bryman and Morstar's fighting style and now the two warriors found it harder to land blows upon the shadmar. The two were in a merely defensive position, trying not to be skewered by the deadly spears.

It was in this moment that Edras and Kinrithir rushed into combat. Their swords pierced many shadmar soldiers from behind, causing additional chaos and confusion among the soldiers, who had left their flank exposed while concentrating on the intruders pinned in the hallway. It was in this moment of confusion that Bryman and Morstar

294

released their fury upon their attackers, cutting through their ranks quickly.

The two warriors cut down the last of the shadmar soldiers, finding themselves face to face with their rescuers. Bryman's axe went high again for a deathly blow upon Kinrithir's head, but before he could swing downwards, his axe was blocked by a sword. Behind the blade were fierce blue eyes.

"This shadmar is not your enemy," Edras said through gritted teeth. Her entire strength was stretched trying to hold back the war-priest's attack.

Bryman lowered his axe and Edras stepped back to catch her breath.

"We cannot dally here. More soldiers will be upon us," Kirithir said to Edras and their new allies. The shadmar then waved his hand for the others to follow him down the balcony ledge along the avenue.

Edras followed without hesitation. Morstar shrugged and followed the sulmar with his friends close behind him, scurrying out of the dark hallway single-file.

After a few twists and turns along the balcony, Kinrithir led the group into a side corridor and through a steel door into large, empty chamber. The room was silent for a few moments as the others gathered and listened for sounds of soldiers following them.

In consternation, Morstar turned to question the two elves. "Who are ye who aids us?" he asked in the Nomen tongue.

Kinrithir stepped up to the dwarf and smiled, "I am Kinrithir Velmir. I am a member of the rebellion who fights to free the shadmar laborers from the soldiers and sorcerers who proclaim to speak for us."

"How do we know you are trustworthy?" Thes asked. He eyed the shadmar warily.

"I can vouch for this shadmar," Edras offered. The sulmar stepped between Thes and Kinrithir. "I am Edras Nemarian, Captain of the Knights of Song."

"The Knights of Song?!" Sia exclaimed with excitement. "The tales of your deeds have reached even my remote village."

"Then Elienspar has heard the calls for aid from the eastern villages?" Thes asked the sulmar.

"I am afraid not," the knight replied. "We have heard no such word in the Glimmering City." Edras then explained the fate of her cohorts and her capture, how her knights were vanquished during their regular patrols.

"I am sorry to hear of the plight of your knights," Sia offered.

"It is no worry. My comrades will be avenged." The knight bowed her head in reverence.

The notion of vengeance brought Thes's eyes back to Kinrithir, who stood stoically by Edras's side. "Who is this shadmar that follows you?" Thes continued to eye Kinrithir distrustfully.

Edras smiled and clasped Kinrithir's shoulder. "It is I who follows him. He leads an army of farmers and miners who rebel against the evil deeds of their overlords."

Kinrithir waved the comment away. "Nay, I am but one of the few who is bestowed with such honor." Edras and Kinrithir then briefly explained to their new companions how they came to start a rebellion beneath the shadmar fortress.

"Now," Kinrithir continued, "who are these warriors of elves, men, and dwarves who come to our aid? And why are you here in Valraen?"

Thes and his friends quickly introduced themselves and explained how they have been monitoring the shadmar forces in the region and how they ended up fighting together. Thes then explained how Sia foresaw the conflict with

296

Delrith and his hypothesis concerning the weakening of the separation between worlds.

"You bring grave news, wizard," Kinrithir responded after considering Thes's information. "If what you say is true, then all of Enelis is at risk."

"Indeed. Now you see why we would risk life and limb to enter Valraen."

"We have seen these demons from the other world, the enemies' sorcerers have sent these abominations against us."

The wizard paused for moment. "I do not wish to speak for my friends, but I believe we would join your rebellion and help you free your people from this tyranny."

Bryman's arm shot up and his lips extended into a warcry. However, he stopped himself, realizing that such a cry would give away their position. He looked down to find Morstar with a wary eye on him. The war-priest smiled and shrugged. The others chuckled quietly.

"We would welcome your help, travelers," Kinrithir smiled eagerly. "We too will help see your mutual quest to the end. I was wary about confronting Delrith, but if your magic is as powerful as the sorcerer's, I think together we could see to his demise."

The gathering of conspirators then felt the mild tremors of more soldiers in the nearby halls. The vibrations gained momentum and the adventurers believed a great number of soldiers to be gathering.

"We have run out of time for idle chatter, the tide of battle is upon us," Bryman said, his eyes flickering with eager excitement.

"Yes, I will need to gather the rebel forces from below. I will need time to bring them together," Kinrithir pleaded.

"Go! Gather the rebels," Edras insisted. "With these new allies, I shall create a distraction. We shall keep the soldiers busy." She pulled out Kinrithir's sword from his scabbard and handed him the dwarven-made Kalavarian-steel sword.

Kinrithir looked into Edras's deep blue eyes and nodded. "Good luck, friend."

Edras nodded in reply before Kinrithir exited the chamber quickly and scurried off towards a descending stairway.

"We shall not be able to hold them off for long," Morstar protested to the sulmar.

"We can employ the ranger's skirmish," Artemis interrupted. He then quickly explained his plan. It was a maneuver he often employed as a Ranger of Lilayan. They would split into small bands, taking turns attacking the enemy from afar or in quick attacks, then fleeing back into the woods. Then the next group would attack the enemy's flank. This tactic would continue until the enemy was forced into an immobile defensive.

Morstar and Edras, the more tactically-minded members of the band, agreed with the ranger's plan. Bryman, Thes, and Edras splint into one group while Morstar, Artemis, and Sia splint into another.

For a moment, Sia looked to Thes, not wanting to be parted from him while they were in Valraen. But she could not argue against separating their magical skills to balance the groups. The druidess quickly embraced the wizard, kissing him lightly. She then whispered something into Edras's ear as they prepared to leave the room.

The two groups exited the chamber into the main avenue where many groups of soldiers could see them from higher balconies. Many crossbow bolts fired down at them, though their aim was haphazard. The two groups of intruders then broke into a run, into two different directions, finding cover among the crisscrossing archways and balconies of the wide avenue.

298

Thes gifted Edras with the same magical sight he gave his other companions. The elves then quickly sprinted across a walkway from one side of the avenue to the other. Crossbow bolts projected at them from above, but the elves were too fast to offer easy targets. \Bryman, on the other hand, was a large and bulky target. The war-priest managed to block the majority of the bolts with his shield raised high above his head. However, a few managed to graze the edges of his chain armor.

Likewise, Artemis and Sia had little trouble avoiding being seen, but Morstar was not as graceful as the other two. Thankfully, the dwarf was a smaller target than Bryman, and could easily protect himself with his shield. The three of them continued along the walkway along the avenue, climbing stairs at one point and descending another set shortly thereafter. Artemis would throw an arrow at any soldiers that appeared to gain an advantageous vantage over their friends. The arrows did little to harm the shadmar soldiers, but helped confuse and disorient them.

The plan seemed to be working. The various packs of soldiers would give chase to one group before an arrow or spell would send them chasing the other group. There were at least six bands of soldiers, with at least half a dozen or more in each band.

Meanwhile, Kirithir had reached the large steel door at the bottom floor and was sprinting down the stairwell to gather the shadmar rebels.

(23) March to the Surface

A chorus of cheers and cries echoed down the long tunnel heading up into the Valraen common chambers. At the front of the long line of former miners and farmers marched Kinrithir, Owkba, Kryther, and Gharin. The line of spears, swords, and makeshift weapons marched like a moving forest of war behind them.

The army reached the top of the tunnel and the leaders carefully stepped into the bottom portion of the wide avenue that once served as the main throughway of the ancient shadmar city. The sound of soldiers could be heard high ahead, the occasional sound of ricocheted crossbow bolts and angry cries echoed off the stone walls. The shadmar rebels quickly gathered into small bands and separated to the left and right, trying to remain out of sight from the upper balconies. The designated rebel captains whispered hushed words to their warbands as they quietly expanded upwards towards their enemies.

Gharin took command over the final band of rebels, leaving Owkba, Kryther, and Kinrithir to head out on their own. Kinrithir was eager to find Edras and see what became of his new allies. It had taken him at least a half-hour to gather the rebels and organize them for attack. He only hoped that his new allies had been able to stay away from harm during his absence.

The two shadmar and the orc found their own way upwards, carefully monitoring the advance of the other rebel groups. They could not move as fast as the others, since Kryther was still weak and sore. The stubborn shadmar insisted on joining his half-brother, despite his injuries. Kinrithir knew he couldn't stop Kryther from joining him, but he was somewhat frustrated that his half-brother was slowing their progress.

The three then heard the sounds of battle nearby. Two rebel groups had flanked a group of soldiers on a side balcony. Kinrithir and Owkba rushed in to aid their comrades as Kryther aimed and fired a crossbow from a protective position. Together the rebels made short work of the smaller band of soldiers, although the farmers and miners sustained a few injuries and one casualty.

Kinrithir then ordered the group to break back into their small bands to continue their ascent. Owkba joined one of the shadmar bands, leaving Kryther and Kinrithir to work alone in their slow ascent to the higher levels.

"You really should have stayed back at the guardhouse," Kinrithir muttered to his half-brother in frustration.

"You would want all the glory for yourself," Kryther sneered.

"Glory?! Nonsense. I fear for your safety, brother."

"I won't let you gain all the credit for the rebellion. I would be a far better ruler than you." Kryther's words were harsh and envious.

"Is that what this is about, brother?" Kinrithir turned to face him. "I do not wish to rule anyone. Just like I didn't wish to lead our House after father passed down his leadership."

"Lies!" Kryther hissed. "You always tried to gain father's favor, to try and keep me from my birthright."

Kinrithir sighed. He looked his half-brother in the eyes. "I simply wished for father's love and respect, as you did. I wished for him to look upon my deeds with admiration and pride. Yet, he only cared for his own desires. We were but extensions of his own perceived greatness."

Kryther slowly accepted his half-brother's answer. "He was quite the unloving brute, wasn't he?"

Kinrithir nodded. "If you want to gain the people's favor and attempt to rule our scattered people, I will support you, brother. You would be a wise ruler."

Kryther's eyes lit up at the prospect. "And what of you? What do you wish?"

"If we succeed here, I wish to explore the surface world; to learn what I can of this new place, free from obligation."

"You are a fool to walk away from such opportunity. The people love you."

"Perhaps, but I care not for such leadership." The shadmar looked above them, hearing the sounds of another conflict. "Come, brother. There is still much to do before our dreams can come to pass."

*   *   *   *   *   *   *

Chaos and battle echoed through the large multi-story chamber. Shadmar rebels were using skirmish tactics against the shadmar soldiers. The clinking of armor and the ringing of steel on steel could be heard everywhere. The soldiers were slowly becoming overwhelmed by the rebels, but more soldiers continued to descend from the upper chambers. It became harder for the rebels to maintain their tactics as the soldiers began to hold bridges and walkways. Soon, the battle had slowed to a near-halt as the shadmar controlled one side of the chamber and the rebels the other. Small battles still erupted here and there as each side tried to take advantage of gaps in the other, shifting their troops around to various positions.

Meanwhile, Thes, Bryman, and Edras were high in the chamber, on the top-level balcony looking down upon the obstructed war zone. They had been cut off from the rebels when a band of quick soldiers relentlessly followed them. They were forced to turn around and face them in combat. Thankfully, between Edras and Bryman's combat skills, and Thes's magic, they had been able to defeat the soldiers without sustaining any injuries.

"It seems we are cut off from our friends and allies," Edras stated, watching the battle begin to slow below them.

"Yes," Thes replied, absentmindedly. He was worried about Sia. "I cannot see a way that we could rejoin them without fighting through a large band of soldiers."

"Aye," agreed Bryman, though his tone suggested that this was a good thing and he was eager to try it.

"Now is not the time for such heroics," Edras whispered to Bryman.

Thes only smiled wryly at the sulmar, as she had not yet fully appreciated Bryman's lust for battle. Bryman wanted to respond to her with a Noradrie battle creed and the oath he took upon becoming a war-priest of his people, but he knew he could not speak such words quietly. The warrior simply grinned and nodded, hoping that was enough to convince them to take the bold action.

"Sorry, friend," Thes replied. "We shall rejoin the battle when the time is right, but for now I think we have another opportunity." The sulmar and man looked upon Thes to hear his plan. The wizard instead pointed to a shadowy staircase within a wide and dark archway down the balcony corridor. The archway was recessed slightly and the balcony in front of it was expanded in a wide arc. A magical light at the ceiling of the chamber shined bright upon the balcony, which made the area quite exposed.

Edras looked at the archway then down again at the nearest band of soldiers. It was risky. They would likely be seen if they tried to enter and climb into the upper chambers. "It could work," she whispered, "but we need to exercise the greatest stealth." She made a small nod to the hulking man next to her.

304

Thes nodded, also not sure how well Bryman could avoid being spotted.

"Don't worry about me," Bryman whispered. "I'll try my best to skulk like an elf, but if we are spotted I'll rout them to me. You two can go on ahead and see to their leaders." The elves hesitantly agreed to Bryman's suggestion. Neither of them were comfortable leaving Bryman to face the soldiers alone, even if it was something the warrior desired himself.

The three of them began to creep along towards the widened balcony. The magical light bathed the stone in a pale, purple glow. With the enchantment Thes placed upon their eyes, the small light seemed as bright as the summer-time sun. Edras went first, crawling low on the left side, keeping a hesitant eye on the band of soldiers down and to the right. Due to the wide openings in the balcony's railing, she could be easily spotted if they chose to look up towards her. Thankfully, they were focused on something below them. Some new chaos had erupted in the chamber below.

*   *   *   *   *   *   *

Sia was trying to catch her breath. A panting Morstar and equally exhausted Artemis sat next to her. They had been relentlessly pursued by a band of soldiers. The shadmar soldiers began to catch on to the ranger's tactical skirmish. They sent some of their lightest soldiers to pursue the would-be skirmishers. Sia and her friends were pursued by two such bands of these shadmar runners. There were too many to face in combat, especially with the slower, heavily armored shadmar reinforcements behind them. So, they ran. Now they finally found some respite as the runners faced a side ambush from the rebels. The rebels fought them back and now held the balcony in an ongoing stalemate. Both sides continued to fire across the divide, but even that had diminished in intensity.

Sia was worried about Thes. She was worried he would face off against the sorcerer as she foresaw. She shuddered as the image of the wizard's final moment dominated her mind.

Morstar put a comforting hand on the elf's back. "Worry not, lass. The elf will be fine." Morstar was also worried about Thes, but he was trying to stay optimistic about the situation. The dwarf felt largely responsible for separating the group. At the time, he was only thinking tactically and did not consider Sia's vision. The dwarf now felt somewhat concerned that even though they had knowledge of the future, they were still powerless to change the tides of fate.

"Should we try to look for our friends?" Artemis asked. "Perhaps they, too, are hiding among the rebels' side of the chamber."

The others agreed with the ranger and they began to sneak their way along the corridors and balconies. At each major crossing to the other side of the chamber, they would find bands of rebels trying to hold a bridge against entrenched soldiers.

The three eventually came across a group of rebels led by Kinrithir and Kryther on the higher side of the chamber. It was the largest stand-off between rebels and soldiers, although it was just as stymied as the other conflicts. The rebel leaders were gathered in a back chamber down one of the side corridors.

"There are our new allies," said Kinrithir as the trio stepped into the small room. The shamar was earnestly happy to see them. Though he was obviously disappointed that there was only three of them. The two shadmar half-brothers sat hunched on the ground with another aged shadmar. They were leaning over a crude map that had been scratched into the floor with a dagger.

"Greetings, elf" Morstar replied. He was somewhat tense as he stared at Owkba standing in the corner of the room. Kinrithir recognized the tension and introduced the two. However, the orc and dwarf gave little more than a diplomatic nod to each other. There had been countless wars between orcs and dwarves, and it was quite a strange occurrence for each to find themselves on the same side of a conflict. Kinrithir then introduced Gharin and Kryther, but Morstar was careful to keep a wary eye on the orc.

"Have you seen our friends?" Sia asked, trying to diffuse the unnecessary tension.

"I was about to ask you the same question," Kinrithir replied. "I fear Edras might have dragged the others on her errand." He then explained how the sulmar knight was looking for her sword. "I have sent messengers through our ranks, but no one has seen them. I fear they may be trapped on the enemy's side."

Sia's anxiety was evident on her face. She had suspected this was the case, but Kinrithir's confirmation diminished her remaining hope.

"I would not worry," he said reassuringly. "Edras is quite the combatant. She will not let harm come to your friends."

Sia politely agreed, but in truth she worried that her vision would play out exactly as she had foreseen. To her surprise, Morstar was the one who voiced an objection.

"We need to get to the other side," the dwarf huffed.

"What?!" Artemis was surprised that Morstar would pursue such an uncharacteristically reckless action. "I doubt we can pierce through the enemy's barrier. Let us wait until the rebels can gain an advantage."

"We may not have that time!" Sia interrupted.

"Aye, I won't let the elf face that sorcerer alone." Morstar was unyielding.

Kinrithir did not want to risk losing the rebellion. "I am as concerned as you, but we are already spread too thin. We will not be able to strike through the enemy without some change in the current stalemate. If we move any of our troops, they will take advantage and we will lose precious ground." Tactically, Morstar agreed, but he was not thinking tactically at the moment.

"Why rush into such danger, your friends might already have fallen to the enemy," Kryther added, somehow thinking this would reduce their desire to take a dangerous action.

Morstar suddenly rushed at Kryther with a snarl on his face. Two shadmar guards acted quickly and intercepted the dwarf. Owkba raised his large mace threateningly.

"Take that back you shadmar coward," the dwarf growled at Kryther.

The frail shadmar scrambled behind the guards, "I'm only being realistic! You cannot risk the rebellion over just a few."

Kinrithir only shook his head in dismay. His half-brother had never been very diplomatic.

"Morstar, please," Kinrithir begged. "I will offer what help I can. Perhaps we can make a distracting false attack to help you get to the other side."

The dwarf calmed down. "Fine. I will not sit idle. Ye must do something soon."

A loud scream echoed in the chambers outside. All tension in the room dissipated and the leaders grabbed their weapons and scrambled out into the avenue. The rebels immediately outside the chamber seemed nervous and uncomfortable. The screaming could be heard below them.

A shadmar messenger rushed towards them, "Captains!" he exclaimed. "There are demons! A horde of small demons have besieged the lower levels."

Kinrithir grew panicked. The enemy soldiers on the far side of the balcony bridge were slowly retreating. He and the others scrambled towards the balcony to peer down below. It looked like the enemy soldiers were pulling back at all levels. From somewhere in the deepest regions Kinrithir saw numerous small dog-sized shadows scrambling along the floors and walls like a herd of large rats. They moved quickly, leaping and striking at anyone who was unfortunate enough to be caught in their way. They did not seem to discern between rebel and soldier.

"Pull back!" Kinrithir screamed down below. "Rally up here!"

The rebels around him began to form a new barricade at the top of the stairways heading to the lower levels. The shadmar below them were racing upwards, trying to get away from the crawling, snarling demons.

Morstar and Sia were so surprised by what they saw, they almost forgot about looking for their friends. Artemis, however, had not forgotten and began poking his friends to gain their attention. He pointed across the bridge which the soldiers left open when they scrambled into a side chamber.

Morstar eyed the open bridge and the chance to enter the enemy's side of the chamber. However, he also was compelled to help the rebels fight off the abominations. Sia, on the other hand, had no such hesitation. She rushed towards the bridge with abandon. Artemis pulled on Morstar has he followed her. The dwarf reluctantly came along.

*   *   *   *   *   *   *

Edras rushed up the stairway with Thes and Bryman behind her. Whatever had distracted the soldiers, it was sufficient for the trio to reach the stairway without being seen. They climbed the wide stairs upwards, trying to keep to the side shadows. There were magical lights glowing from small recesses in the ceiling every few paces, bathing the stairs in that pale, purple glow.

The three soon reached the top of the stairs into a large square chamber. Back in the ancient days, this chamber likely served as a primary entranceway into the shadmar city. Another wider stairway heading upwards could be seen on the far side. The ceiling of the chamber was quite ornate, with many beautiful concentric arches and designs carved into the dark stone. In each recess above, glimmered a magical light, providing the barest of illumination to the chamber below. Along the walls arched rows of elegantly carved columns. To the sides, numerous wide corridors with arched ceilings exited the chamber. There were a few iron crates stacked to the side, near the lower stairway. The trio had been able to sneak behind them as they entered the large room.

On the far side of the chamber, there was a band of soldiers in a semi-circle, listening to their captain give them instructions. The chamber was too large and echoic to make out the words, but it was clear there was some urgency to the orders. Soon the soldiers marched with their spears leading the way down the stairway. Thes and his friends scrambled to the side of the crates as they came past. Bryman stood upright behind the large stone column, it's immense size easily hiding his bulky figure.

Edras watched the nervous faces of the shadmar soldiers. Whatever their orders, the soldiers seemed hesitate to carry them out. She then peered back to the captain who had come towards them before turning down the nearest side corridor. The elf silently gasped. She could see a glimmering hilt on the captain's scabbard. It was the hilt of her sword.

310

Edras turned to Thes and pointed it out to him just before the captain stepped out of sight.

Thes was hesitant to go after the elf's sword, seeing her mission as somewhat unnecessary. "I would rather try to find the sorcerer and put an end to all this."

"I agree, but my sword is integral to that quest." Edras insisted. "Have you heard of the Swords of the Three Crowns?"

Thes was surprised. He *had* heard of the ancient blades. They were probably the most ancient pieces of elven heritage. They were the swords once wielded by each of the three monarchs of the ancient elven civilizations. After the shadmar betrayal, and the forming of the Kingdom of Three Crowns, the swords fell out of importance and the Crown of Three Kingdoms became the primary symbol of the new united elven monarchy.

"Your sword is one of those ancient blades?" Thes was dumbfounded.

"Yes, two of the swords have been in possession of the knightly orders since the forming of the Kingdom. The third I believe was lost. As the leader of the Knights of Song, I was given the ancient blade as a symbol of my oath to the elven people."

"I would agree we should recover such an important relic, but I do not see why that cannot wait until after we win this war."

"It is the sorcerer's demons I worry about confronting," Edras replied. "As you may know, the ancient swords were forged of star-metal."

"Yes, of course!" Thes now understood the sulmar's eagerness to find the blade. "You believe your blade would be able to harm these demons like in the old tales?"

"Yes. We have learned that Kalavarian steel can especially harm them." There was a rumor that the dwarves blended star-metal with steel to create their fabled alloy.

Edras had meant to pull out the dwarven sword to emphasize her point, however, she realized she had given the dwarven blade to Kinrithir in case he ran into demons while gathering the shadmar rebels.

Thes suddenly realized that he too had witnessed this truth about Kalavarian steel. When the panther-like demon attacked him many weeks before, in the tunnels of the crypt, Morstar was able to fell the beast rather easily. The dwarf's hammer, of course, was composed of Kalavarian steel.

"Let us stalk this captain and recover your blade." The elves snuck over to Bryman and informed him of their plan. The three then began to sneak down the side corridor in pursuit of the shadmar captain.

*   *   *   *   *   *   *

"Hold the line!" Gharin shouted over the nervous shadmar. The aged general's voice was hoarse from trying to yell over the din and chaos. The remaining rebels had pulled together to form a barricade against the demonic swarm. They had three lines to hold. One on each stairway to either side, and the large bridge in front of them. The enemy soldiers had disappeared from the other side of the bridge as they sealed themselves into side corridors and chambers. The swarm of demons proved to be a far greater challenge than the soldiers.

The demons were shaped like small, rat-like dogs, but covered in spiny scales of a blood-red hue. They had wide, almost humanoid-like mouths with rows of tiny serrated teeth. The creatures leapt at them without regard for self-preservation, snapping and snarling at the shadmar rebels. The rebels had trouble striking back at them, as their weapons could barely penetrate their hard exteriors. They had concentrated on knocking them back with shields or charging them off the side of the balcony. It was clear to

312

Gharin that this was a losing battle. Kinrithir stood firm on the front line, the silvery dwarven-made sword was the only weapon that seemed to be able to harm the beasts. The demons seemed aware of this fact and avoided Kinrithir as much as possible.

One such demon however leapt off the ceiling, trying to catch Kinrithir from behind. Thankfully an ally managed to slam his shield into the demon before it landed upon the shadmar's backside. Kinrithir turned quickly and chopped his sword down upon the creature. It's snarling head was split from its body. Crimson motes of light swirled out of the felled creature.

There were many gasps and cries around them as they saw the remains of the creature. It was now a beheaded shadmar child. Cries of despair and outrage echoed around them and the line of shields began to dismantle. Kinrithir himself felt dizzy and sick seeing what he had done to the child, who now seemed to be a harmless young girl. Her dead eyes staring up at him from her discarded head. He nearly dropped his sword and stumbled as the revelation fell upon him. The sorcerers had turned the shadmar children into demons.

Gharin remained firm and resolved, shouting to get the rebels to reform and hold the line. It was now evident that they would lose one of their side walls, the demon swarm was chewing through the front-line shield-bearers.

Behind the mass of demons, a gap began to form in the swarm's ranks. The creatures began putting distance between themselves and something unseen. Then a flash of green light could be seen parting the demons, coming towards the shadmar rebels. Morstar was slamming his mighty hammer, sweeping the demons aside and crushing those unfortunate to be caught in his wide arcs. Behind him, Artemis and Sia, their swords glowing with a faint green energy, were cutting through the demons. Their weapons did not seem as effective as Morstar's, but the demons seemed just as wary of the swords as the hammer.

Upon seeing the help coming their way, Kinrithir regained his senses and began to lead the shadmar rebels forward, driving the demons between the two forces. Tears streaked down his cheeks as Kinrithir furiously cut through the demonic swarm, trying to avoid looking at the remains of the dead children that formed in his wake.

*   *   *   *   *   *   *

Edras entered the chamber quietly. It was a small office-like room. There was an ornate desk of iron in the corner with an equally ornate chair beside it. A weapon rack was along one wall with an armor stand beside it. The shadmar captain was now donning his armor, seemingly preparing to join those soldiers he had sent down below. He was currently dressed in loose clothing, the type typically worn for comfortable sleeping in chilly, stone chambers. As the captain reached for his chain greaves he felt cold steel pierce him from behind. The sword reached up through his torso, blocking his windpipe from his lungs. He gargled what was meant to be a shout as he slumped to the ground.

Thes and Bryman then crept into the chamber, closing the steel door behind them. Edras pulled off the ornate scabbard from the captain's corpse and tied it upon her own waist. She then drew the long sword carefully. It was a beautiful blade with a pale blue shimmer to the otherwise silvery steel. The hilt had many sun-like symbols and lines of radiance, and the crossbar had two sun-like globes on each end. Ancient elven script was carved along the side of the blade, inlaid with gold and platinum.

"This is Sulenthuil, Sword of the Sun," she said. "The sword of the former sulmar crown." The other two were amazed at the craftsmanship of the weapon. It was both

314

elegant and enduring. She sheathed the sword and opened the large iron chest in the corner of the room.

"Yes!" she exclaimed. The chest contained the scattered pieces of her armor. It was a fine, silvery chainmail composed of tiny chain-links. The shoulders and chest were fit with white plates of steel embossed with gold trim and curved designs. The armor seemed like it would be more ornamental than practical. Edras immediately began putting the pieces on over her clothes, strapping and tightening them to her body. When the knight was fully clad, it was clear she did not sacrifice any mobility for the increased protection. Edras looked truly regal in the outfit of her post.

She eyed her new friends from within her majestic, winged helm, "Now let us hunt this sorcerer."

(24) Sorrow and Despair

Edras led the way to the end of the corridor. Bryman and Thes waited behind her as she peered into the larger chamber. There was a large gathering of soldiers near the descending stairway, with more soldiers marching into the chamber each moment. The sulmar pulled back to her allies.

"They are retreating to this chamber," she was puzzled by the turn of events.

"We'll have to charge through them to join our allies," Bryman stated, tightening the grip on his axe.

"I don't think we can take that many soldiers," Edras replied, not sure if the warrior was being serious.

"Certainly not," agreed Thes.

"I tire of skulking," growled Bryman.

"I, as well, friend," reassured the wizard. "But let us be tactful and cautious."

The trio then heard a commanding voice echo out of the larger chamber. Though they had not heard the voice before, they knew to whom it belonged. All three of them peered out into the chamber, their curiosity getting the best of them.

A tall shadmar with a mane of jet-black hair strode into the chamber. He wore red robes that shimmered like flames. He was flanked by six large, panther-like demons that growled as they came towards the large gathering of soldiers. The creature's looked much like the ones Edras faced previously, with crimson scales, pointed, forked tails, and rows of razor-sharp teeth. Their eyes were long slits emanating a faint red glow. One of the demons was twice the size of the others. Behind the shadmar patriarch walked four robed sorcerers who wore expressions of superiority.

It was obvious to the three onlookers that there was immediate tension among the soldiers when Delrith entered

317

the room. The patriarch walked slowly towards the soldiers with his entourage. The soldiers created plenty of distance between themselves and the demons.

"Why is everyone lazing about in here? Is there not a rebellion to be quashed?" the sorcerer's voice was magically enhanced and easily reached all corners of the chamber. Thes and his friends could not hear what was said in response when one of the captains replied to the sorcerer.

Edras suddenly had an uneasy feeling and motioned for her allies to join her as she pulled back into the corridor. They followed her down the corridor and she kept going at an increased pace. Eventually, they reached a side passage and they hide around the corner. The passage seemed to connect to the other long hallways that joined to the main chamber.

Edras's instinct was well founded. Soon they heard a soldier marching down the hall. A series of loud, metallic thuds echoed down the hall as the soldier knocked on a steel door. The three intruders looked at each other knowingly. They then scrambled deeper down the passage. Panicked shouts were soon heard behind them.

*   *   *   *   *   *   *

The demons were relentless, but their numbers had begun to diminish. Morstar and his friends had carved a path through the beasts, reaching the rest of the shadmar rebels. Despite their success, the rebels were losing the battle. Each blow was harder to strike than the last. The sight of the crumbled bodies of shadmar children made each fallen demon a painful assault to their psyche and morality. Yet, if they did not fight back, they would be devoured, eaten and torn asunder by the demonic swarm.

Morstar, Sia, and Artemis reached the top of the stairway, and turned to help a grief-stricken Kinrithir hold the line. The shadmar's eyes were red and puffy and the half-hearted strength of his strikes demonstrated his split between need and desire. Many of the shadmar rebels had to be replaced on the line as they recognized the body of their own child among the growing pile of fallen demons. They immediately lost hope and the will to fight back. The demons did not hesitate to tear into their supple flesh when their guard fell. The rebels were dropping quickly.

Kinrithir pulled Artemis aside and handed the ranger the dwarven-made sword. He pleaded with the ranger to finish the work, to do what he did not have the heart to finish. The ranger accepted the sword reluctantly and rejoined his allies to help keep the demons at bay. Kinrithir disappeared into the back hallway until he could conquer his sorrow.

Artemis brandished the two swords, charging to the beginning of the bridge to protect the many shadmar that had fallen to the ground, stricken by grief. Likewise, Morstar held one of the stairways and Sia the other. Though the task was not any easier for the outsiders, they did not have the added grief of recognizing the slain forms that piled around them. Sia did her best to avoid looking at the corpses as she slashed with her glowing scimitar and discharged shards of ice with her free hand.

Thankfully, the three outsiders were able to hold the demons at bay. The creatures became more hesitate to approach, but they continued to gather around and snap at the outsiders.

Things then got much worse for the rebels. Soldiers began to climb down the far stairwell from the upper chambers. A long line of the armored soldiers began to gather along the high balcony, their shields and spears held ready to defend themselves. The soldiers suddenly parted and frantically made some distance from the stairway.

Five of the large panther-sized demons then charged down the stairs on to the balcony. The monsters displayed their pointed teeth as their tails flicked with a hungry anticipation. They growled an unnatural sound that echoed throughout the chamber.

The sound immediately caused the smaller demons to perk up and they began to scramble away. It seemed the smaller demons were as frightened of the large demons as the shadmar. This change of events allowed Morstar, Sia, and Artemis a moment to regroup. Many shadmar rebels were still scattered about, sprawled upon the floor in grief, but a few regained their senses and stood to deal with the new challenge. Those that regained themselves, helped their allies to their feet, sending the grief-stricken away from the carnage, into the back-chambers.

Kinrithir reemerged behind his allies, with Gharin and Kryther beside him. Owkba also appeared coming up the stairs with another band of rebels. The orc had many bite marks and cuts upon his green-tinted skin. Artemis handed Kinrithir the dwarven sword. The shadmar seemed to have regained his composure, though his face exhibited many signs of strain. Kinrithir commanded the rebels to reform the line on the bridge and stairways as the large demons began to stalk their way towards them. The enemy soldiers, however, stood still, they seemed to be trying to make sense of the carnage around the rebels.

*   *   *   *   *   *   *

Soldiers marched down the hallways, throwing the steel doors open in a furious haste. They were searching for intruders. Someone had penetrated their defenses and murdered a captain.

Those intruders continued to evade the soldiers, using the labyrinth-like corridors to their advantage. However, the soldiers were being quite thorough, forcing Thes, Bryman, and Edras to flee farther away from the

320

descending stairway that headed towards their allies. The trio was now near the main chamber again, but at the end farthest from the downward stairway. The extra-wide stairway that headed further upwards was nearby. Across the main chamber they observed Delrith heading down a side corridor directly opposite their own. Two of his sorcerer minions strode behind him. The trio then peered to their right, down the large chamber, and noticed that the soldiers had been sent back down the stairs into the main avenue, presumably with the demons and two of the sorcerers.

"There he is!" Thes pointed to Delrith as the tall shadmar exited the chamber. Edras was more interested in the descending stairway on the far side of the chamber, as she was eager to rejoin their allies. She feared that their friends would need their help against the full might of the soldiers, sorcerers, and demons. Bryman, on the other hand, was looking down the corridor behind them, eager to face off against the soldiers pursuing them.

"Perhaps we should try to rejoin our friends and strike the enemy from behind," Edras offered. Bryman enthusiastically nodded to the knight.

Thes shook his head, "No, this may be our only chance to end Delrith's control of the shadmar people." The wizard believed that putting an end to the sorcerer would cause the soldiers to abandon their cause. Bryman nodded equally enthusiastically at this option.

"We cannot be sure these soldiers are magically swayed," Edras replied. "Also, I fear that the three of us cannot take on such a powerful sorcerer on our own." Bryman huffed in disagreement.

Before Thes could respond to Edras, the sound of soldiers could be heard down the corridor behind them. The time to choose an action was upon them.

"I'm going after him," Thes said as he darted across the chamber. A burning hatred was growing inside him, the thirst for vengeance began to dominate his mind.

Edras was surprised by the wizard's reckless action and scrambled to follow Thes. Bryman, however, was ill-prepared and stumbled against the wall. His armor *chinked* against the stone, drawing the attention of the soldiers down the hallway. The warrior looked at the soldiers and was glad that the time for sneaking around was at an end.

"Go help the wizard!" he commanded to Edras. "I'll take care of them." Bryman stood tall in the hallway, glad to stretch his frame after so much crouching. He brandished his axe and pulled his round shield from his back, strapping the hard wood to his muscular arm. He stepped towards the shadmar soldiers and made a defensive stance. He peered at them from behind the shield, his eyes shining with eager excitement beneath his helm. "Come and get me."

Edras ran across the chamber as quietly as she could, catching up to Thes at the entrance to the corridor on the far side. Thankfully, there were no soldiers remaining in the main chamber to see her pass. The two elves continued to stalk their way down the corridor seeing their quarry enter a steel door at the end of the long hallway. After the door shut with an echoic thud, Thes strode determinedly down the hall, the knight a few paces behind him.

*   *   *   *   *   *   *

The first of the panther-like demons reached the bridge as four more were climbing around to face the rebels from each of the stairways. The first beast approached cautiously as Artemis stood firm on the wide bridge, with Kinrithir beside him. The beast leapt suddenly, knocking Artemis and Kinrithir aside with its great bulk. They both struck hard against the stone railing as the beast charged through the line. Shadmar rebels were struck and knocked back by the strong creature. Chaos erupted into a defensive melee as the other demons attacked on the flanks. The rebels tried to hold the beasts back, but their weapons could not harm them. The rebels began to scatter and flee as the beasts hunted the stragglers, tearing apart their frail bodies as a cat would toy with a mouse.

Kinrithir was trying to climb to his feet, but his body was sore from the impact against the stone. His sword had fallen out of his hand and was laying in the center of the bridge among the bloodied remains of dead shadmar children. He attempted to crawl towards the weapon when he realized he could not easily rise. He saw Artemis on the other side of the bridge, the ranger's body sprawled on the ground near the railing, a bloodied wound upon his head.

As Kinrithir neared the weapon, he heard the beast returning towards him. A crunching sound accompanied the beast as it chewed through a disembodied shadmar's arm. The creature stalked over to Kinrithir, playfully swatting the sword behind it, leaving the shadmar without any hope of retaliation. It opened its massive jowl to display its serrated teeth and forked tongue. Drips of ichor sizzled around the yellow fangs and its hot, caustic breath dizzied the shadmar. Kinrithir looked upon the red eyes of the demon and accepted his death.

The beast then howled in pain as the dwarven blade landed firmly through its flank. The sword caused its flesh to sizzle and burn, and swirls of steam rolled out of the wound. The sword glowed with a pale blue light in Kryther's hand as it came down again and again in a maddened fury. Kryther did not have much strength for his strikes, but thankfully the blade cut through the demon's flesh with ease. The creature desperately turned to face the injured shadmar and leapt upon him. Kryther managed to get the sword in front of him before the beast's bulk landed upon him. The sword cut through the monster's mouth piercing up through its jaws into its skull. The beast's razor-sharp front claws, however, had managed to pierce into Kryther's torso.

Kinrithir cried out as he and his half-brother looked at each other across the bridge. The light in Kryther's eyes went out and he collapsed on the stone. The demon turned back into the corpse of a shadmar soldier, the blade still embedded in its skull.

"Brother!" Kinrithir cried, crawling towards his fallen half-brother. When he reached his half-brother's body, it was clear there was no life left in the shadmar.

Sia had finally reached the stone bridge after helping to fell one of the demons that had penetrated the scattered shield wall. She pulled the dwarven-blade from the shadmar corpse and tried handing the sword to Kinrithir. The shadmar ignored the weapon as he stared at his half-brother in despair.

Sia tried to console Kinrithir, but he was too distraught to hear her words. The druidess then saw Artemis nearby and rushed to the ranger's side. Artemis was knocked out cold, but alive. Sia summoned the spirits to her, using some of her diminishing magical reserves. She healed the ranger's head wound with her glowing hand, then dragged the unconscious man away from the bridge before the other demons returned.

Meanwhile, Morstar and Owkba were facing off against one of the large demons at the top of a stairway. The dwarf held his shield high, egging the beast to attack him. Owkba used the distraction to strike the creature's flank. Unfortunately, even the orc's considerable strength did not help his blows injure the demon. The orc landed a hard blow upon the beast's spine. It spun around angrily, swatting wildly at the burly orc. Owkba blocked the slash with his large mace, but was knocked to the ground by the raw power of the blow. He rolled down the stairway and sprawled at the

324

landing below. Morstar took advantage of the distraction and slammed his hammer into the beast's back leg. The Kalavarian metal crushed the demon's leg, crumbling the bones underneath with ease. The beast scrambled to remain its balance and fell half-way down the flight of stairs.

Morstar raised his hammer high and leapt upon the demon. The blow cracked into the monster's outstretched jaw, shattering through its teeth and crushing its skull. The beast then reverted to a shadmar corpse, which sent Morstar rolling and sprawling down the stairs besides Owkba. The orc had returned to his feet and offered a hand to the dwarf.

"You brave warrior, little one," Owkba said as he pulled the dwarf to his feet.

"Ye ain't so bad yerself, greenskin," Morstar said grinning at the orc.

The two climbed back up the stairs to help the shadmar face off against the final two demons.

* * * * * * *

Thes hesitated at the steel door, his other hand made a gesture and sparks of energy swirled around his fingertips. Edras reached the wizard and pulled on his arm.

"What do you think you're doing? You can't face them alone," Edras did not let go of his arm.

"Then come with me," he stated. "I'm going in there to finish this."

"This is foolish, we should wait for the others to help."

Anger was in the wizard's eyes, "There's no time! And there are too many soldiers between us and them."

"I promised her I wouldn't let you go in there," Edras said quietly, releasing her grip on the wizard.

The bloodlust in Thes diminished slightly. The wizard could see Sia's pleading eyes in his mind. He felt ashamed for what he was about to do, but knew it was also the best course of action. "I believe this is my fate. This confrontation seems inescapable… inevitable." He looked past Edras, seeing Bryman facing off against the soldiers in the far corridor. "There's no more time. Come with me."

Edras sighed, "I do not enjoy breaking a promise, but you are right. We are unlikely to get this opportunity again."

Thes turned back to the door and pulled it open slowly. He stepped into another stone hallway on the other side, there were two open doorways on either side of the hall and a closed, steel door on the far end. A few large, crimson runes shimmered on the door's face.

"I bet he is in there," Thes whispered. The wizard carefully crept down the hall, keeping his hand raised, energy still silently arcing between his digits. Edras was one step behind him. As Thes came to the intersection of the two doorways flanking the hall, he peered to his left and right.

"Die, intruder!" a shadmar screamed as a jet of flames shot out from the side room. Thes was ready, however, and his outstretched hand swirled in a circle, forming a shield of energy instantly. The flames were diverted away from the two elves, ricocheting into the other side room. A painful shout then came from that room as the diverted flames burned the other shadmar sorcerer.

After the flames died down, Edras rushed past Thes, her sword cutting down at the flame-spurting sorcerer. Thes let his magical shield dissipate. He then pointed at the other shadmar, who was still nursing a burned arm, unable to make the gestures appropriate for spellcasting. Thes blasted lightning into the shadmar's chest, knocking him to the ground.

Edras sliced at the other sorcerer, but her sword kept striking an unseen magical barrier. The sorcerer then summoned a sword of pure flames and slashed wildly at Edras with the fiery weapon. The knight back-pedaled out of

326

the room as the sorcerer made frantic strikes. Thes was forced to move out of Edras's way, further down the corridor towards the rune-marked door. The sorcerer's flame-blade could not be blocked by steel and Edras had to be careful to dodge the strikes rather than parry them. She switched to a defensive stance and kept her slashes wide to keep the sorcerer at a distance. Thes stood behind her ready to unleash his spells upon the sorcerer.

The entry door behind the shadmar sorcerer then opened, revealing a score of soldiers coming to the sorcerer's aid.

"Go on ahead!" Edras shouted to the wizard. "I will hold them back!"

Thes did not want to leave the knight to face these foes alone. However, he also did not want to give up this chance to strike at Delrith. Ultimately, the burning vengeance inside him made up his mind, and the wizard turned and rushed to the rune-marked door.

*   *   *   *   *   *   *

Morstar and Owkba climbed back to the rebel's broken line on the other stairway. The demons were slowly peeling away the remaining shield-bearers. The shadmar rebels were a few stairs down, giving the two warriors a good view over their heads down to the clawing demons below them.

"Can dwarves fly?" Owkba asked in his characteristic broken Nomen.

Morstar took a moment to understand the orc's question. The dwarf then grinned wide and nodded to the orc, "Aye, we do indeed."

Owkba then used his incredible strength to grab the back of Morstar's armor and hurled the dwarf at one of the demons. The dwarf sailed through the air with his warhammer leading his charge. The demon saw the mass of metal hurling towards it and swatted at it. However, Morstar's hammer slammed into the creature's paw, cracking the bones within. Morstar then slammed into the side of the beast, the two of them rolling down the stairs away from the desperate shadmar rebels.

The orc then charged in past the rebels at the other demon. He leapt upon it, using his bulk to pull the creature down the stairs with him, granting the rebels a much needed respite from the attacks.

Back on the bridge, two shadmar rebels had picked up Artemis from Sia, taking the ranger to one of the back chambers until he recovered. Relieved, Sia went over to Kinrithir, placing a reassuring hand on his shoulders. The shadmar was still weeping over his dead half-brother, overwhelmed by all the loss and grief. Kinrithir could not see a future for his people any longer.

As the final large demons began to fall, the enemy soldiers began to march towards the bridge. Sia tried to help Kinrithir to his feet so they could create a new defensive line, but he refused to leave his half-brother's side. Sia was forced to draw her scimitar again, calling for the rebels to join her. Gharin answered her call, bringing rebels to hold a new line on the bridge near Kinrithir and the fallen Kryther.

"Rise, son of Thirinar!" Gharin called to Kinrithir, hoping the rebel leader would pull back and join their line before the soldiers reached him. However, he ignored the general. "Damnit Kinrithir, you are the heir of House Velmir now. The champion of the People!" Gharin's words seemed to do little to stir the forlorn shadmar.

The soldiers reached the bridge, forming their own line on the far side. Once their line was formed, they slowly marched forward towards the rebels. The strike of their metal boots on the stone echoed in a stirring unison as they stepped

328

forward together. The absent-minded Kinrithir, still upon his knees, was caught between the two lines. Morstar and Owkba joined the front line with Sia and Gharin, having felled the two final demons. They bore a few cuts and scrapes, but otherwise fared well in the confrontation.

Step. Step. Metal on stone echoed through the quiet chamber. Tension filled the air like a dense fog.

As the shadmar soldiers reached a third of the way across the wide bridge, Kinrithir finally rose to his feet. He left his sword upon the ground and stepped determinedly towards the soldiers, weaponless and weary.

He mumbled something that was lost in the large chamber, his eyes looking upon his hands, which were still coated in his half-brother's blood. He raised his hands up towards the enemy in a gesture of peace, or was it surrender?

Gharin shouted at Kinrithir to return, knowing that if Kinrithir surrendered or was killed, it could be the end of the rebellion. But the rebel leader ignored him, stepping slowly towards the soldiers.

"See the blood on these hands!" he shouted at the soldiers. His piercing eyes coming up quickly. The startled soldiers braced their spears defensively.

Kinrithir seemed unaware as he stepped slightly closer. "See this blood," he repeated. "This is the blood of my kin. This is the blood of my brother. Killed by his own kin. We killed him as we continue to kill each other. This is madness!" His words quickly rose to maddened, exasperated shouts. "We have killed our own children!"

"Silence, traitor," came a dark voice among the soldiers. A spur of blood-red energy shot out and quickly wrapped around Kinrithir's throat like a lasso. Kinrithir gasped for breath as he rose up into the air. A robed sorcerer stepped forward with the end of the magical cord extending out from his outstretched hand.

The rebels began to charge forward in anger, but the sorcerer raised his other hand to halt them. "Hold back or he will be decapitated."

The rebels stopped in their tracks. Morstar angrily gripped his hammer, eying the sorcerer with discontent. A second sorcerer then stepped beside the other one with outstretched hands.

"It is time to surrender this pathetic rebellion," he said. "Drop your weapons and we will let all loyal and true shadmar live."

A mixed response echoed among the rebels. They knew they could not win. There were at least three times as many soliders as rebels remaining. Additionally, the rebels were quite fearful of the sorcerers and their demon allies. Yet, with the corpses of their children at their feet, many felt there was not much to live for and would fight on to the end.

"Drop your weapons!" the sorcerer repeated as he tightened the grip on Kinrithir's neck. The rebel leader continued to squirm and pull at his throat, desperate for air.

(25) The Price of Vengeance

Thes entered the chamber cautiously, preparing another shield spell. He entered a large chamber. There were many candles and braziers burning with a strange reddish glow. The room had three tiers with shallow steps leading down to the center of the room where a large red pentagram was inscribed in the floor. A small candle burned with an unnatural red flame at each of the five points of the star.

Above the pentagram was a large flaming rift, high in the air. The circular rift was quite large and burned with intense energy. Through the strange portal, Thes could see a burning landscape with glowing brimstone and relentless flames in the distance. It had such a dark, unnatural feeling within. Through Thes's magical sight he could also see, surrounding the edge of the portal, a swirling mass of blood-red energies. The wizard recognized them as the demonic spirits he had used to create the portal into Valraen. The spirits seemed eager and malicious as they raced around the edges of the portal, likely maintaining the connection to the demon world of Xelenvar.

"So we meet at last," a confident, yet curious voice said. In the shadows of the far side of the room stood a handsome, robed figure. He had a wild mane of jet-black hair and was unusually tall for a shadmar. His crimson robes shimmered like living flames.

Thes was cautious, his hands still raised to defend himself, but he was now curious as to how the shadmar leader knew of him. "Do you know me?"

"In a way," Delrith said mysteriously. "You are the key to my victory. I have foreseen our confrontation and, in many ways, ensured it would take place."

Thes swallowed. He did not anticipate their enemy also seeing a vision of the future. He suddenly felt very foolish for coming here. Suspecting that his enemy had ensured Thes's arrival here to fulfil the tragic destiny that Sia had foreseen.

"You are right to fear me," Delrith stated. "I have felled wizards far more capable than you."

Thes became determined. "Perhaps it is you who fears me," he said, gaining confidence. "You waited to speak from the shadows rather than striking at me as I entered."

"Hardly!" Delrith spat, his obvious anger giving away that Thes had spoken some truth. But Delrith regained his composure. "While I knew of your arrival, I was curious as to who it was that would ultimately serve as my sacrifice."

"Sacrifice?" Thes was curious. He gestured to the portal. "Is that what this is for? You intend to sacrifice me to the demons of Xelenvar? Is that how you control the hearts and minds of the shadmar?"

"Hate and intolerance can twist a person's heart far better than any magic." Delrith sneered as he stepped slowly towards Thes, his own hands defensively raised. "Show someone their enemy and they will sacrifice themselves to see that enemy devoured."

"And what do you gain from all of this? Do you even care what happens to the shadmar people?" Thes slowly circled around the chamber, trying to learn what he could of the portal.

"I care enough to take up their cause. Just as I will take up the cause of the surface elves. The elves of Elienspar will need us to do what they cannot. Mutual hate will bring them into the fold as easily as it has for the shadmar."

"What cause? There is nothing you can offer the surface elves."

"I offer survival," he stated. "The surface elves of Enaarvis preach their tolerance and acceptance of the other races. But they cannot ignore the fact that dwarves, men, and orcs continue to expand upon their borders, encroach upon

332

their sovereignty. Elves have become a minority in a world where they once dominated. Their precious culture and values are in danger of being snuffed out. The lesser races breed more quickly, expand more rapidly, and spread like a plague invading the lands the elves once called their own. Survival is the primary concern for the elves. We must dominate and enslave the other races before they choose to do the same to us."

Thes felt anger grow within him. He could feel his heart swaying to the sorcerer's words. There was a magical quality to them that attempted to penetrate the wizard's heart and stir his mind toward mindless hatred. However, a burning desire for vengeance already overwhelmed that part of Thes's mind. The sorcerer's words failed to gain a foothold in the wizard's heart. As Thes evaded Delrith's mental manipulation, he understood that the sorcerer could indeed convince the surface elves to take this course. He had a powerful way with the words of hatred and intolerance.

"You will not sway me with your evil words, sorcerer."

Beads of sweat appeared on Delrith's brow as he expended the magical energy for his charm. Thes's eyes could see the demonic spirits swirling within the sorcerer. It was a strange sight, since Thes could not normally see such a concentration of magic within an individual. Yet these demonic spirits seemed to have infused themselves inside the sorcerer as if he was a great reservoir of energy. It was clear, however, that the sorcerer had very little energy remaining. Deep in the sorcerer's core there was a darkness, a void, as if the sorcerer's very soul had been hollowed out for some sinister purpose.

Delrith must have sensed the wizard's peering gaze. He suddenly became angry and lashed out with a blast of fire from his hand. The ball of fire slammed the far wall and exploded into a fiery burst. Thes had leapt to the side, rolled to his feet, then used a magical shield to block the intensifying flames from reaching him.

Delrith threw more explosive balls of flame at the crouching wizard. Thes concentrated on expanding his shield until it surrounded him like a protective globe. The explosion roared around him, unable to reach within the magical sphere. The explosive blasts knocked a nearby podium to the ground, scorching its stone.

The smoke slowly cleared as Delrith peered eagerly at where the wizard had stood. Out of the smoky cloud, a blast of lighting pierced across the room and struck the sorcerer. However, a golden ring on the sorcerer's hand seemed to draw in the electrical energy and absorb it.

Thes charged forward with a magical shield in front of him. He released another blast of electricity, sending a continuous wave of energy at the sorcerer. Delrith simply held out his ringed hand to absorb the blast, a domineering sneer on his face. But as the electrical stream gained intensity, the sorcerer's ring glowed brighter and brighter. It was not capable of absorbing that much energy. The ring suddenly burst in a flash of light. Blood splattered across the sorcerer's face as his finger was blasted from his hand. Delrith screamed in pain, but then gritted his teeth and as he sent more flames at Thes.

The wizard was exhausted from overexerting himself. He had crossed half the room along the wall with his shield raised. Delirth then poured a continuous jet of flames at him. Thes was forced to stop his approach and concentrate on his shield. The sorcerer likewise concentrated on his flames, the magical incineration slowly growing brighter and hotter. The flames turned to a blue-white hue and began to lick through Thes's magical shield. The wizard grimaced in pain as his arms took small burns. He then leapt to the side, rolling down the stairs into the center of the chamber to get away from the fire.

Delrith smiled at his success and ceased the blast of fire. Sweat poured down his strained face as he stepped towards the wizard. Thes climbed to his feet, finding himself standing beneath the fiery portal. He could see an expansive hellscape above him. In the distance, winged demons circled in the red, fire-scorched sky.

Delrith then leapt upon him. The sorcerer's unmarred hand glowed with blood-red energy. He grasped Thes's arm with the glow and the wizard's skin seared. Thes managed to kick Delrith away. The wizard tried to scramble to his feet, but the sorcerer was upon him again. Delrith's four-fingered hand grasped at Thes's throat as his glowing hand came dangerously close to the wizard's skin. Thes swatted and kicked, desperately trying to keep that deadly hand away from him. Delrith then overpowered Thes, pressing his deadly hand down into the wizard's chest.

*　　*　　*　　*　　*　　*　　*

Edras continued to slash wildly, keeping the sorcerer and his sword of flames from reaching her. She kept her eye on the soldiers entering the corridor behind the sorcerer, thankful that they did not draw crossbows. The knight refused to allow them to pass and aid their leader, hoping Thes was capable of defeating Delrith on his own.

"Give up, sulmar," the sorcerer hissed. "You are defeated and outnumbered."

Edras narrowed her eyes at the sorcerer. She then gritted her teeth and charged at him. The sorcerer did not expect her sudden charge, but easily struck at her with the tongue of flame he held. However, Edras ignored the searing wounds of the blade as she spun her body violently. Her sword whipped around behind her in a wide circle. At the end of her spin, she faced the sorcerer, who was desperately clutching at a thin slice across his neck.

"Outnumbered, but not defeated," she corrected the sorcerer, before kicking him back into the soldiers behind him. The sorcerer's body dropped to the ground as the soldiers hastily withdrew, keeping their spears and shields towards the sulmar. Edras remained in a deadly stance, her sword out before her, her glimmering eyes shining from beneath her winged helmet.

Edras gave chase to the soldiers, hoping to finish them quickly and aid Thes. The shadmar backed out of the corridor into the large entranceway chamber. She charged at them, entering the chamber herself. The knight saw Bryman behind the soldiers, who were so preoccupied with her that they failed to notice the noradrie warrior charging across the room. By the time they heard him coming, it was too late.

Bryman slammed into the soldiers, his axe cleaving off one of their heads, his shield slamming another to the ground. The other three turned to face the wild-eyed warrior but were then cut down by Edras's quick and deadly sword. The two made short work of the remaining soldiers.

"Let us hurry and help Thes," Edras called to Bryman, who seemed to be looking around for more challenge.

A loud ferocious growl then erupted down the large room, towards the descending stairway. A large, prowling demon was staring at the two warriors. It was much larger than the others, the size of a great ox. It had rows of serrated teeth and razor-sharp claws. Its muscular body flexed in a fluid motion as it stalked towards the elf and man.

"We can take this beast," Bryman growled as he readied his shield and axe.

"Circle it for a flanking strike," Edras commanded. She then readied her sword and stepped towards one side of the chamber. Bryman followed her command and stepped to the other side.

As the beast came towards them, it was forced to choose one over the other. It quickly leapt towards Bryman, trying to pin the warrior to the ground with its considerable bulk. Bryman dived out of the way, just barely avoiding the grasp of its paw. The noradrie rolled and climbed to his feet, bringing his shield to bear just as the creature snapped its gaping maw.

Edras rushed behind the beast, slashing at it wildly with her star-metal sword. The sword easily cut into the creature's flank and sizzled the flesh into steam. Its long, spiked tail then whipped back at Edras, throwing the knight sprawling to the ground.

The distraction proved useful for Bryman, who slammed his shield into the creature's face as he scrambled below it towards its neck. However, the demon lurched itself high to the side, slashing at Bryman with its razor-sharp claw. The warrior still had his shield held above him, so the claw struck him directly, before he could raise his axe. One of the claws pierced his face, cutting through his left eye.

Bryman screamed in pain and rage, channeling his emotions into wild swings with his dwarven-made axe. The steel managed to slices small gashes along the creature's leg as Bryman pulled away from the demon.

Edras was back on her feet and slicing at the demon's flank again, this time keeping her eye on its tail. She cut it hard along its back leg. It let out a howl of pain and spun its body around wildly. This maneuver forced Bryman to roll away from the beast. Edras was then facing the furious demon's claws. It clawed and bit at her in a flurry of wild strikes, but the agile elf was able to duck, roll, and dodge the blows.

Bryman leapt high upon the backside of the beast, using his axe to cut and climb up the top of the creature's back. It howled again in a loud screech that echoed painfully in the large chamber. The enraged warrior squeezed tightly with his legs and slammed his axe down upon the creature's spine, hacking repeatedly. The demon began to falter and lose its step. Edras then rushed to its exposed neck and sliced a long gash in a wide arc.

Bryman could not see anything through the blood gushing out of his eye-wound and the swirling steam from the eviscerated flesh beneath him. He continued to blindly hack at the creature. It suddenly dissipated into a cloud of steam, dropping Bryman hard to the ground. The hacked and gutted body of a hill giant was on the ground nearby.

Edras rushed to the warrior and helped him to his feet. It was clear that the war-priest's eye was pierced and slashed through, but the warrior waved the elf away and would not accept her help. He pulled out a makeshift cloth as a bandage, balled it up and shoved it into the bleeding socket. He then tied a strip of leather around his head to hold it in place. Before Edras could protest, the war-priest was charging towards the far corridor to find the wizard. She followed.

*   *   *   *   *   *   *

The deadly, glowing hand came closer and closer to the wizard's chest. Thes felt this was the moment. This was where Sia's vision became his destiny. That deadly hand would press against his heart and he would fail in his quest. He would fail his friends. He would fail to fulfill his promise of revenge for the villagers of Escailar.

A surge of resolve then reverberated through him. He would not accept this 'destiny'. He would not let the divines decide the course of his actions. The desire for vengeance fueled the wizard and his blood boiled with latent energy.

Delrith's hand just began to sear the wizard's skin when Thes's form illuminated and surged with radiance. His body became composed of pure electricity, which made the sorcerer's hand harmless against him.

"No!" Delrith screamed. "This is not how I foresaw. This cannot be!"

Thes shouted in rage as the energy within him exploded outward. Delrith was flung up into the gaping, burning maw of the fiery portal. Thes watched in horror as he saw the sorcerer's body torn apart by a swirl of the demonic spirits that composed the magical portal.

Through his magical sight, Thes saw the deep void within the sorcerer expand. It was not a hole. It was a tunnel. The strange magical void that was within the evil sorcerer stretched out and connected to the edges of the burning portal and merged into it. The demonic energy at the edges of the portal burned with greater intensity and the thin barrier separating Enelis with Xelenvar dissipated. The portal began to grow wider, no longer inhibited by the separation between worlds. A deep, guttural laughter could be heard on the far side of the portal.

Thes scrambled to his feet. He was horrified by what he had done. He realized that Delrith was being cultivated by the demons of Xelenvar. The years of channeling the dark, demonic energy had transformed the sorcerer into a conduit between worlds. Thes had unwittingly delivered the conduit to its origins and completed the bridge. There was now nothing to stop the demons of Xelenvar from fulfilling their long-awaited destruction of Enelis.

A great seismic tremor shuddered through Valraen, sending Thes sprawling back to the ground. It was as if the entire mountain roared in discontent as the demon world gained a foothold on Enelis.

The ground continued to shake and tremor, but the initial shockwave had passed. Bryman and Edras charged into the room finding Thes scrambling to his feet again. Thes was surprised by Bryman's bloodied eye, but the warrior seemed to be ignoring the wound. Edras had some burns and cuts, but otherwise seemed okay. They tried to help Thes to his feet.

"You defeated him!" Edras cried jubilantly.

"Yes, but I have done a terrible thing." He gestured towards the growing portal. He had to yell this to them as the roar of the portal became quite loud. "The world is in danger and it is all my fault." Thes climbed to his feet and stepped towards the portal.

The wizard summoned every bit of energy he could muster. He began to glow again with electricity. He cried out to Edras and Bryman, "I can only hold them off for so long. Go to Elienspar and tell them to prepare for the demonic siege." His body then exploded into a blast of electrical energy. Arcs of lightning leapt from where the wizard stood and surrounded the portal, encasing it in a magical cage. It was a much larger version of the cage Thes had once used to encase the demonic spirits. The portal tried to grow against the edges of the energy cage and the two forces expanded and compressed as they struggled against each other.

Bryman and Edras were dumbfounded. The wizard's body was nowhere to be seen.

*   *   *   *   *   *   *

The magical lasso around Kinrithir's neck suddenly disappeared. He fell to the stone bridge and panted to catch his breath. There was a look of surprise and horror on the sorcerer's face. His command over the demonic spirits had ceased.

Morstar grabbed the dwarven blade near his feet and tossed it across the bridge. It clattered on the stone near Kinrithir, who was still kneeling upon the ground. The sorcerer stood before Kinrithir, moving his hands wildly, trying to make the demonic spirits obey him.

340

Kinrithir grabbed the hilt of the sword and rose, pointing the tip of the blade towards the sorcerer. He noticed that the soldiers behind the sorcerer were lowering their spears. Many had expressions of concern and horror as if they could finally see the rebellion unfolding and their slain children in the broken piles across the bridge. Spears began to clatter upon the ground as the soldiers lost the deep hatred that was driving their actions. They no longer had the heart to wage war on their own kin.

The two sorcerers became panicked, knowing that their lack of magic likely meant that Delrith had fallen. The sorcerer in front of Kinrithir angrily charged at the rebel leader, brandishing a dagger from his belt. Kinrithir, however, easily whipped his sword down on the robed shadmar, cutting him deeply across the torso. The sorcerer dropped to the ground in a pool of blood. The other sorcerer turned to run but was grabbed by two nearby soldiers. A third soldier then purposefully pierced him through the heart with a spear.

Kinrithir looked sadly at the bloody mess. He looked upon the soldiers, the corpses strewn about the bridge, the broken pieces of shadmar children, and the tire and worn band of rebels standing in a line on the far end. This would be the end of war for the shadmar.

"The war is over!" he shouted. His voice echoed through the chamber. "We are no longer slaves to a mad sorcerer. We are free to make a new life upon the surface. One without the promise of war and hatred."

Before the shadmar could continue, a great shockwave of energy shook the chamber. Nearly everyone fell from their feet. The walls and ceiling of the chamber cracked as a wave of tremors continued to rock the stronghold. Fear and panic seized the shadmar. The soldiers turned and began running towards the stairway upwards. The rebels were hesitant to follow, but as the tremors ebbed and flowed in intensity, many rebels scrambled behind the soldiers towards the stairway.

"They did it!" Morstar said happily to Sia as he pulled her back to her feet.

Sia was very relieved. She felt that if Delrith had fallen then Thes must have lived. She was eager to find the wizard. However, she also had a bad feeling about the continuous tremors.

Morstar and Sia found Owkba carrying Artemis, coming towards them. Sia joined the orc, making their way to the climbing stairway. Morstar headed to Kinrithir, who had returned to the side of his half-brother's body. Gharin was kneeling beside him.

"Sorry about yer brother, elf," the dwarf said, laying a friendly hand on his shoulder.

Kinrithir was silent a moment, but then smiled. "Half-brother," he corrected. "He shall be remembered as a hero of the rebellion."

"Yes, indeed," said Gharin. "But we must be going, Kinrithir. I fear these chambers may collapse upon us." He pointed to bits of rock falling from the ceiling as more cracks stretched across the stone.

"Is there even an exit to this place?" Morstar asked.

Gharin only shrugged at the dwarf. The two convinced Kinrithir to say a final farewell to his half-brother and the three of them scrambled up the stairway as the last to leave the chamber. The quiet scurrying of small creatures could be faintly heard behind them.

*   *   *   *   *   *

In the large entranceway chamber, a mob of shadmar were scrambling towards the upper stairway, everyone trying to push their way out. The tremors seemed to be at a greater intensity at this level of the complex, causing rocks

342

and stones to crack and fall from the walls and ceiling. Everyone was in a panic to get out before they were crushed by a collapse.

Sia was ignoring the imminent danger as she sprinted across the stone chamber towards Edras and Bryman. The elf and man were standing at the far end on the right side. Edras was tending to Bryman's bloodied eye.

"Where is he?!" Sia asked exasperated.

Bryman only solemnly shook his head at her.

Edras stepped over to Sia and took her by the shoulders. "I'm sorry," she said quietly.

Sia's lips quivered and tears began to trickle down her cheek. She did not want to believe it. "No, let me see him!"

"There's nothing left to see, dame" Bryman explained. "He's nothing but light now."

Edras then quietly explained to Sia what happened in the spell-chamber. The druidess was horrified. She could not accept that Thes was lost to her and that a portal to Xelenvar was now open.

"We have to get everyone out of here!" Edras continued. "Before the portal reopens and the demons break free!" She beckoned Sia to join her, following Bryman towards the stairway.

"No! I must see for myself!" Sia rushed down the corridor towards the spell-chamber.

There were now many hundreds of shadmar filling the chamber, trying to push their way up the stairs. But then a new panic spread through them, starting from the top of the stairway. There was no exit to the surface. The ancient entrance had long been sealed in.

Bryman charged to the front of the crazed mob, offering his strength to help move stones. Edras instead went down the corridor, knowing that Sia's magic might be their only way out of the ancient stronghold.

The knight sprinted into the chamber. Sia was standing just inside the doorway, staring forlornly at the crackling cage of electricity around the red portal. Edras stepped beside her and gently tugged at her shoulders.

"We need your help," she shouted over the din of the portal. "The way out is sealed. Can your magic breach a path?"

Sia nodded slowly. She took off a small pendant from around her neck. It was a silver medallion with the detailed drawing of a songbird inscribed in the metal. The druidess said a few words quietly to the pendant and kissed it. It glowed with a faint yellow light for but a moment. She then placed it upon the ground at the bottom level of the three-tiered chamber.

The two elves then ran down the corridor back into the main entranceway. They found Morstar, Gharin, and Kinrithir entering from the far end. Sia headed towards the top of the stairway as Edras went down to explain to the others what had transpired in the spell-chamber.

When Sia reached the top of the stairway, she found many strong shadmar and Bryman in a wide corridor that was partially filled with stone and rubble. It seemed like the grand hallway had collapsed. A very faint light could be seen in the distance. A pin-sized hole pierced through the rubble to the world outside.

The red-eyed druidess strode to the beginning of the rubble as Bryman signaled the other shadmar to back away. Sia closed her eyes and concentrated. She reached into her sorrow and pain and let the emotion flow through her. The ground began to tremble independently from the ongoing tremors of the portal. The ground beneath her feet began to get soggy and pools of water formed. Soon the water roared upwards into the surge of a stream, striking at the rocks and flowing through the holes and cracks between them.

Sia stood there with her arms outstretched. The flow of water seemed to rise near her feet and did not flow back towards the shadmar behind her. Tears poured down her face and in unison, the flow of the stream grew in strength. Eventually the water had enough strength to pull the rocks and boulders with it, tearing a gaping hole through the corridor. The makeshift stream flowed down the side of the mountain and bright daylight flickered into the dark corridor for the first time in millennia. The druidess opened her eyes and the water flow ceased. She stepped through the long dripping tunnel and stepped out into the sunshine.

She stood on a high masonry walkway connected to a long, crumbled stairway that headed down the mountainside. There were tall trees everywhere. Many were evergreens glimmering in the sunlight, others were mostly-bare deciduous trees. There was a cold wind flowing from the north which blew the elf's hair behind her, whipping it around playfully.

Sia stepped aside as the frightened shadmar came streaming out of the corridor. Many of them squinted and covered their eyes as they caught their first sight of the daylight sun. There was much awe and bewilderment among them. However, another tremor reminded them of the danger. The shadmar began to scramble down the long stairway into the forest. The shadmar were free.

(26) Parting of the Ways

The broken entrance to the ancient stronghold of Valraen gleamed in the fading autumn light. A wide stone platform was constructed into the side of the mountain with a crumbling, broken stairway descending into the deep forest below. Artemis sat on the stone platform near Sia, his head had been bandaged. Morstar stood nearby at the top of the stairs next to Bryman. The noradrie warrior had a bandage over his left eye, tied to his head with a leather cord.

"What is next for you, clan-brother?" Bryman said to Morstar. "Will ye join the elves in this coming war?"

The dwarf sighed. This war would be bigger than any conflict that was known to Enelis in many ages. He knew what he had to do, but he feared how successful he could be. "No," he finally said. "I must do the right thing. I will head to Kalavar and gather the Seven Kings. I will try to convince them to aid the elves against the demon hordes."

Bryman turned to look at the dwarf. He knew that Morstar had not been in his homeland for many years. Morstar had deserted his post and would likely face charges if he returned home. "You are a brave warrior and have earned the honor for a second chance."

"Thanks, clan-brother." Morstar grinned up at the warrior. "Where does the path of war take ye?"

"Alas, I will join the elves. I cannot leave this battle unfought. Perhaps when it is finished, I will have earned enough honor to return home myself."

"Don't think I be abandoning our fellowship," Morstar huffed. "If these dwarves have half a mind, ye be seeing me return with a fierce army."

The ground shook again in a mild tremor. Edras then stepped towards the two, Kinrithir and Owkba behind her.

"We should be going soon. The danger of this place increases with each moment."

"Aye, I have me quest," Morstar mumbled. He stepped over to Owkba. "Ye are a great warrior, greenskin. I would not wish to face ye in an opposing battle."

The great orc nodded respectfully to the dwarf. The orc had previously stated that he was heading northwards to return to his tribe.

"Let me come with you, friend," Artemis begged the dwarf. His head had been bandaged and he was still a little light-headed, but otherwise capable of travel. "I have never seen the halls of the dwarf-lords and you may need someone to vouch for your warnings and deeds."

Morstar looked down at the man. He seemed to be weighing the idea carefully. "I suppose I could use the companionship," he muttered. Artemis smiled at his friend.

The sun was growing orange, glimmering through the trees on the western horizon. Edras seemed eager to leave.

"Anyone else coming to the city?" she asked. "We have a long road yet to travel."

"I will join you," Kinrithir told Edras. He had spoken long with Gharin after the shadmar exited the ancient stronghold. They decided it was best for Kinrithir to go to the elven city and speak for their people. In the meantime, Gharin would gather their people together and convince them to head towards the city. Kinrithir looked into Edras's deep blue eyes. "I hope to ensure my people are still welcome."

"They will indeed be welcomed, on my honor," Edras reassured him. "I will make sure Queen Alilledra is ready to accept the shadmar refugees." She paused thinking a moment. "It is in fact good that you come. If you can speak on behalf of your people, you may help convince the Queen

348

that the old prejudices are ready to be put to rest. What of the rest of your people, will they travel with us?"

"No. They are scattered in the forest. Gharin is gathering them together, but I imagine it will take some time. I believe many will accompany him, but no doubt others will flee this place to seek a new life elsewhere."

Edras nodded. She knew that Kinrithir would be a good spokesperson for the shadmar. The prejudice against them was strong and Kinrithir's kind and thoughtful demeanor would help their case for asylum.

"And what of you, lass," Morstar said to Sia. The druidess was sitting nearby on the stone platform, her legs dangling over the edge. She had been oddly quiet since they reached the outdoors.

Sia turned slowly to the dwarf. "I will stay here," she stated solemnly. There were many surprised expressions at her statement.

"Ye can't stay here, lass!" Morstar exclaimed. "Head to the elf city with the others."

Sia stepped up and looked at her new friends. They were genuinely concerned for her. "I cannot go, I am needed here."

Morstar stepped over to Sia. "Please, lass. Don't let yer life go to waste."

"I'm not," she stated unemotionally. "Thes's magic will break in time. I will work on magical fortifications here to slow the demons' progress."

"Ye can't stay here alone," the dwarf mumbled.

"Yes, I can and will." Her voice was firm.

"If you change your mind, you are always welcome in the Glimmering City," Edras offered. Sia nodded her thanks, but was determined to stay.

"He ain't coming back," the dwarf whispered sadly.

"You don't know that," Sia snapped. The druidess couldn't explain it, but she still felt Thes's presence here.

The magic the wizard used to surround the portal was something the druidess had never seen. She felt that Thes was still present within the energy cage. He had not completely consumed himself as it had seemed. However, she still had some doubt as to whether he was truly alive, or it was just her own wishful thinking.

Morstar seemed to accept that there was nothing he could say to convince her to go. "Fine. Ye do what ye wish, lass," he grumbled. "At least make those demons suffer!" He gave her a toothy grin. Sia nodded to the dwarf.

"The day grows dim, we must be off," Edras stated, eyeing the setting sun. Everyone said final farewells to the three. Then Edras, Bryman, and Kinrithir, a most unlikely combination of travelers, set down the stairway on the long journey to Elienspar.

"Well," Mostar said to Sia. "Ye can come with us if ye like."

The druidess sighed. "I appreciate your concern. But I'm not going anywhere."

"Alright, alright, I'll stop proddin' ye." He turned to Artemis. "At this point, we could wait until the morning if you need the rest."

Artemis knew some rest would help his injuries, but he was wary to stay so near the demon portal. "Is it safe to stay here?"

"I do not know for sure," Sia replied. "I do not completely understand the magic Thes used, nor how long it will last."

Morstar grumbled to himself, trying to decide what to do. "Let us stay here until dawn. Ye and I do not have as far to travel." The dwarf knew that Kalavar was much closer than Elienspar from the shadmar fortress. The dwarf also hoped by staying he could convince Sia to join them in the morning.

Morstar went into the woods to gather some supplies, insisting that Artemis rest. Sia offered to help, but the dwarf only grumbled and waved her away.

"You must think I'm mad," Sia said to Artemis, who sat down nearby.

He shook his head. "No, I understand your sorrow." Artemis knew it took time to accept a loved-one's death. He had lost friends, family, and his own partner during the gnoll raid on Layu. During his forced exile, he spent much time dwelling on their deaths. But in many ways, leaving his homeland made it easier to deal with the loss. He was forced to start anew. If there was not the threat of war, he thought perhaps Sia could do the same.

The druidess sighed. She looked over the forest which seemed to stretch out endlessly before her. The brown and gold sea shimmered with the last orange crescent of sunlight behind. The sky was so clear that Sia could barely make out more mountains in the distance and hints of green in the valleys beyond. In that moment, she felt the joy of an unbound freedom, the entire world available to explore. Yet, inside she felt the incredible sorrow and despair of having no dreams or purpose to drive her on that exploration. The juxtaposition of having everything and feeling nothing.

The twilight faded to darkness as Morstar returned. Artemis was sleeping against a tree off the platform and Sia was nowhere to be seen. The dwarf pulled off his backpack, pulling out his bedroll. He was amazed at how well the pack had survived the combat of the past day. He laid out his leather roll and went to sleep upon the stone platform. The dwarf quite enjoyed the firm comfort of the rock.

Over the night, the tremors subsided, allowing the travelers to find rest and fade into a deep sleep. The next morning, just as the dawn sun began to provide faint light, the dwarf awoke, finding Artemis kneeling above him. It was still somewhat dark, since the west-facing platform was completely overshadowed by the mountains.

"Sorry, friend," the ranger whispered. The dawn sun rises and we should be on our way." The dwarf grumbled in response as he packed his things.

"Good luck, on your journey," Sia said to them. Her eyes were red and it was clear she did not gain much sleep over the night. "May the dwarves see the wisdom in honoring the old alliances."

"Last chance, lass," Morstar offered. "Join us and leave this foul place behind."

Sia smiled and held back her tears. She could only shake her head in response, but she was glad to have friends who cared about her. She gave each of them a firm hug before they began their descent down the long stone stairway.

Sia watched the two figures zig-zag their way downward for a long while, somewhat regretting her choice to stay. She then turned towards the broken archway that led through the rubble-strewn corridor into Valraen. The druidess did not get the rest she had hoped overnight, but at least felt renewed enough to lay warding and protective enchantments. She would do her best to block the exit from the shadmar fortress.

The druidess spent much of the day placing magical wards and traps throughout the corridor and hallways, from the demon portal out to the exit. There were many moments when she expected the magical cage around the portal would break, and a horde of demons would come rushing out in a destructive rage. But nothing happened. The portal was blocked. Thes's sacrifice was not in vain.

Sia sat outside on the stone platform to rest. It was late in the afternoon and the sun shined brightly upon the fitted stone blocks. The druidess was growing hungry, but dared not take time to forage in the woods. She would rest her body and mind, then return to her work.

The druidess stared out over the forest again, watching birds of prey spiraling over the tops of the trees. For a moment, Sia desired to take the form of a bird and soar among them, to embrace mindless freedom among the high winds.

As her mind wandered through daydreams, she suddenly heard a song-like tone reverberate through her mind. The chime-like melody was the result of an enchantment she had placed upon her medallion.

Sia leapt to her feet and charged down the corridor. Her magical sight glowed with the outlines of countless wards and enchantments on the floors, walls and ceilings. Thankfully, the snares and deadly magical traps would not trigger upon an elf, so she charged through them without heed.

The druidess mind was racing as she sprinted down the long stairway from the surface into the large entrance-chamber. Her feet were contacting every fifth step in graceful, bounding strides. She charged through the side corridor towards the spell-chamber. Her heart was beating wildly and a rising, desperate surge of hope brought her beating heart into her throat.

Sia flung open the rune-marked, steel door and gasped. Exalted jubilation overtook her senses as she saw, upon the hard, stone floor, an elf. A travel-worn, unconscious ethmar wearing an open, green robe was sprawled upon the floor. His hand stretched out in front of him, wrapped around Sia's faintly-glowing medallion.

"Thes!"

BACK COVER

In the deep and hidden reaches of the Aegis Forest, underground-dwelling shadmar elves have come to the surface to raid upon the unsuspecting villages of the surface elves, bringing fire and bloodshed. Thesomber Ambreaia, an elven mystic and scholar, faces this new peril after the destruction of his home and community. United with unlikely friends, the elven wizard gathers allies to fight against this force of darkness. The cycle of revenge and reprisal sets the wheels of fate in motion. What will be the final price of that retribution?

Chains of Vengeance is the first book of an epic, fantasy trilogy.

356